WILD GROWS THE HEATHER IN DEVON

Books by Michael Phillips

Best Friends for Life (with Judy Phillips)
George MacDonald: Scotland's Beloved Storyteller
A God to Call Father†

THE HIGHLAND COLLECTION*

Jamie MacLeod: Highland Lass   *Robbie Taggart: Highland Sailor*

THE JOURNALS OF CORRIE BELLE HOLLISTER

*My Father's World**   *Sea to Shining Sea*
*Daughter of Grace**   *Into the Long Dark Night*
On the Trail of the Truth   *Land of the Brave and the Free*
A Place in the Sun   *A Home for the Heart*

Grayfox (Zack's story)

THE JOURNALS OF CORRIE & CHRISTOPHER

The Braxtons of Miracle Springs   *A New Beginning*

MERCY AND EAGLEFLIGHT†

Mercy and Eagleflight
A Dangerous Love

THE RUSSIANS*

The Crown and the Crucible   *Travail and Triumph*
A House Divided

THE SECRET OF THE ROSE†

The Eleventh Hour   *Escape to Freedom*
A Rose Remembered   *Dawn of Liberty*

THE SECRETS OF HEATHERSLEIGH HALL

Wild Grows the Heather in Devon

THE STONEWYCKE TRILOGY*

The Heather Hills of Stonewycke *Lady of Stonewycke*
Flight From Stonewycke

THE STONEWYCKE LEGACY*

Stranger at Stonewycke   *Treasure of Stonewycke*
Shadows Over Stonewycke

*with Judith Pella   †Tyndale House

WILD GROWS THE HEATHER IN DEVON

MICHAEL PHILLIPS

BETHANY HOUSE PUBLISHERS
MINNEAPOLIS, MINNESOTA 55438

Published by Bethany House Publishers
A Ministry of Bethany Fellowship International
11300 Hampshire Avenue South
Minneapolis, Minnesota 55438

Printed in the United States of America by
Bethany Press International, Minneapolis, Minnesota 55438

Library of Congress Cataloging-in-Publication Data

Phillips, Michael R., 1946–
    Wild grows the heather in Devon : a story of early twentieth century England / by Michael Phillips.
        p. cm. — (The secrets of Heathersleigh Hall ; 1)
    ISBN 0-7642-2062-4
    ISBN 0-7642-2043-8 (pbk.)
    I. Title. II. Series: Phillips, Michael R., 1946– Secrets of Heathersleigh Hall ; 1.
PS3566.H492W55 1997
813'.54—dc21
                                                  97–33862
                                                      CIP

To Gregory, Heidi, and Penny,
and those dear and loyal friends
who have loved and supported us
in this difficult time.
Thank you all!

MICHAEL PHILLIPS is one of the premier fiction authors publishing in the Christian marketplace. He has authored more than fifty books, with total sales exceeding four million copies. He is also well known as the editor of the popular George MacDonald Classics series.

Phillips owns and operates a Christian bookstore on the West Coast. He and his wife, Judy, have three grown sons and make their home in Eureka, California.

Contents

———— ◆◆◆ ————

Introduction
Ideas and Change

———— ♦♦♦ ————

$\mathcal{M}$y objective as a writer is more than to just tell stories. Though I certainly want my books to be enjoyable, it is important to me that they contain more than entertainment value.

I approach every new project, therefore, by asking myself what unique elements I might bring to a book or series to make it a distinctive literary experience for those who eventually read it.

"What human struggles, historical issues, and spiritual concepts can I explore," I ask myself, "that haven't come up in quite the same way in previous books? How might I develop a new range of characters whose lives will be fresh and interesting? What thought-provoking challenges can I cause these characters to face that will enable them to grow? How will the individuals in the story interact emotionally with those around them and within their specific historical and cultural milieu? Most important, how will they respond to God when he makes his presence felt in their hearts?"

All this no doubt stems from what I as a reader look for in a novel. When I read, I want to grow and be changed from the experience. I enjoy finding myself intellectually and spiritually challenged. I want to think and learn. I want to feel that I've met real people whose experiences will stay with me. I want to know that I've genuinely experienced some place on the globe or some period in history about which I was unfamiliar before. When I finish a book, I hope I will be a little different than when I began. I want to feel that I've enjoyed a full-course literary meal rather than just a snack. When I took to writing myself, therefore, it was with the hope of producing the sorts of books that I personally like to read, with the kinds of characters and issues that I myself find intriguing. After all, if *I'm* not fascinated by the lives of my characters, how can I expect readers to be?

It is the qualities I have described above that make the Scottish novelist George MacDonald my favorite author. Some complain that these complexities cause my books, like MacDonald's, to be too long and involved, that every title is really two books in one. I take such comments as great compliments, signs that readers are getting their money's worth. For I happen to enjoy best those books that take weeks to read, that are *journeys* rather than two-hour television programs. One of my favorite MacDonalds is 786 pages! That book is not just a story. It is an *experience!*

The era in which I chose to set THE SECRETS OF HEATHERSLEIGH HALL is a historical period I find especially fascinating from several different perspectives. I would sum it up by calling it an era of *ideas* and of *change*. Both play significant roles in this first book of the series.

In most historical novels, a strong sense of historical *events* (war, revolution, social change, and so on) is intrinsic to the story. The particular setting of this book, however, is one of relative tranquility. The late Victorian period in England was an era characterized by a free flow of new *ideas* rather than by *events*. Some of these ideas would later be proved to be fallacious (communism). Some would stand the test of time (universal suffrage). About others (evolution, universal reconciliation), debate rages on a hundred years later.

At the outset of this project, I found myself intrigued by the question of what stresses would come to a thoroughly "modern" family in this pivotal age, one with little prior spiritual inclination or background, if suddenly confronted by the Gospel in a new and personal way. What would be the *ideas* they would wrestle through? What *changes* would result? What would be the impact on each family member, on the relationships of husband and wife, on the family as a whole, on their views, on their world outlook?

This was something I had not done in a book before. The more I considered it, the more fascinated I became. Especially, I became curious to consider how a man and woman confronting God personally for the first time might wrestle through issues of spirituality as the intellectualism of the times worked in combination with the deep emotional tugging of the Holy Spirit on their hearts. I am extremely intrigued by this interplay between the rational and the emotional. It is a component of the spiritual life often overlooked in today's occasionally pietistic spiritual climate.

Furthermore, I found myself wondering what tension such a fundamental change as conversion might bring to a family in that age. What if the husband and wife were not in agreement in all things? How would the children in such a family react? What if the change were not welcomed by some family members? (These questions, of course, could apply just as easily to our own time.)

The thought of such potential familial stresses led to another question I thought it important to explore—that is, why *do* people without religious background become Christians, and what happens to them afterward?

I think too often we base evangelism on what God can do for us— *Accept the Lord and he will give you a happy life.* That's backward to my way of thinking. If salvation is not based on the truth of God's character, on his inherent goodness and love for us, and on our obedience as we respond to give back that love, then I think its foundation will always be faulty. Happy lives, sunny skies, abundance, blessing, and ideal circumstances do not necessarily follow giving one's heart to the Lord. We live as God's children because he is our Father, not because he lavishes us with blessings. Some lives are hard. Some questions are not answered in this life. But that does not change who God is and how we are called to respond to him.

For all these reasons, I felt it important that everything not necessarily go smoothly and rosily because the characters in this story encounter God. Real life doesn't usually work that way. Neither do the lives of the family Rutherford, whom you are about to meet.

With these comments about my objectives as foundational, I would also like to tell you a little more about the time in which the Rutherfords lived and why I find it such an intriguing period of English history. As I said, it was a time of ideas and change—and that's putting it mildly. Late nineteenth-century Great Britain was a positive intellectual greenhouse for new concepts. In every field, from politics to science to theology, thinkers and policy makers were pushing past boundaries in ways that would have been inconceivable a hundred years before. Societal concerns gave rise to socialism. On its heels, communism was born in England during the final two decades of the nineteenth century. Scientific advances were changing the way people viewed the natural world. Darwin had already proposed an evolutionary foundation for the animal kingdom. Within the first decade of the twentieth century, Einstein would propose his theory of special relativity.

This surge of new ideas brought with it rapid and enormous societal change. Industrialism had already revolutionized both commerce and daily life. Electricity was changing the way people lived. Telephones were revolutionizing communication. Motorized engines were moving people faster and more conveniently than ever before. Cities were doubling in size every few years as life became increasingly urban.

The changes in British politics were just as rapid and as powerful. The British monarchy was losing power and influence while Parliament, once a bastion of conservatism and the aristocracy, was witnessing the birth of the Labour party. The middle class was rising in influence. All men, not just nobles, could now vote. That right would soon come to women as well.

Clearly, some of this change was for the better, some was not. Few will quarrel with the wisdom behind giving working men and women the vote and protecting children from grueling factory labor. The wisdom behind evolutionary and communist theory, however, might be more open to question. (It could be conjectured that most of the *social* change proved generally beneficial to people and culture, while many of the new *philosophical* ideas of the times produced a deviation from traditional and biblical truth.)

Absolutely central to this historical milieu was a climate of vigorous rationalism, which was applied not only to scientific matters, but to religious ones as well. Generalizations are always dangerous, of course, for they are never entirely true. But it seems nevertheless to be a valid observation that churchgoers of a century ago, in Great Britain especially, were more comfortable with intellectual dialogue as an integral component of spiritual life than are many of our own time.

People a century ago discussed and analyzed and thought issues out for themselves—far more, I believe, than many in Christian circles today. People attended public lectures as a pastime. Intellectual debate was a standard drawing-room activity. Such discussions often formed the evening's entertainment. There was no radio or television. Instead, people sat in parlors and drawing rooms and *discussed* the current ideas being circulated in church and society and in the day's magazines and newspapers.

This climate of discussion and debate shows itself quite clearly in this series. Not only are the ideas you will encounter here historical in themselves, so too are the dialogues in which these ideas are prominent. Readers accustomed to today's "quick read" fiction may find this surprising and even, at times, a bit uncomfortable. Yet this style of writing and interaction is deliberate and, I hope, ultimately rewarding. My goal is to help you not just read about these times, but fully to *experience* them. Thus I hope you will be drawn into these discussions with the characters and *feel* a little what it was like to be a Christian in turn-of-the-century England.

So for those readers who occasionally desire more "action," I would simply offer a reminder that 1890s England was not, in general, a fast-moving time. It was, however, a fascinating time, and one that was critical in shaping the world we live in today. If you can allow yourself to settle into the pace of the book and "live" it as intended, I believe you will find it fascinating as well.

The specific topics that people were debating at the turn of the century will be familiar to you, for many of today's hot issues were born at approximately that time. Traditional norms in every discipline and walk of life—science, society, business, politics, industry, art, music, and religion—were being questioned. The debate between God and science, evolution and creation, was at the forefront of everyone's thinking. Everything from women's rights to Darwin's ideas about natural selection was vigorously and heatedly debated—as they are in the book you are about to read.

Three topics in particular which come in for their share of discussion in this volume may perhaps raise red flags in your thinking. To this day Christians feel heated about all three—evolution, the roles of men and women, and universalism.

In those days, the idea of evolution was seen as one of the most serious threats to Christianity itself. If evolution was true, many people assumed, then God simply could not exist. For a thinking person of the times, therefore, the idea of evolution was one of the serious stumbling blocks to faith and belief. This issue arises in the book as rationalist Charles Rutherford wrestles through the foundational truths of the Christian faith and attempts to reconcile them with his evolutionist assumptions.

Later in the story, a lengthy discussion arises concerning the roles of women and men and the seeming disparity between what modern society was saying about equality and what the Bible appeared to indicate. When working on this book, I found myself intrigued by the situation that might develop if a relatively "liberated" and modern woman—and these were the days when the seeds of today's feminism were being planted—encountered a more traditional, conservative viewpoint concerning the wife's role in marriage and a woman's place in society. I therefore attempted to frame the sort of dialogue that might well have taken place in England at the time.

It might help as you read to know that my wife helped me write this particular section! We attempted together to envision the kind of discussion two women of the time might actually have had in sorting through such a complex issue. Judy's help was invaluable toward this end because she has approached these issues from both vantage points represented.

Whereas the debate over evolution was for the most part between the conservative church and the scientific community, and the issue of the roles of women was largely between the conservative church and a societal movement, another equally heated controversy existed within the church itself. No more divisive point of contention existed in the church of those days than the theological controversy over "universalism," or, more properly, universal reconciliation. It was a conflict that furiously raged in all denominations and seminaries, split churches, spawned countless books and pamphlets, and sparked thousands of parlor debates throughout England and Scotland. As today, a belief in universal reconciliation was considered heresy in some circles, enlightened thinking in others.

The discussion in two later chapters of this book, therefore, is intended to be read—as are the discussions on the other topics mentioned—in its *historical* context, rather than as an apologetic for or against any particular point of view. My goal is to present ideas, not sway opinion.

To help in this regard I might remind you—as I occasionally tell readers who write, taking me to task for something or another in one of my books—that characters in a book must be true to *themselves*. Obviously, not every character in fiction represents either author or publisher. It would be a narrow-minded publisher and unimaginative author who wrote and published nothing but what tightly reflected his or her own limited perspective. If *life* is to be accurately represented, a certain range of thought and opinion must be allowed for among the characters.

I suppose it cannot be helped that every character contains elements of the author who creates them. At the same time, none of these characters—Charles or Jocelyn Rutherford, Timothy Diggorsfeld, Bobby or Maggie McFee, nor anyone else in the story—is *me*. They are themselves. Not every word they say represents my particular viewpoint. Without such diversity there would be no way for characters in a book to engage in meaningful dialogue.

The topics debated by characters in this book were on everyone's minds. They were heated issues then. They remain heated issues today. You will no doubt find yourself agreeing with certain of the characters at some points, disagreeing at others. I encourage you, therefore, to keep in mind the historical context of the discussions where these issues are raised, not mentally arguing for or against any particular point of view that a certain character may voice. My desire as an author is not necessarily that we all reach agreement about these or any other doctrinal issues, but that we all think, that we learn, and that we grow closer to God as a result. If in the end you find yourself honing your own faith on the sharpening stones of these various controversial issues, then I will feel I have done my job well.

In closing I should say, too, that perhaps even more than any other series of mine which you may have read, THE SECRETS OF HEATHER-SLEIGH HALL truly is a *series*. Each of its titles will, I hope, give you a sense of completion and satisfaction. Yet at the same time it will be clear that "the whole story" has not yet been told with this one book. The first several books all combine to form a unity which none of the individual titles can achieve on their own. I beg the patience of my readers as the series develops, hoping you will remember that the various entrees of a "full-course literary meal" take longer to prepare than they do to consume.

I hope you enjoy the literary, historical, spiritual, and personal "journey" we are about to embark on together. As always, I can be contacted through the publisher or at PO Box 7003, Eureka, CA 95502.

Michael Phillips

Prologue

◆◆◆

The Secret of Heathersleigh Hall

1829-1865

Stormy Tryst

1829

A blustery wind swept down from out of the north. The sky steadily blackened through the afternoon hours as thick ominous clouds swirled overhead.

Darkness gradually descended over the south of England. The violence of the gale increased.

It whipped about unprotected corners of stone or wood with a frenzy that seemed determined to blow every dwelling in the region off its foundations and into the sea. Alas for those poor cottages with roofs of thatch, for the likes of such a storm had not been seen in a generation.

Reasonable men and women had long since taken to their beds. Children slept through the tumult with happy visions of angels dancing in the windy heavens. Their parents lay awake, praying the covering over them would remain intact till morning.

In the hours shortly before the stroke of midnight, fierce gusts now howled through every crevice, across slate roof tiles, and about the gables and turrets of the largest house in the north Devonshire downs. Even a tempest such as this could not hope to shake such a massive structure from its underpinnings. Yet its moans and eerie otherworldly sounds were enough to strike dread into the heart of anyone whose misfortune chanced to find them out in such a gale.

Behind the house—not so close as to threaten the structure, but only to cause wreckage to the garden nearby—large pines and firs swayed dangerously. Now and then a loud crack of breaking limb added a sharp report, as of cymbals, to the frenetic natural symphony, though the wind swallowed up their fall, and no soul heard them as they crashed to the earth below.

That the dead of winter had come there could be no doubt. Why the Creator had chosen a night such as this, full of evil forebodings, for the momentous event, none could say. Perhaps because what should have given great joy was destined instead to result in deceit, selfish ambition, and greed.

Before the darkness had passed and the wind gone to continue its mischief further south, death would visit this house. Generations would have to pass before the lie that followed would be brought, as must be the fate of all lies in the end, into the light.

A scream sounded from somewhere within the place. It was not the sound of terror, but of anguish and pain, for indeed the moment of woman's travail had come. It was followed by a distant rumble of thunder.

A lone window shone with the flickering of candles that somehow managed to stay alight despite the blasts from the heavens against the panes of glass. Inside, a second woman made what preparations she could for the hour of her calling, though she was not hopeful.

A rider approached, galloping hard through the impending storm. How he had won through the blackness was no less a miracle than that the servant lad sent to fetch him had gotten to the manse at all. Where the boy was now, no one paused to wonder.

The woman behind the second-floor window heard nothing of the hooves. She was busily engaged.

A flash of lightning lit the sky. Already the thunder which answered was closer than that which had sounded minutes earlier.

The rider dismounted, tied his horse to the rail with some difficulty, every piece of clothing on his body blowing about and doing its best to detach itself from his person and fly off into the night. A momentary gleam of white clerical collar revealed itself as the heavy cloak flapped open, though there was no one to see it.

He approached the entry. One knock was sufficient, for he was expected. A hand reached out and pulled him inside. Even before the wind had swallowed up the dull echo of the door's closing, the visitor was hurrying up the stairs after the master of the place.

The beginning as well as the end came quickly.

Within thirty minutes both midwife and vicar had carried out their respective offices.

The rains arrived in the meantime, and now pelted the glass windows and stone walls with furious force. With its first heavy drops the wind began to subside.

Not eager to brave the storm again, but even more reluctant to spend the night here—stories abounded in the region concerning the lord of the manor and his relationship with things of the night; if the house was not haunted already, it would surely be so after he was gone—the vicar offered his final condolences, then prepared to make his departure. Downstairs, he quietly accepted the proffered sheaf of one-pound notes, a huge sum to any man in his position.

From the landing above, the midwife silently observed the clandestine exchange. The services which the man of the cloth had come to render accompanied his position—he was not being paid for that. She knew well enough that the final words now spoken went well beyond what the parish ordained. What was being bought at this moment, she had no doubt, was silence. She only prayed the vicar would yet somehow do his duty before God.

She turned and tiptoed back. She must see to her charges until a wet nurse arrived in the morning. This room was no longer a fit place for new life, and the undertaker would be wanted before long.

It took not many minutes after discharging the vicar for the master of the house to seek like interview with her, although she became the immediate recipient of no such fortune. With intimidation, not cash, the unlikely pact was sealed between the highest person in the area and, in his judgment, one of the lowest. That he had required her services when the night began, and now needed her more than ever, did not raise the woman one speck in his eyes. If anything, it caused him to resent the very sight of her, and he spoke with disdain.

"You'll keep quiet about what you have seen here tonight," he said, in a menacing tone that hovered in the debatable region between question and threat.

The midwife said nothing.

"Do you hear me, woman!" he growled. Any doubt of his intent was suddenly gone. "My eldest *son* shall be the heir to all I possess. I presume my meaning is clear enough."

"Your meaning is perfectly clear," she returned.

What few remaining words passed between them were not uttered in pleasant tones. In the end the lord of the manor had his way, for he was a powerful man.

◆ ◆ ◆

It was not until the next night, alone in her own cottage with her prayers and her conscience, after husband and daughter were asleep, that the midwife decided what to do. She had scarcely slept in twenty-four hours. Her soul was ill at ease in the knowledge that she was party to a falsehood. Even more, that she had not summoned the strength to resist Lord Rutherford's sinister threats.

An inner sense told her that the events of the previous night carried a significance beyond what she could see. Despite the promise the man had extracted, she must yet seek some means to bring the truth to light.

She would hide a clue.

If her own mouth was silenced, the vow she had uttered could not prevent *another* from discovering the secret. She would pray a day would come when the facts of the incident would emerge. Meanwhile, she would take what steps her conscience dictated.

She opened the Bible which lay on her lap, and began thumbing through the pages she knew so well. The stories of this Book were dear to her heart. She found herself pausing at the midpoint of its first book.

As she read through the significant passage again, suddenly the words leapt off the page into her brain. As they did, involuntarily she glanced up and sent her eyes roving around the room. Suddenly the next phase of her plan came into focus.

She would leave her clue here, and hide it there! And then pray the Lord to bring faithful eyes to discern her hidden message.

———— ♦♦♦ ————

A fortnight passed.

The night was again late. The solitary figure of a woman crept through the silent corridors of the great house.

She who had been here in the midst of the storm two weeks earlier to attend life's miracle had now come on a far different errand. Something else was on her mind on this night, something she prayed would set right—however long it took—the lie she had been forced to tell. She had stolen through the wooded region nearest the west wing. After fall of darkness she hurried from the cover of trees across to the cold stone wall of the Hall. She knew the place well, for certain long-forgotten circumstances of her childhood had made her a frequent visitor here and playmate to a maid of the present lord's now-departed aunt. A little-used door near the servants' quarters had always remained unlocked until a late hour. By it on this night she gained entrance.

Another wind had risen, exactly as on that fateful night, though not so fierce. She hoped it would keep her footfall from being heard as she made her way through the darkened passageways.

Seen by none, she climbed the narrow stone staircase. Reaching the landing at the top, she fumbled in the darkness. At length her hands fell upon the key. She turned it with painstaking care lest its mechanism betray her. The bolt gave way, sounding only as a dull thud absorbed by the surrounding stones. She pulled the door toward her, then tiptoed inside.

Thin light from a pale moon shone into the small enclosure. She hadn't been in the old haunt for years, but remembered it like yesterday. In a few seconds she located a second key in its hiding place. She inserted it into the cleverly concealed lock which could not be seen even in broad daylight. She turned it and waited for the invisible door to give way in the wall. She had no right to know of such things inside a great mansion like the Hall. But her own father had carried out a good deal of the construction of the mysterious affair for the present lord's uncle. Overhearing him talk of it, she and her friend had sneaked here on more than one occasion to see what they could see. What the two young girls discovered proved essential to her purpose on this night so many years later.

The occupation of midwife was one that conjured images of individuals more acquainted with the unseen world than most mortals. This woman was in truth a God-fearing soul. Yet an observer upon this present occasion would likely have spread the report that she was a witch, seeing as how in the few seconds of blackness which resulted from a cloud's windy passage past the face of the moon, the woman disappeared through the wall of the room without a sound, and vanished.

It took some time to reach her destination. She could have brought a candle, but the faintest odor escaping into the occupied portions of the house might prompt inquiry and a possible search. She chose instead to rely on feet grown older, it was true, but whose memory of these precincts as they felt their way along was accurate and true. They would not lead her wrong.

The door she must exit at the other end was more perilous. One false move and she would be detected. She reached its reverse side. Here was no lock. With careful fingers she gently probed against the ancient wood. It moved an inch, then two.

She set an eye against it, and peered through the crack thus created. The room into which she must carry her mission was dark and unoccupied. Slowly she swung the heavy frame further on its hinges, then stepped tiptoeing out of the blackness onto a carpeted floor. Warm air and an unmistakable musty smell of accumulated knowledge greeted her.

She entered the room noiselessly, leaving the strange door open behind her.

She had only seen the large family Bible once years before, and hoped it had not been removed to some other place in the mansion. She could afford no time for a lengthy search. Surely her presence would be discovered if she tarried too long.

The grey reflection from the moon through a window again aided her design. She glanced around.

There was the Bible on the library table.

She breathed a sigh of relief, then continued forward. She stretched out her hand, then turned back the heavy, dark, ornate cover. She flipped through the first leaves until she came to the genealogical pages.

The woman squinted in the eerie light.

The lord of the manor had already entered the birth into the family record. She would add a notation beside it. Only one curious about family beginnings would investigate. She would pray for that person, whoever it might be and whenever he or she might lay eyes on this reference.

Here she would leave the clue which would set things right.

Her note took but a moment. Now she must hide the sacred book where only she for whose eyes they were intended would find them when time came for her to claim her rightful legacy. She closed the book and lifted it from the sideboard, then carried it to the hiding place where it would lie for a season. Her father had been not only a mason, but also a skilled craftsman who had cunningly fabricated one of the very pieces of furniture in this room with a tiny secret chamber. She would have known nothing about it except that he had perfected the design with an earlier model for their own humble dwelling, and she had discovered the nature of the working mechanism.

It did not take long to conceal the book.

She now closed the secret panel in front of it, slid in the drawer which hid the lock from visibility, removed the key to the inner chamber and took it with her, then finally closed the outer door to the secretary. There would the book lie until the appointed time for its unveiling.

She returned the way she had come, joining the small key onto the ring of the larger by which she had gained entrance to the hidden passageway.

She then hid both in the wall of the ancient tower.

Mysterious Alliance

1847-1856

These were difficult years for everyone in Britain, rich and poor alike. The failure of the previous two years' potato crop in Ireland had caused a famine with repercussions for the poor throughout Great Britain.

The troubles of the rich, however, were caused by a failure of financial markets, not potato harvests, and Henry Rutherford, Lord of the Manor of Heathersleigh,* had grown frantic to save his Devon estate amid badly declining fortunes. Keeping the full truth from his children, he had sold off small portions of several outlying tracts of land, though the receipts from such sales had done little to arrest the financial slide.

Lord Rutherford's difficulties were in no small measure amplified by certain questionable speculations which had soured with the commercial crisis and collapse of credit. In truth, Rutherford feared legal repercussions if the details of two or three of these investments were discovered.

His one hope of exoneration lay in the fact that an invisible partner in one of the most lucrative of his pursuits was a longtime personal

---

*Pronounced Heathers-lee

friend and high-placed cleric in the Church of England. In exchange for continued discretion, Bishop Crompton let it be known that any large donation or deed of land to the Church would reflect with favor upon Lord Rutherford should future legal unpleasantnesses be visited upon him. The bishop would personally, he said, vouch for Lord Rutherford's innocence insofar as complicity was concerned with those who had hatched the scheme.

Such a benefaction on Lord Rutherford's part, the bishop implied, would have the added benefit of insuring his own silence concerning certain events of a night long past. What had happened that evening, when the bishop was still vicar in Milverscombe, was a secret the two men held with only one other.

"A certain parcel of land comes to mind," the bishop added when the two met to speak of the matter. "With a little house on it—you used it formerly as a gamekeeper's cottage, I believe."

Lord Rutherford eyed him skeptically.

"Seeing as how you no longer employ a gamekeeper," the bishop continued, "and the place, as I understand it, is vacant, I should think it a fair exchange in order to insure that you are able to retain the larger portions of your estate."

"But I still have immediate obligations."

"There may be an additional cash advantage to you in such a transaction," replied the bishop. "Let us propose your making a grant of the land and a small portion of the woodland, and my paying you personally for purchase of the dwelling."

"What could you possibly want with such an out-of-the-way place?" asked Lord Rutherford.

"I have always coveted it," replied the bishop, "thinking what an enjoyable country home it would make when the pressures of my position become too much to bear. A spiritual retreat, as it were."

Henry Rutherford smiled wryly. The idea of his gamekeeper's cottage being used as a site for meditation and prayer was altogether too humorous.

He was loathe to part with the cottage, yet realized he had little choice. His ancient ally had become an extremely influential man. This one transaction could significantly alleviate both his legal and financial anxieties.

The deal was soon consummated, secretly of course. Only one other soul would ever know of it. She who already possessed one secret with the two men would in time share this one as well.

———————— ♦ ♦ ♦ ————————

It was several years later when the bishop chanced to see the woman on the streets of the village. Whether it was ill luck or divine providence that caused their paths to cross, the reader himself must determine.

Bishop Crompton did not make a habit of visiting the village when at his retreat. On this present occasion, however, a pang of nostalgia swept over him for the old parish where he had begun his ecclesiastical career. He was no longer a young man, and in recent months his conscience had begun to whisper to him concerning many things he had done, as well as what manner of man he had been.

Suddenly approaching along the street near his former church, he saw the woman he had not laid eyes on since that fateful stormy night. He knew her in an instant, as she did him.

In truth, the events of that night had begun gathering themselves more forcefully about the old midwife's memory, for the year approached when she had planned to divulge that which would unlock the mystery only these two knew. She had, however, begun to harbor doubts concerning such revelation. The young woman had turned out not of altogether virtuous character, taking more after their father than her brother. The notion had come to her recently that perhaps providence had decreed the deceit for future good of both estate and village.

She was in a quandary over what to do. Seeing the former vicar thus jolted her, as if the meeting carried divine import.

The bishop nodded stiffly, thinking to pass her by. But the midwife paused, then spoke.

"I know why you are in Heathersleigh Cottage," she said.

"Yes, and what is that to me?" he replied.

"Just that there you are with plenty to eat, while me and mine have nothing but gruel to keep us alive. You received fifty pounds and the house. What have I got to show for my silence?"

"What do you expect me to do about it?"

"I have a married daughter who now has a young one of her own and another on the way. It's all any of us can do to put food down our throats. These are evil times, vicar, especially for one who knows what

I know. Surely a man such as yourself is not beyond feeling compassion for the likes of us."

Squirming behind his collar, Crompton managed a few moments later to conclude the awkward interview.

But for days thereafter he was plagued with the woman's words. He could not deny them to be true. He had all his life enjoyed plenty. She, whose need was greater, possessed next to nothing. Yet what could he do? What *should* he do?

The bishop's health decreased as his age advanced. Still further did his conscience waken as the years added to their number. He retired from his official position, took up permanent residence in his wooded cottage in Devon, which had from the moment of dubious transfer belonged to him rather than the Church.

———————— ♦ ♦ ♦ ————————

When the good bishop Arthur Crompton died a year or two later, all thought it strange and highly irregular that the unmarried man who had risen so high in ecclesiastical circles should leave his home to an aging local peasant woman with whom not a single individual could recall seeing him talking even once.

Perhaps not so many would have considered it strange had they heard the words feebly whispered from between his dying lips: *"My Father, it has been a life too much wasted loving myself, too little given to listening to you and doing what you told me. I cannot help it, for this life is done. I shall serve you more diligently in the next. Forgive my foolishness. You have been a good Father to me, though I have been a childish son. Perhaps now you will be able to make a true man of me. In the meantime, do your best with this place. Make good come of it, though I obtained it by greed. Bless the woman and those who follow. Give life to all who enter this door. May they know you sooner than I."*

He paused, closed his eyes in near exhaustion, then added inaudibly—

And now . . . I am ready . . . take me home.

None heard the words, save him to whom they had been spoken. He heard, and he would answer.

Most vexed of all by the curious turn was the aging Henry Rutherford, who, now that his fortunes had again reversed, would have done anything to resecure the property and oust the old woman. But he had no legal recourse. The will, brought forth by the bishop's solicitor, was legally irrefutable.

There were now only two alive who knew the connection existing between the man of the cloth and the woman of swaddling clothes—she herself, and he whose secret both had sworn to protect. It was a secret she never revealed as originally planned. In the end, she could only conclude that the blessing had indeed been passed on as God intended.

Both bishop and peasant carried the knowledge of their unknown alliance to their respective graves.

Everyone said the woman's former profession must have made her privy to some fact which resulted in the strange bequest of the former bishop's country home. No living soul ever discovered what that secret was.

Thus did a second mystery come to be added to the first.

Root of Strife
◆◆◆

1865

A five-year-old boy tiptoed toward the darkened bedchamber where an old man lay, as the boy thought, asleep.

He had seen the nurse leave and walk down the hallway a few moments earlier. Now curiosity drove him toward the door. It stood half open.

He paused and cast a peek inside. The room was dusky, for heavy curtains were pulled to keep out the sunlight. He inched through the opening without touching the door, entered the room, and now paused.

Across the floor, on a bed between sheets of white, lay the thin form of Lord Henry Rutherford, who had always seemed to him ancient, and now looked to have left the reckoning of earthly years behind altogether. One of his thin arms lay outside the bedcovers at his side, appearing even whiter to the youngster than the sheet, though not quite so white as what hair he still possessed atop a skull over which the skin seemed to have been stretched rather more tightly than seemed comfortable.

With eyes wide in fascinated awe, the boy crept forward.

Instinctively he knew his grandfather was dying. He could not help being afraid. Everyone had been walking about the Hall and speaking in hushed tones, with doctors and nurses coming and going, for a week. For just such reason they had come from the city to visit. A faint odor in the room contributed to the dreadful terror of the place, a smell which indicated something other than health was present.

He reached the bedside and stopped. He stared down upon the ashen and wasted face. Lord Rutherford had not spent his life putting others ahead of himself. This flaw of character contributed to the fact that as he now came to the end of his earthly days, he was exceedingly wealthy, and at the same time nervously ill at ease over his prospects for the future. As yet he had found no way to make use of the former fact to alleviate the latter concern.

The expression on his countenance, as he now slept fitfully, looked as if he were having an uncomfortable dream over precisely this moral dilemma. No slightest twitch of facial feature, however, betrayed that life still existed within him.

The boy was well aware of the old man's peculiarities, for Lord Rutherford and his cavernous old manor house were the stuff of many a family legend. Into the eager ears of wide-eyed nieces, nephews, grandchildren, cousins, and servants had been passed the certain knowledge that portions of the Hall were haunted, some said with the ghost of Lady Rutherford and various of her also-departed sisters.

Truth being no requisite ingredient to the receptive acceptance of such tales, they had grown through the years, gaining credibility from the strange noises that issued from the upper portions of the house in winter—the very time of year when, as everyone knew, Lady Eliza had breathed her last. Old Lord Henry himself believed that she had returned to the Hall to haunt him, confided two or three of the eldest servants, for had he not undertaken to board up that region of the garret through which she always contrived to slip between the here and hereafter? It was failure of these efforts, they said, that in the end had driven him mad.

All this, along with the spookier embellishments of a rising generation, went through the boy's brain as he continued to stare at the bed. His heart pounded, wondering what was happening deep inside the frail form.

Suddenly both the old man's closed eyelids fluttered and twitched, as if his eyes were rolling about inside their sockets.

In panic the boy thought to flee. But his feet remained nailed to the floor. Now the ancient eyes began to open, as if the sense of some presence beside the bed had awakened him. He spied a form, yet knew it not as his grandson from London. His pupils widened, but he yet lived within the fading fragments of the dream which left him more slowly than his consciousness returned.

The old man's eyes widened and locked onto those of the boy, which returned their gaze with mute terror. It was indeed as if a ghost had come to life right before the boy's eyes.

Suddenly the thin arm shot from the bed.

The grip of ancient fingers closed around the youngster's arm with a strength they had not exercised in years.

In abject horror, the boy's heart pounded within him like a drum. But he remained still as a statue.

"Cynthia ... my dear young Cynthia," the old man whispered, "—you've come back, just like I prayed you would."

The boy tried to speak and identify himself. But his tongue could find no more power of movement than his legs. His grandfather was mistaking him for his mother!

"God forgive me ..." said the old man, his voice gaining strength, "... we'll set all to right now that you've come back—"

He closed his eyes and relaxed a moment to draw in a breath.

"I ... I was a fool ..." he tried to begin again, in a faltering voice, "... they were terrible times ... I had to protect ... they tried to take the Hall ... it was your mother ... if she had only—"

The terrified boy could not begin to grasp the significance of the few cryptic words that followed. And then they were cut short.

Suddenly light blazed into the room.

"Giffy!" cried the nurse, bounding through the door. "What are you doing disturbing your grandfather?"

"I ... I only came in for a look," stammered the boy.

"Don't you know he is weak and mustn't be disturbed!" she reproached, hurrying toward the bedside as if her rights of both ownership and protection had been seriously violated. "Go back to your cousin—he's playing outside. You stay with Charlie, do you hear!"

She took hold of Lord Rutherford's thin hand, unwrapped its fingers from the boy's arm, and laid it back at his side on the bed. In the few seconds since the nurse's entry, the last lingering remnants of the man's dream dissipated into forgetfulness. He lay back on his pillow and breathed easily.

While the fussy nurse attended to him, muttering angrily and chastising herself for leaving the room, the boy crept silently out, the possessor of a secret whose significance he was as yet unaware of. The shock of seeing the dying man pushed the odd message for some time from his mind.

It was a secret no other mortal would ever share. His grandfather died later that same night, speaking not another word to a living soul.

WILD GROWS THE HEATHER IN DEVON

PART I

◆◆◆

A Happy Family

1894-1897

1

A Mother's Dream

✦✦✦

*A*n observer overlooking the southwest tip of England in the summer of 1894 would have beheld a rocky and historic coastline. From Land's End to Bournemouth stretched harbors and shipping centers from which centuries of pilgrims, merchants, sailors, and pirates had set sail to all points of the known world.

In front of that coast spread a deep blue sea, its water not warm like the Mediterranean, yet more temperate than any other spot surrounding the many isles that combined to make Great Britain. Above it rose a sky which on this summer's day shared its bluey vastness with an abundance of white moving clouds.

Coastal cliffs and inlets, river mouths and coves, all met the splashing water at the dividing edge between sea and land. Beyond rose the hilly downs of the shires of Cornwall, Somerset, Dorset, and Devon, those counties of England's great southern peninsula which protruded westward into the Atlantic. Their inland domains gave way to green rolling hills, occasionally rugged, many patches of wooded forest, and great green stretches of grass and pastureland.

The terrain that surrounded the village of Milverscombe in the county of Devon was a particularly gentle and inviting one, with sufficient change to offer infinite interest, yet without any aspect that a traveler viewing the landscape would consider severe. No mountains could be seen, though hills rose and fell from horizon to horizon. No seascape presented itself, though in fact the rocky shores of the Bristol Channel lay only some fifteen miles northward. No great forest of fairytale depth worried local youngsters at play, though trees and wooded areas abounded. The nearest city of size was Exeter, but villages and hamlets were numerous.

It was a land good for doing most of the things man has been given to do upon the earth, and the many cattle, occasional sheep, and yet fewer horses, along with cultivated fields of grain and potatoes, gave evidence that the men of the region were doing them. The greater proportion of the terrain, however, yet remained untilled and ungrazed, and thus unspoiled and untamed for the walkers who enjoyed exploring its fields and public footpaths with no more concern for property boundaries than common courtesy would dictate.

Today, on just such an excursion, a small boy and girl sprinted with carefree abandon up a grassy knoll toward where a single daisy had popped its white-and-yellow head out of the ground.

"I got it! I got it!" cried the girl, reaching the crown first, not because she was faster than her older brother, but because the competitive fires burned less brightly in him.

She plucked up the flower in a single motion. She turned clutching its slender stalk and ran back down the hill to where her smiling mother strolled with slow contentment, a few beads of perspiration beginning to gather on her forehead.

"Look, Mummy—look at the pretty flower."

"It's beautiful, Amanda," said the woman, stooping to give the daisy a sniff as her daughter held it up, though she knew the fragrance would not be an appealing one.

"I got it before George!" added the girl.

"I saw that, dear. My, but you are swift for such a little girl."

"I'm almost five, Mummy. That's not so little."

"How right you are, Amanda!" laughed the mother. "Not so little after all." Together they continued on up the knoll, as the woman contentedly glanced about her at the peaceful countryside.

It was not exactly a solemn region, as the highlands of the north are solemn. Once at the remote edge of England's borders of civilization, this land was now ever more thoroughly crisscrossed with roads and railways. Industry, invention, and progress were steadily coming to the entire isle. Yet even in such modern times at the close of the great century there remained a hint of wildness here, reminding one of the days when ancient Celts fled westward to escape the invading Saxons. Many open, remote, and unspoiled places still could be discovered where human progress had left no discernible imprint.

Devon was not *quite* as modern yet as London, Surrey, and Kent. And that was perfectly agreeable to Jocelyn Rutherford. She preferred a home in an out-of-the-way place, far from the staring eyes of London society.

Six-year-old George was not so much interested in the flower in his sister's hand as in the barely recognizable shape just poking its head out of the ground beside the stalk Amanda had so unceremoniously severed. As Jocelyn and Amanda approached the spot, he bent down on his knees, with face six inches off the ground, to examine it.

"What are you looking at, George?" asked his mother. A little sigh as she spoke betrayed her fatigue from the walk.

"I think there's another daisy inside this little green ball," he said.

"I want it!" cried the girl in gleeful enthusiasm, squirming down energetically beside him.

"It's not ready, Amanda," said the boy. "It's not a flower yet. It's only a bud."

"What's a bud?"

"Like a rolled-up flower before it gets to be a flower."

"When will it be a flower, George?"

"I don't know—when it gets enough sunshine to open it."

The boy jumped up. "Come on, Amanda—let's find another!"

Off he ran across the grass. His sister scampered after him as fast as her tiny but determined legs would carry her. Already she had forgotten the daisy. It dropped from her hand not far from where it had grown out of the grass to attract her notice.

Gently Jocelyn Rutherford lowered herself to the warm, fragrant grass and watched the two as they raced off down the slope. The walk out from the Hall had taxed her, for she was six months along toward bearing her third child.

Absently she picked up the forgotten daisy, then held it up and gazed a moment at the simple glory of its happy face.

And I'm happy here, too, she thought to herself.

Out here on the downs, there were no mirrors to mock her. Here, her eyes had only to gaze *outward* upon all that she had been given— the home behind her, the countryside she so loved, and her two treasured young ones. Here, she did not have to gaze inward nor to think about her face . . .

But now, of course, she *had* thought about it. Almost of its own accord, her hand came up to trace the familiar outlines of the bright red birthmark that stretched from neck to forehead . . . the mark that for so many years had defined not merely what she looked like but who she was.

But not *here*, she told herself, deliberately lowering her hand. *Not here at Heathersleigh.*

Jocelyn especially loved the peaceful seclusion of her home. Knowing what her face looked like to acquaintances and passersby, how could she not feel out of place in the society of which her husband was a part? Charles was always such a great encouragement. But she knew how people were. Here at Heathersleigh she could be content, and not have to wonder what people were thinking.

George and Amanda did not look at her strangely. In such young eyes their mother was just what she had always been. Out here Jocelyn could be happy that no one else's eyes were upon her, not even her own.

And Charles ... for some reason she could never understand, her husband had always seen beyond her marred face and loved her for the woman she was. Even now she could not fully fathom the happy circumstances that had come to her life.

A happy face, thought Jocelyn, looking down at the daisy again.

She had all any woman could dream of—a husband who loved her, two dear children, another on the way—and even a home in a stately manor house. She was, after all, the wife of the new lord of the manor of Heathersleigh. With only a bit of imagination and will, she could convince herself to stop wondering when it all would end.

Still clutching the smiling little flower, Jocelyn pushed herself up carefully from the hillside and set off after her children with an energetic and determined step. What was this newfound happiness in her life but an opportunity, a chance to redeem her pain and turn it into good?

Here she could do what was the one thing she wanted most in life— to be the best wife, and the best mother, in all England.

She would lavish upon her children what she had not had—affection and acceptance. If her own mother had been unable to love her, she could still turn the pain to good in the lives of George and Amanda and the new baby growing inside her. She would love them and accept them and pour herself into them with all the energy she possessed. Never would any of them have a single doubt that she loved them fully, exactly as they were.

As George's and Amanda's happy shouts and cries receded into the distance, Jocelyn's gaze followed them toward the village—the peaceful little cottages, the narrow streets, and the church with its steeple stretching so straight and high into the sky. Then, slowly, her eyes swept back over the warm summer's landscape toward the Hall which was now her home.

Unknown to Jocelyn Rutherford there was One who beheld her even now as she gazed out over the hills of her home. He it was who had given her the mark of love for which she would one day thank him. She would learn of that gratitude which lies at the root of all true joy. The lesson, however, would not come without change and pain. He is never content for us to be merely content. He desires that we be always becoming more. His will is that our contentment arise from gratitude rather than safe or pleasant circumstance. Toward such a true contentment he was already taking Jocelyn Rutherford, though she did not yet recognize that it was on such a pilgrimage she was bound.

"I really am happy here," she murmured as she watched her children play on the next hilltop. Here, she had been given a chance for love ... and motherhood. Here, she had the opportunity to make her pain almost seem worthwhile by making sure her own children never had to suffer.

Here at Heathersleigh Hall, she was at home. If she had her way, she would never leave this place as long as she lived.

2

A Father's Vision

♦ ♦ ♦

The physical landscape of the county of Devon had not changed dramatically in the three hundred years since the mighty Spanish Armada dropped anchor off its rugged southwestern coast, intent on invading England.

The vast Spanish empire of the sixteenth century had been at its height when the huge fleet of 130 proud warships, merchantmen, and transports first laid eyes on the rugged coast of Plymouth in the year 1588. There, in blustery seas, the Armada anchored in preparation for invasion.

The entire island looked southwest to Devonshire ... and trembled.

What awaited the Spanish, however, was humiliation and defeat at the hands of Francis Drake and Charles Howard. After a century of world domination on the high seas in worlds old and new, the empire of Isabella, Cortés, and Philip II began a decline from which it would never recover.

A new power was rising in the world in this sixteenth century—*England*.

Given impetus by its triumph in the landmark sea battle, the influence of earth's most strategic isle rose through the seventeenth and eighteenth centuries to dominate the future of Europe.

And now as the nineteenth century drew to a close, mighty Britannia not only ruled the seas, but held influence over the entire globe. In politics, finance, industry, and ideas, the progressivism of England led the world toward a new century.

It was a good and happy and proud time to be English, notwithstanding changes looming on the political scene and rumblings of many strange happenings on the Continent. Queen Victoria was still on the throne at the seasoned age of seventy-six. And when the new century dawned a mere five years from now, there was every reason to believe the coming years would continue bright with the promise of peace and prosperity for the citizens of the greatest kingdom on earth.

Epitomizing this modern era of which she was a part, a young girl now walked hand in hand with her father along the main street of Milverscombe. By the light bounce of her step an observer would conclude she possessed no care in the world. Indeed, she looked like the leader of the two as she pulled her father energetically along with the same enthusiasm she had shown for the daisy with her mother the year before.

Charles Rutherford, a well-proportioned and distinguished gentleman of thirty-eight years, was clearly pleased with his eldest daughter's vigor and enthusiasm.

Little Amanda was already thoughtful beyond her years because her father had taught her to be so. A thorough modern himself (though his title was ancient), his greatest joy was teaching his young son and daughters to *think*. He engaged them in constant dialogue. The subject mattered little. Whatever came into his head or one of theirs was fit grist for their strengthening intellectual mills, whose stones he had begun to harden and hone long before they could even talk.

He never addressed them as children. He intelligently answered any question they thought to pose as if speaking to a mature man or woman. But such answers more often than not drove the questioning back upon them, probing yet more aspects of the matter at hand. He answered by raising points they had not considered, urging them to observe and ponder, to weigh and analyze, and to form their own conclusions. Always did he push them deeper into their own thoughts and minds, forcing them ever and again to face those basic queries so essential to mental curiosity and growth—*Why* are things as they are? *How* do things function?

His own perspectives mattered less at their ages than that they used their powers of logic and reason. He would let them develop each according to his or her personal bent. His chief goal was to give them the intellectual stimulation to do so, rather than force his own views upon them.

"Do not accept what you cannot understand," he was fond of saying. "Do not take what comes merely because such has it always been, or because by such traditions have people formerly been taught. Question *everything*." At the same time he emphasized that they could do and be anything they chose. There were no limits to what man, or woman, might achieve.

Such tenets defined the reformist creed he espoused. Those of like outlook, whose ranks were swelling to great numbers these days, took them as foundation stones of truth because they sounded so enlightened. These men and women were more *products* of their age, however, than *authors* of its modernism. In actuality, most knew less about truth than they realized.

Charles Rutherford was an advocate of the new order in every sense of the term. The time had not yet arrived in his own life when he would send his probing mentality toward the sources of that modernism, and inquire into his own role in it. When it came he would do so with the same incisive scrutiny with which he now engaged the millstones of his liberal brain toward societal concerns.

Then indeed would he confront truth. In anticipation of such an encounter, unknown to himself, others were already praying. But it would not come until his personal soil was ready for the reception of ideas which at this moment could not have been further from his consciousness.

As a result of their interactive dialogue, seven-year-old George had become engrossed in the whys and hows of mechanical things. Young George shared his father's passion to understand gadgets, devices, and the workings of the physical world around him. Father and son let pass no chance to observe locomotives and other engines, and they were tremendously excited by the steam, electric, and gasoline-powered motorcars that Charles saw from time to time on the streets of London. At home, they liked tinkering with machines in their workshop and attempting to build inventions of their own.

His current companion, however, cared little for the engineering marvels of the day. Her fascination lay with society. Already motions stirred within her, encouraged by her father's promptings, to rise high in that order and make her mark upon it. Not for some time, however, would she grow to recognize that society was composed of *people* with individual needs.

Charles glanced down at his daughter with an admiring smile. *What a time to be English*, he thought. *What a time to be a young woman, facing advantages as never before in history. It's a wonderful age in which to live!*

A man approached. He was clearly of humble origins. His shirt and trowsers were soiled with the dirt of honest labor in his fields and among his sheep. Face and hands were rough and showed the weather.

"Good day to ye, milord," he said, placing hand to a cap as worn and dirty as his boots.

"And to you, Mudgley," replied the girl's father, pausing a moment. He dropped her hand and held his own out to the man. "How are your sheep?" he asked. "About ready for the shearing, I would say."

"Next week, it is."

"I thought so—does it look to be a good yield?"

"Middlin', sir."

"Will you be needing help? I've been attempting to perfect a mechanical apparatus to speed up the process without drawing so much blood. If you're short I can send some of my men over for the day. It will give me a chance to try out my device."

"That's good of you, sir," replied the man with grateful and humble smile.

As they spoke, Amanda watched silently. She beheld the two as if they symbolized opposite poles on the social spectrum, as indeed they did, and revolved the differences, to the extent that she was capable of, in her young mind.

As the two continued on their way a few minutes later, Amanda twisted her nose and glanced back at the sheepherder.

"He smelled bad, Papa," she said.

"The smell of honest labor is nothing to be ashamed of, Amanda," her father replied, "nor something for others to despise."

"I still don't like it."

"Men of the land like Mudgley are the true noble breed of our nation, Amanda. Without them, where would any of us be? We must always seek to do what we can for them."

Amanda glanced around again, then turned and fell in step beside her father. She still wasn't convinced.

3

Of Tomatoes and the Future

♦♦♦

$\mathcal{H}$eathersleigh Hall, the Devonshire mansion which Jocelyn and Charles Rutherford and their family called home, had been originally built in the mid-seventeenth century and added to numerous times in the intervening years. It had reached its present form during the occupancy of Charles' grandfather, Lord Henry Rutherford, who had added extensively to the west wing. The impact of some of his lesser-known interior changes had long since been forgotten.

And certainly there was little talk of building inside the mansion's massive grey stone walls on this lovely June morning in 1897. Instead, voices could be heard in lively discussion around the breakfast table—and one voice in particular.

The venerable queen of mighty Britannia who ruled the globe seemed a fit model for the determined young monarch of this home, who enforced her dominion with both energy and charm. That she had learned to exert herself yet more forcefully in the years since the incident of the daisy and the encounter with the sheepherder was clear enough.

"I do not think I want the tomato today," she announced.

"It's all right, dear," placated her mother's gentle voice. "You don't have to eat it."

"In fact," persisted the girl, "I don't even want to see it. I want it taken away. I do not want it on my plate again."

The kitchen staff exchanged amused glances as they listened to the conversation from the breakfast room. Such exchanges were hardly new. The girl was one who knew what she wanted and usually got it.

At the table, the young lady paused and smiled sweetly and irresistibly.

"You know, Mother," she added, "I think I just realized I hate tomatoes."

Jocelyn returned the smile.

"The plates are all prepared the same in the kitchen, Amanda, with the whole breakfast," she said. "But you can choose what you want to eat of it."

"But I don't even want to *see* a tomato on my plate, Mother. There is no reason for it to be there day after day."

"That is the way the plates are always prepared, dear."

"Then it can change," rejoined the girl. "Papa says I shouldn't do things just because that is how they have been. Papa says we should demand change."

"On some mornings you may *want* the tomato. You ate everything off your plate just yesterday. Perhaps if we just left—"

"That was yesterday," interrupted the girl with perfectly pleasant countenance, though unmistakable tone, "but I do not want to see it there ever again."

Jocelyn glanced helplessly over toward her husband, while young George ate his breakfast as if nothing out of the ordinary was going on.

Charles Rutherford looked at his wife with obvious amusement.

"I'm afraid Amanda is right, Jocie," he chuckled. "I have told her that very thing."

"Then you explain it to her," laughed Jocelyn.

"Quite right, Amanda," the man now said, turning toward his daughter. "Do not accept anything simply because it is tradition. Think for yourself. Why *does* every plate in England have to display a tomato every morning? Is it a worthy tradition? We must challenge any practice that has become outdated and is no longer relevant for our times.—There, is that what you had in mind, Jocie?"

"I'm not certain you conveyed what I was trying to say, Charles," she laughed. "But I concede your point. Amanda is as free a thinker as her father!—Sarah," she said, turning toward the kitchen.

A maid appeared.

"If you please, Sarah," she said, "could we have a new plate for Amanda . . . *without* a tomato?"

The maid complied cheerfully, and everyone was content, the parents no less than the daughter.

Mother and father did not consider the exchange indicative of conflict. If their daughter did not want a tomato, who were they to insist otherwise? Self-rule was the order of the day. The family thus continued happily with their breakfast, none realizing the import of the seemingly trivial event.

How insignificant do some matters appear at the time, yet how large later do they loom in the memory, when the perspective of years sharpens the lens of truth. It is not many in this world who are wise enough to heed what lies beyond the earth's curve. If the sun is shining, it is enough . . . though perhaps it ought not to be.

The Rutherfords were a family representative in many ways of the well-to-do of the times—affluent and enlightened. Similarly did the European family of nations look toward a new century in the midst of unprecedented comfort, prosperity, and self-contentment.

Neither nations nor family, however, knew that much different times lay ahead than they envisioned. Out of sight behind the horizon, like a new and unseen Spanish Armada, storm clouds were already gathering. Little did the would-be heir of her father's reformist ideas know what the new century would hold, or how the comfortable realm over which she now presided would one day be turned upside down.

On this particular morning the father of the family Rutherford was even less inclined than usual toward anything that might disturb the harmony and pleasure of existence. Other things than tomatoes were on his mind throughout breakfast, for a great honor was about to come to him. On a day such as this, he would have given his daughter anything she asked.

"Well, Jocie," Charles finally said when the children had been excused and taken away by their nanny, "our big day is almost here."

"*Your* big day, don't you mean?" replied his wife, taking a last sip of her tea.

"You are part of it all with me, Jocelyn—you know that."

She smiled but said nothing. Charles was so kind to her. Yet sometimes she wondered if he would ever really understand the anxiety and stress being out in public caused her. Would her lingering doubts ever disappear?

She dabbed her napkin to her lips and then laid it beside her plate. "You know that I am proud of you," she said. "And I will be there at your side, as I promised. But now," she added, rising from the table and giving him a kiss, "I have some things to do."

"If you want me," she added, disappearing through the doorway, "I'll be in the kitchen."

4

Reflections and Dreams
••••

An hour later, Charles Rutherford stood gazing absently out his study window.

The final reminders of an early summer's storm swirled about overhead. A tempestuous wind had preceded last evening's warm drenching rain, and now its lingering gusts were blowing and pushing the last grey clouds ahead of them in the direction of Land's End and out to sea.

Through constantly opening and closing holes between them, a bright sun was doing its best to shine out. Its rays, working in harmony with what rain still wrung itself from the clouds in occasional spurts, produced now and then a momentary curve of rainbow. The clear sky above the eastern horizon was steadily lightening, and by afternoon it would doubtless be blue overhead. Pastures and trees, hedges and meadows, forests and cultivated gardens, dripped clean and fresh from their dousing, and the sun, when it finally triumphed, would send sparkles reigning across every inch of the earth's showered surface.

But this silent, blustery music of the universe was lost on its observer this morning. Heedless of both rainbow and its meaning, Charles gazed out over the landscape of the estate. Though all thought of tomatoes had long since left his mind, the morning's incident had put him in a temporarily nostalgic mood. As he gazed out over the landscape of the estate, images from his own childhood came back to him.

Actually, he smiled to himself. Amanda was not so very different than he had been at her age. The realization brought to mind the old couple of the woods to whom as a youngster he had more than once voiced his *own* independent spirit.

———————— ♦♦♦ ————————

A_y, Master Charles," came the slightly high-pitched but melodic voice of the Irishman, and he could hear the words as if it were yesterday, " 'tis any fool can see what's wrong with the world and ought to be changed. But 'tis the wise man who can see what's right and ought to be preserved."

Bobby McFee's Irish accent gave the words almost a mystical import in the boy's youthful imagination. This reaction was strengthened no doubt by a somewhat wild appearance, as well as the fact that he was in the habit of saying such odd, out-of-the-way things.

"New is not always better, Master Charles," the man went on. "It may seem better, God only knows. But it may be a step backward in the end."

It was a day not unlike this. The sun shone and the wind blew. Charles peered across the mown and hedge-lined field to the edge of the woods beyond. In his mind's eye he could almost make out the remnants of the well-worn path across the grass, which then disappeared into the trees.

He continued to smile with almost a nostalgic longing. Those were happy times, the days of his childhood. During the summer months he must have tromped over that path to the McFee cottage nearly every day. And as his reflections carried him away, he recalled one such visit.

The stone and timber dwelling where Robert McFee lived with his wife, Margaret, known to everyone for miles as Maggie, was in actual fact far more than a mere cottage, though such it had always been called. The very size of the thatch-roofed structure indicated an original ownership higher on the social scale than any of the peasant dwellings scattered throughout the hills and dales surrounding Milverscombe.

The commonly accepted legend concerning the place was that it had been constructed in the early eighteenth century as a lodge for the gamekeeper of Heathersleigh Hall, for at that time the land upon which the cottage rested had lain well within the expansive borders of the estate. The passage of time, however, and the financial misfortune of Charles' grandfather, had succeeded in vastly diminishing those borders and forcing the sale of much property, including at one point the gamekeeper's cottage.

It was a credible theory. There was no reason to doubt the truth of it, and no one did. Old deeds and records buried somewhere within the Hall's thick stone walls would have in fact confirmed most of the details of the cottage's early history, if they ever chanced to come into the light of day. The story of its later years, however, was another matter.

How exactly the property came into the hands of the McFees, if they knew the details at all, Bobby and Maggie never said. The villagers speculated that if a father or grandfather of one of the two had bought the place, then he surely must have had considerably more resources than had come down since, for the old couple lived very simply and frugally, keeping to themselves.

Some called them queer; others called them quaint. The townspeople in general considered them a strange lot, though Bobby's knowledge of animals was so vast that none of them could have gotten along without him. They were therefore willing to put up with his eccentricities. And his wife made herself indispensable to the villagers in a thousand ways. She knew much that was not commonly known, about medicine and weather, about herbs and other plants, and about humanity in general. In times long past Maggie would doubtless have been burned as a witch. The poor of the region now thought of her as an angel. The well-to-do didn't know what to think of her, and cared even less.

Charles had heard his own father comment on their various peculiarities more than once. But when he was young he never saw anything so unusual about them—only that they were old-fashioned and looked as woodsy as their surroundings, as if they had indeed stepped out of the pages of a fairy tale.

There was nothing he liked better, in fact, than visiting the McFees. There was always so much interesting going on about the place, Mr. McFee in his barn and his wife busy in her garden. Whenever he came they made time for him, and never minded the childish importunity about modern things which had possessed him even as a boy.

He had made the mistake of taking his cousin to visit them once. But he had been just like the rest, and had come away making fun of the two, and him along with them. But on the day of the visit he now remembered, he had been alone.

"Come, Master Charles," said McFee, laying down the blade with which he had been planing a plank of wood. "I think Maggie's about t' call us for lunch. Then afterwards, you and me will go up into yon hills t' see if we can fetch a trout or two from the lake for ye to take back t' yer mother."

He led the way from the barn into the dwelling which sat in front of it, where his wife awaited them in her kitchen.

"Sit down, Master Charles," said the woman, "and be welcome as always to our humble fare."

As the future lord of the manor took his seat, she placed a plate of sliced brown bread on the plain wooden table in front of them.

"We have white bread every day," said the boy in a boastful but innocent tone.

The two McFees glanced at one another and both smiled.

"You'll discover one day that sometimes the simple pleasures are best," said Maggie. "And that what comes from the earth satisfies more than what comes from the hand of man."

"Why is that?" asked the lad.

"Because it's closer to the hand of God," she replied. "The further back and nearer to God's making of a thing you can get, the better and purer it's likely to be. The hand of man spoils more than it improves what God has made."

"But God doesn't really make things, like people do."

"Oh, doesn't he, then? Who do you think made the world? Who do you think made you, Master Charles, if not God himself?"

"My father says this is the age of science. He says God is just an old-fashioned story."

Again the two smiled, this time with sadness.

"He's much more than that, lad," now said McFee. "But that's something ye'll have t' discover for yerself. For now, we're going t' give him thanks for providing for us. Bow your head, Master Charles."

He did so. The man prayed.

"Lord, our God, we thank ye for taking such good care of us. Thank ye for the earth and the sun and the rain that makes things grow so that we might have bread t' eat. Thank you for my good Maggie's hands that serve both yerself and me so faithfully and lovingly. Thank ye for our wee friend, Master Charles. Take care o' him too, Lord, and when the time comes show him that he owes his life t' you, and that he came from no-where but yer own heart. You are ay good t' us, our Father, and we'll never tire o' saying thank ye. That's all we can return t' you for the life you've given us, our thanks, and the obedient work o' faithful hands. Amen."

The boy scarcely understood the words, though every time he sat at the McFee table young Charles Rutherford felt a strange sense of contentment. He neither took offense at the couple's words, nor found them peculiar. He accepted them as he accepted the air he breathed. There was a simplicity and serenity here that drew him, and thus he came to visit whenever he could.

As Maggie McFee now handed him a thick slice of the rich earthy bread, he spread on a generous supply of the fresh butter he and Bobby McFee had churned only an hour earlier from milk taken from their one cow the day before. The boy's teeth bit into the hearty slab with greater vigor than would have been required for the white bread back at the Hall. When he and Bobby set off along the bank of the stream toward the lake an hour later, poles and lines over their shoulders, laughing and chatting freely, the lad who would one day be lord over all this region felt refreshed and invigorated. Truly indeed had he partaken of the food of life.

———— ♦ ♦ ♦ ————

Charles Rutherford's thoughts returned to the present.

His youthful fondness for the strange couple in the woods had not diminished, though he had seen not nearly as much of them in the last twenty years as perhaps he should have. When they crossed his mind, as they had a few moments ago, with their faces came wistfully pleasurable reminders of days gone by.

Yet he was the little boy of his reminiscences no longer. He was a man who now stood at the very center of that modern empire he had only dreamed of then.

He turned from the window into the room and glanced down once again at the invitation on his desk.

"The honour of your presence is requested..." began the ornate script, hand-lettered by the royal calligrapher. He must have read it over a hundred times since it had been delivered by special courier a month before. And now at last the appointed day had nearly arrived.

This is the moment I've been waiting for all my life! thought Charles Rutherford, Devonshire landholder, and by reason of his inherited position, Lord of the Manor of Heathersleigh.

He was to be knighted in the chivalric order as a Knight Grand Commander. Tomorrow he and his family would travel to the capital. The following afternoon, at one of the many Diamond Jubilee celebrations honoring the sixty-year anniversary of her coronation, Queen Victoria would receive him personally and bestow the honor herself.

The event represented the high point of a career that showed all the signs of becoming yet the more noteworthy, for he was but thirty-eight years of age. The London *Times* had already dubbed young Charles Rutherford one of England's top ten politicians to watch. Though the title of lord of the manor, which had been his father's, grandfather's, and great-grandfather's before him, was legitimate and of ancient date, it was a feudal title that did not entitle him to sit in the House of Lords.

This blemish, as some might have considered it, upon his rank, was actually, for a modern like Charles Rutherford, a great blessing. For it made him eligible for election to the House of Commons, a position not available to English or Scottish peers, and which Rutherford had enjoyed as a Devonshire M.P. for some years.

He allowed his eyes to wander up from the royal seal and drift about the expansive office on the second floor of the west wing which he called his study. The hardwood floor, well worn in places from centuries of use, was accented by two Persian rugs. A leather couch sat before a wide fireplace in which a small fire crackled. Several ornate high-backed oak chairs stood about, along with one leather chair and footstool that matched the couch. The ceiling was high, painted in white. Tall windows framed with heavy gold drapes, nearly always pulled to the side except on the bitterest of cold winter's days, opened in a northwesterly direction. Around the room, rich paneled wainscoting separated wood floor from walls, white like the ceiling, and upon these walls hung numerous paintings and small tapestries.

His gaze now passed across two oil paintings, one of his father, the other his grandfather, then his eyes moved to the adjacent wall where they fell upon an original pen drawing of Leonardo's he had purchased some years back at a London auction. It was of some unidentified mechanical device, which, as far as Charles could fathom, had never existed anywhere but in the great artist and inventor's clever brain. Its gears were not so hard to understand as the way they had been arranged together and the means by which they connected and moved, as well as what purpose they had been designed to achieve.

Perhaps the most fascinating aspect of the drawing, which made it priceless, was the incomplete sketch in one corner of the face of a woman. If it did indeed represent the beginnings of *Mona Lisa*, as he suspected, painted between 1503 and 1506, that would date the mechanical drawing in the neighborhood of 1502, when the great artist was engaged in various engineering projects in northern Italy. Placing the drawing in its historical perspective, however, did not unlock its secrets.

From the drawing his eyes moved to the shelf nearby which contained his own attempt, in iron and bronze and links of chain, to duplicate Leonardo's two-dimensional drawing in the three dimensions of reality, a fabrication which still sat incomplete and revealed no more clue to the potential use of the thing than did the original. Charles had tinkered away at it in his shop down in the basement of Heathersleigh Hall for three or four years with forge and various tools, before finally giving up.

On the corner of his desk, however, next to the gold-plated hand-telescope his father had given him on his twenty-fifth birthday, sat an invention of his own which *had* come to fruition, emerging largely out of his work on the Leonardo project—an ingeniously designed miniature electromagnetic motor, mounted on a base of wood. He was in the process of securing a patent for it, and hoped eventually to find some industrial function, once electricity came into more widespread use in the nation's factories.

It was not that Charles Rutherford needed the money that this invention, or any of a half dozen others he was working on, might potentially produce. He was a creative man who admired the likes of Leonardo, men of vision in advance of their fellows, men who changed the world with their intellect and their daring, men who inquired into the unknown and challenged the norms of their times.

Notwithstanding Bobby McFee's words to him as a child about the value of the old, his was a brain that by nature could not help probing the new. He had grown up doubting tradition, questioning established methods, asking why such-and-such couldn't be, and dreaming about what might be and *could* be. And he was already teaching son and daughters to think in like manner. His mind persistently sought to push the limits of his own personal creativity and mechanical skill to see what he might be capable of thinking or designing or making— when he was not, that is, writing some political manifesto for presentation in the House of Commons, or for publication in one of London's progressive political or socialist magazines.

Rarely, however, did his questioning mind turn itself inward. Charles Rutherford was a man of supreme personal confidence, and thus had yet no need to question himself.

Beside the motor, between two carved ivory bookends, sat one of Charles' other most prized possessions, along with the Leonardo drawing—an autographed first edition of the 1859 printing of Charles Darwin's *Origin of Species*. He had met the great naturalist personally in 1881, shortly before his death, when he was himself yet a young man. Both the meeting and the book had exercised a profound impact upon him. He had read the *Origin* four times.

Along with Thomas Huxley, H.G. Wells, Bernard Shaw, and others in the new wave of socialist and progressive thinkers, Mr. Darwin had helped formulate his views on life and the universe. The modernistic perspective conveyed to him as a youngster by his father expanded and grew within him with the years. His personal development in many ways paralleled that of the age.

Rutherford was no scientist himself. But the Darwinic worldview of rationalism and scientific determinism resonated with his youthful brain during his years at Cambridge, where he had discovered the book. At the university his socialistic tendencies sent the roots down further that would define his later views and political orientation. Afterward, his outlook grew yet stronger during his stint in the navy.

Like Leonardo before him, Charles Darwin was a bold pioneer in his field, unafraid to challenge long accepted ideas, though religious conservatives were doing their best to tarnish his reputation and ban the *Origin* altogether. They would never succeed, thought Charles. Progress was on the side of scientific advance, and religious intolerance could do nothing to stop it.

Western civilization had not come to this high point of industrial might by sitting on its laurels, or by clinging to a religion for old men and women, with little practicality in its ancient creeds. As fond as he was of the McFees, they were the sort of people that progress left behind. Religion had been replaced by science, progress, invention, and rationality. Men like Leonardo and Darwin had challenged men's minds and forced them forward into new eras and new times.

Such was his dream, to exercise similar impact, to change the world in his *own* sphere—perhaps not invention like Leonardo, perhaps not science like Darwin, but in the world of practical parliamentary politics where he was growing to be recognized as one of the nation's leading free-thinking progressives.

And now, with the queen's vote of confidence, his reputation was secure.

5

A Kitchen Mêlée

*D*istant shrieks from downstairs interrupted Charles' thoughts.

They sounded alarming. He turned and ran quickly from the room. As he hurried along the corridor, then down the wide flight of stairs to the ground floor, voices echoed in his direction from the kitchen. Now, however, he detected laughter amidst the rest. Whatever was wrong, it no longer sounded dangerous. Gradually he slowed his pace.

He entered the kitchen and beheld a scene quite unlike anything he had ever witnessed. There knelt his wife on the floor, face flushed, her abundant hair escaping from its pins. George's face was buried in some contraption on the table. All around, the servants displayed various expressions of mingled humor and terror.

"Papa! Papa!" cried Amanda, running toward him. "Mother's caught three mice!"

———————— ♦ ♦ ♦ ————————

Daughter of an officer in the Royal Army, Jocelyn Wildecott had spent most of her early years in India. Growing up with the privilege of her position, for reasons highly personal she possessed a large heart that opened itself with compassion to the less fortunate native population. Though from a family of plenty, suffering had touched her closely, carving a well of sympathy within her heart even as it likewise set within her a determination to rise above the handicap that caused it. This tenderness of spirit, along with its corresponding energetic demeanor, first drew the young Charles Rutherford to her when they met at a military social event at Portsmouth. He had just begun his commission in the navy at the time, and Jocelyn's father and family were in England on furlough from India.

The encounter was brief, yet neither forgot the other. Their paths did not cross again for several years. Then suddenly they found themselves simultaneously engaging in second glances—she, at the time, working in a London hospital, he visiting an ailing friend.

As Charles strode down the corridor, he paused at the nurse's desk.

"Miss, uh . . . Wildecott, is it not?" he said hesitantly.

"Why, yes it is, Mr. Rutherford," she replied, bringing his name back to mind in the second or two since she had first observed him. She smiled as she spoke. The words which followed, however, were accompanied by an uncertain curling of her lips in which was mingled the faintest touch of sarcasm. "You have a very good memory."

Indeed, she was used to being remembered. Once they laid eyes on her, no one forgot Jocelyn Wildecott. The realization always brought with it a reminder of the pain that was constantly with her.

"No better than yours, it would seem," replied Charles, displaying his teeth in a winning grin. "It is nice to see you again. Let me think, it must be, what, four or five years."

"My family was back from India in '78. I believe it was—"

"Ah, yes—'78 . . . the Navy fête down in Portsmouth—so . . .

four years. You're back in England for good now?"

"My father retired two years ago," nodded Jocelyn.

The two spoke for another minute or two before a call took Jocelyn away.

She was relieved, for the exchange was unnerving. The dashing young Rutherford had looked her so straight in the eye, with such unflinching sincerity, that she found herself wondering if he even noticed.

The thought was absurd. How could he not notice!

But never before had a man of quality spoken to her without her detecting a darting back and forth of the eyes toward the ugly bright red birthmark. But this young man, handsome enough to turn the head of any young woman in England, had gazed at her so directly, and spoken so genuinely that her appearance almost didn't seem to matter to him.

Charles Rutherford returned to the hospital the following day, this time not to visit his injured friend but to make arrangements to see the daughter of Colonel Wildecott at some other location than her place of employment. But already her uncertainty from the day before had returned. Doubts were creeping in about the fellow's intentions. What else could it be but that he felt sorry for her?

An hour with him on horseback, however, put her anxieties to rest. During the following month they visited nearly all of London's parks together in such a manner. Never in her twenty-two years had she experienced such a thing, but when riding at Charles' side, there were times she even forgot how different she was.

Within a year and a half, Miss Wildecott became Mrs. Charles Jocelyn Rutherford, wife of an aspiring politician and the future lord of the manor of Heathersleigh . . . and herself future mistress of Heathersleigh Hall.

----------- ◆ ◆ ◆ -----------

All the maids and domestic help, male and female, loved Jocelyn Rutherford. Several had come with her to Heathersleigh when she married Charles.

Breeding and title notwithstanding, Jocelyn Rutherford was no stuffy aristocrat. Was it because of or in spite of the disfigurement on one side of an otherwise lovely face that she seemed so endearingly real? In the secure environment of her own home she was able to let her hair down. When she did, even those of her servants who had known her for years sometimes did not quite know what to do.

The evening before, it had seized Jocelyn's fancy to show seven-year-old Amanda how to make paté from the lamb they had enjoyed at dinner that day. It would neither do for the cook to prepare it, nor to buy it in the village. Jocelyn herself would demonstrate the process exactly as she had learned from her own mother in India.

Assembling the necessary ingredients took some time following breakfast, for no one could remember the last time anyone at Heathersleigh had requested lamb paté, either Jocelyn herself or Lady Rutherford, Jocelyn's mother-in-law, dead now four years.

When all was at last ready, she turned and addressed a simple and loyal hardworking woman by the name of Sarah Minsterly, who served as cook and housekeeper's assistant. "Sarah," said Jocelyn, "would you please find me the meat grinder?"

"I don't know where it is, mum. I doubt I've used it even once."

"It must be in the pantry."

"I'll have a look."

Sarah disappeared. A few moments later her voice called out, "Ah, *there* it is—up on the very top shelf. Just be a minute, mum."

"George, go help Sarah get it down, would you?" said Jocelyn to Amanda's brother. "It may be heavy."

George disappeared after the cook. The sounds of a stool dragging across the floor and climbing followed. A minute later nine-year-old George reappeared, carrying the seldom used grinder, trailing not a few cobwebs along with it, in both his hands. His mother took it while she and Amanda continued with mother-daughter chatter.

"We'll clean it up and get it ready after we've anchored it down," said Jocelyn. "—Amanda, lay a tea towel on the edge of the table. I'll hold it, and George, you tighten up the clamp underneath."

Amanda and George were curious now—mechanically minded George to see how this contraption worked, and Amanda to see what the big rotating handle could possibly have to do with making a delicate thing like paté.

A minute later the grinder was solidly attached.

"Now," said Jocelyn, reaching inside, "we'll remove this plunger and clean it—"

A bloodcurdling shriek sounded from the woman's ordinarily composed mouth.

She leapt backward as the wooden plunger dropped to the floor with a crash. At the same instant three of the tiniest mice imaginable scurried out of their suddenly disturbed nest and ran in confusion across the table.

A chorus of screams followed from Sarah and two housemaids who had drawn in closer to watch. They sprang backward from the table and ran for the furthest wall they could find. Only the two youngsters remained, watching the mice scamper to the edge of the table, stop, then resume their flight in the opposite direction.

Coming to herself and thinking quickly, Jocelyn now grabbed up a nearby bread basket. The kitchen by now echoed with shouts and screams and laughter. Obviously in more panic than the humans, the terrified mice did not pause this time, but ran like lemmings off the opposite end of the table, where they found themselves falling straight into the ready basket. The next instant Jocelyn plopped it upside down onto the floor. Kneeling, she held the basket over the baby mice.

When Charles made his entrance, he surveyed the scene, mouth open. Then he broke into laughter.

"Mrs. Rutherford," he said, "if I may ask—whatever are you doing down on your knees on the floor?"

"It is exactly as Amanda said," she laughed, still breathing deeply from the excitement. "I've got three little mice underneath me."

"I see. And I thought the Saxons had overrun Devon again and you were all being put to the sword. I am very relieved!"

More laughter followed. The servants drew closer again. Curiosity now replaced anxiety. With the man of the house present, things seemed not nearly so alarming.

"I can't see inside," said Amanda, kneeling down and trying to peer through the webbing into the basket.

"Stand back, Amanda."

"I want to see them," she insisted.

"Hmm, let me see—what shall we do?" said Charles, thinking to himself and glancing about. "Ah yes—that should do it."

Spying a large baking sheet across the kitchen, he walked over and brought it back, himself kneeling down at his wife's side.

"Don't hurt them, Papa!" exhorted Amanda.

"I shall be careful," he said.

"This should take care of it," he said. "All right, stand back, Jocelyn."

"Papa, Papa . . ."

"You too, Amanda."

"I'm not afraid!"

Charles slid the sheet slowly and gently under the basket.

Holding one hand underneath and the other on top of the basket, he now lifted the entire assembly and carried the mice toward the door. Both children followed.

"May I have them, Papa?" said Amanda at his side.

"I think we should let them find a new home outside," laughed Charles.

They reached the door. George opened it and Charles stepped outside and across the drive.

"Here, George, why don't you take them out to the woods."

He carefully handed sheet and basket to his son. George took it and walked off across the grass. Amanda sprang after him.

"George, don't let the cat get them!" she cried, scurrying along at his side.

"I'll let them go in the woods."

"Don't hurt them!"

"I won't."

Charles watched them go, then turned to see Jocelyn joining him. She slid her arm under his.

"Thank you for rescuing me," she said as they slowly made their way back inside.

"I have to admit," he said, "that when I came into the kitchen, and saw you there on the floor with such a delighted but perplexed expression on your face . . . it was wonderful. You looked like both George and Amanda all at once."

Jocelyn laughed. "I am just glad you came along when you did. I didn't know what I was going to do. I wouldn't have thought of the bread sheet."

"Amanda would no doubt have figured something out and *told* you what to do."

"She usually does," smiled Jocelyn.

"Is there *anything* she doesn't think she can do better than anyone in the world!" said Charles.

"If so, I haven't discovered it," rejoined his wife.

"I suppose it is our own fault," he mused. "We *have* taught her to be independent."

"As in the matter of tomatoes! You were no help—I was trying to talk her into not making such a fuss over it!"

"Sorry," laughed Charles. "She's just so adorable when she asserts herself. Such a tiny thing, and yet she sounds like a little grown-up. I just can't be cross with her."

"No one can," agreed his wife. "I sometimes worry a bit when she orders the servants around, yet she does it so charmingly that none of them seem to mind."

"Our precocious little daughter has indeed learned to get her own way," Charles mused with another chuckle.

Even as they spoke of her, they heard the high-pitched sounds of the rambunctious and assertive object of their words shouting out orders to George regarding every phase of the operation concerning the mice.

They walked together into the house.

"All ready for tomorrow?" asked Jocelyn.

"I think so," replied her husband. "How about you?"

"I am nervous," sighed Jocelyn. "You know I don't like such events. I cannot but think people are always staring."

"If they are, it is only because you are so beautiful."

"Charles, please—you know what I mean."

"Of course I do," he replied. "But you must believe me too. You know that I think you the most beautiful woman in England."

"One side of my face, at least."

"Perhaps, in the eyes of those who don't know you. But to my sight, *all* of you is lovely, especially what is inside."

"How could I ever have been so lucky to have a man like you love me?" said Jocelyn. "I never expected to be married at all. I must still sometimes pinch myself to realize how happy you have made me. Yet I still wish there was some way I did not have to go tomorrow and mingle with all those people. Wouldn't you really rather not be seen by the queen . . . with me?"

"Jocelyn Rutherford! I will not have any more such talk. I love you and am proud of you, and I want the whole world to see you at my side!"

Jocelyn smiled. "I'll try to remember," she said. "But that isn't the only reason I'm nervous."

"What else?"

"I thought what might happen if Amanda smuggled one of those mice into her pocket, to show to the queen."

He laughed at the thought. "I wouldn't put it past her."

"She has everyone here at Heathersleigh around her little finger, but somehow I don't think Victoria would be amused."

"When she turns on the charm, she seems able to win over just about anyone."

"All the same, perhaps we should check her pockets before we leave."

6

Lofty Objectives

———— ♦ ♦ ♦ ————

*C*harles Rutherford returned to his study while his wife returned to the kitchen to resume the making of the paté, now with an *empty* meat grinder.

Again he read over the queen's invitation which had prompted his earlier reflections.

He recalled the first day he and Jocelyn had met. That same look had been on her face then which had appeared momentarily just a few minutes ago—an expression of energy and zest that could not help compel the eyes of any observer. It was a vitality that combined vigor of personality with the need to prove herself, a combination which only made her all the more interesting in his eyes.

Charles and Jocelyn Rutherford had married in 1884, just two years before his first stand for Parliament. He was twenty-five at the time, she twenty-four. That was thirteen years ago. He had been elected to the House of Commons two years later, at twenty-seven, as a liberal, a progressive.

Many said initially that Charles' father's money had secured him the post. Very quickly, however, the young Rutherford began to make his presence felt in the Liberal party. When his father died suddenly, Charles had stepped into his position as lord of the manor and used the respected family name to even greater advantage than before. Soon he was one of Liberal leader William Gladstone's right-hand men, and a recognized leader in the House of Commons.

Two years later he rose to yet greater prominence when the Gladstone Liberals joined ranks with the Irish Home Rulers to oust the Conservatives from control of the government. Charles Rutherford's name and picture regularly found its way into the *Times* as he and his colleagues strove to steer British politics in a new direction.

But their dominant role was short-lived. Effective Liberal government proved impossible, with a Conservative House of Lords blocking their every move.

In 1895, two years ago, new elections were held. The Conservative Lord Salisbury was soon back as prime minister with a solid and powerful Conservative majority. Young Charles Rutherford managed to keep his seat in the electoral swing, however, and with Gladstone now retired, his star continued to rise in Parliament, despite the minority role of his party.

Reminded of his father by the painting in his study, Charles found himself wishing he could share tomorrow's momentous event with the man who had given him life. His father, known affectionately as Lord Ashby, had now been gone seven years. When Charles' mother died three years later, Charles and Jocelyn had become the new eldest generation at Heathersleigh, although Charles had resisted the appellation of "Lord" for himself, both because of his liberal views and because his title was not of the peerage.

Now, the day after tomorrow, at a mere thirty-eight, Charles Rutherford, Esquire, would become *Sir Charles Rutherford*, the first in his family to be knighted. There were many places in society one of his position and reputation might do good and make his influence felt. For one desirous of achieving maximum impact on the world stage, however, the Commons certainly seemed the most logical and influential platform.

Secretly Charles Rutherford cherished the ambition to be prime minister one day.

But most important was that one day people look back on his life in the same way that he looked upon his two daring and innovative mentors Leonardo and Darwin—as a man bold to move the world forward in new directions, and one of whom in consequence it would be said that he had changed history.

It was no small objective.

But then Charles Rutherford was a renaissance man in his own right, and had all his life been driven by an ambition toward greatness.

7

Shadowy Schemes

A well-dressed man in fashionable suit glanced about two or three times, then walked into the upscale London pub on Charing Cross Road not far from Cambridge Circus. *The Owl and the Rose* was noted less for its ale, although a variety could be had, than for who might be seen there. It was reported to be one of Dickens' favorite haunts, and both Prince Edward and Rudyard Kipling were said to have been fond of its rich, though private, atmosphere. It is true that plots had been hatched between its walls, though mostly literary, and certainly not of the sort which on this day were to be discussed.

The newcomer looked about in the dim light, then strode forward and sat down at a vacant table alongside one of the rear walls. He ordered a light ploughman's lunch for two, and waited.

Fifteen minutes later, another man entered, not so finely attired as the first, though obviously a cut above working class. The two were soon engaged in low but earnest dialogue as they partook of the meal and a light amber brew.

"You have the men you need lined up?" asked the first man. The accent in which he spoke, though the English was refined enough, was clearly continental.

"The roughs will be there," replied the other, an Englishman through and through. "All it took was a quid apiece. They're a greedy lot, those street types. They'll do anything for a bit of brass."

"They know nothing?"

"As far as they're concerned, I'm a bleeding antireligious nut just wanting to give the evangelists what for. They don't know an evolutionist from a communist, and care even less."

"Just make sure it stays that way."

"What good is it going to do to rouse up that crowd, if you don't mind my asking? Neither side's got any clout."

"All we're after is a ruckus, not a cause. Agitation is what we want from the masses. Any public gathering serves our purpose equally well. Once the pot is boiling, but not before, it will be time to incite them further with ideas. For the time, all we want is to rouse people against one another, to produce a general spirit of unrest. Such must always be the unseen foundation for revolution."

"Then rest easy. These bounders I got are a rowdy lot. If it's unrest you want, that's what you'll get."

8

Difference of Outlook

You know what I'm in the mood for?" said Jocelyn at lunch.

"What's that?" asked her husband.

"A ride," she replied. "I need to get out for some fresh air before I think *too* much about tomorrow. How would you like to take me for a romp?"

"Oh yes—I'll go!" exclaimed Amanda before her father had the chance to answer.

"I was speaking to your father," said Jocelyn good-naturedly.

"I want to go too," persisted Amanda.

"Sometimes your father and I like to get off by ourselves so we can talk. Men and women do that, you know."

Amanda said nothing. She returned to her meal with an expression that was certainly not indifferent, yet fell short of an outright pout.

"What do you say, Charles?" said Jocelyn, turning once more to her husband.

"I'd love it. You and I haven't been out into the hills for months."

"Good. I'll do my best to forget London for a couple of hours."

As soon as lunch was over, both older children disappeared. The children's nanny, Constance Dimble, took three-year-old Catharine upstairs, and Jocelyn and Charles went to change into their riding clothes.

As she was dressing, Jocelyn Rutherford found herself thinking back to her first ride with Charles, which had been in Hyde Park in London only a few days after the encounter in the hospital.

———————— ♦ ♦ ♦ ————————

Do you intend to work in a hospital forever?" Charles had asked as they had ridden along.

"I don't know," Jocelyn had replied. "Forever is a long time. I don't know that I've thought of it in such permanent terms."

"What do you dream about then, when you think of the future?"

"I don't think about it that much."

"Oh, but you must."

"Why? I am content with each day as it comes."

"Of course. But the accumulation of days won't amount to anything unless we leave the world a better place. How will we change the world if we don't think about it ahead of time?"

"Change the world!" she laughed. "Whoever said anything about changing the world? That's not my goal in life."

"What other goal is there? All great men who aspire to significance want to change the world."

"But I'm not a man," smiled Jocelyn.

Charles laughed. "A good reply. You have a sharp wit, Miss Wildecott. But what does being a man or woman have to do with it? Surely you are one who believes in equality between the sexes. Even in India you must have been aware of this question." As he said these last words, Charles glanced sideways with a twinkle in his eye.

"Of course," Jocelyn answered. "But equality is yet far off when women are not even permitted to vote."

"Touché! Then I will modify my statement to accommodate the new age—you can be a great woman who changes the world."

"Perhaps," she rejoined. "In fact, I heartily agree. Women can do most anything men can do."

"There—we are on the same side after all."

"On the discussionary point, perhaps. But who says I desire to exercise great influence, as you obviously do? I may admit to wanting to do something worthwhile, even to prove myself. I try to make a difference with my nursing. But someone like me has no illusions about changing the world."

"Why not?"

"Come, Mr. Rutherford. Look at me."

"You mean the mark on your face."

"What else would I mean?"

"That is no limitation. These are new times in all ways. You can do and be anything you want. That's one of the things I first noticed which drew me to you. Here you are, a woman of standing who chooses to work in a hospital. I like that about you."

Jocelyn could not prevent a smile creeping to her lips as he bestowed his approval. Yet despite the obvious sincerity of his tone, she could hardly believe him. She had listened to him first with a certain humorous detachment. She liked him, but how could such a good-looking man possibly understand? Eventually, however, Charles Rutherford's infectious enthusiasm to do and become and achieve could not help but begin to exercise its influence on young Jocelyn Wildecott's way of thinking. Especially once she began to fall in love with him. Before many months were out he was taking her to women's rallies and liberal speeches and other political and activist lectures. She found herself becoming so involved in the issues that she thought less about her appearance than at any other time in her young life. He had helped her begin to believe in herself.

"I don't know if I'm cut out for this kind of life," she said one day when they were talking seriously on their way back from a lecture. "I am interested in the issues. But I don't find myself as eager as you seem to be to join in."

"Why not? You have good ideas and much to offer. I don't understand you."

"I'm not like all the other women who are talking about rights and all the social causes."

"Not like them . . . in what way?"

Jocelyn did not answer immediately. When at last she spoke,

her voice was soft and thoughtful.

"You've hardly ever mentioned my face," she said. "Even after that day we were riding when I brought it up, you've never said another word about it. Surely you notice how people stare."

"It means nothing to me—either the mark or people's stares. If they want to think less of you as a result, that's to their shame, not yours."

"Perhaps you're right. But I'm the one who must live with it. A sick person in a hospital, or a child in an orphanage—well, there is a need I can fill, and they are very accepting of my help. Perhaps even more so because I too am an individual, as it were, with a lack, a handicap. But being involved in social issues means mixing with people less likely to be accepting than a poor sick child."

"But don't you want to show that kind of people how wrong they are about you?"

"I suppose there is a side of me that always feels I must prove myself, that I have to make up for my looks by doing what I do better than someone else. At the same time, it's so difficult to realize that wherever you go and whatever you do, people are looking at a red splotch on your skin rather than at your character, at who you are . . . on the inside."

"Perhaps you don't give people enough credit?"

"I only wish I could agree with you, Mr. Rutherford. Unfortunately I have twenty-two years of experience on my side. I've lived with the stares, the pointing fingers, the snickers from children, the polite drop of the eyes."

"But you are a very attractive, intelligent, and articulate young woman. Why would anyone—"

"Believe me, I have suffered much from the silent glances of people who stare at me as if I am some kind of a freak, even the looks of pain in the eyes of my own mother, to whom I have always been a great disappointment."

"Your own mother? Surely not."

"I'm afraid so."

Her response silenced him for a moment. He could hardly believe what he'd heard. Deeply affected at the thought of her pain, he reached out and touched her hand. But quickly his irrepressible optimism rose up again.

"Well, what of it? All the more reason to show people what you're made of—to stand up and be who you are and make something of yourself."

"That takes a great deal of courage in light of a challenge such as mine."

"You do not strike me as one lacking in that virtue."

Jocelyn smiled. "I have been known to be feisty at times, even to be more outspoken than was good for me. Whether that is the same as being courageous, I couldn't say. But as to your point, I am not sure I am willing to pay the personal price of, as you say, standing up and showing people what I am made of. I think I would rather simply live my life and avoid the stares."

"But I return to my conviction that you don't give people enough credit. If you stood up and showed people who you are, they wouldn't even notice your face."

"It just may be that you give people too much credit. I am not at all certain I want to risk my future on your theory. If looks don't matter as much as character to you, Mr. Rutherford, then you are an unusual man."

◆◆◆

She had been right in that, thought Jocelyn to herself. Charles Rutherford was indeed an unusual man, and a good one. In their thirteen years of marriage he had shown himself to be a thoughtful and loving husband.

Sometimes she could hardly believe her good fortune.

9

A Ride

*H*alf an hour later, Charles and Jocelyn left the house and walked toward the stables, chatting freely and looking forward to the afternoon.

They entered the barn to see Amanda atop a tall chestnut mare, comfortably ensconced in the saddle and waiting with what patience she possessed, a look of knowing conquest on her face.

Heathersleigh's groom and stable man, Hector Farnham, greeted Charles and his wife as they walked in. "Miss Amanda, she said you was all to have a ride together," he said cheerfully.

Charles and Jocelyn glanced at one another with an expression of thwarted resignation.

The groom had just tossed a saddle onto a second horse's back and proceeded to gather the leather straps underneath its belly, utterly unsuspecting of the plot in which he had been made an accomplice. "She told me I should saddle up Red Lady here for her with the gent's saddle," the man went on. "She said you and Mrs. Rutherford would be along presently, and that I should saddle Celtic Star for you, ma'am, and Clydon for you, sir."

Jocelyn glanced at her husband. Red Lady was her favorite horse, a gift from Charles three years ago on their tenth anniversary. But she knew from experience that there would be no reasoning with Amanda, and she was reluctant to spoil the pleasant afternoon. Besides, she was comfortable on any horse, though Celtic Star was showing signs of her age.

"Yes, Hector," said Jocelyn with a smile, "that will be fine."

Charles sighed and nodded his like assent. He had hoped for the time alone with his wife. Like her, however, he quickly realized the inevitable.

"—But, Amanda," said Jocelyn, glancing up, "you must let Mr. Farnham put the small lady's saddle on her."

"I want to ride like George and Papa."

"Ladies ride sidesaddle," answered her mother in a calm voice. "It would never do for a girl of your position to ride like a boy."

"Why?"

Jocelyn glanced helplessly at her husband. She knew the reply that had been about to escape her lips, *Because that is the way ladies are supposed to ride*, would carry no more weight with Amanda than a feather.

As Jocelyn Rutherford stood struggling for an appropriate reply, Amanda appeared like a tiny general atop her horse looking down upon her troops. Amanda herself was perceptive enough to realize that her mother's pause was her own greatest ally in this present contest of wills.

"Since this appears to have become a family event," said Charles, rescuing his wife from the necessity to reply, "we might as well see if George would like to join us.—Saddle up Raith too, will you please, Hector."

He turned and ran back to the house while Amanda smiled from astride the tall chestnut mare.

Even at the young age of seven, Amanda Rutherford was well accustomed to such triumphs. Strong willed and precocious, she had walked and talked at an early age . . . and begun even then to exercise her dominance over her older brother. Before much longer she was the acknowledged queen of the whole household. Whether barking out orders like the little commander she was, slyly orchestrating events so they conformed to her liking, or simply charming others into complying with her wishes, she had become adept at getting her own way.

Nor did either father or mother strenuously resist such tendencies. Times had changed, and they were enlightened parents. Laws and educational advances, not to mention socialist ideas of equality for every man, woman, and child, all combined to heighten their respect for childhood. The thought that indulging their daughter's willfulness might be detrimental to her never occurred to such modern thinkers as Charles and Jocelyn Rutherford. For the most part, they *admired* her independent spirit, and they were confident that through education and example they could shape it toward the good.

By the time Charles and his son returned to the barn, two horses were ready for them and the two ladies sat in their saddles, mother toward one side, Amanda's tiny legs undaintily straddling Red Lady. Father and son mounted, and the four set out.

Charles led northward across open grassland. Within a few minutes Amanda passed him and struck a course more westerly toward the highest of the hills on the estate. Soon George followed her.

Charles and Jocelyn communicated as much with their eyes and facial gestures as with words. The expression that passed between them as the children rode off ahead was one of amused pride. Young George sat well upon his roan gelding, and Amanda, more determined than graceful, stuck like a burr astride the oversized mare. They had no concern about her safety, for Red Lady was always a gentle and responsive mount. And neither stopped to reflect that it was their little daughter, not the mare, who might require the discipline of bridle and reins.

For Charles, it was enough that he teach her and guide her bright young mind toward enlightened thinking.

For Jocelyn, all that mattered was that her daughter feel her accepting and unconditional love—the love she herself had never felt.

She had been aware of her mother's disappointment in her from before she could even remember. An aloof woman by nature, the colonel's wife could hardly find it in her power even to take her firstborn into her arms, so loathsome did she find the hideous red birthmark. The attending physician had assured her the redness would disappear over the course of several months.

Mrs. Wildecott was content to leave her first daughter with the nurse as soon as she was able to resume her social appointments. No one would expect her to take such a child out. For a time she held out hope in the doctor's words. By the time Jocelyn was five, however, Mrs. Wildecott had resigned herself to the inevitable.

By then she'd given birth to a second daughter—a delightful girl unmarked by nature, into whom she could pour her attentions and what measure of love the rigid woman may have possessed. Her firstborn would have known she was different without ever once looking in a mirror, simply from the cool, detached way her mother behaved around her. While her baby sister was often in her mother's arms, young Jocelyn could not even remember the feel of her mother's hand upon her own.

As a result, trying but in vain to win the approval of her mother, she gradually became all the more attached to her father. Yet he was not an emotive man, and found her childish desire for loving relationship not repulsive as did his wife, but nevertheless awkward. He did his best by the girl. But his tentative touch, and the stiffness of his lap, were woefully insufficient to give her the affection future men and women require.

Jocelyn's parents were not religious people. In India, the British contingent gathered at church to see and be seen. Jocelyn knew her mother was embarrassed by her very existence. The Sunday bonnets with which she outfitted her each week were large and unattractive—but they served their purpose well, keeping one side of her face under perpetual shadow.

When Jocelyn thought of God, she thought of her father—a good enough man, but distant and impersonal. Her father was kind. God probably was as well. It had never yet dawned on her to consider that God had created her. If the thought had come into her young brain, it would have sent shock waves through her system to imagine that God would make someone so ugly and so deformed. What kind of God would do such a thing?

As she grew into her teen years, Jocelyn Wildecott never allowed herself to think or dream about the future. She set herself to serving in the hospitals and orphanages, and took each day as it came.

Then Charles Rutherford had unexpectedly entered her life!

It was not long after their engagement that the subject of children first came up between them. It was almost as great a surprise to Jocelyn as to Charles for her to realize she had no clearly defined notions of what sort of mother she wanted to be.

But that changed soon enough. Once the idea of having children of her own—actually being a mother!—was a real possibility, Jocelyn knew that she desired nothing more than to instill good feelings within however many children she had.

She would do for them what her own mother had been unable to do for her—enable them to walk with head high. Her own children would believe in themselves, believe that they possessed worth. She would give to her own children what she had never had—self-confidence and happiness.

Now at last she had a son and two daughters, and the chance to do just that.

George and Amanda and Catharine would never know the pain she had felt. Theirs would be a happy and contented childhood and youth!

———————————— ◆ ◆ ◆ ————————————

The course they followed rose steadily, though not sharply, toward a range of low-lying hills that could be seen from the windows of the Hall facing northward. From these hills in the opposite direction, on the clearest of days, hints of the Bristol Channel still farther to the north could be imagined.

It was not a thickly forested region, yet between the open grassland and fields, it was covered with clumps of pine, fir, birch, and grand old maples, some oak and ash and hawthorn, under all of whose leaves and needles spread various grasses and wild shrubbery, some varieties of heather among it, from which the estate had doubtless drawn its name. When tramping through such woods, one might well imagine oneself in the midst of a dense forest. But just as suddenly could one emerge bathed in sunlight on the pleasantest of open grassy green vistas upon which sheep grazed as if they hadn't a care in the world.

It was altogether a delightful place for riding, although Charles and his family did not avail themselves of it as often as might be expected. The Heathersleigh stables contained some of the finest specimens of horseflesh for miles, and Hector Farnham knew and loved every one of his equine gentlemen and ladies as well as most mothers do their own children. Charles himself was absent from Heathersleigh much of the time, however, and Jocelyn had little taste for riding on her own.

10

Encounter With a Woodcutter

$\mathscr{A}$s they went, and as the four horses gradually drew up even with one another, Charles chatted casually to his family as was his custom, explaining now how the windmill in the distance was able to operate machinery, now how the hair of the grazing sheep could be transformed into clothing, then posing some question or other for George and Amanda to consider.

"There are so many changes coming," he was saying as they entered a small wooded area. "It is an exciting time to be alive. Soon people will be riding everywhere in motorcars. Why, George, your children probably won't even know how to ride a horse!"

"There will *always* be horses, Papa," said Amanda. "Nothing could replace them."

"I'm sure you're right. What do you think, George—*will* there be machines one day to take people flying in the sky?"

"You mean motorcars with wings?"

"Exactly!" laughed Charles.

"I cannot imagine people flying, Papa."

"Neither would our ancestors have been able to imagine railroads. I doubt there are limits to what man's ingenuity can accomplish given enough time and experimentation."

A kind of pounding or whacking sound began to filter into their ears faintly through the woods.

"What is that noise?" asked Amanda.

"Let us investigate!" replied her father, urging his horse off at increased pace in the direction of the sound. "Who will be the first to discover the origin of this mystery?"

Caught up immediately in the game, Amanda and George dashed after their father, passed him, and soon left him trailing their two steeds. He reined in Clydon until Jocelyn drew even with him.

"You are always such fun," she said. "What a father our children have! Everything with you is a game, a challenge, an opportunity, a mystery!"

Charles threw back his head and roared.

Five minutes later the parents emerged into a small clearing to see their children's horses stopped beside a stocky and robust man whose axe had gone silent in a thick block of fir the moment George and Amanda appeared.

The woodsman raised a friendly hand in greeting toward the couple on horseback. His head was as bald and shiny as a pig's nose, though with occasional stray porcinelike bristly white strands extending out from random parts of it, most erratically around his ears. Yet although his mane had long since disappeared from above his forehead, his eyes shone from under thick white eyebrows with the sparkle of youthful enthusiasm.

"Good afternoon to you, Bobby!" Charles called out as he rode up. "Getting a start on next winter's wood early, I see."

"Aye, Master Charles," replied the man in his thick brogue. The man had made no more attempt to rid his tongue of its Irish heritage than had his father who had come over to England fifty years before. Bobby's use of an old-fashioned word or the turn of an odd phrase still revealed lingering reminders of his roots across the water to the west.

"I'm not as young as I once was," he added, wiping his forehead. I need an earlier start.—But excuse me, *Lord* Rutherford. I'm forgetting myself..."

"Tomorrow you may call him *Sir Charles*," said George proudly.

"Call me anything you like," laughed Charles. "I'm not sure anything but 'Master Charles' will ever sound quite right in my ears coming from you."

The woodcutter set down his axe, then reached up to give Charles his hand.

"It was Mr. McFee chopping wood!" exclaimed Amanda. "That's what we heard. Mr. McFee's the mystery, Papa."

"So it would seem! How do you fancy being the object of a family search, Bobby?"

"I'm always pleased t' provide my betters entertainment with my presence in their woods, sir," said the man with a twinkle in his eye.

"I'm neither your better, nor, unless my sense of direction as we rode misleads me, are these my woods," rejoined Charles.

"Nonetheless, it's much appreciative I am that ye allow me t' cut here."

"The woods belong to the cottage as well as the Hall, Bobby," replied the lord of the manor. "No one in my memory has quibbled over that. It may have all belonged to my grandfather or great-grandfather at some former time. But the cottage is yours now, and you've as much a right to the wood as myself. Besides, you and I've been friends too long even to discuss such things."

"You're right, Master Charles, and I'm appreciative o' yer friendship."

"Why don't you have one of your servants cut the wood for you, Mr. McFee?" asked Amanda with precocious innocence.

"Amanda," began Jocelyn with embarrassment, "Mr. McFee—"

But she was cut off by the rustic chopper of wood, who would rather Amanda hear the truth from his own lips.

"I'm a poor man, Miss Amanda," he said. "I wouldn't know what t' do with a servant if I had one. But even if I weren't poor, I'd still be out splitting my own wood. For there's nothing I quite enjoy so much as hard work in the fresh air on a bright day such as this."

Whether the significance of his reply could be grasped by the young mistress of Heathersleigh—who was as innocent of realities in some aspects of life as she was advanced of her years in her powers of persuasion and manipulation—was doubtful.

"Well, we are out for a bit of a ride and had best be off," said Charles. "—Come children, let's leave Mr. McFee to his work."

"Give your wife our best, Bobby," added Jocelyn.

"She'll ask me why I didn't bring ye back for a visit," replied the man.

"Tell her we *shall* come over to the cottage one day before long."

"That we shall indeed," added Charles. "I must see if my fingers still remember how to coax milk from your cow. It's been quite a few years since I tried that."

"Too many t' be sure," rejoined Bobby McFee. "Ye're always welcome."

Charles led off through the woods and the other three followed. The woodsman leaned on his axe and stared after them, remembering.

♦♦♦

He and Maggie had not seen Master Charles for two years, and that had been but a brief encounter. They had not had a visit and chat over tea for probably five or more. The aging man and wife knew he had changed. He could not forever remain the youngster they had been so fond of years earlier.

But they were unprepared for just how different he looked when he came tramping through the wood and up the winding path toward the white-plastered and thatched-roof cottage and barn. Though merely nineteen, he had become a man—tall, handsome, articulate, and self-assured.

"Well, Bobby," he said approaching, "I'm off tomorrow to see the world on one of Her Majesty's great ships. I wanted to come say good-bye."

McFee rose off his knees from the midst of the potato patch, brushed his hands two or three times across his trowsers, then offered it to the onetime frequent guest who was now taller than he.

"We're privileged that ye'd think o' us on yer last day in Devon, Master Charles," he said. " 'Tis good o' ye t' come.—Maggie!" he cried. "Maggie, Master Charles is here!"

She appeared from around the house a few seconds later, fairly skipping toward them with delight. A wide smile spread across the face around which patches of grey had begun to gather, though she was not yet fifty. She was not satisfied with a handshake, but threw her arms around the lanky lad.

Charles laughed with delight. He still loved these two as much as ever, notwithstanding the infrequency of his visits in recent years.

"Still the same dear Maggie!" he said.

"I haven't changed, Master Charles," she exclaimed, standing back now and eying him up and down, "but you surely have. When did you get so tall?"

"Last year I think," he replied with a grin. "Right around my eighteenth birthday, as I recall. Suddenly I looked in the mirror . . . and there was a stranger staring back at me!"

"Ah, well, you're a fine-looking man now. Isn't he, Bobby?"

"Ay, that he is. He'll be turning the head of every young woman in London afore long."

"Come in, come in, Master Charles," said the woman, turning

toward the cottage. "We'll have tea once more before you go."
She led the way and the two men followed her inside.

"Your garden is lovely, Maggie," said Charles, glancing around
as they went. "I don't know that I've ever seen it so full of color."

"The Lord surprises me every year with new hues of his paint-
brush," replied Maggie.

"No doubt your own hard work has something to do with it."

"Not so much as what the Lord put in the soil. His things will
grow whether I am here or not. It's God's life that gives beauty
to the world, Master Charles, not the work of man's hands."

They reached the cottage, and walked into the cool, dim light.
Maggie put water on to boil, while Charles and Bobby took
chairs at the table.

"Today's scientists have a different explanation of why things
grow," said Charles, resuming the previous thread of the conversation. "They might say what you just did, but with a different
conclusion—that the chemicals and particular arrangements of
elements that nature has thrown together will grow things, with
or without God."

"But they don't recognize the source of life, so they know no
better," said Maggie from her place at the stove. "That's just the
nonsense of your university talking."

Charles could not help laughing, but good-naturedly.

"You consider what the university teaches nonsense?" he said,
still chuckling.

"By no means—only the part of it that leaves God out, and
says that life came about without him."

"What do you think, Bobby?" said Charles, turning to her husband. "Do you agree with your wife?"

"I tell ye, Master Charles, if ever a body needed it proved t'
them that God was in his heaven, that he'd made the universe
and everything in it, and that he's the reason you and me's got
life within us, Maggie's flower garden out there gives all the proof
he'd need. That is, if such a one had eyes t' see the proof that
was right in front o' him."

"Proof—what kind of proof?"

"I mean no proof for the head, Master Charles, but rather the
kind o' proof God intended that only hearts could understand."

"Why would he intend such a thing?"

"The Creator gave us our intellects t' help in our journey. But he gave us our hearts t' complete the job. In fact he made it so that the mind can't get across the last barriers at all. The mind can only take ye so far. After that, ye got t' rely on something else. 'Tis why only the humble o' heart can see the proof o' God's truth that he put right in front o' everyone's noses."

Charles pondered his words a moment or two. Maggie took the opportunity to pour hot water into the teapot.

"You'll see what we're talking about one day, Master Charles," she said.

"All men's eyes are opened eventually," added Bobby. "Though some take a little longer about it than others. Ye'll remember the flowers. Then suddenly all the arguments o' man, and all the human reasonings ye learned at the university, and all the science o' this modern age—suddenly none o' it will matter. Yer mind has taken ye as far as it can. Then 'twill be yer heart that'll realize God is God."

Again Charles laughed.

"Well, Bobby, we shall see!" he said. "Though it's hard to imagine it happening. I'm a rationalist, Bobby. I believe in science, in progress. Not that I hold your beliefs against you. But they're too outmoded for a young man like me."

"Yer day will come," Bobby replied.

"It comes to all," added Maggie.

"As I said, we shall see," said Charles.

The young man paused, laughed lightly, then added, "And the two of you shall be the first to know of it, when and if it does. You'll always be friends to me, however much we may differ in our opinions of what orders the universe, faith or reason."

When Charles disappeared through the wood back toward Heathersleigh Hall some time later, Maggie and Bobby McFee glanced at one another. Then, as if in one accord, they knelt where they were, amid the glorious abundance of floral color surrounding them in Maggie's garden, and lifted up their young friend to the Father they prayed he would one day acknowledge, and then desire to know more intimately.

———————— ◆ ◆ ◆ ————————

Bobby remembered the words, because he and his wife had prayed them many times in the years since.

And now as he stared after the retreating riders, he uttered the simple prayer yet again:

"Lord, open his eyes t' yer truth. He's got a good heart, Lord, and is a fine young man o' noble character. Only one thing he's missing—he doesn't yet know his Father. Make him complete, Lord, so he can be a whole man. In yer time and in yer way, Lord God, reveal t' him that place in his own being that his modernism and his science can't explain . . . without looking up t' you for the answer."

11

A Family Discussion About Changing Times

◆◆◆

They had been riding for a while, after leaving behind the woodcutter Bobby McFee, when Charles asked:—

"Once the wood is gone, George, what will people use for fuel?"

"Some people use coal, Papa."

"What if there is no coal? What if the coal runs out like the wood—what then?"

George thought a minute.

"I don't know."

"I know—I know, Papa!" exclaimed Amanda.

"What then, Amanda?"

"They will burn something else."

"What?"

"I don't know—something."

"Then you haven't answered my question."

Again the only sound for a few moments was the clomp, clomp, clomp of the horses' feet on the ground, broken by an occasional snort from one of their wet noses and thick fleshy lips, and accented every three or four seconds by the dull thudding sound through the trees behind them of axe striking wood.

"What about electricity?" said Charles at length.

"Can electricity make heat?" asked George.

"People are experimenting with it. Why, by the time you are master of the Hall, George, my boy, there will doubtless be electric lights in every room. Candles will be as obsolete as horses!"

"What is electricity, Papa?" asked Amanda.

"Would you like to answer your sister, George?"

"Current moving through wire," said George.

"Well done," said Charles. "That expensive tutor I hired for you must be earning his pay. Now, what is *current*?"

George did not answer immediately.

"There are tiny bits of electric charge, Amanda," said Charles, "called electrons. We have only just learned about them; Professor Thomson over at Cambridge discovered them. These electrons move through wire at the speed of light—"

"I didn't know light moved."

Her father laughed.

"It moves so fast you can't see it," he said. "So does electricity."

"But I *can* see it. I see everything. Light does not move."

"You see everything because the light from the sun shines upon it and makes it visible. That light from the sun is moving faster than anything else in the whole universe."

"But it's *not* moving, or else I would see it."

"You'll have to take my word for it, Amanda, light *moves*. And it is that same kind of movement, within a wire, which causes electricity."

"How does that make light?"

"If the wire is thin enough, and the electric current flows exactly in the right amount, the wire will glow. If you place a glowing wire inside a small vacuum bulb, then that glow will—"

"What is a vacuum?"

"An enclosed and sealed area from which the air has been removed."

"How do you remove air? Air . . . air is nothing!" exclaimed Amanda, throwing her arm about her as she rode.

Charles and George both laughed.

"Don't laugh at me, George," said Amanda. When her father laughed in the midst of a conversation, that was one thing. But she would not tolerate being ridiculed by her brother.

"He meant nothing by it, dear," interposed Jocelyn. "It was only that what you said had a funny sound to it."

Soothed for the moment, Amanda let the incident pass. George and Charles gradually resumed the discussion, but now without Amanda's participation.

As was often the case, their talk diverged from fuel and electricity after a time, and came around eventually to various of the political issues he was presently thinking about, on this occasion prompted in Charles' brain by the encounter with his nearest neighbor.

"What do you think, George," he said as they rode, "—should all men be treated equally, even if one is more intelligent, capable, and knowledgeable?"

"How do you mean, Papa?"

"For instance, take two men—one well-educated, informed on the issues, responsible and clear thinking, and the other a peasant who can neither read nor write and knows nothing of the world situation. Now—should both be allowed to vote, and should their votes have equal weight, even though the one is more qualified to render a rational, intelligent, and well-informed determination about what is best for the country?"

George did not answer immediately, but pondered his father's query.

"Or," Charles went on, "turn it around. Take a man like Mr. McFee, and assume him literate and knowledgeable on the issues and yet at the same time he is poor. Put alongside him a wealthy landowner who is perhaps a drunkard and knows little about the state of his nation. Should the wealthy man possess the power to vote and determine policy, while the well-informed poor man has none?"

"What about women?" interjected Jocelyn.

"A good point," rejoined Charles. "What indeed?"

"You know Emmeline Pankhurst and some of her crowd would have women equal with men at every turn."

"Mrs. Pankhurst may carry it further than anyone. But what do you think? How would you, George, my boy, weigh the relative value to society of the vote of a poor, uneducated, illiterate *man*, or a drunken, uninformed nobleman, alongside that of a conscientious, educated, thoughtful, intelligent, and well-informed *woman*?"

Again the four rode a few moments pondering the implications of

Charles' inquiry. Amanda had remained thus far curiously silent, but it would not last much longer.

"At present," Charles went on, "the man has the vote, not the woman, however qualified she may be to wield it perhaps more wisely than he in a given instance. Is that how it ought to be?"

"Why don't *you* change it, Mother?" said Amanda.

Jocelyn laughed. "Even if there was something I could do, it is still the men who have to decide."

"Why only men?"

"Because they're the ones who sit in Parliament."

"Is this state of affairs right?" Charles now persisted. "If the matter came before the Commons, what ought I to say to my colleagues concerning such a matter?"

"You should say that—" Amanda blurted out.

But she got no further before her father's hand went up to silence her. These were no frivolous questions, and he wanted to carry the dialogue with his son through to its conclusion.

It was silent a few moments. Young George Rutherford was one of those rare individuals who had realized early in life that the best thinking is done with the mouth closed. He was not anxious to speak until he had something to say.

"I know, Papa!" interposed Amanda impatiently, when several more seconds had passed. She could hardly tolerate her brother's slow deliberation over things.

"I'm sure you do, but give your brother the chance to answer."

"Why should I?"

"Because I asked him the question."

Again it was quiet. Amanda's impatience was visible as she fidgeted in her saddle.

"Something other than wealth and social standing ought to be the measure—is that what you want me to see?" said George tentatively.

"You've begun to get hold of the thing, but only around the edge of it yet. Grab hold of the center.—*Think*, George! What is that other thing?"

"Is it that character should be more important than wealth or standing?" said George after another minute.

"You're getting closer," said Charles.

"*Deserving* people ought to vote," interjected Amanda. She had been patient long enough.

"Not a bad answer, Amanda, insofar as it goes," replied her father. "But it doesn't go far enough. Who *are* the deserving?" he asked, turning toward her.

"Good people."

"Who defines that goodness?"

"Parliament, people in power . . . the queen—people like *you*, Papa."

"Ah, my dear," replied Charles, "but the queen and I and people like us . . . what if *we* become greedy and selfish and want to keep all the power for ourselves?"

"The queen would never do such a thing."

"England has had its share of rogues on the throne."

"Not Queen Victoria."

"And when Victoria dies?"

Momentarily Amanda was stumped. It had never occurred to her that the ageless lady was other than immortal. Charles took the opportunity to comment further.

"If we are the ones who define *good*, and we become *bad*—then where will the country be?"

"*You* would never become bad, Papa."

"Some people do, Amanda."

"But not *you*."

"Perhaps not. But one never knows. All men and women possess the capacity for good, as well as for evil. Some people *do* become greedy and selfish, even though no one thinks it could happen to *him*. How does a nation protect against that?"

Amanda's lips had no ready reply.

"If there is an elite—*however* it is defined . . . by wealth, by property, by education, by one's knowledge of affairs—then the possibility exists for a class system in which one segment of the population will be able to lord it over another. In other words, if there is an elite—whoever it is—the possibility exists for slavery . . . even if a society turns itself upside down, as the French did theirs in 1789, and the elite becomes comprised of commoners. The French revolutionaries made the aristocrats *their* slaves. *Any* elite has the capacity to abuse its power. Such has been true, even of our own nation at times past in our history. Thankfully we are more enlightened in these new days, though we still have much work to do. But there are some nations on the Continent where such slavery yet exists because elite ruling classes still wield far too much power."

He paused, then continued.

"You only considered one side of the question, Amanda—that is, that the present system is incomplete. That was accurate, but only *partially* so. But you must learn to look at all sides of a thing to get inside the full truth of it. If you had done so, you would realize that seeing the problem doesn't always yield a solution. You must see not only what is *wrong*, but what needs to be *done* about it—what change must we make in order to set things *right*. You did not stop to *think*. The instant I asked George the question you wanted to begin talking. You cannot get to the bottom of things when your mouth is moving."

In the moments his father and sister had been thus occupied, George had begun to get hold, as Charles had said, of the center of the thing.

"It is not just their character or goodness or wealth or even being informed, is it?" he said, "that ought to determine who votes. It is just that they are . . . *people*—that *all* people ought to be treated equally and ought to be able to vote no matter about all the rest—whether they are rich or poor, men or women, or even educated or not. Is that it?"

"Exactly!" exclaimed Charles. "Good boy! Equality mustn't be regulated, or eventually it will break down into some new form of *ine*-quality. It is the fact that we are all *humans* together that makes us unique. That fact alone ought to make us equals before the law."

Amanda gave her horse a kick and galloped off ahead. She was no expert horsewoman, and her seat was considerably less than graceful. But she would not listen to such correction of her ideas and praise of her brother's without *some* demonstration—even a silent one—to display her disapproval.

12

Something Strange in the Garret

*B*eing out in the woods had invigorated George's brain. He returned from the ride with his mind bent on exploration.

Even as they rode up to the great Hall which was his home, he looked up and let his eyes rove over its walls and turrets, three wings, and the fearsome eastern tower, with the gaze of potential adventure. Its three floors, basement, and mysterious garrets full of tiny rooms presented such a plethora of possibilities, he had not even set foot inside all of its seventy-five or hundred rooms. In days long forgotten, most had at one time or another been occupied and used by family, staff, and servants. Now many stood vacant or were filled with musty-smelling boxes from the dim past, adding a quiet odorous aura of antiquity to the place.

It was a home that offered endless intrigue to the boy, whose inquisitive mind was alive to adventure wherever he might discover it . . . and especially eager to understand the way the physical world was put together.

"May I explore the garret today, Papa?" he asked as they dismounted outside the barn, where Hector Farnham now began taking charge of their mounts.

"I suppose so, George, my boy," replied the lord of the manor as they walked toward the house while Amanda ran ahead. "What is your plan?"

"Just explore."

"In hopes of finding something?"

"I don't know. What *is* there to find, Papa?"

"Nothing that I know of, George," laughed the father. "No ghosts— that's for certain, no matter what people may say."

"What about the noises, Papa?"

"What noises? I've never heard them."

"Amanda says she has."

Charles laughed. "I have the feeling your sister's imagining things. But why don't you go up there and see if you hear them."

"Thank you, Papa!" said George excitedly.

"I doubt I've been in the garret since I was a boy," added Charles. "I don't remember much very interesting then. I'm sure it hasn't changed, except that more cobwebs are likely hanging from the beams."

Later that same afternoon, George's puttering in the attic regions of the house had led him to the end of a corridor where an odd-looking wall blocked further exploration.

He stared at it a few moments, then glanced about. The paneling was different, both in coloration and mode of construction, than in the rest of the upper portions of the Hall. It seemed to be of a different wood, and not so old.

George approached, then rapped lightly against it with his knuckles.

Was he imagining it, or did it have a hollow sound?

Without pausing to think through the implications, the next instant he had turned and was hurriedly striding back the way he had come. He would carry his search further. Quickly he left the low-ceilinged garret, descended to the second floor, and made for the north wing. From its attic spaces he hoped he might be able to approach the same region from the opposite side.

"Amanda, Amanda, come with me," said George excitedly as he went, seeing his sister leaving her room. "Come see what I found!"

"What is it?" she asked.

"Something strange up in the garret."

"The garret—ugh! I wouldn't go up there for anything. There's nothing but spiders and horrid old webs hanging about."

Undaunted, and not realizing he had stumbled upon the threads of a generations-old mystery concerning the Hall that was his home, George continued on his way.

♦ ♦ ♦

Lord Rutherford's instructions had been plain enough, though it was the most curious assignment Webley Kyrkwode had ever been called upon for at the Hall.

Both Lord Rutherford and his nephew were strange ones,

Kyrkwode thought to himself as he carried two long planks up the servants' stairway to the second floor, and from there up the narrow flight to the garret. If young Henry inherited both the Hall and the title from his uncle, as all supposed inevitable, who could tell what the grand place would come to?

His own young Orelia had spent half her childhood at the Hall while he had been engaged in one construction project or another for the lord of the manor, playing with her young friend, daughter of one of the lady's maids.

But he no longer allowed her to accompany him from the village. Orelia was now fifteen and growing into a buxom and comely young woman. Kyrkwode had seen more than sufficient glimpses into the character of Lord Rutherford's eighteen-year-old nephew to know that he did not want the young man's eyes roving in the direction of his daughter.

The brawny laborer set down the two heavy boards, stood straight to stretch his back, then descended for another load. Building these walls would be the easy part. Keeping an entire corridor hidden from view would be more difficult. And he would have to contrive some locking mechanism not readily detectable from the other side.

The locksmith in the village would help with that, although Kyrkwode would not be able to divulge the purpose for his inquiry. That should not be too hard to do, thought the builder to himself. He had always been fascinated with unusual doors and clever locks. He had installed any number of such things—usually with the help of both blacksmith and locksmith—not only at the Hall and the cottage for Lord Rutherford, but also for many of the villagers.

One more should not raise too many questions. Whatever masonry work was required, he would see to himself. When it was completed, only he and Lord Broughton Rutherford would know of it.

PART II

❖❖❖

First Glances Inward
1897

13

We Can Change the World!

*O*n the morning following their ride into the woods, in the first-class carriage of the Southwest England Express, the family of Charles Rutherford, Lord of the Manor of Heathersleigh, sped eastward toward their destiny.

On Charles' part, the future about to overtake him was one he neither anticipated nor would have chosen. The effect of the next two days upon him would be far different than what he envisioned. Neither could any of the five know what inheritance in unseen realms awaited them, or what sacrifice would be required before each could lay claim to his appointed share in it.

For Charles Rutherford was a *sought* man. Not by the queen of England, however . . . but by the King himself. He was about to be made far more than a knight in the world of men. The calling upon him was far higher, into *sonship* in the eternal royal family.

"What do you think, Amanda?" he said ebulliently to the daughter sitting at his side, heedless of the higher things at work which had his own heart at the center of their heavenly vortex. "Are you excited to be going into town?"

"Oh yes, Papa," his daughter replied. "I can hardly remember anything about the city."

"That is scarcely surprising, seeing as you were but three the only other time you and George and I accompanied your father," smiled Jocelyn Rutherford from the seat opposite, where she sat holding little Catharine. The nanny, Constance Dimble, sat beside her, silent but listening interestedly to the conversation.

"You will love the city," remarked Charles. "What about you, George? Do you remember London?"

Before her brother could reply, Amanda spoke up again.

"Why, Papa?" she said, wide-eyed with anticipation. "Why will we love the city?"

"Because of all it represents!—It is a great time to be alive, is it not, Jocie?" Charles added, turning to his wife sitting across from him. "It's the age of man, of invention, of progress. No other time in history has offered so much—and here we are with the chance to be right in the middle of it."

"And you in the *very* middle of it," added Jocelyn, "being honored by the queen personally. Just think, in a short while you shall be *Sir Charles*, a knight of the realm."

Charles smiled with satisfaction to hear the words fall from his wife's lips.

"I still can hardly believe I am going to meet her myself," she added.

"But you shall, my dear—you shall! No more anxiety?"

"Some. But I keep telling myself that Victoria will be as kind to me as you have always been."

"I am certain she will. It is an honor for us to share together."

"Is this really the greatest time there has ever been in history, Papa?"

"Indeed it is, Amanda!" he answered, turning to face their daughter again. "None of us even grasp just how great an era this is. We have the opportunity before us literally to do what no people before us has done."

"What, Papa?" asked Amanda.

"Change the world, Amanda. Change it for the better—wipe out disease and poverty and suffering and injustice. Mankind will soon be capable of controlling its own destiny."

On the other side of his mother, young George sat staring out the window, quietly contemplating the workings of the magnificent invention in which they were seated. He had inherited his father's fascination with things that *worked*, and trains were a particular love of his nine-year-old mind. He had not, however, inherited his father's interest in politics. Of a more thoughtful and melancholy temperament, he showed little interest in the conversation in progress across from him. He contented himself instead with the passing countryside and the sounds and sensations of mechanical motion.

Amanda had inherited her father's passion, however, not for the workings of machines but for the workings of society. If he said they could change the world, why would she think otherwise? He was a leader in Parliament, was he not? He was about to be made a knight by the queen. Didn't he know everything? Amanda was seven and impressionable . . . and she trusted whatever her father said.

"Is that what you will do when *you* are prime minister, Papa?" asked Amanda. "I know it is what I shall do when I am in Parliament like you."

Charles laughed.

"One day you shall *indeed* accompany me, Amanda. You shall go with me to London, and for no mere visit of two days such as this, but to take your own place in its society."

"Do you really mean it?"

"Of course. When you are seventeen, we shall present you to all of London society. You and your mother shall accompany me when I go into London, and you shall stay for the entire social season."

As he spoke, he glanced toward his wife with fun in his eye. She was shaking her head at the thought of such societal involvement. But Charles continued:—

"Your coming out, Amanda, will be the talk of the city."

"Oh, I can hardly wait!"

"Indeed. And I shall introduce you to princes and princesses, to M.P.s and lords and ladies. You shall go to parties and wear fancy dresses. There will be music and dancing and balls. You shall become one of them, and along with me, we shall make England and the world a better place. What do you say to that?"

Charles could not help being caught up in his moment of triumph, and his enthusiasm overflowed with high-spirited prognostications. The predictions he lavished on his daughter were a bit grand, perhaps. But she took in his words as certainties only awaiting time to be fulfilled. In her young ears they were statements of what someday *would* be fact.

"Oh yes, Papa! When may I go to a ball and meet a prince?"

"Charles, you shouldn't fill her mind with such expectations," said Jocelyn with a smile. "A young lady's coming out is one thing—meeting princes is something else. She might just take you seriously."

He laughed again. Despite his wife's protestations, it was music to his ears to hear his daughter speak so, for he eagerly anticipated the day when he could share his active life at the center of English affairs with not only his son but also his daughters. That his wife had not been presented to society with a formal coming out, and would have loathed the very thought of it, did not enter Charles' mind. Jocelyn had always considered herself extremely fortunate to have been in India at the time of her seventeenth birthday. She had thus been spared both possible humiliations—either the ritual itself, or the knowledge that her mother might have prevented it even if they had been in England.

Amanda was so young, her parents had never before even spoken of the matter.

"Of course she will take me seriously," Charles replied. He turned again to Amanda, and spoke again. "All in good time, my dear," he said. "Perhaps when you are twelve—no, let me think," he added, assuming a serious tone, placing his forefinger against his lips for effect, and looking her over approvingly from head to toe, "—I think you *may* be ready by ten," he said slowly, emphasizing the word, then nodding thoughtfully. "What do you say to that? Would you like to go with me to a London ball at ten?"

"Oh, may I, Mother—please!" she exclaimed, beaming under her father's approbation.

"We shall see, my dear," said Jocelyn. "But seventeen is a more traditional age for being presented than ten."

"And one day I shall be prime minister too," Amanda added, including her own prophecy as the finalization of the discussion.

"Whatever put the idea of being prime minister into your head, dear?" asked her mother.

"Papa did, Mother."

"What—I never hinted at such a thing!" laughed Charles.

"Papa says he will take me to the city with him to help him change the world," said Amanda, still addressing her mother.

"Don't you know women are not allowed in the House of Commons?" said Jocelyn.

"If he is in the House of Commons, why should I not be as well?"

Charles and Jocelyn Rutherford glanced at one another and smiled. Both knew well enough that it would be pointless to argue. Once an idea came into their determined little Amanda's head, nothing short of the very divine intervention Charles would have scoffed at was capable of removing it.

"Well, Amanda," he said after a brief pause, "perhaps you *shall* be prime minister one day at that."

"Do you *really* think so, Papa?" said Amanda, for she was shrewd enough to have seen the look which passed between her father and mother. "Or are you just teasing me?"

"Why not?" rejoined Charles, almost as if debating within his own progressive mind the viability of his daughter's incredible and far-reaching suggestion. "What's to stop you? Of course, we'll have to get women the vote first," he chuckled as an afterthought.

"Why shouldn't women vote?" said Amanda, with a little more persistent edge in her tone.

"I do not say they *shouldn't*," he replied. "But we have to give the rest of the country time to catch up with some of the other reforms we have made. It hasn't been that long since working *men* have been able to vote."

"I think women *ought* to be able to vote," said Amanda, and now the voice of the young politician was resolute, as if her indomitable declaration should make it so.

"Many women would agree with you, dear," said Jocelyn, "wouldn't they, Charles?"

"Indeed. And a number which is growing daily. But these things take time. For that to happen we first have to get the Liberal party back on top. At the moment the Tories control the government and they are extremely powerful just now."

"What are Tories, Papa?"

"The Conservative party," he answered. "As long as I am a Liberal, and they are in power, there is very little I can do ... other than speak out. But if there is anything you can depend on in politics, it is change. Our day will dawn again. The time for such change shall come."

A brief silence followed as the train clacked along. Its massive wheels along the iron tracks created the most beautifully clanking rhythmic music in George's ears.

"You know," mused Charles, "I believe someday there *shall* be a woman prime minister. You mark my words, Jocie," he said, turning again to his wife, "whether it's ten years or ten generations from now. England is a land of progressive ideas, and has been ever since Magna Carta was signed."

In the seat across from them Amanda's mother listened but offered no further comment for now. She was proud of Charles. And despite a few lingering anxieties, she was thrilled for the opportunity to meet Queen Victoria. But when the celebration was over, she would be happy to return to Heathersleigh. Even as Charles' wife, London society was not the life for her. Notwithstanding her husband's promises about their daughter's future, it would have suited Jocelyn Rutherford for Amanda to avoid the trappings of society altogether.

"Our political system is the envy of the world," Charles was saying.

"Certainly women will vote one day. Forces are already gathering in other nations in such directions. Once the presence of women has been established in the Commons, it will only be a matter of time before a woman rises to the top of her party. Perhaps our Amanda is onto something after all."

Though in most bloodlines, political legacies were passed down from father to son, in the family Rutherford it was upon young Amanda that the political psyche of her father had already, even at seven, come to rest. He had noted the gleam in her eye as they talked. By his words, even if unconsciously, he had built into her a sense not only of energetic determination, but also invincibility. Whether there ever would be a woman prime minister—who could tell? But *if* it ever happened, he wouldn't put it past his energetic and dogged little Amanda to grow up to be the woman who achieved it.

Of course these controversial views concerning women's suffrage, not to mention the notion that women might share the hallowed corridors of the Houses of Parliament, were not ones he voiced even amongst his most liberal and farseeing colleagues in the Fabian society. Nor did he pause to reflect upon what the socialist writers who had influenced him would think of his own aristocratic blood. It was enough, he thought, if he used his privilege for the betterment of mankind.

As Amanda sat contemplating what she had heard, and dreaming of what fortunes lay before *her* in the great city, she was aware of no such reservations on the part of her father. How was she to think of his every word other than a *fait accompli* of his political program? If her father said that she could change the world with him, she adopted his word as fact. If he said she might become prime minister someday, that too became solidified in her tenacious and visionary brain.

Amanda had been an astute observer of her father's rise in prominence, more so than either Charles or Jocelyn realized. Indeed, hadn't she listened to her father's views and speeches? She was a young socialist, just like him, with just enough youthful naïveté to accompany her ideals to think that if her father might aspire to the prime ministership, why shouldn't she? That women did not yet even possess the power to vote represented no obstacle in young Amanda's mind.

She was too young to concern herself with practicalities. And as the train carried them along, her father's words sunk deep into the fabric of her being.

She would make herself as influential as he ... perhaps greater.

14

Center of Civilization

◆◆◆

If ever a single dot on the globe could claim to be the hub of man's activity on the earth as the nineteenth century after the birth of Jesus Christ wound to a close, that place was surely the great city to which the Rutherford family was traveling.

As the train pulled into Paddington Station, their eyes widened and their senses heightened with anticipation. All around them was noise and bustle, and Devon seemed a million miles behind them.

The family disembarked. Charles arranged for a cab that would hold them all, and they set out for their hotel. The *clickety-clack-clack-clack* of the sturdy horse's four shod feet along the cobbled street from the station toward the center of the city continued the mesmerization of George's brain begun by the train's wheels and tracks. His sister, however, sat heedless of the occasional snort, the creak and groan of leather, the rubbing of wood and metal, or the faint odor of horseflesh that wafted back into the carriage. Horses were of the country, and everything associated with them was familiar and boring.

But the city—that was something different. She gazed this way and that, her senses tinging with the electric atmosphere of the huge, sprawling metropolis. From every direction, sights and smells and sounds of the biggest gathering of human beings on earth called out to her in ways her Devonshire home never could. She could scarcely contain the enchantment welling up in her heart as she glanced about in the continuous energy of delight.

No more exciting place in all the world could possibly exist, she thought, as she bounced gently along at her father's side in the horse-drawn cab. The city's very activity stimulated her brain as nothing back on the downs of Devon ever had. Tall buildings loomed above them. Horse-drawn carts of every size and shape imaginable filled the streets. Some, like theirs, bore visitors or residents from one place in the city to another; others transported vegetables or fruit or other produce to market. Still others were filled with boxes and freight of unknown content.

A few motorcars sped about, whose *put-put-put*s of white exhaust smoke and oddly tooting horns drew both George's head and his father's with more than idle curiosity. Peddlers shouted and called to potential customers concerning a great variety of goods. Many turned toward their carriage as it passed, holding up now a dead chicken by the neck, now a bouquet of roses, now a fresh melon, with a tone that was at once imploring, demanding, and inquiring.

Dozens of open-air market stalls spread along the sidewalks. Businessmen in suits and carrying leather satchels walked in and out of the tall buildings. Every inch of the place bustled with activity and movement.

"Do you see that wall there, George?" Charles was saying, pointing out a stone structure to his son. "It is said to be one thousand years old."

"A thousand years!"

"Can you imagine, George?—it was built before the Norman invasion. But there are ruins from Roman times almost *twice* that age! We shall go across the river tomorrow to the old city and Southwark, and I will show you. It was called Londinium then."

As they now came along the street named for their queen, the sight of the magnificent Abbey met their gaze. Even modern, progressive, forward-visioned, spiritually agnostic Charles Rutherford could not but be filled with a sense of awe at its grandeur. Who could not be stirred by memory of the history contained within the walls of the great cathedral?

"When the Normans conquered England in 1066, George, my boy," Charles said, "William the Conqueror marched straight up from the south coast to London. He had himself crowned right here in the Abbey."

He spoke a few words to the driver of the cab, who, as a result, called out several unintelligible sounds to the horse whose business it was to pull them across town. Whatever language of man or beast they were, the horse apparently understood the meaning well enough and slowed his gait. Charles took the opportunity to point out various elements of the exterior design of the cathedral to George, while Amanda busily watched the people going in and coming out.

Gradually the pace of the carriage increased again. A minute later they came within sight of the magnificent Palace of Westminster, where the two Houses of Parliament met. It was here that Charles' duties kept him busy during the parliamentary season.

"William the Conqueror made Westminster his home and the center of his government," he said. "Ever since then, this has been the site where kings and queens and parliaments have presided over our nation, though of course the queen now lives at Buckingham Palace."

"Is it as old as the Abbey?" asked George, gazing in wonder at the ornate spires and the clock tower at the top of which Big Ben presided regally over the city.

"No, George. Much of Westminster Palace was destroyed in the fire of 1834. Certain portions of the old eleventh century Hall survived, but most of what you see was built during my father's time."

"Isn't it wonderful, Papa!" exclaimed Amanda. "Everything is just as you said."

"It is indeed a city beyond equal."

"Will we really meet the queen?"

"Indeed, all three of you shall be presented to her," replied her father. "It will be a moment you will never forget as long as you live."

"You must be the most important man in all London!" said Amanda, still gazing up at the brown and gold parliamentary palace.

Charles laughed.

"Do you hear that, Jocie?" he said to his wife, still chuckling.

"I heard," replied Jocelyn. "But I have always told you that."

Again he laughed.

Amanda hardly heard their banter. She felt more alive and invigorated than ever before in her young life. All the more deeply, as they now passed this nerve center of the nation, did the words her father had spoken on the train penetrate the depths of Amanda Rutherford's soul.

She was growing up more rapidly than either father or mother realized. At seven, Amanda yet stood, as it were, on the threshold of seventeen, ready and eagerly awaiting the moment of her *own* entrance into this bright, gay, exciting, historic world of power and influence.

Nothing could suit her more than to be the prime minister's daughter, as she fully believed one day very soon she would be—the belle of every ball, attending the most spectacular events of London's social season. Then she would take her place, like her father, at the vanguard of England's progressive political movement.

♦ ♦ ♦

In every era, two seemingly contradictory forces work to move civilization forward. History spawns the times, even as the times give birth to men and women who step forward onto the world stage and exert their influence on the course of events. Does the march of *history itself* produce the people who are swept up in it? Or do those *people* dictate which directions the drama of man will take?

The history of this particular land, almost of itself, had given rise to the family who now gazed out the window of their carriage at the sights of London. Charles and Jocelyn Rutherford and their children were people of their times. Yet equally were they the product of the long history of the England they proudly called their own. Their personas, their character, their vision, could no more be separated from this era in which they lived than from the two millennia which had preceded it.

The carriage now entered Whitehall and made its way along the broad avenue to Trafalgar Square. As they turned onto Haymarket, a building which housed a certain prestigious bank came into view. Charles eyed it with more than casual interest. His wife noted the expression, but said nothing. She did not know exactly *what* he was thinking at the moment, but she knew well enough *who* was on his mind.

Charles' thoughts quieted. For the next several blocks, despite the noise and hubbub around them, he reflected abstractly on the growth of the great capital and the legacy its magnificent history had left its modern leaders—men like he himself, and even perhaps his cousin in the bank they had just passed. The two had grown up, if not exactly together, at least in proximity to one another, though their courses in life had diverged early. It was men such as they, each in their own way, who would influence the directions this city and this nation would take in a new century.

If history could produce greatness, so could cities. And none more than this.

Those who would impact the world, those whose potency and leadership would be felt by their peers, those who would be remembered by their achievements and by the historians of the future—to London they looked to fulfill their dreams. In London dwelt opportunity.

His little daughter was right. Surely this city was the center of all things.

"Well, here we are!" announced Charles, as the cab pulled up in front of the Grosvenor House Hotel on Park Lane.

15

Clandestine Arrangements

♦♦♦

*A*s the Rutherford family settled down for the evening in their hotel, a late-night meeting was taking place some two thousand kilometers to the east. Though but two individuals were involved, it was destined to exercise an equal impact upon the future of England as the momentous festivities being planned in London for the following day.

A woman by appearance in her late thirties, though in the dim light it was impossible to say for certain—handsome though with somewhat course features, possibly Slavic in origin—had just spoken.

"I vill certainly be vatched," she had said.

"Of course, but your very visibility gives us our opportunity. And you must *watch* your accent. W's are troublesome."

"I *will* pay closer attention," she replied, emphasizing the proper English pronunciation. "Usually, it's not so much the problem with me—when I'm with you, I get nervous. You don't have to *worry*."

He ignored the hint of accusation. "The new arrangement will enable you to move about freely at the highest levels of society."

"It is not always good for a sleeper to be much seen."

"You will not be alone."

"How will we maintain contact?"

"I will arrange everything. As long as you are able to travel to and from the Continent, and can come and go as you please, there will be no difficulty. As the wife of an important dignitary you should be able to do so at will."

"It vill be much different than evading the eye of the Austrians."

"And much *easier*. The English think they are invincible. That fact alone is our greatest weapon. Even when one of our number is discovered, they are usually sent back after but a brief disciplinary action. Not only are the English a proud people, they are a soft race."

"If *our* leaders found one of *them* out, he would be shot."

"Precisely. As I said, you have nothing to fear.—Tell me, do you love the man?"

"I learned long ago that love must subserve the cause."

"It can nevertheless be put to good advantage."

"I am a realist," she replied, then smiled thoughtfully. "I am fond of him, in a daughterly sort of way. He is kind to me."

"Will that be enough?"

"For a woman in my position, one takes what opportunities one is presented. As I said, I am a realist. If it helps the cause, I will be content. Besides—" she added with a shrewd grin, "you are paying me too well for me not to be satisfied."

"I see we understand each other," returned the man, the edges of his lips turning upward in a cunning grin.

"I will stand to inherit a fortune, I hope before I am too old to enjoy it. This should presumably help advance the new order. I vill have the best of all worlds."

"And your son?"

"He is but nine. He will adapt to the change. He speaks flawless English. No one will suspect his origins."

"Good. Then I wish you much happiness as the new lady Hal—"

The woman put her finger to her lips to silence him.

"Please," she interrupted, "do not speak my new name here. These are uncertain times. Unfriendly ears are everywhere. I would rather get used to it over there first."

"As you wish."

The man rose from the table.

"You will be contacted," he said. "Once you are in touch with our network, you will receive notice of an antique auction to be held in Rome in the fall. Make sure you attend. We will meet again at that time."

The man turned and exited the cheap restaurant, leaving the woman alone with thoughts of her new future in a foreign land.

16
Last-Minute Reflections

♦♦♦

$\mathcal{T}$he morning of June 28 dawned as bright as Charles Rutherford's optimism concerning the future of England and his part in it.

When his wife Jocelyn first became aware of the light streaming through the window into the bedroom of their hotel suite, she rolled over in the bed to discover herself alone. She sat up and glanced about, then sought her small pendant watch, which she had placed on the nightstand. The hands displayed ten after six.

She rose, put on her dressing gown, and walked into the sitting room. There stood her husband at the window, already dressed. His back was to the room as he stared over the rooftops of London at sunrise. Softly she approached.

"Couldn't sleep?" she said.

Charles turned and smiled.

"Ah, Jocelyn—creeping up behind me?"

"I didn't want to disturb your solitude with too loud a step."

He took her in his arms and they stood together a moment. "Yes, you're right," he said at length, "I couldn't sleep."

"How long have you been up?"

"An hour."

"Nervous?"

"Excited. Perhaps a little nervous . . . I was thinking, too, of my father."

"In what way?"

"Realizing what this means, being given an honor that never came to him."

"What does it make you feel?" asked his wife.

"One part pride," he answered, "—for I know *he* would be proud of me. Another part melancholy . . . and of course how is it possible not to feel humbled to be given so great an honor? It is impossible to pinpoint all the thoughts and emotions that come and go on such an occasion."

"You know I am very proud of you too," said his wife softly.

"I do know, Jocie," replied Charles. "I cannot say it means more to me than all the rest," he added with a smile. "But it means a great deal. I love you with all my heart."

Jocelyn Rutherford laid her head gently on her husband's chest. Again they stood a few moments in silence. For her, this was worth all the knighthoods of a thousand kingdoms. She was willing enough to enjoy the wealth and prestige that came with rank and position. But she would have been just as happy as a pauper living in a stone cottage in the highlands . . . as long as they were together.

"Shall we have some tea sent up?" he asked at length.

"That would be nice. We can enjoy the morning before the children are awake. I think we have another hour before Constance and the children require us."

"Then I shall go downstairs and see about the tea, while you are getting dressed."

17

Annoying Disturbance

About midday on the 28th of June, after a thoroughly English breakfast of eggs, toast, tea, thick bacon, mushroom, and tomato—which even Amanda consumed without comment—and a morning spent dressing and making sure everyone looked just right, the Rutherford family left the hotel for Buckingham Palace.

The actual anniversary of Victoria's sixty years on the throne had passed a little more than a week earlier, on the 20th of June. The Diamond Jubilee celebration had been going on ever since, and would culminate with today's huge garden party on the grounds of Buckingham Palace. The event would last informally most of the afternoon. Though she had been receiving accolades and gifts all week, yet more honors would be bestowed upon the queen. Numerous speeches would be made. Receiving of dignitaries by the queen was scheduled for four.

Their carriage driver maneuvered his way through bustling traffic, deftly dodging pedestrians and vehicles alike, until they drew near a crowded thoroughfare where a hundred or more people blocked the street. Sounds as of a commotion of some kind filtered back to them, but they could see nothing other than a mass of humanity. The horse slowed, then finally stopped.

"What is it?" called out Charles.

"Can't rightly say, guv," replied the driver in thick Cockney. "Some kind o' parade or wot—blimey, but if it ain't got the street all tangled up ahead."

Charles leaned out the window and peered forward.

"It's the St. James Lecture Hall," he said.

"Right you be there, guv."

"There must be some event scheduled today."

The sound of music coming from somewhere did suggest a parade, yet the unmistakable tone of angry voices indicated a serious disturbance.

"Are the police about?"

"Ain't a bobbie in sight, guv," replied the driver.

"Well, I shall see what's to be done," said Charles, opening the door and jumping down out of the carriage onto the street.

"Charles, do be careful," implored his wife. She had heard several angry shouts in the midst of the din.

Dismissing her concern with a few words and a wave of the hand, he strode forward, disappearing quickly into the thick of the crowd. Pushing his way past those who had gathered to watch the spirited row, he arrived within a minute at the eye of the maelstrom.

On the placard attached to the front of the lecture hall he noted an announcement in bold print reading, EVOLUTION AND GENESIS: SCIENTIFIC FACTS REPLACE CREATIONIST MYTHS. Beneath this title were the words, "Open to public, 15d admission. Noon—June 28."

"What's the trouble?" he asked an onlooker.

"Bunch o' chapelgoers came t' protest the lecture, mate," replied a man, who then paused to scrutinize Charles' expensive attire. As he looked from polished boots up to black top hat, the man's thick bushy eyebrows raised in wonderment.

On the sidewalk ahead a salvation band made what attempt it could to continue a rousing gospel hymn. Some of their number passed out anti-evolution leaflets among the crowd—much of which had come to attend the lecture—doing their best to convince whoever would listen to change their plans.

The horns and voices of the little band, however, were mostly drowned out by the shouts being tossed at them from about a dozen young men who had recently emerged from the hall, carrying a banner in support of their cause and attempting to put a stop to the protest so that more listeners could be drawn in. In the meantime, the more rowdy elements of the crowd had sided with the latter. Gradually they added their own taunts and threats to what had until a few moments earlier been mostly a civilized, albeit a heated, exchange.

"—back to your church and hold a service there," one of the men from the hall was saying. "You are welcome to attend the lecture and listen respectfully. Otherwise we ask you to leave so these other people can do so. We are happy for you to join us, but you must not prevent others from doing so."

"Get out of here, yer scruffy chapelgoers!" cried one of the newcomers. "No one needs the likes of you!"

The evolutionists were doing what they could to exhort and encourage the crowd into the hall. Several young troublemakers in their twenties grew rowdy and belligerent. These now edged their way closer to the center of the confrontation. They shoved and pushed at the two men who stood in front of the dwindling congregation. The band leaders did their best to ignore them and continue singing, while their troops passed out their tracts.

"We want none o' yer hymns, so sod off!" shouted a particularly surly fellow to the leader of the band. Despite the early hour, he appeared to have been drinking heavily.

One of his cohorts sidled up to an attractive young lady of the band. The same instant Charles arrived, the fellow stretched his arm around her.

Nervously she stepped back, then tried to hand him a leaflet.

"Hey, good-lookin'—how 'bout you comin' home with me? I'm more interestin' than's these preachers o' yers. I'll let you preach t' *me* when we's alone!" he added, eying her with a leering grin.

She drew away. He met her resistance by pulling her more forcefully toward him. Suddenly noticing what was going on behind him, one of the band leaders now turned and hurried forward.

"Please, sir, leave her alone," he said. "She's done nothing to—"

He did not have the chance to finish his sentence. The burly troublemaker let go of the terrified young lady. He grabbed the man's lapels in his two huge fists, and now sent the slightly built evangelist sprawling back into the midst of his band.

The music stopped with a crash. Preacher and drummer toppled in a heap onto the ground, the former's leg through the middle of the latter's broken instrument.

Amid laughter and more jeers from the roughs, Charles now ran forward into the middle of the fray.

"Please, all of you," he cried, "stop this at once!"

He approached the young lady, but was met by the brute who had instigated the incident.

"Mind yer own business, guv!" he growled. "Who are you anyway—what's it to you?"

"I'm Charles Rutherford," he answered, "and until the police get here to take these people away, I'm here to tell you—"

But the man's blood was flowing hot. Emboldened by what he judged his success with the preacher, he now likewise sent Charles flying back. It was no mere shove this time, however. A massive clenched fist landed with a vicious thud just above Charles' left ear.

Charles stumbled and fell back onto the sidewalk. His hat rolled into the crowd of onlookers.

A few of them, seeing clearly enough that he was a gentleman—one or two by now recognizing him as a Member of Parliament—helped Charles back to his feet.

Angered but forcing himself to remain calm, again Charles strode forward. This time he was on his guard. And he was handy enough with his own fists, as the young woman's assailant would discover soon enough, a skill he had developed to some level of proficiency in Her Majesty's navy.

Laughing while Charles picked himself up off the ground, the troublemaker quickly lost his mirth. Warily he eyed the re-approach of the well-dressed man. He had no idea that by day's end this new adversary would be a knight. But he recognized the glint in the fellow's eye well enough, and the set of his lips. They were fighting expressions with which he was well enough acquainted.

The ruffian raised his fists defiantly. The edges of his thick lips turned upward with an evil grin of anticipation. This would be an easy contest!

Only a moment more he waited, then took a lurching but ill-advised step toward Charles, cocking his arm to swing.

Suddenly Charles' feet danced sideways. The same moment a luring flick of his head drew a great blow from the man. But the roguish fist met only air, and his feet stumbled in consequence. He spun back, surprised that he had missed. Again he lumbered toward Charles.

None of the onlookers could say how it was accomplished exactly. The two punishing jabs which came next were delivered with such lightning speed that no one quite saw it clearly. The next moment, the brute lay unconscious, measuring his own length on the ground.

"All right," said Charles, turning toward a couple of the troublemaker's cohorts, "take your friend and get him out of here."

They came forward and dragged the man to his feet. Groggily he came to himself, scarcely knowing what day it was, and having no recollection of what had just happened. They retreated without further incident.

"The rest of you," he said to the crowd, "go on about your business. You who are in charge of the lecture, and you people planning to attend, I suggest you proceed. Perhaps I shall even join you—the topic sounds intriguing!" he added with a laugh, which helped diffuse the tension.

Laughing and talking about what had just happened, slowly the crowd disbursed. Some continued along the street. About half began moving in the direction of the lecture hall. A short man walked up with Charles' hat and handed it to him.

The leader of the small Christian band had been helped by his comrades out of the drum. He rose to his feet and now came forward to express his appreciation.

"I can't thank you enough," he said. "I don't know what we would have done had you not come along."

Behind him the young lady approached with a radiant smile of gratitude.

"Thank you so much, sir," she said sweetly. "I was so afraid."

"Don't mention it," replied Charles a bit gruffly. His head was already beginning to ache from the blow.

"But I implore you, sir," the preacher went on, "not to attend the lecture. Evolution is not a teaching that comes from God."

Partly because of his throbbing head, partly because his black frock coat and elegant striped trowsers were now spotted with dirt, but mostly because the sound of religious sentimentality struck such an irritating chord of unreality in his brain, Charles felt a wave of anger and disgust sweep through him.

"I'll thank you to give *me* none of your sermons!" he said sharply, turning on the man. "This would not have happened at all if you people had not attempted to interfere with this lecture in the first place. When are you going to realize that your protests and hymn singing and absurd leaflets cannot stop progress or silence the voice of science?"

"Claiming that man is descended from apes is hardly progress," replied the man calmly. "If you would just read this leaflet, sir, the truth about evolution is explained clearly."

As he spoke, the man handed Charles one of the small tracts with which the street was now well littered. Charles grabbed at it rudely, crushed it in his fist, and threw it to the ground.

"Don't give me any of your religious claptrap," he rejoined. "Just get your people out of here before I call the police and have you all thrown in jail for disturbing the peace."

Charles turned to go.

Before he could take a step, however, an expression of mortification seized him. The face of the young lady whom he had rescued caught him with a force almost physical. She was looking at him stunned. Her eyes shone with profound hurt. She was saddened, rather than angered, by the rudeness of his angry remarks.

Charles had the sense . . .

The thought was ridiculous! *He* was on his way to see the queen. *She* was the worst form of commoner, one who allowed her life to be ruled by religious nonsense!

Yet it almost seemed . . . that she felt *sorry* for him.

He dismissed the notion from his brain. He spun around, and strode back through the disbursing crowd. Unaccountably agitated, he walked hurriedly to the carriage to join his waiting family.

18

Sir Charles Rutherford

◆◆◆

*C*harles . . . what happened?" exclaimed Jocelyn as he climbed in beside her.

"Nothing.—Get us out of here," he called brusquely to the driver.

"But your trowsers. And—good heavens! You've got a cut on the side of your head!"

But she could only get a scant account of the incident. He was in no mood to talk. It was too late to return to the hotel, he said. He would clean himself up as best he could, and see to his scrapes in one of the guest sitting rooms after reaching the palace.

They arrived without further incident.

Charles was able to make himself sufficiently presentable that he was confident no one would ask if he had fallen into a gutter on his way. Soon he was busy greeting his parliamentary colleagues and other dignitaries in attendance. The incident at least served one purpose—Jocelyn hardly thought about herself all day. She was too concerned for Charles. If the welt above his ear grew any larger, people were going to notice his face more than hers!

The atmosphere of the palace grounds was gay and festive.

Flowers bloomed abundantly in every direction one looked, every bed and walkway groomed to perfection. The expansive lawns and gardens were exquisitely manicured, not a weed in sight anywhere. Hedges bordered several theme gardens, one containing full-blooming rose bushes, another different species of dwarfed conifers and other trees, and a third a mazelike series of raised flower beds displaying more color per square inch than any other spot in the whole of London.

At two o'clock, Queen Victoria was honored by representatives of most countries in the Commonwealth, by the heads of several of England's leading families, and by the kings and princes, queens and duchesses, chancellors and heads of state of several of the Continent's nations. Many of her foreign relatives were present, as well as stage personalities and concert artists.

For most of the afternoon the queen traveled along the lawns in a victoria—a light, four-wheeled carriage with seat for two and perch for coachman—drawn by two greys. As she passed through the crowd, men bowed, women curtsied, and everyone looked happy. She then retired to a large tent set up for the occasion, filled with flowers, and wide open in the front so she could be seen. She had tea and toast, and readied herself to meet those upon whom she would confer special honor on this day.

As the hour of four o'clock approached, those who were to be recognized as knights assembled with their families outside the queen's tent, waiting their turn to be taken inside by Lord Lathom, the Lord Chamberlain. Charles was easily the youngest by a decade. With Jocelyn and the children, he waited patiently behind three or four of his colleagues for his audience with the queen.

Jocelyn leaned over and adjusted Catharine's cap, then straightened. Just for a moment her gloved hand strayed toward the side of her face. Then she lowered it, clasped her hands in front of her, and took a short, determined breath.

This day has not been easy for her, Charles realized with a little start. *Sometimes I forget.* . . . He reached over and touched her arm gently, and when their eyes met she gave him a weak smile.

At length they found themselves slowly approaching the tent across the red carpet which had been laid out before it. Victoria's fifty-six-year-old son Edward, who would one day be King Edward VII, stood at his mother's side—stoic, sturdy, and silent.

"Charles Rutherford, Esquire, Lord of the Manor of Heathersleigh," came the formal announcement. "The order Knight Grand Commander!" Then came a brief, formal résumé of Charles' accomplishments.

Charles walked forward with Jocelyn half a step behind him, holding little Catharine's hand. George and Amanda followed. And then they were all standing before the grand lady.

The queen stretched out a white, slightly pudgy hand. He took it briefly, giving just the proper bow for the occasion.

"*Lord Rutherford,*" she said, and though her voice was soft, in it were contained the memory and mystery of countless centuries. "You bring esteem to your nation, and to your queen, by your achievements."

"Thank you, Your Majesty. I am deeply honored."

She tilted her head slightly, in acknowledgment.

"Your Majesty," he said, "may I present my wife, Jocelyn . . ."

The queen's glance drifted momentarily toward Jocelyn's birthmark, then quickly found her eyes. The sight seemed to add a timber of tenderness to her tone as she spoke. "Lady Rutherford," she said with a smile, "I am happy to meet you today."

"Thank you, Your Majesty," smiled Jocelyn.

" . . . and my son George and daughters Amanda and Catharine," added Lord Rutherford.

George bowed, Catharine and Amanda curtsied. Victoria smiled at all three.

"I'm going to be prime minister someday!" announced Amanda confidently, looking brightly into the queen's eyes.

The right side of Jocelyn's face suddenly turned nearly as crimson as the left. How mortifying!

"Are you now, dear?" smiled Victoria. "—I had been told," she added, turning to Amanda's father with the hint of a playful grin, "that you were a progressive, Lord Rutherford. I even flatter myself that I may have been a trifle progressive in my early years. But I must admit your daughter's statement goes a bit farther than even I am prepared to go. Does she come by such a notion from you?"

"No doubt I must admit to a certain role in her views," replied Charles with a smile not quite successful in masking his embarrassment. "Yet there are times I do confess myself absolutely bewildered by what comes into her brain!"

"Well, I am sure she will turn the world on its ear when her time comes.—Won't you, my dear?"

"Yes, Your Majesty," smiled Amanda brightly.

At a sign from the Lord Chamberlain beside the queen, Charles now knelt before her. A moment later he felt the delicate touch of the flat of the Sword of State upon first one shoulder then the other, held by the Lord Chamberlain with Victoria's hand upon it. Tingles surged through him.

"Rise, Sir Charles," she said.

This was the greatest of all England's queens, he thought, and she had just conferred upon him the status of knighthood.

He rose and stepped back.

The queen turned. The Lord Chamberlain handed her a small package from a stack of several on the table behind her. She now handed it to Charles.

"I would like you to have this book," she said. "It is one of my favorites. I have given copies to all my grandchildren. I have inscribed this one to you, in commemoration of this joyous day."

"Thank you, Your Majesty," replied the new knight. "My whole family shall treasure it."

Victoria smiled briefly. Then it was over.

The new Sir Charles Rutherford and his family were led out of the tent, while the great lady occupied herself with the next of those who would receive like honor on this day. Charles and Jocelyn glanced at one another as they went, with silent expressions of mingled humor and horror at what had just transpired.

Amanda had always been unpredictable, but this one took the Yorkshire pudding!

19

Which Direction the Future?

*A*n hour later, with the day's formalities concluded, a group of three men had gathered and were chatting informally, sipping at the drinks they held in their hands.

It fell silent momentarily as they took notice of the interview in progress at the queen's side on the dais. An elderly, white-haired man, in full military regalia, had just been shown a seat next to her.

"I say," remarked the earl of Westcott, "isn't that chap with Victoria there Bismarck?"

"The queen and the old Prussian chancellor chatting like old friends," added Baron Whitfield. "I heard they weren't inviting foreign dignitaries and royalty."

"Some insisted on coming. I suppose they could hardly prevent it."

"Who would have thought it?—Victoria and Bismarck. I daresay, these are indeed changing times we live in."

They watched the two aging rulers a moment with a silence bordering on reverence.

"The old guard is passing," remarked Chalmondley Beauchamp, the third member of the trio.

"No doubt about it, Chalmondley," rejoined Whitfield. "She's seventy-eight . . . what's the old man?"

"Bismarck must be close to eighty.—Ah, Charles," exclaimed Beauchamp, seeing the new Sir Charles Rutherford approaching, "come join us!"

"Congratulations, my good man!" added Westcott, a liberal colleague from Parliament.

"Thank you, Max . . . Chalmondley . . . James," he said, shaking hands with each of his colleagues in turn.

"We were just commenting on the queen's guest of the moment." Rutherford turned and briefly took in the scene.

"Did you hear," he said, "that the German Reichstag voted *down* a resolution to send the former chancellor birthday greetings two years ago, when he turned eighty?"

"Rather peevish of them, I would say," observed Whitfield with customary English scorn.

"Yes, they're quite a different breed," added Westcott in like tone. "—If socialism ever takes root in Germany," he added, a trifle more seriously, "I shudder to think what they might do with it!"

"Fortunately, it seems old Karl Marx made little impact on his own people, even if the Russian workers were quite fond of him."

"Do you think anything will come of Marx's view—communism, you know?"

"How can it? The thing's totally impractical—peasants running the country, aristocrats and merchants digging ditches. It's an absurd notion! The Frenchies tried it in their revolution back in 1789 and look what came of it—chaos."

"It is a commentary on our times, is it not," observed their friend, journalist Paxton Brentford, dryly—now joining the four with a nod of his head in the direction they had all been looking. "The two old war horses, Victoria and Bismarck, with the twenty-nine-year-old Russian tsar not far away—" He gave another nod of his head, this time in a different direction across the lawn. "All of them surrounded by a hodgepodge of English conservatives and socialists—a duke's mixture, like you four."

His listeners chuckled as Brentford spoke.

"Ah, my political colleagues," he concluded, "the world is changing faster than any of us realize."

"And we . . . we are changing . . ." began Charles, then paused as he became unaccountably distracted, "—and . . . and we . . . are changing with it," he struggled to continue in his reply to what Paxton Brentford had just been saying.

He shook his head, trying to clear it. What had come over him!

"We will face the new century as a challenge," he went on, his voice steady again. "We are the English, after all. We rule the world."

"Spoken like a true champion for progress!" laughed Brentford, "even if you did fumble a bit over your words. What's the trouble, Charles? You cannot still be nervous over meeting the queen?"

"No doubt that is it!" laughed Charles uneasily, wondering *himself* what had caused the lapse.

"But for how long *will* we rule the world?" asked Westcott. "We are being challenged on all fronts."

"Tut, my good man—the British Empire shall endure forever," confidently asserted Beauchamp, a Conservative M.P.

"What about the Russians?" interjected a young man, walking up and launching himself straightaway into the midst of the lively conversation. He appeared to be in his early twenties and wore the full garb of Her Majesty's army.

"They are our allies—what about them?" said Beauchamp, turning toward him.

"There are allies, and then there are *allies*," remarked Brentford.

"It is true, they may be a force to reckon with in the future," put in Sir Charles. "The new ideas, in some respects, seem to be taking hold over there more rapidly than here."

Again his concentration wavered. He heard the words from his own lips, and the voice sounded like his own, but a strange detachment from the conversation came over him, and his focus again lost sense of the conversation.

"In worrisome ways, however," said the earl of Westcott. "They are a race that knows how to make change only through violence."

"I don't know if the Russian people are intelligent enough to know what to do with socialism if it bit them in the face," remarked the newcomer.

"You had better keep your voice down, Churchill," said Beauchamp.

"The tsar's here, you know. He's practically family."

"Nicholas II—he would be the first to agree with me," rejoined the young army officer. "He's nearly an Englishman himself, married to Victoria's granddaughter, tutored by an Englishman."

"Alexandra may be Victoria's granddaughter, but she's German, not English," added Whitfield.

"And there, if you ask me," commented Beauchamp, "is the real problem—the Germans, not the Russians."

"The Germans are a sensible lot," said Churchill. "They don't go in for these revolutionary ideas."

"Perhaps not, but they are a people skilled in battle," rejoined the count. "Bismarck will not be the last of the Teutonic race who makes war, I daresay."

The new knight tried to keep up his share of the conversation and focus on what the others were saying. But the words of those around him continued to grow fuzzy in Charles Rutherford's brain. He heard the sounds of the reception fading distantly away and becoming faint in his ears. He was there with his friends, but *not* there.

Even as the voices of his companions dimmed, *another* conversation—unsought, unwelcome—intruded into his consciousness. . . .

◆ ◆ ◆

I can't thank you enough . . . a strange voice was saying in the ears of his mind, . . . *don't know what we would have done* . . .

Charles Rutherford tried to rid his brain of the memory.

But now came two eyes to join the voice—silent, imploring, sad eyes . . . eyes that betrayed shock at what they had just witnessed.

With steely resolve, Charles closed his own eyes for the briefest of instants, forcing the apparition from him. He drew in a quick reassuring breath.

◆ ◆ ◆

"Wouldn't you agree, Charles?" the earl was asking.

Hearing his name broke the reverie.

In the mere second that had passed, Charles' brain had taken a long journey inward in the direction of his conscience. Confusion was his initial response.

"Uh . . . oh, yes—right," he floundered unevenly. "German through and through," he said, doing his best to shake off the lapse of concentration.

"I say, old man," said the earl of Westcott, "are you quite all right? I daresay, you seem a bit off your game for such a high point in one's career."

"Yes . . . yes—quite fine, thank you, Max," replied Charles. He attempted a laugh. "The day's just, you know, been too much for me, I suppose."

The baron nodded, but did not seem altogether convinced. Meanwhile the conversation continued.

"Tut, tut. I still maintain Nicholas is secure," commented Beauchamp with all the assurance of his Tory bearing.

"I say, Churchill," now put in Brentford, changing the subject, "when are *you* going to stand for the Commons like your father?"

"After my father's problems in Parliament," laughed Churchill, "I don't know that I ever shall."

He turned to Charles in a sideways gesture, drew his hand to his mouth, and said in pretended confidence but loudly enough for all to hear, "—and if I *was* planning a political move," he added, "I would not announce it in the hearing of a newsman looking for a story!"

Everyone laughed, Brentford loudest of all. He could take a good joke, even when it was at his own expense.

♦ ♦ ♦

Amid the laughter which faded eerily away, unsought voices and images again forced their way back into Sir Charles' brain.

He had hardly heard Churchill's joking aside.

Again the young lady's eyes stared at him, haunting him with their pleading, sorrowful expression of pain. Why was he suddenly so ill at ease? What could account for it?

He had saved the young lady from a ruffian.

Why did he feel such an overpowering sense of condemnation? What was it about her eyes that possessed such power to wound him?

Her expression made him feel that a knife had been plunged into his heart!

20

A Changing World

*B*rentford was speaking once more to young Winston Churchill. "So," he said, "you've been off fighting the Spaniards in Cuba, I understand."

The young man nodded.

"Careful, young man," chided Westcott. "He's after an interview!"

"You forget that I'm a newsman too," smiled the young soldier. "I can handle myself.—Actually," he went on to the journalist in his gravelly voice, "since then I've been on two campaigns in the northwest frontier of India."

"You *do* travel about!"

"One follows orders, Baron Whitfield."

"Even when one is the grandson of the seventh duke of Marlborough?"

The young Churchill smiled, but did not reply.

"Where are you off to next?" asked Westcott.

"I have been engaged as a correspondent for the London *Morning Post*," answered Churchill. "There is talk of my joining General Kitchener in the Sudan."

"Ah, the *Morning Post*—my competition!" lamented Brentford.

With great effort Sir Charles forced himself to concentrate. *This was not how I envisioned this day*, Charles thought. This was his moment of triumph. Yet he felt as if he were losing his mind trying to keep his attention focused!

Once more the conversation drifted back to a discussion of the changing world situation. Charles was happy to let the others carry it. He took another sip of the wine from the glass in his hand. Perhaps he had had a little too much of it. That must be it! The wine had muddled the clarity of his brain.

"Returning to a remark you made earlier, Churchill," asked Baron Whitfield, "are you saying Nicholas is not fit to lead the Russian people?"

Churchill did not reply immediately.

"I will answer for him," said Westcott," by saying that he is as aware of their, shall we say, *backwardness*, as any of us here."

"He's a peaceful enough man," commented Brentford.

"But will the revolutionaries allow him to remain in power?" queried Count Beauchamp. "That is the vital question. These are new times. Whatever you say about the Russian people, the leaders of their revolutionary movement—anarchists, communists, the whole lot of them—are stirring things up over there more than we might like."

"You're right there."

"You know how Nicholas's grandfather met his end—they blew up his carriage right after it left the Winter Palace. Where we use the vote, they use bombs. At least in this country we adapt to new social trends peacefully."

"Not a very civilized lot in my book," commented Westcott.

"So, Churchill—what do *you* think the future holds?" asked Brentford.

The young officer's face showed a thoughtful maturity beyond his years. His eyes gleamed with the unmistakable look of leadership in the making.

"Forces in eastern Europe concern me," Winston answered at length. His voice bore the same expression as his eyes. "I must admit I agree with Count Beauchamp. I confess that I trust the Germans and the Russians no farther than I can throw a good cigar. If they should ever draw equal to us in military and naval capability, then I should be far more anxious for the stability of Europe than I am at this moment."

The small group of listeners took in the young soldier's words with nods. A few sipped at their drinks.

A silence followed. Still again Charles Rutherford felt the strange sensation come over him of living in the midst of two conversations at once.

♦♦♦

Thank you . . . I was so afraid . . . said a woman's voice—a sweet voice.

... implore you, sir ... not a teaching that comes from God.

It was a man now speaking. The tone was gentle and sincere, however misguided.

But now came a third voice—an angry voice ... a voice neither gentle nor kind.

... none of your sermons! it said, *... protests ... absurd leaflets ... have you all thrown in jail ...*

It was a voice he knew ... its tone was mean and harsh.

◆ ◆ ◆

Charles glanced around, determined to force himself back to the present.

"Von Dortmann!" said Sir Charles, happy to seize upon a distraction that might rescue him from unpleasant reflections. He strode a few steps from the others and greeted a new acquaintance he had met only an hour earlier. He led the man back at his side. "Come join us."

"I would like you all to meet Johann von Dortmann," he said, now speaking to his English friends, "over from the Continent for the celebration."

Again handshakes and greetings followed.

"Of the Prussian von Dortmanns?" asked Whitfield.

"That is correct, Baron," replied von Dortmann in perfect English.

"I believe I've heard the name—a banker, are you not?"

The newcomer nodded.

"As one of his countrymen, what is *your* opinion of Chancellor Bismarck?"

"A grand man," replied the Prussian.

"How well do you know him?"

"He is a guest upon occasion at my estate. I accompanied him over from Berlin."

A few nods of significance followed. The man was of more prominence than they had realized.

"What do you think will come on the Continent in the new century?" asked Westcott.

"The Continent!" he repeated, "—I'm concerned with what will come for *Britain*," replied von Dortmann, with hint of a smile.

Everyone laughed.

"My new friend is a diplomat as well as a financier!" said Charles. "He has resisted your bait, James, to commit himself in a thorny query involving his own nation."

"Shrewdly put, von Dortmann, I daresay!" said young Churchill at the Prussian's remark.

"Britain is secure, I assure you," said Paxton Brentford. "My parliamentary friends here will see to that, Tories and Liberals alike. Victoria may just live forever. If she doesn't, Edward will keep the ship steady. He's a prudent enough fellow—no worry there. But the Continent, what with the Germans and Prussians and Austrians and Serbs and Bosnians and Turks—I don't like to think what the new century may hold.—Have you spoken with Lord Salisbury on the subject?" he said, turning his head to Beauchamp.

"The prime minister is watching everything closely."

"Another diplomat!"

"And you, Sir Charles, have you spoken with your former leader?"

"I have not seen the honorable Mr. Gladstone for several months. When I last spoke with him, domestic affairs were far more on his mind than the state of the Continent."

"How was he?"

"Weary," answered Rutherford sadly. "His deafness increases. He is eighty-eight—older than either the queen or Bismarck."

"I fear the grand old man will not understand these new times," said Brentford, with almost a prophetic tone, "even if he should live to see the century. The Liberals must leave the new century to its rising new leadership."

A brief silence followed.

"With the year 1900 will indeed come a changing of the guard in many ways," remarked the earl of Westcott. "We old political war horses will gradually be turning affairs over to the likes of you, Rutherford—excuse me, I forget the occasion! ... *Sir Charles*—and to you, young Churchill. The two of you should get together and plot out a strategy for securing Britain's fortunes throughout the new century, whatever it may hold."

Charles and the young soldier glanced at one another and smiled briefly, but no more was said on the subject.

21

Breaking of the Cocoon

♦ ♦ ♦

The gala celebration did not leave the lord of the manor of Heathersleigh as full of joy and the satisfaction of achievement as he had anticipated. Instead of exhilaration, an undefined heaviness of soul burdened him. Gradually its weight increased.

Something was wrong inside. He did not know what.

The ride back to the hotel from the palace at about five-thirty was oddly subdued. Even Amanda seemed to recognize something amiss with her usually enthusiastic and talkative father. Jocelyn attributed her husband's silence to a heart perhaps overfull of emotion from the occasion just past. She did not intrude nor worry. He would be himself before long.

But Jocelyn Rutherford's husband would never again return to what he had been accustomed to calling *himself.*

The essential core of his being that defined what he referred to when he used that simplest yet ultimate defining word of human language, the pronoun "I"—that entity was in the process of undergoing the most significant and wonderful change to which all men and women must come in the end. That which Charles Rutherford called his "self" was about to experience the change of being born again.

It was a process of which he yet knew nothing. He had heard the expression only through the Gospel readings in village church services, which he had attended as a boy and which, by reason of his position in the community, he still attended on occasion. His ignorance, however, lessened not a hair the reality of the transformation which approached. That it was invisible as the wind which blows where it will, took nothing from the fact that he *felt* its peculiar and unmistakable stirrings within him. They were uncomfortable stirrings at present. He knew only that something strange—was it something terrifying or something wonderful?—was at hand.

The butterfly embryo cannot know to what winged heights it will soar when its own birth is complete. The unborn infant in the blackness of its mother's womb is incapable of apprehending the wonder of life awaiting it in the region where light and air and freedom reign. The new birth must therefore always seem terrifying with its first pangs. To whatever degree they have been comfortable in their death-wombs of self, will those to whom Life comes initially resist breaking through the shell of darkness.

To be freed from the confines of that cocoon requires a momentary shock to the former individual's comfort system, a jolt of electric, life-beginning pain. Only so will the wings of the butterfly be released to stretch. Then indeed will it fly. Only so will the eyes and lungs of the infant child be opened. Then indeed will he see. Only so can the old self die, in order that a newer and deeper and truer self—the self that was God's idea of us when he made us—might be born.

A high place in an earthly kingdom had been granted to Charles Rutherford. But he would soon be heir to a kingdom of which he scarce possessed an inkling. How could it be other than that he would fear the first sensations of its approach?

For the heavenly must always seem awesome—yea, fearful—to the mere mortal, until he yields himself to the blissful death out of which God's life in his heart is born.

22

The Beast Hand

*C*harles felt increasingly uncomfortable all evening following his honor at the queen's palace garden. He had finally retired to a fitful and uneven sleep. But his slumber was filled with weird ill-shaped phantasms that only added to the gnawing discomfort of soul.

Unwelcome dreams intruded.

He was walking ... hurriedly, glancing back frequently, then hurrying onward again ... quickly onward. He was in a city—it must be London. He recognized nothing. It was a strange part of the city, unfriendly, dark, dirty, cold ... he must get someplace. He broke into a run. Crowds of people were about ... many people now, blocking his way. He tried to squeeze through ... the mass of humanity was thick. He pushed and shoved his way ... running again ... another glance backward ... he must make haste ... important matters were at hand.

Suddenly a girl blocked his path. He crashed into her ... stumbled ... fell onto the pavement. *You fool!* he cried. *Watch what you are about ... do you not know I am on the queen's business?* The voice sounded strangely unlike his own, but he felt the words falling from his own mouth. *Out of my way, you little urchin!* he yelled.

Picking himself up, he tripped into a run once more ... looking back only long enough to see tears of pain from the injury he had caused pouring from the child's eyes. She stared after him, beseeching him for help. But he had no time ... he had more important things with which to concern himself. Again he was running ... running ... he had to get there ... couldn't be late.

The crowd was gone ... he was alone now ... running along a deserted walkway alongside a tall building. He rounded a blind corner ... suddenly a great beast appeared in his path.

In mute agony he tried to scream, but only a peep sounded from his terrified lips. Unable to stop, he stumbled into the horrid creature, staggered backward, and fell into the street. He glanced up. Alongside the great monster *he* was now as small as an urchin gazing up in fright ... tears now rose in his own eyes ... *he* had become the child!

The beast approached. Again he tried to scream but his tongue clung to the roof of his mouth. He struggled to regain his feet. But his muscles had no more power than his voice. The hideous thing drew nearer. It was going to kill him! A huge hairy arm reached forward. His heart pounded with fear greater than any he had known. In terrified panic he tried to free himself from the trance. Still he could not move.

A clawed hand stretched toward him ... but it did not reach for his neck to slit his throat with its sharp claws ... instead the palm opened, as if in entreaty. Slowly he put out his own hand, the only part of his body he could move. Terrified yet unable to resist the invitation which he knew also to be a gesture of command, he placed his own hand timidly into the huge hairy claws.

But no hand of beast met his touch ... rather, that which closed about his was the soft, gentle grasp of royalty. He had felt it somewhere earlier ... he could not remember ... when he had knelt before some important personage. Other images now mingled with the dream in confused disarray . . . the gentle beast hand whose inside was that of a queen—or was it a King's son—now pulled on his.

The beast hand drew him to his feet. He yielded, and gradually rose. Slowly his eyes rose to see what manner of strange but gentle creature was this beast with the soft regal hand. He looked up . . . and now gazed into the beast's eyes. A great cry of terror at last burst from his lips— it was his *own* face! *His* countenance sat upon the beast's frame! But why was it smiling and radiant . . . did it not know itself a beast . . . and what of the royal hand . . . were there two beings in the one . . . what—

23

Unexpected Claim of Conscience

♦♦♦

Suddenly Charles awoke with a start.

He sat up in his bed, eyes wide, perspiring freely. It was sometime after one in the morning. He remained still a moment in the dark, breathing heavily, trying to gather his wits about him.

Slowly the dream faded. His breathing calmed.

At yesterday's reception he had wondered why the incident with the salvation band seemed bent on intruding into his thoughts. Now he saw it clearly enough. He was tormented by *guilt*. The dream illuminated that fact clearly enough. The urchin's eyes were the very eyes of the young Christian woman he had seen in front of the lecture hall. He had behaved reprehensibly. There was no way around it. He felt what any honorable man would feel . . . a sense of shame.

At last he knew where the inner struggle was taking place within him—in the depths of his own soul.

Why could he not dismiss the incident from his mind? The encounter had been insignificant enough. He tried to tell himself so for the tenth time. He had felt pangs of guilt before. This was not the first time he had behaved as less than a gentleman. But he had never felt like this. This time, for some reason, the guilt went down to the core of who he was.

He could not shake himself from the haunting claim on his conscience. It was not the magnitude of the thing. Small or large—it hardly mattered. It was what the incident revealed . . . about him—that however good he might be most of the time, the potential of downright meanness, even cruelty, lurked within him.

Charles rose and crept softly into the other room so as not to disturb his wife's sleep. He sat down in the blackness. The night was silent. The *last* thing he wanted to do at this moment was think. Thinking had become torture. Over and over his brain spun with thoughts that were as new to him as the stings of wrongdoing that plagued him.

A new world began to open to Charles Rutherford as he sat alone— as he thought—in the darkness of the hotel in London. In actuality he was less alone than he had ever been in his life.

The world now dawning upon his being was one of which he knew nothing. It was a world which terrified him and from which he would have fled had he been able. Yet it was a world whose approach he could do nothing to stop. Suddenly he felt the presence of a *lordship* he had never acknowledged. Beside this, his new title seemed paltry and unworthy.

Salvation must always begin, more or less, with discomfort. Spiritual hunger is the foundation for growth. Salvation cannot approach the soul basking in contentment. It is the *dis*content who feel the pangs of their own character-hunger and eternal emptiness. It is this very gnawing disquietude of *unrightness* that enables the hungry soul to be filled.

Charles was at last hungry for the only sustenance capable of satisfying his soul's deepest need. For he had become disturbed with what he saw when he gazed inward. Finally he was less than happy with the man he was. And finally, therefore, he was ready to become the man he was meant to be.

The eyes of the young lady tormented like a fire in his heart. The memory of the incident triggered a host of unwelcome images from out of his past, occasions when he had been short with the servants, impatient with the children, thoughtless of Jocelyn, and less than fully gracious to his colleagues in London.

And then, as the young woman's eyes burned yet deeper, at last he realized what he had beheld in them: he had seen love. She had *loved* him with a compassion unlike anything he had observed on human face before that moment.

Charles was no stranger to what the world called love. Jocie loved him, and he loved her.

But that young woman's eyes had contained something ... different.

And he had thrown the compassion back at her and the others with no less force than had he slapped her across the face. How was he better than the ruffian he had laid out on the street?

He was no more open-minded than he had accused the Christians of being. How tolerant had *he* been toward them? He, the progressive, open-minded liberal thinker, had been anything but open-minded! He preached the equality of humanity. He preached progressivism of ideas. But now it was clear that he remained filled with his own hidden prejudices. How prophetic had been his own question to his daughter: what happens when good people become bad?

You would never become bad, Papa. Amanda's words rang in his brain. Now he wasn't so sure they were true.

What inconsistency—to defend the young woman one moment and then verbally attack the poor preacher the next. Had he even stopped to think about what the man had said? And then to be made a knight by the queen so shortly afterward, as if he were some paragon of English virtue. He was nothing but a hypocrite!

The Savior of the world was called Jesus because he would save his people from their sins, and from the sin nature that lies within them. The fact that sin resides deep in the heart of *every* man and every woman ought to be the most fearful and terrifying fact in all the universe. It is the single circumstance of the human condition which we ought to combat with more vigor than any other.

Rarely, however, *is* it so. Instead man fights all known evil *except* that one overarching evil at the root of everything. Thinking to rid the world of its problems, its inhabitants labor against every plague of society, while ignoring that which causes the rest—their own sin nature.

Alas, our need of a Savior is greater than our cries for deliverance. We battle the world's ills, not recognizing that those ills can *never* be cured until the great evil is cured.

Charles Rutherford perceived at last the mortifying truth to which all must one day come, the truth that within *himself*—within even what he had considered the goodness inherent in his social standing and his seemingly forward-looking ideas—dwelt selfishness, self-satisfaction, hypocrisy. Within him dwelt sin.

And he detested it. He felt its horror. His own being had become the beast of his nightmare.

He was ready at length to say, though he yet knew not who might be capable of answering . . . *Heal me of this wickedness I find within myself!*

♦ ♦ ♦

Jocelyn Rutherford's first indication that something more serious was plaguing her husband came about an hour later. She opened her eyes and rolled over in bed, only to realize that the room was dark and that once again she was alone. How late was it? The light from the windows gave her no clue, for the gaslights on the street outside shone far into the night. Once more she rose and tiptoed into the adjacent room.

There sat her husband. He stared into the candle he had lit and placed on the table beside him as if its flickering yellow movement might be able to console him. On his face was an expression such as Jocelyn had never seen before. Had she been asked to describe it, against all reason she would have said he looked like a lost child who did not know where to turn.

At first she was terrified, thinking perhaps he had suffered an attack of some kind. Charles observed her approach, glanced up, and forced a smile. Though it contained pain, at the same time his look reassured her.

"Is there something . . . wrong, Charles?" she asked hesitantly.

Again he smiled thinly.

"Yes, Jocie," he said, "I'm afraid there is."

"Something you want to tell me about?"

"I don't know," he sighed.

"Did something happen at the reception I do not know about?" she asked.

"No—nothing *there*," he said, smiling ironically. The word contained worlds of meaning she could not fathom.

Jocelyn sat down beside him. A brief silence followed.

"It's funny," said Charles after a moment. "One anticipates something for so long, but then it invariably turns out differently than expected. I thought yesterday's celebration would be the high point of my whole life. Yet a few hours later, all I can think about is the incident that happened on the way."

"With the crowd ... when you were hurt?" asked his wife.

He nodded.

"I'm afraid I behaved badly, Jocie," he said with a sigh. "I lost my temper. I was quite beastly to some people. I said some things I had no right to say."

She slipped her arm around him and laid her head on his shoulder. Charles proceeded to tell her in more detail about yesterday's incident and its unpleasant and unpredictable effect on him.

PART III

❖❖❖

Unexpected Change
1897

24

A Morning Walk

$\mathcal{I}$t was the second time in as many days that Charles Rutherford found himself approaching Jermyn Street. Today, however, he was alone and on foot. It was a little before ten o'clock in the morning. Jocelyn and the children had remained at the hotel.

They were scheduled to return to Devonshire today, but he had delayed the trip home. He did not know why exactly. Something told him he could not leave the city quite yet.

While Jocelyn still slept he had dressed in simple street clothes and gone out without waiting for breakfast. That had been about six-thirty in the morning. He had been walking ever since.

He had slept but little following his unsettling dream. He and Jocelyn had talked, and she had finally returned to bed. He sat awhile longer and eventually followed her, but only to doze off intermittently.

Once away from the hotel he felt a little better. It was good to be out, to breathe in the fresh, crisp morning air, to be *doing* something after the long and unnerving night.

The early morning air held a chill, although the bright rays of rising sun promised later warmth. Charles made his way first to the Mall and into St. James's Park, walking its length toward Buckingham Palace, then into Green Park, across Knightsbridge, and into Hyde Park. The greenery and flowers all spoke more noticeably to him today than before. Something in his mind seemed to be slowing down. He was acutely aware of his surroundings. The voices of trees and grasses and hedges and flowers and birds spoke in an unfamiliar language of feelings, not words, and on this day, for the first time in his life, he found himself beginning to understand their subtle meanings. They drew his heart. Eventually he had effected a great circle through the park all the way to Oxford Street.

The city by now bustled all around him. Oxford Street was at the height of its morning commerce. People and markets and peddlers and carts filled the broad boulevard. Charles found himself detached and therefore more tolerant of the busyness than before. Everything he saw reminded him both of the dream and yesterday's ride to the palace. The vague urgency of the nightmare was not present. He was in no hurry now. He had no definite destination in mind. As he walked, the sunlight and city atmosphere, and even the crowded streets, ministered encouragement to his troubled soul. He found his eyes more than usually observant of what was taking place around him. He looked into the faces of those he passed with heightened sympathy and compassion.

As he made his way along, absorbed in thought, he saw not far in front of him a raggedly dressed girl of about five. She held a bouquet of flowers she was hopeful of selling. Glancing about, she bumped carelessly into a hurrying pedestrian. The girl stumbled and fell. The flowers flew from her hand and scattered about. Several wound up in the street, where they fell under the hooves and wheels of a passing carriage.

Charles hurried forward. He stooped as the girl struggled back to her feet, and reached down to her. She glanced into his face, eyes full of tears. Tentatively she reached up and took his hand. It felt so small and soft in his, so much like his own daughter's. He closed his palm around the tiny thing and drew the youngster to her feet.

"My flo'ers," she whimpered.

"I'll help you, missy," he said cheerfully. "We'll gather them together."

He let go her hand, then set about picking up what he could salvage from the street. The girl meanwhile scrambled about the sidewalk. Presently between them they retrieved most out of the dirt, though several now had broken stems.

"Here you are, missy," said Charles, handing her those he had gathered.

"Thank 'e, sir," she said, drawing a dirty sleeve across her tear-splotched cheeks. She forced a thin smile.

"How much do you want for them?"

"Ha'penny fer two flo'ers, sir."

"And for the whole bouquet?"

"Sixpence the lot, sir," replied the girl, the pitch of her voice rising several degrees in hopeful anticipation.

"Well, my little lady, here's half a crown," said Charles, as he brought a coin from his pocket. He knelt to one knee, and handed it to her.

"Thank 'e, sir!" she exclaimed, eyes wide as she clutched the enormous sum. The little hand had never before possessed such wealth.

Charles took the flowers. He stood, smiled again, then continued on his way.

As he went, unconsciously he drew the clump—he did not even know what variety of flowers they were—to his nose. With the recent memory of the girl's face in his thoughts, he drew in a deep breath.

His heart smote him.

Something in the young girl's expression, working now in combination with the sweet pungency from her flowers, filled him with an indescribable longing, though he knew not for what. There was only one possible response. And now tears welled up in Charles Rutherford's eyes.

He paused, sniffing and dabbing at both eyes and nose, then turned momentarily into a side alley. He had to be alone until the sensation passed.

He had never wept in his adult life. What was becoming of him? he wondered. What had caused this inexplicable and baffling assault of tears? Here he was, a Member of Parliament and a Knight Grand Commander, leaning alongside a stone building in a deserted alley off Oxford Street and weeping from the scent of a handful of dirty flowers!

Yet he did nothing to stop the flow. Even as he blinked his eyelids and wiped at them with the back of his hand, he felt no shame. He did not at that moment recall Bobby McFee's words to him from years before, nor realize how faithfully Bobby and Maggie McFee had prayed for him since. But nevertheless, the flowers and their prayers were accomplishing their work.

A few minutes later, Charles Rutherford resumed his trek along Oxford to New Bond Street, refreshed in some strange way, as if the tears, like a spring rain, had carried out some soul-cleansing work. A lump remained in his throat, however, perhaps as a reminder that tears would never hereafter be quite so far from his eyes.

Charles now turned to begin making his way back toward the center of the city.

In the distance again he heard music. It was similar to yesterday's. He continued on. It grew louder. Another salvation band came into view. They were everywhere these days, it seemed. He approached, glancing hopefully over the ten or a dozen participants. He recognized no one. They wore uniforms and were clearly not associated with yesterday's group. A middle-aged woman stood in front of the others, singing and directing the small choir and band.

Charles watched a moment. Seized by a sudden impulse, he walked briskly forward, straight toward the conductress. Her mouth paused in midnote, half-open, though her arm continued its rhythmic motion.

"I just wanted to tell you thank you for the enjoyable music," he said, handing her the bouquet of flowers.

Momentarily speechless, the poor woman's mouth now broke into a gradual smile of pleased bewilderment. She clutched the strangely delivered bouquet as if it were some priceless fortune. But she could utter nothing in reply.

Already her anonymous benefactor was disappearing down the street!

25

Jermyn Street Again

*S*miling as he went, Sir Charles rounded another corner, the memory of the lady's pleased expression lightening his heart considerably.

He had not exactly planned Jermyn Street as his next destination. In the midst of his morning wanderings, however, it was no doubt inevitable that he would unconsciously find his way there in the end. He was curious whether he might discover any landmarks from his strange dream. Perhaps he hoped to resolve something in his mind.

He drew near St. James Lecture Hall, the scene of yesterday's incident.

The street was still now, nearly deserted. It was such a contrast from yesterday, and from the busy parts of the city through which he had recently come. He glanced at the signboard. Nothing was scheduled for the hall. The street was a quiet one. A few pedestrians passed by, but there were no bands, no peddlers, no girls with flowers.

Charles found himself reliving yesterday's altercation. In his mind's eye he envisioned getting out of the cab, then walking forward into the crowd, exchanging blows with the ruffian, and then—

He closed his eyes at the painful memory. The lump in his throat struggled to rise.

He saw himself angrily lashing out at the frail preacher and innocent young woman.

What manner of beast dwelt inside that could cause him to do such a thing? Was he indeed the beast of his dream? If he had been capable of this, without provocation ... what might he—Sir Charles Rutherford—what might he be capable of if he were seriously provoked?

As Charles walked about, gradually came the further question—was this the sort of man he wanted to be, a man whose anger could erupt without warning, a man in whom cruelty and rudeness lay dormant? The words he had spoken to his daughter about good people becoming greedy and bad and selfish continued to haunt him.

Struggling, he sought to enlist his familiar philosophies to counter the new and discomforting thoughts. Maybe he wasn't perfect. But he was generally a good and moral person. Besides, men were not able to determine their intrinsic nature. Darwin had proved it. They were accidents of selection. He himself had been one of the lucky ones. How could he wonder about changing himself, about becoming different than what he was? The notion went against all of his carefully constructed beliefs.

Suddenly the implication of his question of a moment earlier probed yet deeper into the unknown. Might a man want to be someone other, someone different than he was? Might a man actually step outside Darwin's natural selection process ... and by an act of the will, alter who he was?

Darwin himself would scoff at such a question. Charles' colleagues in the Fabian Society would say such quandaries were mere illusions of the mind. The only real world was that of physical reality. No one could alter predetermined forces. Men might change the world. He had given his life to such a hope. But change themselves, their nature ... that was not something whose implications he had considered.

What about character? thought Charles now to himself.

What about virtue, kindness, and human integrity? Might a man make more, or less, of himself in those areas of personal growth and individual maturity?

What could evolution have to do with any of that?

Might those important regions of humanity be places Darwin's theory could never touch?

What if a whole parallel world existed—an *inner* world, where such things as character and conscience and virtue dwelt—a world *unseen* by men like Darwin, a world with which mere physical theories never intersected?

He had heard men talk about the *physical* world and the *spiritual* world, but he had never paid heed to such distinctions, assuming the latter to be a figment of unenlightened men's imaginations. Now he found rising up within himself sensations for which no mere physical theory could account. What could evolution have to do with conscience? How could a sense of right and wrong evolve from a worm? What in Darwin's natural selection theory could explain why flowers brought tears to the eyes of a sophisticated man of the world?

There *was* another region of life coming awake within him—that fact could not be denied. But it was nothing covered by any chapter in the *Origins*!

Was it . . . could all this be prompted by—he could hardly utter the words even in the solitude of his brain! . . .

—by the *spiritual* side of his being?

Charles Rutherford had never thought of religion in a personal way before. As a child, he had attended the village church with his family from time to time. Charles himself had continued the practice when he inherited the title, although in recent years his attendance had been limited to funerals, weddings, and other ceremonial occasions. But he had always regarded the high Anglican services in much the same way as he regarded Westminster Abbey—part of England's history and worthy of respect as such, but in many ways a relic of past days, with little or no relevance to modern life or thought.

The *religious* content of the services he had come to disregard completely. Christianity seemed to him the most impractical of creeds. But now he was beginning to wonder. Might there be more to it than he had realized?

What could be more *real* than the tears which had fallen down his own cheeks onto the dirt of that alley off Oxford Street?

Charles shook his head and drew in a deep breath and looked about, as if to rescue himself from delving too deeply into a matter he was not yet prepared to face.

Beneath his feet, as he slowly walked, his gaze fell upon several of yesterday's leaflets scattered about. Many lay mud smeared in the gutter. However many the small salvation band had handed out, it was clear a good many had been tossed down right here and never read.

His eyes chanced upon a tight little wadded ball of paper. It was the leaflet he had *himself* angrily thrown down. He stooped and picked it up, an altogether different feeling coming over him than yesterday's. Slowly he opened it.

Evolution versus the Genesis Account . . . read the title.

He scanned the first few lines. He was familiar with the gist of the argument. He went no further for the moment, but gazed over the leaflet absently.

At the end of the text he read the handwritten words: New Hope Chapel, 37 Bloomsbury Way, Holborn. The place was not many blocks away.

Without pausing to think what might come of it, Charles turned and made for the address of the church. Glancing down again at the leaflet as he went, he now walked briskly along the sidewalk toward a new destination.

26

New Hope Chapel

♦ ♦ ♦

𝒯imidly Sir Charles Rutherford walked up the several steps to the stone chapel on whose front stood the words, NEW HOPE CHAPEL, T. DIGGORSFELD, PASTOR, and tentatively tried the door, expecting to find it locked.

Instead it yielded to his touch and swung open. Slowly he entered the darkened building.

He saw no one at first, nor heard a sound. Slowly he walked forward. Uncertain sensations filled him.

It was a simple enough chapel, constructed like so many of its kind in a simple stone rectangle. The edifice itself inspired no sense of grandeur. Yet the silence of the high vaulted ceiling, the dim light filtering through the muted blues and reds and yellows of a single stained-glass window depicting the crucifixion of Christ, caused an atmosphere to descend upon Sir Charles Rutherford of what he could only call awe.

But awe of what? the rationalist side of him asked. Nothing was possibly here but old stones, colored glass, and superstition. Yet his heart told him differently. Two sides battled in his brain—the physical and the spiritual, the rational and the emotive.

Try as he might, he could not ignore the latter. He could scarcely admit it to himself . . . but he felt a *presence* as the solemn mood deepened.

Slowly he walked down the center aisle, almost afraid to let his footsteps make a sound on the cold tile floor.

A sound made him start.

Charles glanced up. Someone stood in front of the large room, a short distance to the right of the lectern.

Charles continued tentatively forward as his eyes grew more accustomed to the dim light. Now he saw the man's face—it was the preacher from yesterday's encounter on Jermyn Street. He stopped, some fifteen feet from the altar. He recognized the man at about the same moment the minister realized he had a visitor.

The two men stood a moment gazing uncertainly upon one another. An expression of anxiety suddenly spread over the other's face as recognition dawned.

Charles saw the change and was mortified that his mere appearance should make another so uneasy.

"Please," he said hesitantly and with a pang of sorrow, "I mean no harm."

"I thought perhaps you had come to . . ." The man stopped.

"To cause you more trouble than I did yesterday?" suggested Charles.

The other did not reply.

"I assure you, nothing could be further from my mind. Actually—"

Charles hesitated, and looked away with uncharacteristic nervousness for one of his social stature.

"—actually," he repeated, "I came . . . to apologize for my rudeness."

The word came as such a surprise to the young minister that he stood for a second or two speechless.

"I . . . I assure you," he began after a moment, "there . . . there is no need—"

"But there is," interrupted Charles. "I was boorish beyond belief, both to you and the young lady."

"As I tried to express," said the young man, gaining his poise and now desirous of putting Charles at ease, "we are most grateful for what you did."

"Nevertheless, I beg you to accept my apology."

"Granted."

"Thank you."

"As a matter of fact, I do not always accompany my people on such outings as yesterday's," added the minister. "It is not exactly my preferred method of spreading the news we have been given to communicate. Yet I go with them upon occasion to demonstrate my support. I am glad I did yesterday—otherwise, you and I might not have met. In any event, you are entirely forgiven. Set your mind at ease."

Charles sighed. A momentary silence followed.

"Did you have a chance to read the pamphlet?" asked the pastor. "I see it is still in your hand."

Charles glanced down and smiled.

"Yes . . . yes, actually I did manage to read most of it on my way here, just now as I walked along. This is the one you gave me yesterday. I am embarrassed to think what I did with it. I went back to retrieve it a short while ago."

"What did you think?"

"I disagree with almost every point this pamphlet makes."

"Yet still you came?" the pastor asked.

"My conscience could not live with the memory of my behavior. I had to apologize. I hope you do not take offense by my saying I disagree with what is said here," Charles added, nodding toward the pamphlet in his hand.

The man smiled. "Not in the least. Intellectual agreement is at the bottom of my list of spiritual concerns. The intellect is important, don't misunderstand me. But nothing is more unnecessary for faith than intellectual conviction of rightness at every point."

"I am hoping you will be able to tell me where I might be able to pay a visit on the young lady," said Charles. "I must make apology to her as well."

"That will be easy enough. She and her husband live not far from here.—Before you go, would you like to come into my study and have a cup of tea with me?"

"Tea—my, that does sound good!" replied Charles, laughing lightly. "I haven't had a cup all day. I suppose the time got away from me."

"Then, please—come," said the minister, turning and gesturing his arm forward in invitation. "I do not get the pleasure of many morning visitors. I will enjoy having someone to chat with—probably more in fact than you will enjoy the tea!"

Charles followed him to one side of the small sanctuary. They passed through a narrow door, down a dimly lit corridor, and at length into a small but comfortably furnished study, into which the late morning sun streamed with cheery silence. A thin trail of steam was already rising from the spout of a copper kettle which sat on the flat black top of a small iron stove. The pastor offered Charles a chair, while he opened the tiny stove door and tossed in another scoop of coal. He then proceeded to place three spoonfuls of tea in a porcelain pot that stood on a small oak table and to pour hot water from the kettle over the leaves.

"There, that should do it, I think," he said. "It shouldn't be long."

He turned back to face his visitor.

"I am Timothy Diggorsfeld," he said. "I am the pastor here."

"My name is Charles Rutherford," his visitor replied simply. It was the first occasion he had encountered where he might legitimately have introduced himself as *Sir Charles.* Yet he strangely shrank from mentioning either title or property.

"I am delighted to meet you, Mr. Rutherford," said Diggorsfeld, shaking Charles' hand. "Whatever may have been troubling you yesterday," he added, taking a chair opposite his guest, "I can already ascertain that you are a man of character, simply because of what you have done here today."

"I'm afraid I still have a good deal to learn," confessed Charles.

"To *learn*—how do you mean?"

"About life, I suppose," replied Charles, uncertain himself what he had meant.

The pastor took in his words without comment, then rose again to check the tea. He gave the pot two vigorous stirs with a spoon, then prepared two cups.

"Milk?"

"Please."

"Sugar?"

"Only milk, thank you."

Diggorsfeld poured the tea from the pot, handed his visitor one of the cups, then returned to his chair with the other.

"Well worth the wait!" said Charles, smiling with satisfaction as he breathed in deeply of the aroma, then probed with a few tentative sips with his lips.

Both men were silent for a minute or two. The pastor considered what to say to this unusual man who had obviously been antagonistic to the Christian faith the day before, but who today seemed strangely and warmly open.

"Do you mind if I ask you a question, Mr. Rutherford?" he asked at length.

"Not at all," replied Charles.

Diggorsfeld was not a man much given to the popular version of small talk called *chatting*. His question, therefore, was probing and straightforward. It bore not a trace of prying insensitivity. The conversation which ensued as a result of it was stimulating, and would prove life changing for both men.

27

Unusual Errand

*E*ven as Sir Charles sat talking with his new acquaintance in London, another man slouched in the corner of a Devonshire pub, silently cursing himself for having hired an imbecile to carry out an important task. Drumming his fingers impatiently, he peered once more toward the doorway of the *Hedge and Fox*, wishing there had been some way to avoid coming to Milverscombe himself.

He was confident no one in the village would recognize him—especially since he had hardly set foot inside this miserable aggregation of cottages for years. He had allowed four days of beard to accumulate on his face before coming and was now dressed in what he hoped would pass for workingman's attire. Even someone who knew him could stare directly into his face without making a connection. No more opposite station from his own could be imagined than that of which he now appeared a member. Still, he knew he must exercise caution and take every care possible.

He sincerely hoped, however, that his disguise would not be required much longer. He was used to finery, and these clothes made his skin crawl.

Where is the fool? he thought, taking a sip from the warm pint of stout in front of him.

The man hadn't shown himself yesterday morning as per instructions. By late afternoon the man in the pub had concluded himself swindled out of the ten pounds he had paid as down payment for services. But the fellow had finally arrived when it was far too late in the day to carry out the plan. The visit to the Hall had had to be postponed another day.

It was a delay the watcher could scarcely afford, for it was rare indeed to find an occasion when the entire Rutherford family was away from the Hall. He was well enough aware of Jocelyn's aversion to society and of the momentous occasion that had persuaded her to venture forth, accompanying her husband and children to London. The family was due home later that day—their arrival now much too close for comfort.

But he wasn't about to let this opportunity slip through his fingers. So he had decided to chance it, to conduct the search this very morning, before their return. But the fool should have been finished by now. . . .

Had he known of Charles' visit to New Hope Chapel, he would not have been so agitated. But he did not know of it. Therefore he continued to drum his fingers and steal surreptitious glances at his pocket watch, carefully concealed in his ragged pocket.

———————— ◆ ◆ ◆ ————————

Meanwhile, three miles to the west and about an hour earlier, a stranger had presented himself at the front door of Heathersleigh Hall. He had ridden up in a small buggy, not expensively appointed yet neither of the plain functional sort which might be seen in the village. By appearance it would seem to confirm him to be exactly what he presented himself—a tradesman of some skill and knowledge, from Exeter, sent on a mission most urgent. He was dressed as befitted his supposed calling and carried a leather satchel in one hand.

The bell was answered by Sarah Minsterly.

"Good morning to you, mum," said the man in an official tone. "My name is Oscar Saxelby. Might I have a word with his lordship? It is a matter of the utmost importance."

"Mr. Rutherford is in London, sir," replied Sarah.

"Perhaps Lady Rutherford, then."

"She is with him."

"Ah ... I see," said the man called Saxelby in somber tone. These were facts he knew only too well, although the expression that passed across his face was very convincing. "That does present us a bit of a problem," he said. "It is urgent that I inspect Lord Rutherford's library. I am afraid I would not be able to get back for—hmm ... let me see," he said, opening the satchel and now consulting a small appointment book, "—for at least a week," he concluded. "I have been hired by the office of the Secretary of State for National Heritage, and you see, I must call on all the estates and large houses in Devon ... and time is of the essence, mum."

"Time ... I don't understand—what's it all about, Mr.—" She hesitated.

"Saxelby, mum."

"What is this all about, Mr. Saxelby? Certainly it can wait until Mr. Rutherford—"

"Silverfish, mum," interrupted Saxelby. "I'm afraid I have the unpleasantness to report that there has been a serious outbreak of silverfish infestation in the region."

"Silverfish infestation?" repeated Sarah, growing more and more bewildered by the minute.

"Yes, mum—books being destroyed by the nasty little creatures at an alarming rate. They eat the glue and the paper, mum. It is a rather dreadful development for anyone who loves books. They can destroy an entire library, mum. No one even knows they are on the attack until it is too late. They have also been known to get into a lady's linen and destroy whole closetfuls."

A gasp of astonishment now escaped poor Sarah's lips.

"I see you grasp the seriousness of the situation, mum," said Saxelby. "Which is why I simply must inspect Lord Rutherford's library at once, as I am all the private libraries in Devon. In cases where we discover the infestation in time, we can take steps to—"

"Please ... please, Mr. Saxelby," interrupted Sarah, "come in."

She fairly pulled him through the door, which she closed behind him.

"Follow me," she said. The next instant she was making for the main staircase with as rapid a walk as she felt was dignified, with Saxelby hurrying to keep pace with her. In less than two minutes he found himself standing in the dark, quiet, musty library of Heathersleigh Hall, Sarah Minsterly gaping at him with huge eyes, as if awaiting an immediate verdict on the state of Lord Rutherford's prized and priceless literary possessions.

He lifted his nose in the air and sniffed notably a few times with significant expression, then nodded slightly.

"No odor that I can detect, mum."

Sarah sighed in visible relief. Gradually her countenance returned to its normal state, which, even when nothing in particular was amiss, seemed to border on an undefined anxiety.

"But," he added, "I will suggest that you leave me alone to conduct the actual search and investigation. I must make use of several unpleasant mineral spirits. You would not enjoy the odor."

"Oh ... oh yes—of course, Mr. Saxelby," said Sarah, retreating quickly toward the door. The next moment the stranger was alone in the library.

With stealthy step he went to the door just shut and noiselessly locked himself in.

He now turned to begin his search. In truth, his name was not Saxelby. Nor would he know a silverfish if one were crawling upon the end of his own long and rather thin nose. But the housekeeper or cook or whoever she was had believed him, and that was all that mattered.

Now, it was something *other* than silverfish he had been hired to find.

♦ ♦ ♦

An hour and a half later a buggy drew up to the door of the *Hedge and Fox*. The man whose name was not Oscar Saxelby got out and walked inside.

Spotting the man who was assuredly not the Secretary of State for

National Heritage, he walked toward the table.

"Did you find it?" barked his employer in as loud a whisper as he dared.

"I tell you, guv, I searched them bleeding bookcases from top to bottom, and every table and cabinet and sideboard in the place . . . and it just weren't to be found."

"How is that possible!" cried the other, slamming his hand down on the rough oak table. Heads of the few other patrons of the place turned around. He glanced down and covered his face with one hand.

"How is that possible?" he repeated. "It has to be five times the size of any other book in the library, with decoration as would make it stand out. Are you sure you saw nothing?"

"I looked at every book in the ruddy place."

"You checked everywhere?"

"Everywhere but in one secretary."

"Why not there?" Again his voice began to rise.

"It was locked."

"You fool! Why didn't you open it?"

"I tried, but you told me to make no noise. What would you have me do, guv—throw the thing on the floor and smash it to pieces? You told me the housekeeper was a daft one. But even she'd have come running if I'd done that."

The other was silent a moment.

"Yes . . . yes, I suppose you're right," he sighed, then fell into a dark reverie. He would have to get into the library and get a look inside that secretary himself.

"What did you tell the woman?" he said at length.

"That there was no sign of silverfish. I said the library was in no danger, and that she needn't trouble Lord Rutherford about it."

28

Where Does Conscience Come From?

◆◆◆

$\mathcal{M}$emories of his lengthy talk with the young pastor Diggorsfeld still swirled through the mind of Charles Rutherford as the carriage bearing him and his family approached Heathersleigh Hall on their return from London.

He knew he was a different man than the one who had journeyed to London three days earlier. And not primarily from what had happened at Buckingham Palace. Even memory of the honor he had gone to the city to receive no longer stirred his passion.

Upon their arrival, the station master in Milverscombe had greeted him boisterously, "Welcome back to Devonshire, *Sir Charles!*" said the man, deliberately emphasizing the new title. The people of the village were as proud of the honor as if it had been granted to them.

"Thank you, Bob," smiled Charles sincerely. Inwardly, however, he winced at how meaningless the designation now seemed. The very sound of it reminded him of the mental discomfort his trip into London had precipitated.

Later that afternoon he walked upstairs to his study. How different everything appeared now. On his desk still lay the invitation to the queen's reception which had stirred such excitement only a few short days ago. Now it lay in front of him as an ordinary sheet of parchment, dull and lifeless, with scarcely interest to draw his eyes for a second look.

The new Sir Charles gazed about his study, then began to wander aimlessly about the small room. He felt trapped by a past which now offered few answers to the questions which had haunted him ever since his long talk with the London pastor of New Hope Chapel. He walked to the window and stared passively over the countryside a few moments. He turned again into the room. Nothing in it drew him now.

Absently he picked up his first edition of Darwin and began thumbing carelessly through it. Here and there his eyes fell upon familiar passages, some underlined and with his own marginal notes.

"... *the existence of closely allied or representative species in any two areas, implies, on the theory of descent with modification ... admit that the geological record is imperfect to an extreme degree ... innate tendency toward progressive development ... natural selection tends only to make each organic being as perfect as, or slightly more perfect than, the other inhabitants of the same country with which it comes into competition ...*"

He now noted something to which he had paid no attention during his previous readings of the book—Darwin's repeated references to a Creator's occupying a role in the process of natural selection.

It was curious, thought Charles. From popular rhetoric on both sides of the debate, he had always assumed Darwinism and Christianity to be mutually exclusive.

"*To my mind it accords better with what we know of the laws impressed on matter by the Creator ...*" he read, then paused to reflect on the spiritual implications of the author's statement. It was strange in Charles' ears to hear *Charles Darwin* speak of "the Creator."

Darwin ... a creationist *and* an evolutionist!

Obviously Darwin was not the atheist many Christians made him out to be. As much as Charles thought he knew of the man he had so greatly admired, he had never stopped to inquire about his beliefs other than as they applied strictly to science.

He continued on the few pages to the conclusion of the book, where he read:

"*There is a grandeur in this view of life, with its several powers, having been originally breathed by the Creator into a few forms or into one, and that ... from, so simple a beginning endless forms most beautiful and most wonderful have been, and are being evolved.*"

An interesting blend of evolution and creation, mused Charles Rutherford.

His thoughts returned to his own personal inner dilemma.

Whether Darwin was right or wrong was beside the point of that inquiry. The young pastor had pointed out unmistakably that there were many matters that evolutionary theory could not touch, those areas concerning our *humanity*.

Charles closed the book and replaced it on his desk. How much longer would the *Origin of Species* remain there in its place of honor? Would a Bible soon be joining it?

He sat down, and soon found himself reflecting back on his conversation with Timothy Diggorsfeld in the latter's study at the New Hope Chapel.

◆ ◆ ◆

The young pastor had asked Charles whether he would mind a question.

"Of course not," Charles had replied.

"You mentioned your conscience when we were in the other room," said Diggorsfeld.

Charles nodded.

"You said your conscience could not live with the memory of your rudeness. In consequence you felt you had to apologize."

"That is exactly how I have felt this past twenty-four hours."

"Why do you think that is?"

"Do you mean, why did I find myself confronted by a guilty conscience?"

"Precisely."

"Because of what I did."

"How exactly?"

"I behaved badly, I did wrong."

"But how do you *know* it was wrong?"

"I felt ill at ease. As I said, my conscience began to torment me."

"But why?"

"Because . . . I don't know—" laughed Charles uneasily. "You are questioning me the way I question my children!" he added, not understanding the direction in which the pastor was probing. "I suppose because that's what the conscience is supposed to do—tell us when we've done wrong."

"But *wrong*, if you don't mind my asking, Mr. Rutherford, according to whose or what standard?"

"How do you mean—isn't right and wrong universally accepted?"

"I hardly think so. And if, as you suggest, the conscience points to some higher standard, then what *is* that absolute right and wrong to which it points? Especially is that question important if that conscience itself is merely a chance product of millions of random mutations, as your Mr. Darwin, if I understand him correctly, would have it?"

Charles smiled, at last perceiving the progression of thought into which he had been drawn.

"It would seem, Mr. Diggorsfeld," he said, "that I underestimated your gift of logic. You have lured me into a denial of my own point of view."

"I meant no trickery," said the pastor with a shade of anxiety on his face. "I have no desire to offend you."

"Not to worry," said Sir Charles with a wave of the hand. "I meant the comment good-naturedly. I did not see where you were headed with your questions, until suddenly you had snapped the trap shut.—Well done, I must say!" he added with a little chuckle. "Caught at my own game!"

Delighted to find his new friend the possessor of a sense of humor, even to the detriment of his own side of the argument, the pastor smiled in return.

"I only meant to illustrate how your *own* internal thoughts and feelings," he went on, "—the guilty conscience—if examined logically and rationally, *in itself* undoes the very theory of evolution you espouse."

"I admit, that is an argument I have not encountered before now. I have never met a cleric who set forth his cause with quite your skill."

"Christians are not fools, Mr. Rutherford," the pastor retorted mildly. A look of bemusement crossed his face. "At least, we are not *all* fools. The Bible does not come to us as if we were numbskulls."

"And yet you must admit that many of your persuasion plead more with passion over traditions than they employ logic to enforce the ideas of their belief."

The pastor nodded.

"That some Christians *happen* to be fools," he replied, "leads no more to the conclusion that Christianity is in error than that the foolishness of some of our kings and queens justifies calling the monarchy a farce."

"A good point!" laughed Charles.

"Fools occupy the throne as well as intelligent men and women. But the monarchy remains its magnificent self notwithstanding. Likewise, there are Christian fools and Christians of great wisdom. I daresay Darwinism has fools in its ranks as well as men and women of great intelligence."

"No doubt."

"What is before us, however, would you not agree, is to find the truth, independent of these variations of humanity who espouse many views?"

"I would agree."

"Well, it is my conviction that Christianity is and remains the truth, however much or little men understand it, and however skilled or unskilled its proponents may be in articulating it."

"A well-put train of thought, I must say," replied Charles. "It certainly frames the discussion along somewhat different lines."

"But let me return to the matter at hand. If evolution is true, and we are the chance product of a chance universe, then why do we possess a conscience at all? More to the point—how could we ever come to possess it? What can atoms and mutations have to do with right and wrong?"

"Perhaps it is learned—a product of culture and upbringing?"

"Upbringing certainly contributes to one's view of what constitutes right and wrong, I grant you that. But do you not honestly believe that the pangs you felt which brought you here on this day originated in some deeper region of being than from what could be accounted for by what you were taught as a child?"

Charles thought a moment, then nodded.

"Yes . . . yes, you're right," he said. "I *know* they came from someplace deeper than what I was taught. I suppose that is what made me so uneasy."

"It is that *deeper place* which intrigues me!" the young pastor continued. "I believe it is hugely significant."

29

The Proof... Is Within You!

$\mathcal{C}$harles stood and strode about his study.

After a few minutes he was back at the window, staring absently out, reflecting further upon the previous day's thought-provoking conversation.

———— ♦ ♦ ♦ ————

Diggorsfeld had just paused in the discussion for a sip or two of tea. He was clearly thinking through what next to say.

"Let me ask you another question," he said after a moment. "Why do we sigh when we behold a breathtaking sunrise or sunset? Why does the glorious scent of a rose call alive such deep yearnings within us? All these clearly speak to something higher than the mere physical makeup of our bodily selves."

"I'll admit I've never thought about evolution in connection with sunsets and roses before," replied Charles.

———— ♦ ♦ ♦ ————

He reflected on his own experience with the girl's dirty bouquet, and the remembrance brought him momentarily back to the present. From deep in his memory, reminders of the McFees' flower garden across the way at the cottage began to steal into his consciousness. A fondly nostalgic feeling accompanied them.

He peered out across the countryside from the Hall with a smile. He could almost smell the place from here! Maggie's flowers would be in full bloom now, Charles thought.

He must visit his old friends again. And soon.

Nor do most people think of God except in connection with churches and hymns," Diggorsfeld was saying. "But I find far more evidence of the Creator's existence in sunsets and roses, and in this deeper place within us that you and I are investigating, than in any sermon I or any other man could preach."

"As I said, I have never thought of such things before."

"Has your conscience ever made you quite so uncomfortable before?"

"Never."

"You see, the conscience is man's proof that something higher and deeper than evolution is at work within the heart of man."

"Proof?"

"Indeed—I see it as no less than proof, in its full rational sense. This uneasiness you feel—it is something that *must* be accounted for. It must be explained. If there is an actual right and wrong, a standard of behavior to which something within calls us, it must originate in thoughts and feelings no Darwinic natural selection could produce in ten billion billion years of evolution."

"Why do you say that?"

"Because science itself simply has nothing to offer on the matter. Darwin altogether ignores man's *morality*—a thing utterly distinct in man from all other living creatures."

"But *proof* remains a strong word," commented Charles.

"Man *knows* right from wrong. Every man and woman possesses a live conscience. It had to come from somewhere."

"Perhaps it evolved, as has our brain," suggested Charles.

"Come now, Mr. Rutherford," rejoined the pastor, "you strike me as an intelligent man. Surely you see the fallacy in such a hypothesis. Evolution is a physical, natural phenomenon. I'm talking about morality. I do not think you seriously believe such a thing could come about by Darwinic evolution, by mere chance."

Charles smiled. "You won't let me off with shoddy thinking, I see that!"

"You wouldn't respect me if I did," rejoined Diggorsfeld, returning the smile.

"No doubt you are right."

"It is a *spiritual* component of our makeup," Diggorsfeld went on. "Therefore *even if evolution were true*—to which view I do not subscribe, and which I do not believe even the scientific evidence supports—but even if it were, it *cannot explain the conscience.* The sense of right and wrong is a spiritual dimension of human nature. It lies altogether outside our physical bodies. Thus, the question again: How did it get there? Where did it come from?"

"I . . . I assume you will say that it . . . came from God."

"Precisely."

"To be honest," Charles said, "I have to tell you that I have not been one who considers myself a believer in his existence."

"Your belief or non-belief cannot alter the factual data of the case, which you yourself have produced just by coming here."

A look of question spread over Charles' face.

"That sense of right and wrong is *God's* fingerprint within *your* humanity."

"His fingerprint?" repeated Charles.

"Exactly—a fingerprint which has remained behind within man as *evidence* of his creation of us—within you and me and every other man, woman, and child on the face of the earth. Nothing else can account for it. We are told in Genesis that God made man *in his own image.* You see, Mr. Rutherford, the conscience is one small part of that *in-his-image-ness.* As I see the matter, it proves the truth of the Genesis account as much as any fossil record a future geologist might discover and dig up somewhere. Our very *humanity* proves that Genesis is true, and that God created us just as the Bible says."

"You make a compelling argument for the existence of God, I must say," smiled Charles.

"No, you mistake me," smiled Diggorsfeld.

"How do you mean?"

"I have made no compelling argument—it is you *yourself,* Mr. Rutherford, who have made the case."

"I don't understand you."

"The voice of your *own* conscience, speaking to you from the region of that deep place in *your own heart,* has given proof of the existence of the very God in whose existence you earlier told me you did not believe. From out of your own depths the Creator has spoken, and said, " '*I am here, Charles Rutherford. I made you*

*and I placed myself here to remind you that I am your Creator. You may
say you believe or don't believe, but nothing you can say or do removes
this trace of me from your being.' "*

Charles was silent.

The matter had now assumed loftier import than merely having to apologize for something he had done. Suddenly *God* was
involved . . . and involved with him personally!

30

Storm and Rainbow

✦✦✦

*A*nother rainstorm blew across southern England. The following
morning dawned turbulent and wild, with gusts still howling about
and dashing occasional blasts of thick raindrops nearly horizontal
against the windowpanes.

Sir Charles had slept soundly through the storm, his first full night
in many days, and awoke refreshed and full of vigor.

"Look at it out there, Jocie!" he exclaimed, as he stood in front of
their bedroom window after dressing. "Doesn't it make you want to
run out into the middle, like when you were a child, and be part of it?"

"It doesn't make me want to do any such thing," laughed his wife.
"What's come over you, Charles? I've never known a storm to excite
you like this."

"It's just so . . . so wild and tumultuous—the clouds swirling about,
the rain pouring down in sheets, the wind whistling around every corner of this old place!"

"Exactly as it does a dozen times every summer and winter," she
said.

"Don't spoil my fun—if it were midnight, I would imagine us
caught up in the middle of some old gothic tale!"

"And are you the hero or villain?"

"Come out with me!" exclaimed Charles.

"What—it's pouring!"

"All the better!" He dashed forward and grabbed her hand, then began to pull her from the room.

"Charles!" she laughed and pleaded at once. Who *was* this new husband of hers! Was this what happened to all new knights who knelt before the queen? She had never heard of such a peculiar reaction.

Jocelyn's expostulations proved of no use. He tugged her out of their room and down the stairway. Moments later they ran out the front door, hand in hand, into the midst of the mêlée. Charles let go of Jocelyn, ran about in a wide circle, then stopped and threw his arms into the air, and gazed up into the middle of the downpour.

Giggling at her husband's ridiculous antics, Jocelyn did not know whether to be happy or concerned. Something had changed, that much was certain. But she could not help being swept into the joy of the moment. Soon husband and wife were running about together.

"Do you remember when we got caught in that sudden downpour just like this," said Jocelyn, "before we were married?"

"How could I forget—off in the woods over there," said Charles, pointing generally toward the north. "That was certainly our most memorable walk together when we were courting.—But," he added, bursting into a renewed fit of laugher, "—just look at you! You're drenched from head to foot."

"Look at *you!*" rejoined Jocelyn.

———————— ♦ ♦ ♦ ————————

From the window at the staircase landing, where she happened to be standing staring out absently, Amanda looked down upon the madcap scene with a strangely curious expression. She did not smile nor give other indication of reaction, other than a mild wrinkling of her forehead.

She could not have given definition to her emotions or thoughts. She simply detected a change in her father. And she wasn't sure she liked it.

It had begun while they were still in London. And he had been so quiet on the train ride home—a different kind of quiet. He had been so jovial and happy on the way three days before. But going home he sat thoughtful and silent.

They had always been such chums. Yet these last two days her father hardly had a word for her. All his time was spent talking with her mother.

Amanda was accustomed to occupying no position in any situation but the center of attention. George never threatened that role, for he did nothing to compete with it. Now she began to sense the invasion of something unknown. An indefinable change was coming to their family. That she could neither see it nor identify it made her uneasy. More than uneasy, it annoyed her.

Amanda could not have known what was causing this strange sense of childish disquiet. But she knew that she didn't *want* her father changing. She liked him the way he was. It irritated her to see her father and mother playing in the rain together ... without her.

Half an hour after Amanda's silent observations, the family gathered for breakfast in the dining room. Charles and Jocelyn had dressed in dry clothes, though with hair still wet, and sported exuberant spirits. Amanda already sat at the table. George stood waiting. Catharine was just arriving with Miss Dimble.

"Good morning, children!" boomed Charles. "Quite a day, don't you think?"

"It's raining, Papa," said Amanda in a whine. A hint of exasperation remained, punctuated by a wrinkling of her forehead.

"Yes, and what a rain it is!"

"But I won't be able to go out."

"Whoever said you needed to let a little rain stop you, right, Jocie?" laughed Charles, taking his seat at the head of the table.

"It certainly didn't stop you!" rejoined Jocelyn in fun. She poured tea from the waiting pot into all the cups but Catharine's, then took her own seat next to her husband.

Sarah now entered from the kitchen carrying two racks of toast.

"Good morning, Sarah," said Charles. "How are you today?"

"Very well, thank you, Sir Charles."

"Please, Sarah. I am still Mr. Rutherford to you, whatever the queen may call me. I don't intend to be a knight around my own home—that's only for London."

"Yes, sir."

"Yes, sir ... *what?*" said Charles playfully.

"Yes, sir, Mr. Rutherford."

"Again."

"Yes ... *Mr. Rutherford*," said Sarah, smiling with a hint of blush.

"Ah, that is much better to my ear," said Charles, returning her smile.

She now returned to the kitchen and came back a moment later bearing a tray containing four plates, each of which contained one egg, two cooked tomato halves, and three small sausages. There was also a fifth plate which had no tomatoes. She set them before the five family members.

"Thank you, Sarah," said Charles. "Everything looks and smells delicious as usual."

Without preliminaries, they began to eat.

"So, George, my boy—what do you have planned today?"

"I'm going to work in the basement, Papa."

"Still tinkering with that old rusted door?"

"I think I shall manage to have it opened today," said George excitedly.

"I tell you, son, there's nothing behind it but rusted tools and rubbish. My father used to say he locked the place up to keep from having to clean it out, and never wanted to see inside it again."

"Have you ever seen the old door open, Papa?"

"Never. But perhaps I shall come down to help you. With two of us, we might be able to pry the old contraption loose on its hinges."

"Would you, Papa?" said George, his face brightening.

"Indeed—yes, I will. But if we get it open, then we shall have to clean it out."

"I'll do it myself," said George, now with even more enthusiasm at the project. "I don't mind! I'm sure it will lead somewhere."

Sarah walked in from the kitchen. "Excuse me, sir," she began.

"Yes, Sarah?" he said, glancing up.

"I've been meaning to tell you, sir—" she said, "*Mr. Rutherford*, I mean . . . that the man came to inspect the library when you were away, and said everything was fine."

"What man?"

"The man from the Secretary of State's office, sent to inspect all Devon's libraries."

"I'm sorry, Sarah," said Charles. "I haven't the slightest idea what you are talking about. I knew of no such order."

Sarah now related the incident.

An expression of concern passed across Charles' face rather than the relief the housekeeper had expected.

"It is a puzzling affair," he said. "An expert such as he apparently purported himself to be would surely know that silverfish feed only on the glue in books, not their paper. And you can certainly not smell them by simply standing in the middle of a room. Furthermore, they do not eat linens, as is commonly supposed. It sounds to me as if his purpose was as much to alarm you as it was to protect our library. How long was he here?"

"Not more than an hour or hour and a quarter."

"Hmm . . . a thorough search, if it was indeed silverfish he was after, would have taken hours for a library our size . . . perhaps even days."

"I'm dreadfully sorry, sir, if I—" began Sarah.

"No, Sarah," interrupted Charles. "No harm was apparently done. From what you've said, you could not have done other than what you did. Perhaps he was a spy from the British Museum, sent to see what rare editions they might like to make an offer on!"

It fell silent around the table for a moment or two.

"Well," he said decisively, "as there is nothing we can do to get to the bottom of it, we shan't worry about it further."

He took a long swallow of tea, emptying his cup. He poured in a spoonful's worth of milk, then filled it with tea to the rim, giving the mixture a quick stir with his spoon.

"And you, Amanda?" he said, glancing in her direction. "What are you going to do today?"

She shrugged.

"Not quite as exciting on a rainy day in the country as in the middle of London, is it, my dear? Ah well, sometimes we must make the best of it where we are, even though the prospects don't appear altogether—"

A sudden burst of brightness entered the room. Without warning, the sun shone through a hole in the storm. As it did, its rays exploded straight in at the window.

Charles' voice stopped in midsentence. He glanced toward the light. The next instant he leapt from his chair and ran to the window.

"Just look at that rainbow!" he exclaimed.

"It's only a rainbow, Papa," said Amanda.

"*Only* a rainbow, Amanda, my dear!" he replied, "—*only* a rainbow! Don't you know what the rainbow *means*?"

"What *does* it mean, Charles?" said Jocelyn.

"Come to think of it—I'm not certain I know myself," laughed

Charles. "I mean, in school we heard a story about old Noah and such, but..."

He paused, a strange expression crossing his face. "But ... you know, I think I do know what it means. I think it must mean that God loves us," he added.

The room fell silent.

Charles turned slowly to face the rest of his family. All four of the others, as well as Sarah Minsterly, stared blankly at him, incredulous at the words which had just fallen from his lips. None of the four had ever heard him mention the word *God* before.

"—at least," he added, laughing again, "it *seems* that is what it must mean. What *else* could something so beautiful *possibly* mean?"

The remainder of the breakfast was subdued. It was not the mention of God that had everyone in a state of wonderment. It was how their father and husband was behaving. Jocelyn was unusually quiet. Charles noted the reaction, thought it curious, but said nothing. He resolved to be more circumspect in the future.

Amanda remained quiet as well.

Something strange was going on here. And in her heart, Amanda didn't like it.

31

What Am I to Do?

Several weeks passed, during which the residents of Heathersleigh Hall resumed more or less their normal routine.

Every Monday morning, as was his custom, Charles traveled to London for that afternoon's two-thirty session of Parliament. He spent the week at his London flat while attending the week's sessions, then returned by train to Devonshire each Friday afternoon following the House closing at three o'clock.

During this time he paid as many visits as his parliamentary schedule would permit to New Hope Chapel on Bloomsbury Way, posing many more questions about the Christian faith than he would have dreamed he was even capable of thinking up. He listened with interest to everything Timothy Diggorsfeld told him. As yet he did not commit himself either way.

"But what am I to do, Timothy?" he asked one day, "supposing I come ultimately to the conclusion that the Christian faith is true? Does that mean I must give up my belief in evolution, throw out my signed copy of Darwin, and force myself to adhere to a list of Christian doctrines? I'm not sure I could do all that."

Diggorsfeld laughed lightly. "Put your mind to rest about all that," he said. "As I've told you many times, Charles, the Christian faith is not so much a belief system as it is a way of life. It is a way of life whose core involves men and women relating themselves properly to the God who made them. That means *living life with him*, not forcing their minds to run in certain channels. As far as what you will or will not believe as part of that living, he will show you all those things. But they are secondary to the *living* of life."

"Do you mean that everything can remain for me as before?"

Diggorsfeld thought a moment.

"In one sense, perhaps," he replied. "In other words, God does not come to you with a list, saying, 'Comply with all this and I will accept you.' There's none of that in how God operates. He accepts you exactly as you are. In that sense, one might say things do not change. But in another sense, *everything* changes."

"How do you mean?"

"Just this—that once you *do* come to God, once you accept the Christian faith as true and say to yourself and to him that you want to live by it, then there *are* expectations that immediately go along with it."

"Expectations?"

The pastor nodded.

"You see, God loves and accepts every man exactly as he is, for who he is at any given moment. He loves a commoner or peasant no less than he does any nobleman in the land, or the queen herself. But when one comes to him and says, 'God, I want to be your son or daughter ... I acknowledge you as my Creator and Lord,' God says in return, 'Wonderful. Welcome to my family. Now—there are certain ways my children are to live. Let me instruct you in them.'

"Those, Charles, are the expectations I spoke of that are inherent in the Christian faith—ways God has instructed his people to live. They are not conditions for acceptance. They are not *rules*, so to speak, which you will be punished for breaking. They are simply the way Christians are to live."

"I think I understand."

"For example, what if an aspiring politician were to say, 'I want to join the Conservative party. I want to be a Tory'?"

Charles smiled at Diggorsfeld's selection of analogy but said nothing.

"People would no doubt be curious about his beliefs and his background," replied Charles.

"Now suppose, if you will, this man's entire perspective *opposed* the Tory viewpoint, or his way of life and outlook were blatantly contrary to it. His colleagues would not want him to represent their party then, would they?"

Charles shook his head.

"I realize it's not an exact parallel," Diggorsfeld went on, "yet I think we can still learn from the analogy. If a man is going to be what is called a 'Tory' in the House of Commons, that designation tells people something about how he sees things and what he believes. A *Tory* is distinct from a *Liberal* or a *Labourite*. And these are distinctions all of Britain is aware of."

"Right."

"That is the point I am trying to convey about what a Christian is and does, how he thinks and responds and behaves, his attitudes and points of view—they are *distinct* from how the rest of the world thinks and responds and behaves and views things. God does not set up a list of expectations and rules and say, 'Do this and don't do this or I'll slap your hand.' He simply says, 'This is how my children live.' "

"I see."

"If we don't live accordingly," said the pastor, "how can we call ourselves God's people?"

"But how are we to know what those things are?" asked Charles.

"That is one of the reasons why Jesus came—to show us and tell us exactly how God's sons and daughters are to live and think and respond and view things. So you see, Charles, getting back to your original question—when you ask what you are to do, you have asked the foundational question in all of life, the question that is essential to all growth and meaning in life. *What do I do?* is the quest upon which we are all engaged."

"So," laughed Charles, "answer it for me!"

"You are an intelligent man. You will discover what *you* are to do. God will show you. It is to *him* you must look, not to me. I am but a fellow pilgrim on the same road."

"Further along than me, you will grant that," laughed Charles.

"Perhaps," smiled Diggorsfeld. "But probably not so far as you imagine. In any event, what I am attempting to express is that when a man or woman faces his Creator one day, the questions will not be, 'Did you believe in evolution or a six-day creation? Did you go to church? Did you adhere to every doctrine you were told to believe? Did you tithe? Did you participate in the sacraments? Did you agree to every point in the creeds? Did you go through this or that catechism?' Rather the Father will ask, *'Did you live according to what my Son taught . . . did you do what I told you?'*"

"Are all these matters of belief and doctrine therefore unimportant?" asked Charles.

"By no means. Unimportant—certainly not. What I want you to understand, Charles, is that we do not necessarily *just* believe. Certainly, one's actions proceed out of his or her belief. But Christianity at its core is not a 'belief system,' it is a *do*. And the *do* is this—we are to do what God the Father, and God the Son, and God the Holy Spirit say."

"Which is?"

"What all three tell us through the Scriptures. Jesus was sent by the Father to explain and demonstrate that life and to offer up his own life to make it possible for us to enter into it. Therefore, we are to do what Jesus says—follow his example, obey his commands, put into practice his teachings."

32

Probing Words Out of the Past

The train journey from London this particular Friday in mid-July sent Charles Rutherford's thoughts into more personal caverns of reflectiveness than usual.

Words from out of his distant past crept ever closer to his conscious memory. They were unsought, rising as it were out of the nebulous mental stirrings in which his brain had been engaged of late. But neither did he resist them as they came. Now a word floated to the surface, now a phrase, gradually followed by entire chunks of conversation.

. . . if ever a body needed proof . . . eyes t' see what was right in front o' him . . .

Charles knew well enough whose voice it was. He smiled at the memory of the thick Irish brogue, even as he heard his own voice question in return:

. . . what kind of proof?

. . . no proof for the head, came Bobby McFee's answer. *. . . kind o' proof only hearts can understand . . . intellect helps in the journey. But hearts has t' complete the job . . . mind can only take ye so far . . . only the humble o' heart can see the proof that's right in front o' everyone's noses.*

Charles sat back in his seat and closed his eyes, the rhythmic clacking of the rails blending with fragments of conversation in sleepy, pleasant reminiscence. As he did, his weeks of discussions with Timothy Diggorsfeld and many long-forgotten bits of wisdom from the mouth of Bobby McFee blended together in his mind until he could hardly distinguish between them. He had indeed been given two worthy mentors to guide him through this period of reevaluation and change.

Two hours later, as Charles made his way from the main road up the winding, tree-lined drive to Heathersleigh Hall, dusk had settled over southwest England. It had been a rigorous week, capped by late-Friday business, and he was tired. The methodical *clip-clop* cadence of shod hooves over the packed-gravel drive through deepening shadows of birch, beech, maple, and pine continued the reflective dreamy mood begun by the train. He gazed about with weary pleasure, allowing himself to drink in the quietness of the final two or three minutes of the approach.

It was *so* good to be back in Devon. Never had London seemed quite so hectic. Usually he enjoyed it. But by Wednesday of this week he had already begun anticipating getting back to the country.

It was peaceful here, thought Charles as his eyes took in the idyllic scene. So still as the evening descended. A three-quarter moon was just creeping above the tops of the trees, glowing bright in an evening sky of deepening blue tinged with a faint reminder of vanishing orange. The carriage rounded the final bend at the top of the rise. It emerged out of the trees and the front of the Hall came into view.

Gradually they slowed, then stopped in front of the great house.

"There you be, sir."

"Thank you . . . thank you very much, Hector," said Charles, stepping down, briefcase and small satchel in hand. "I'm sorry you had to make two trips into the station."

"No trouble at all, Mr. Charles. A right peaceful evening it was."

Jocelyn had been listening, heard the crunch of gravel under the carriage wheels, and came to the door, where she now stood. She greeted her husband with a smile and kiss.

"You look tired," she said.

"I am worn out," he sighed. They went inside arm in arm.

"Would you like something to eat?"

"I ate on the train. But tea would be wonderful."

"The water is already boiling."

"The children?"

"Amanda and Catharine are in bed and asleep. George is in his room for the night, probably reading or tinkering with something."

"Just the two of us?"

"I had a feeling, when you weren't on the early train, that you might need some peace and quiet when you arrived," smiled Jocelyn.

"You read my mind."

"Go put your things away and relax," said Jocelyn. "I'll be up with tea in five minutes."

Charles climbed the stairs while Jocelyn returned to the kitchen. After popping in for a brief visit with George, he adjourned to their private sitting room. He slumped into his favorite chair, sighed deeply, and gazed around the room with a sense of well-earned relaxation and well-being. Jocelyn returned shortly, carrying a tray with teapot, cups, milk, sugar, and a small plate of sweetcakes and scones. Charles glanced up as she entered, his eyes brightening.

"Ah, Jocelyn—a feast for eyes, nostrils, and soul! Thank you."

She set the tray down and took a seat beside him. They proceeded to fix their cups while Jocelyn asked about the week just past.

"You had late business, I take it?"

"This African situation is heating up," replied Charles. "A meeting was called with some of the party leaders after the House closed. I had to be there, though my heart wasn't in it."

"Did you visit Reverend Diggorsfeld this week?"

"Twice actually—both very good visits."

"What did you talk about?"

"We continued the previous week's discussion—you know, arguments for and against the existence of God."

Every Friday evening, Charles recounted in detail his recent conversations with the young pastor, to such an extent that Jocelyn felt she knew the man almost as well as her husband did. This also served the purpose of keeping her abreast of her husband's spiritual journey. Because Jocelyn was more or less content with her life, however, her interest at this point was more for Charles' sake than her own.

"I thought you were convinced," she said.

Charles thought for a moment.

"I suppose I am," he replied at length. "But the rational tussle is stimulating. Christianity is far more intellectually rigorous than I ever imagined. It is challenging to try to place matters of faith into practical and logical intersection with the real world."

"So . . . *are* you convinced it is true?" persisted Jocelyn. "Do you now consider yourself a Christian?"

Again Charles was silent. "That is an involved question," he replied at length. "I'm not sure one ever comes to a distinct point in time when you say, 'Ah ha!—all at once suddenly I believe.' It's a gradual process. You look back and realize your thinking has progressed. Timothy has helped guide me along in that without applying any pressure. He's enough of a modernist himself that I feel his sympathy with my doubts and questions. That's one of the things that makes me trust him. He brings such an astute, contemporary outlook to the discussion. Yet now I wonder..." Charles' voice trailed off.

"You wonder what?"

"I wonder if perhaps I have come to that point, or even gone beyond it, without realizing it. I think probably—if you take the thing purely on the intellectual level . . . I think I can say that I *do* believe. I hadn't stopped to put it quite so definitely as that before now. Yet when I hear those words coming out of my own lips . . . I'm not sure what it means . . . what it's *supposed* to mean. What *does* it mean for a man actually to say he *believes* in God?"

Again Charles paused.

"What is it?" asked Jocelyn.

"All at once the McFees came into my mind," he replied.

"Why them?"

"Along with Timothy's modern and erudite approach, perhaps some old-fashioned religion might do me good as well," replied Charles, "—to balance the picture, so to speak. I was thinking of Bobby and Maggie as I rode home this evening. It just may be that they have the answer to what I just asked . . . about what belief actually means."

"Why would you think so?"

"They used to talk to me about God when I was young. I hardly paid much attention then, yet all of a sudden it seems very important to talk to them. I think it's time for a visit. Will you join me?"

"Of course."

"Then we shall go out to the cottage tomorrow!"

33

Old Friendship Renewed

❖❖❖

In early afternoon, with Catharine down for a nap, George contentedly occupied, and Amanda under the watchful eye of Constance Dimble, Charles and Jocelyn Rutherford struck out on foot across the open space at the back of Heathersleigh Hall toward the woods. The McFees' cottage stood about a mile distant.

Charles' fatigue from the previous evening was gone, and he was in high spirits. Though she had no interest in going on a walk, the fact that she was not included in the outing put Amanda in a sour mood. This unfortunate fact would add considerably to the otherwise cheerful Miss Dimble's vexation on this day. For Amanda would vent her annoyance by making the nanny's life very difficult indeed.

"We're going to be talking about grown-up things, Amanda," her father had said at lunch. "You wouldn't be interested."

His words were enough to make her insist on accompanying them. Charles' persistent refusal insured a grumpy disposition for the remainder of the day. Her father never used to refuse her anything.

"What do you think, Jocie," said Charles as they went, unaware of the tempest they were leaving behind, "can you imagine a more wonderful place on the face of the earth than Devon in July?"

"I have not seen enough of the earth to say that with complete authority," she replied with a laugh. "And yet I would venture to agree with you."

"Have I ever shown you my little hideaway off there in the woods?" he asked, pointing to the left as they walked.

"I don't think so. I don't recall your mentioning it. As long as we've been here, do you mean to tell me there are still places you haven't shown me?"

"I just remembered. I'd forgotten about it myself. More and more things from my past are coming back to me these days."

They reached the woods and continued through them. By and by they approached the cottage. Maggie saw them through her kitchen window.

"Master Charles, it is wonderful to see you!" she exclaimed, running outside to greet them. "Lady Jocelyn—it is an honor to have you here ... come in, come in.—Bobby!" she cried. "Bobby—we have guests ... Master Charles is here!"

Charles was already laughing at the exuberant welcome as they followed Maggie inside.

Ten minutes later all four were seated together with cups of tea in hand, visiting like the old friends the three Devonshire natives were. After a few more minutes a lull came in the spirited conversation. A thoughtful expression spread over Charles' face.

"I'm not exactly sure why we're here," he said. "Jocelyn and I were talking last evening, and somehow I knew I needed to see the two of you."

"*We* know why," said Maggie with significant expression. She and Bobby glanced at one another.

"Then perhaps you can tell me," laughed Charles.

"The time has come, hasn't it, Master Charles?" she rejoined. "God's been getting under your skin and speaking to you like we always said he would?"

"How could you have known?"

"We been praying for ye," said Bobby.

"You once told me the time would come when I'd remember Maggie's flowers and would know that God was God. I suppose that day has arrived."

"Lately we sensed the Lord was trying t' get hold o' ye. Didn't we, Maggie?"

Maggie nodded.

"Well, you were right," said Charles. He went on to explain briefly what had happened in London, then told them of his new friendship with the pastor Diggorsfeld.

"He sounds like one o' God's true men," said Bobby.

Charles nodded. "But I can tell I need to do something else," he said. "Maybe there's a decision I need to make. Mr. Diggorsfeld told me I would eventually have to decide which party label I wanted to wear, so to speak. I think my intellect is convinced. Intellectually I would have to say I do believe. I am comfortable with the recognition that God is God. But I don't know what to do now. As Jocelyn and I were talking last night, I realized I didn't really know what *belief* actually meant. I think I believe. Mentally. But I have the feeling there is more to it. I felt the two of you might have something further to tell me."

Charles paused and chuckled. "I said that you would be the first to know if I changed my mind about God. Maybe that's another reason I am here."

The small cottage fell silent. It was Bobby McFee who broke it.

"Do ye recall, Master Charles," he said, "when I told ye long ago that the Creator gave ye yer intellect t' help in yer journey, but it was yer heart that had t' go the last distance alone?"

"I do remember," replied Charles, nodding his head. "I was just thinking of that conversation last evening on my way home."

"The Lord likely brought it t' yer mind on account o' it being time now that he wants ye t' complete that journey he's brought ye on t' this point."

"Complete it—how do you mean?"

"'Tis all well an' good t' talk about spiritual things, and t' talk about whether God be real or not. All that work o' the brain's necessary. But the time comes when a body's got t' go the rest o' the way with what it means t' believe."

"And what is that?"

"Becoming one o' God's family—becoming his son or his daughter. That's something that can't be done with the head, only with the heart."

"Isn't everyone his son and daughter?"

"In a manner o' speaking. He made us all, so we're his children in that way. But most aren't acting like sons and daughters, not living under his roof, if ye get my meaning. They're not living the way his family lives. That's the kind o' children he wants—sons and daughters that *are* living with him, as part o' his household, with him as their Father. That's what life's about—getting back under the Father's roof. It's kind o' like God has two families—the one that's everybody in the whole universe, far-off relatives that don't really even know him, and the close-by family that knows he's their Father and are actively living with him every day. The one's the close-in family, the other's just distant relations."

"How *do* you become part of the immediate family—one that's living as a son or daughter?"

"Open up your heart t' him. Let him inside. Tell him ye want t' live with him and for him now, instead o' for yerself. Tell him ye want t' take up residence again inside the family home."

"Do you mean, pray and say those things to him?"

Bobby nodded.

"But what do you mean about being part of his household?"

"Ye see, Master Charles, God's the best and most loving Father there ever was. He made us because he loves us. He loves us more than we can think. But because we're a dull-witted and stupid lot, we don't pay attention t' how our Father wants us t' live. So we live our own independent ways without asking him about what he might have t' say in the matter. We go about our lives as if we hadn't got a Father above us at all. We just figure that since we're alive, we ought t' be able t' do whatever we want. We never think that maybe we're supposed t' be part o' a household and family that belongs t' somebody else, and where somebody else is in charge. Ye see what I mean about us being a stupid lot?"

Charles laughed.

"So we forget that God loves us. Pretty soon we forget he's there at all, 'cause his is a quiet voice. And though he's everywhere, and speaking t' us all the time, it's easy not t' see or hear him if we close our eyes and ears. So we forget all about him. We live our own way. We don't ask anyone what to do or think—we just do what we happen t' think is right, which may or may not be what he wants us t' do. When we live like that, all we're doing is cutting ourselves off from him and from the family we're supposed t' be part o'.

"Now nothing can *really* cut us off from him, because we couldn't breathe a second without him. We're still his creatures, because he made us whether we call him our Father or not. But we've forgotten t' be sons and daughters. We drift away and forget, and become those distant relatives I was talking about. We're still part o' the family o' God's created world, but we've forgotten all about whose world it is, and what it means t' be one o' his creatures.

"So t' help folks who've forgotten, the Father sent his Son Jesus t' the earth t' remind us that we've got a heavenly Father, and t' show us how we're t' live in his family. And that's what folks've got t' do—come back into the Father's intimate family like Jesus told us, and then t' live as part o' that family.

"He's a good and loving Father, the Father o' Jesus and our own Father too. He's waiting for us to say, 'God, I want ye t' be my Father again. Ye *are* my Father, because ye made me. But now that I know ye as my Father, I want t' start living like yer son.' But there's something else that has t' happen too. Ye see, the Bible says we've not just drifted away from his family—'tis that we've been in rebellion against his fatherhood. So we have t' repent o' that, to stop our rebellin' and go back the other way.

"'Tis what's called repenting o' sin. And we've got t' ask his forgiveness for being wayward children. But when we ask, he does forgive us. 'Tis what Jesus dying on the cross was all about.

"Ye see, Master Charles, 'tis up t' us t' come back under the roof o' the family. There's nothing he can do till we do that. But once we decide t' do it, Jesus makes the way possible."

"How *do* you live as his son?" asked Charles.

"Do what Jesus said. That's why Jesus came—t' tell us how t' live as God's sons and daughters."

"Back to my first question—is that what it means to believe?"

"Believing is more than just saying with yer head, 'I know God is God.' 'Tis also saying with yer heart, 'God, I want ye t' be my Father, and I want t' live as yer son.' It's both things together. Believing means t' *live* as God's son or daughter. Ye can't do that without both the head and the heart working together."

It was silent a long time.

"I want that," said Charles at length. "I do believe with my head, and I want to live what I believe in my heart too. I want to be a member of the immediate family, not the distant one. But . . . well, it's been so long, I don't really know what to say, what the right prayers are. Can you show me how to pray to him?"

"We could pray with you, and help ye through it, Master Charles. But I think ye'd be better t' go t' the Father yerself, just the two o' ye. Find a quiet place—an' ye too, Lady Rutherford, if ye're o' the same mind as yer husband. For there can't be any more wondrous thing in the world than a man and a woman together giving their hearts t' the Father o' them both, and together coming back into his family.

"So just find a place where ye can be alone. It doesn't matter where, or if ye close yer eyes or how ye do it. Just talk t' God like he was yer very own kind and loving Father, 'cause that's what he is. Talk t' him out o' yer heart. Tell him whatever ye want t' tell him. Thank him that his Son Jesus died for ye, t' bring ye back t' his family. Then ask him t' show ye how t' be his son and daughter. Open up yer heart as well as yer brain. Ask him what he wants ye t' do. And then when he shows ye, make sure ye do it. And the way he'll tell ye is from how Jesus lived and what he said. That's how ye live in God's family, ye do what Jesus said. If ye ask, he'll show ye what t' do."

34

A Newly Changed World

*C*harles and Jocelyn returned from the cottage in silence. Charles wanted to ask Jocelyn what she thought, and if she would pray with him. But he was reluctant to intrude. For the first time he began to sense something he had not considered before now—that perhaps she herself was struggling with doubts about this new direction.

For the rest of the day Charles had a sense of approaching change. The following morning, Sunday, he awoke early.

He glanced at the clock on the wall. It was fifteen till six. Jocelyn still slept.

He rose, dressed quietly, descended the stairs, grabbed up his favorite walking stick from the hall tree by the door, and went out into the stillness of the morning.

The sun was only recently up. Her rising left behind a rainbow trail of purples, oranges, reds, and yellows in the eastern sky and a sparkle of dew on the carefully tended lawns surrounding Heathersleigh Hall.

The gardener, Harlan Latimer, always kept the place looking well-groomed, as befitted such a stately and historical residence. But today, as Charles gazed about the meadows and fields around him, which were silent in anticipation of the day and overspread with the glories of the sunrise, all was new. His eyes looked toward the thinly forested hills in the distance. Reminders of childhood romps drifted into his brain and heightened the quiet pleasure of the early hour.

He breathed in deeply of the morning air, then set off across the lawn toward the open countryside, with no particular destination in mind.

There could be no doubt, he thought as he went—everything about his outlook was altered.

Nature—indeed, so many aspects of life—had begun to weave a spell upon him, from flowers and sunrises, to smiles and music. A simple nod from a stranger walking along Whitehall in London, the handshake of a colleague, a smile from dear Sarah Minsterly, the happy tones of the Mozart country dances Jocelyn played on her spinet—any was sufficient to make his heart swell with a vibrant and pulsating love for all humankind. The face of humanity had become dear to him!

Surely, he thought as he walked casually along, this world could be no mere random accumulation of matter, heaped together to produce a meaningless thing called "life." The grass gradually lengthened under his feet as he moved farther from the house. How could he have been oblivious for so long, and not seen what the final paragraph of the *Origin* hinted at, yet which even Darwin himself fell short of grasping in all his years of study.

A live Heart existed at the center of all things, breathing the wonder of life into every inch of the universe!

Why had it taken him so long to recognize that most simple, most obvious, most profound, yet most overlooked fact?

It was a huge thing he had never considered until a few weeks ago. Christianity *had* to be true in a deeper and more personal sense than conveyed by the mere facts which he had long dismissed as irrelevant. And now came again the question of implications he had been considering all weekend.

What obligation did recognizing the reality of the Christian truths place *upon him*? What might it require that he would have to *do* in consequence?

Charles Rutherford was enough of a thinking man and rationalist to recognize that consequences were involved in everything. For him to embrace a personal God, who had a claim upon him in very down-to-earth ways, would most certainly involve *significant* consequences. What would it mean in his personal life? What would it mean to his family? How might it change his priorities and attitudes and perspectives? What would it mean to his career?

Already he had begun to feel a modification in how he looked at things. The honor of knighthood had brought with it little of the satisfaction and sense of achievement he had expected. Indeed the whole political realm in which he had long been involved was beginning to lose its fascination and interest. London—the great city which he had always loved so dearly as the center of his activity, the apex of the world itself—shone now in his eyes with less luster. He had formerly risen on Monday mornings with a sense of eagerness to get back to the city. Now he regretted that he could not remain at Heathersleigh longer, and all through the week anticipated his return on Friday.

Along with such alterations of orientation, he found himself drawn in the most peculiar directions, desirous of taking long walks rather than sitting in his study, wanting to help Harlan with the lawn or prune a hedge himself rather than work on his motor or other devices. Was this the difference between intellect and heart Bobby had spoken of? Were these whisperings of nature being spoken to his heart rather than his brain? Everything upon which his eyes fell reminded him of Diggorsfeld's statement about the fingerprint of God.

Without his realizing it, Charles' walk had brought him to the edge of the heather garden. It had been part of the estate as long as he remembered, lying to the southeast of the house at the edge of a small wood, and containing what his mother once said were over fifty separate varieties of the plant. At least one of those subspecies was in bloom year round. It stood some seventy-five or hundred yards from the house, but neither he nor Jocelyn had paid the area more than passing heed. Nor had he instructed Harlan to bring it within the domain of the rest of the grounds. As a result it was now completely overgrown, the various plants running wild over one another, with weeds and brambles throughout.

Charles had always considered heather little more than an uninteresting wiry shrub, notwithstanding that it gave the Hall a proud name. Now he found himself considering how he might personally cultivate the patch, prune back some of the overgrowth, and see if he could reestablish the pathways he remembered winding through as a child.

This was precisely the kind of change he kept noticing in his thinking. The new thoughts were subtle at first. Yet he could feel them probing steadily more deeply into the soil of his consciousness, stirring up new questions about old values and convictions. Where would it all lead? Would it result only in increased attentiveness to a heather garden ... or would the winds of newness blow through his life in more sweeping ways?

Something told him that even had he tried to forget what had happened last month in London, even if he tried to return to the way his life had been before, he couldn't do it. Somehow he knew that he could not continue along the same pathways as before.

The fact that the Creator was now *close* ... that astounding fact must alter everything!

35

Purple Messenger

❦harles was now a good way from the house, walking aimlessly across a grassy meadow. The sun had put enough distance between itself and the horizon to have left behind all traces of its spectacular waking, and was already beginning to make its warmth felt over the earth.

Nearly in front of him a hint of color low down in the midst of the green arrested his step. He stooped to investigate.

A tiny violet peered out from amid the meadow grasses, casting its happy face up toward the sun as if to gain its strength for the day. Charles did not know the little meadow-lady of the morning's name was "violet." But he found her face no less lovely because he knew not what to call her.

He bent onto both knees to examine the four delicate petals more closely. In their center, a tiny heart of yellow pollen flung narrow rays of darkest purple radiating out into the lighter hues of the petals. The simplicity of the arrangement and colors, all in such miniature, was spellbinding. And to think, he might easily have walked by and never even seen it.

He lowered his head, bringing his nose almost to the ground, and allowing what scent might be contained in the tiny purple thing to invade his nostrils. Its fragrance was distant and faint, speaking not of perfume, but rather of the earth whence it came. It reminded him of . . . of *something* . . . far off . . . something he could not quite lay hold of.

A pang seized Charles' heart. The same feeling that had possessed him on Oxford Street when sniffing at the girl's clump of broken flowers laid hold of him anew. A lump rose in his throat.

He lifted his face from the ground with a sigh, remaining another moment on his knees.

Let evolution explain that! he said with a smile.

Oh, one of Darwin's disciples could no doubt manage to explain the evolutionary purpose of the fragrance, and how the atoms and mutations and weather and geologic conditions all combined to produce this particular flower at this particular time and place with this particular aroma.

But let science explain why his heart leapt at the faint and mysterious aroma! That fact could be accounted for by no chance dance of atoms and random mutation of organisms!

Someone must mean it!

Where else could such a feeling originate but in the heart of a Creator-Father. He had blurted out several weeks ago that the rainbow must mean God loved them. Now he knew the tiny flower meant the same thing. Both bow and blossom came from the same Source.

If the God of Christianity was indeed living and active in the affairs of men as that "Someone" ... then what *did* he mean by making men weep at the fragrance of rose or violet, or by invading his heart with love at the smile from a passing stranger?

What could He possibly mean other than to speak soft reminders of his creative presence, as Diggorsfeld had said?

But why?

Why else than to turn the hearts of men—however their minds argued against His very existence—*toward the One who had made them?*

The language of nature was the language of the heart. Bobby and Maggie McFee had said the heart would take over when the intellect could go no further, speaking what rational intellect was incapable of apprehending. That was the message of the tiny violet!

It was not enough, both Diggorsfeld and his friends in the cottage had told him, mentally to admit to such truths. The Creator desired a personal response.

"The time comes when a body's got t' go the rest o' the way with what it means t' believe," Bobby had told him, "—that's becoming his son or daughter."

36

Private Sanctuary and Decision

*C*harles rose and continued on his way, striking now across a faded path which had not been trod by his own feet in years, but which he remembered from boyhood.

Walking along the overgrown trail reminded him again of the secluded corner in the woods in which he had played as a boy. A longing to visit the old haunt he had told Jocelyn of yesterday rose up within him. His pace began to quicken.

Within ten or fifteen minutes he was scratching his way through the brushy entrance, now overgrown and nearly lost to view. Presently he was standing in the middle of the meadow hideaway, the years tumbling away, remembering with fondness the day he had discovered it so long ago. Around him on all sides rose an enclosing circle of tall trees and tangled brush. The tiny meadow, however, was clear of all but a soft green carpet of sunlit grass. The gurgling music from the small stream running through its midst sent him momentarily back to his boyhood.

He stood absolutely still for two or three minutes, drinking in the silence. The quiet of the morning, and the solitude of being completely surrounded by trees, invaded his spirit with the same sense of awe he had felt upon first entering New Hope Chapel in London several weeks ago. On that day the sense of presence had confused him. Today, however, he realized what—and *Who*—was responsible for it.

This was no imaginary sensation. He was not alone. An almighty Personage was present with him.

At last Charles Rutherford also knew that he was ready to say *yes* to him.

But he felt no hurry. He strolled casually about, remembering this and that about the place from years gone by. Gradually the sense of presence deepened. Through his mind flitted fragments of many conversations. Bobby and Maggie said a moment came to all when the eyes of the innermost being were opened.

He knew that for him that day had at long last arrived.

"Just talk t' him," the Irishman had said, "like ye would t' the perfect Father, as if ye knew such a one loved ye more than ye had ever been loved by anyone before. Don't make great efforts t' make great *prayers*—just talk t' him. Tell him honestly, sincerely, and humbly that ye want t' be his . . . that ye are ready t' be his son. Ye're not giving a speech, Master Charles, ye're talking t' yer Father."

Charles stopped, then slowly sunk to his knees.

"God," he said in a whisper, *"I cannot say I can see you or even know what you are like. But I feel you here in this place with me. I know now that you are in all places, and that I can no longer ignore your existence. I am sorry so much of my life passed when I foolishly did not recognize the many ways in which you were speaking to me. I am sorry I was blind to your presence, and I thank you for the circumstances you brought to open my eyes to the truth that you have been right beside me all along."*

He paused momentarily, took a breath, then continued.

"Therefore, I want to tell you that I acknowledge you, and I am at last ready to be your son. I don't yet even know what that means, or what is involved. But if you will show me, I will do my best to do what you want, whatever it may mean. I acknowledge, too, as Bobby said, my waywardness, my sin. Forgive me. Thank you that your Son, Jesus Christ, died so that my sin could be forgiven. I want to follow him, though I can hardly say I know where he is leading. I am ready to be your son as well. I want to live, as Bobby said, in your house, as part of your intimate family, with you as my Father. Show me what you want me to do, and I will try to do it. Continue to open my eyes to your presence, your fingerprint as Diggorsfeld calls it, both in the world around me and within my own self. I will need a great amount of help because I don't know much about what it means to be a Christian. But if you will teach me, I will try to learn."

His voice fell silent, and he let out a deep sigh. Three weeks ago he may have been a reluctant pilgrim, but now he felt a sense of satisfaction and peace. Beyond that, he felt only a sense of having done what he had to do, of doing what he *wanted* to do, because it was the right and only reasonable way for an honest man to respond to the truth.

He rose and breathed in full lungs of the fresh morning air, which, if possible, smelled even better now. Then he turned to leave.

Bobby McFee had said God would show him what to do.

And then the radical thought came to him as he walked back—after breakfast they would all go to the church in the village!

37

God Can't Love Me

♦ ♦ ♦

$\mathcal{T}$he carriage ride back from Milverscombe to Heathersleigh Hall after the service was quiet. Amanda and George had seemed glad of the outing and curious about the unfamiliar church service, but Jocelyn was strangely subdued. Charles began to wonder if he had done something to offend her.

He tied the reins to the post in front of the house as the children scampered down.

"Let's go for a walk, Jocie," he said. "Just let me tell Hector we're back."

He disappeared around the side of the house for a minute or two, then returned. Jocelyn still stood by the carriage unmoved and expressionless. Charles led her across the entryway to the grass south of the Hall's west wing. A few minutes later they were strolling amongst low-growing shrubs and scattered birches.

Charles groped for a way to begin. Something was obviously bothering her. But what could account for it? As they walked, Jocelyn's arms remained close to her side.

"What did you think of everything the McFees said yesterday?" Charles asked.

Jocelyn shrugged. One of her hands unconsciously went to the marred side of her face.

"I went out into the woods early this morning," Charles went on. "I prayed, like Bobby said."

He paused and took in a breath as he glanced to his side. "I want to say I've never been happier in my life," he said. "It felt good to tell God I wanted to live as his son. I knew it was the right thing to do. But . . ."

He hesitated. Still there was no reply from Jocelyn.

"You seem so distant all at once, Jocie," Charles went on. He could tell his wife was aching inside, and he hurt with her. "How can I be happy if you are unhappy?"

Still she said nothing. They continued to walk. Charles did not want to push.

"Jocie, what's the matter?" he finally blurted out. "You've hardly spoken in twenty-four hours."

Jocelyn was fighting back tears, though Charles had no way of knowing it. She was afraid that uttering a single word would unleash a flood.

"I thought you were on this new road with me. All this time I've been telling you about my talks with Timothy . . . has it bothered you?"

No reply.

"Do you not like my talking about God? Jocie, why are you like this? Please . . . tell me what you're thinking. Don't you want to enter into this new life?"

"It's not that I don't want to," she finally replied. "Oh, I don't know—maybe I don't."

Charles looked at her, waiting. Several long seconds passed.

"What's wrong with how things were?" she asked finally.

"It isn't that something was wrong," Charles replied. "Improving something doesn't necessarily mean it was *wrong*, only that you've discovered something better. But once you discover the better, it seems it might be wrong to hold back. Now that we know about life with God, it would be wrong for us to hold back. Now that we *do* know, how can we not go forward?"

"Why? *Why* do things have to change?" insisted Jocelyn. "I've been happier these years here at Heathersleigh with you and the children than I've ever been in my life. I don't want that to change."

"Even if it's change for the better?"

"Who says it will be change for the better? I like our life the way it is. I don't want anything to upset it."

"But don't you see, Jocie—it can only get better. When I told God that I wanted to belong to him, I was filled with an altogether new . . . I don't know, a contentment and satisfaction. I felt, as Bobby said, that I had become part of a family, that I had a new home."

"But we *are* home," Jocelyn blurted out. "We *have* a family. Heathersleigh is home for me. This is the only place I've ever felt at home and at peace."

She drew in a long steadying breath. She was obviously struggling with great emotion.

"I can believe that there is a God out there," Jocelyn went on. "That's not an intellectual problem for me, as perhaps it has been for you. Maybe it's more natural for a woman to believe in God, I don't know. But that's where I want to leave it. Why can't that be enough?"

"*Enough,*" he repeated. "How can it be enough?"

"I am satisfied with my life."

"Even when more is out there waiting for you?"

"Maybe you can't think that way. But I do."

"Even if it means holding something of yourself back?"

"I'm not like you, Charles. I'm not always on a crusade to find *more*. And I don't want religion taking over our lives. In my own way, I suppose I've always believed in God without even thinking about it. But why does that have to *change* everything?"

"But what if there are things down there deep inside us that need fixing?"

"What's wrong with being good enough?"

"Because everyone has to grow. Change is part of life."

"I don't want to have to get fixed."

"Do you want to be God's daughter?"

Jocelyn did not answer immediately.

"I don't know if I do or not," she replied at length. "Maybe ... maybe I don't. But I don't want someone trying to make me different down inside."

"Even God?"

"I just want to be myself."

"He couldn't want anything but to make you a *better* person. I know that if I could improve who I was as a man, nothing would keep me from it."

"I suppose more than anything, I just want to be left alone."

"I'm not sure we have that option indefinitely. What if God wants more for us?"

"Oh, Charles, why do we have to make such a fuss about growing and improving all of a sudden?"

"Because we've never given our lives to him—well, I have now. When you give your life to him, it *does* change everything. It can't help it. You can't just say, 'Oh, I believe in God now,' and leave it at that. You can't just take him or leave him, like . . . well, like . . . like a tomato at breakfast."

Jocelyn could not prevent a slight smile creeping over her lips.

"If you believe he is there, and you believe what Bobby and Maggie say about him making us and loving us, then you have to do more than just believe. I don't see what else there is to do but give yourself to him—*all* of yourself. I can't see how there can be any middle ground with God."

Jocelyn's brief smile vanished. The look of distance had returned to her expression, and with it a sudden pang of loneliness.

"You can embrace something wholeheartedly," she said, "and give yourself to it. I can't do that. I don't open up all the way like you. I have to protect myself . . . I don't trust anybody else."

"Do you trust *me*?"

"What's wrong with keeping him out there?" said Jocelyn, evading his question.

"It's the difference between the immediate family and the distant relations, like Bobby said."

"Maybe I don't want God to be in my immediate family. I have *you*—why do I need *him*?"

"Jocie—you're not making any sense. Why *wouldn't* you want God to be close, to be a loving Father? I can't imagine not wanting such a wonderful thing."

"Who says it's wonderful?"

"It has to be. God is good."

"You've changed, Charles. It's all those talks with Reverend Diggorsfeld—now *you're* starting to sound like a preacher. How do you know we can trust what he says about God . . . or trust God himself for that matter? *I* don't know that."

"He couldn't be anything but a good and loving Father."

Again Jocelyn fell silent. They continued to walk for some distance through the trees. They were nearly down to the main road now, and gradually turned eastward to begin circling back up toward the open fields in back of the house.

"I can believe God is there . . . that he exists . . . that he is out there somewhere," said Jocelyn at length in a measured voice. "But I don't know that I do believe all that about him loving us so much and being good. I don't know, maybe he is in control of everything, and—"

Her breath caught.

"He is," insisted Charles. "If he is God, then he must be in control and must want what is best for us . . ."

Charles stopped in midsentence. On Jocelyn's face was a look of angry disbelief such as he had never seen.

"He wants what is *best* for us!" she exclaimed.

"Of course. What else could—"

"Is that why he made me like this?" she interrupted. "Do you have any idea what it is like to live your whole life feeling like a mistake? He's in control of our lives! Do you know what that means, Charles? How am I to trust a God who *intended* me to be like this!"

"Is that your hesitation—whether you can trust him, whether he's *good*?"

"Wouldn't you be hesitant?" she returned. "He made me so that my own mother was disgusted with the very sight of me, embarrassed to be seen with me. And now you want me to call him *loving* and *kind* and *good*! You want me to give my life to him and think of him as a wonderful and loving Father?"

Charles listened dumbfounded. He had no easy reply.

"I can't possibly think of God like that," Jocelyn continued. "I will go along with you on all this. I will support you in what *you* do, just like I learned about politics and science to support you. But don't ask me to embrace a God who made me like this. How could he possibly love me? How could I possibly love him?"

Charles had never seen Jocelyn like this. He reached out to put his arm around her, to draw her to him. But she pulled away, then stood like a frightened child, arms crossed, eyes flashing, lips trembling.

"Jocelyn," he said softly, "I'm so sorry . . . I didn't know you felt this way."

Charles gazed tenderly into his wife's face. His eyes saw no stain, no mark, only a woman he loved with all his heart. Therefore, she was truly beautiful in his sight.

"But I can't help thinking you really *do* believe God is good," he added, "more than you admit, more than you want to. And you're angry with him. If you didn't really believe it, you wouldn't be angry. It's because you know he is good that you *expect* God to be good."

"I am not angry at him," she retorted.

"Then tell him thank you for how he made you."

Jocelyn returned his words with a blank stare. *"Thank him?"*

"Can you . . . can you thank him?"

"No I can't thank him!" she shot back.

"Why?"

"I see nothing to thank him for. What do I owe him after what he did to me?"

"Your life."

"Everybody has that. Besides, wouldn't you be angry if you had to wear this every day of your life?" she said, pointing to her face. "You don't have any idea what it is like! How could you possibly understand? Look at you. You're handsome, intelligent ... everyone likes you. But *me!*"

"But, Jocelyn, you're—" Charles tried to begin. But she interrupted him.

"This horrid ... deformity ... is there every morning when I wake up," she said. "I look in the mirror and am reminded of it every day. I wake up sometimes and think it's all been a dream, and that maybe it will be gone. But I don't even need to look in the mirror. I can see it in everyone's eyes. The looks of shock, or embarrassment, of revulsion—they all remind me that it is still there. Every day of my existence! How can God love me! The words mean nothing."

She stood, stiff and erect, shaking, but fighting the urge to break into uncontrollable sobs.

Slowly Charles approached. Gently he wrapped his arms around her tight body and drew her toward him. Gradually she relaxed and allowed him to hold her. After a few moments she began to cry softly.

They stood for some moments; then Charles led her out of the trees toward the overgrown heather garden.

38

Individual Marks of a Father's Love

*C*harles led his wife to a small stone bench.

"Sit down, Jocie," said Charles. "I have something I want to say."

They sat down beside one another. She laid her head on his shoulder. For many minutes neither spoke as they sat quietly together.

"Oh, Charles," said Jocelyn at length, "I don't want our lives to change."

"We are living things. We must grow."

"But we're adults. Haven't we grown enough?"

"We're not like one of my machines that can just get completed and that's that. We're living, breathing, changing, growing creatures. We can't be stagnant—we must always strive for the best. I want the best for you. And I want the best for myself. I want us both to know God as a good Father . . . one who does love you."

He paused briefly.

"You aren't a mistake to him," he went on. "I can't explain it, Jocie, but I know he made you as he did, for some reason we cannot see. A *good* reason, not a bad one."

"How can that be?"

"Just imagine, Jocie—what if that red birthmark on your face is a mark God intended as something special, something wonderful, something to show just how much he loves you, and you alone. *If we could only see what was in God's heart when he made you!*"

It was silent. The thought was too huge to comprehend.

"Everyone has *some* kind of mark, Jocie—something about the way they're made that they don't like."

"Not many people have huge, glaring red birthmarks."

"Perhaps not. Yours happens to be more visible than most. Other marks are invisible—hidden twists on the heart or soul that cause people to think God must not love them. But what if all those hidden scars are really God's special marks of individuality, put there, in some mysterious way we cannot understand, to help us see how much he actually *does* love us? What if your red birthmark is really a sign of great love?"

"But how, Charles . . . how could such a thing be?"

"I don't know, Jocie. But if God is a good and loving Father—somehow I think it has to be so."

"How can you be so sure he *is* good and loving and trustworthy?"

"If he wasn't, he couldn't be God."

Jocelyn stared at her husband blankly.

"The God who made us, and who created the world, *has* to be good," Charles went on. "I can't explain why, but I see no other possibility."

"What does that have to do with how he made us?"

"However he made us has to be *good*. Even the things that don't appear so, things that *we* might change about ourselves if we could.

193

But that's only because we don't see them as God does, don't see their value. It may be that we will never recognize these marks as loving signs of the Father's special and individual fingerprint upon us, until we thank him for them, until we recognize them as coming from a hand of love rather than from a hand of cruelty."

Jocelyn took a deep breath and struggled to find her voice.

"That would be so hard to do," she said as her hand once more came to rest on her face. "To see … this … as a good thing—that's more than I can comprehend."

"I believe it's true," said Charles.

"It's different for you," replied Jocelyn. "You've always had confidence, been content with who you are. For you this is more an intellectual decision. I know everything Mr. McFee said about the heart. But still, you can look at Christianity, and decide whether you believe it or not. You said that very thing to me."

"I see that," acknowledged Charles. "I realize it's different."

"It's not that way for me. I … I just can't think of God without thinking he doesn't like me, without thinking of him as mean, even cruel, without thinking that he must look at me as my mother used to look at me, with cold disdain. Mr. McFee kept saying that God was good and loving. Those are the *last* traits I think of when I think about God. Loving? If he loved me, why would he have made me like this? If he loved me, why did he make me look like some kind of monster? Don't you see, Charles? I don't know *how* to believe that God loves me."

She broke down in sobs. Charles said nothing further until after her weeping began to subside.

"I don't think you can know that goodness," he said at length, his voice very gentle, "until you are willing to give him thanks for it. And Jocie, *I* can give thanks for it with all my heart! I believe God's fingerprint on your face is partially responsible for making you different from other ladies of your standing … and different from your mother. People can be bitter over their marks of individuality. Or they can be thankful and let God use them to deepen compassion and character within them. I believe you are a better and more understanding and compassionate person because of the way God made you, and a better mother as well. Don't you see, Jocie?—you really can thank God for your birthmark because it has helped form your character inside. Oh, Jocie—I love you so much! How could God not love you infinitely more than I do?"

Jocelyn nodded in the midst of her tears. She tried to take in his words, although she was beginning to tire physically and emotionally.

"Jocie, do you love Amanda and Catharine and George?" Charles asked.

"Of course I do. They're my children. How can I not love them?"

"And you are God's child, Jocelyn. He loves you even more."

Again she began to cry softly.

"Do you remember the other night when Bobby read to us from the Bible about God's loving us so much that he sent his Son to die on the cross so that we would know of his love?"

She nodded. "I've heard that verse all my life, but I never thought of it quite the way he explained it."

"Well, I think Jesus was showing us how to give ourselves. We have to trust him and his goodness so much that we would be willing to go that far. But he doesn't ask that much of us. All he asks is that we believe that he loves us. Can you believe that he loves you, Jocie?"

"I don't know," she replied softly. "I never really knew love until you loved me."

"Where do you think we learned to love? *Our* love must be from God. He *loves* you, Jocie."

Gently he stroked her hair and let her weep.

"*You're* the only one who has ever loved me," she said softly.

Silently Charles prayed for wisdom to say the right thing. After a few moments, he leaned away, then reached over and turned Jocelyn's face toward his so he could look directly into her eyes.

"Jocie," he said, "I'm sorry to keep returning to something so painful for you. But I believe you need to thank God for the way he has made you."

She returned his gaze with the bewildered eyes of a wild animal caught in a trap.

"I think," Charles went on, "that you need to thank him for being a good and loving Father, and thank him for your red face, recognizing that he intended it for your good, to remind you of him. It is his fingerprint upon your face, Jocie. When he made you, he touched you in a unique way different from everyone else. He left that mark of his touch upon you in red, to remind you every day—not that he doesn't love you . . . but that he *does*."

Deliberately he reached up and laid his hand over the purplish red mark. She winced at his touch, but he kept it there and held her eyes with his.

"It's God's fingerprint, Jocie!" he said once again. "It's the fingerprint of love."

PART IV

All Things New

1899

39
Silent Witness to High Things

A solitary figure stood peering through the window of her bedroom into the courtyard below.

Outside, the gentle late morning's breeze across the fields and meadows of the Devonshire downs brought with it the sweet aroma of greenery and growth. It was a fragrance which only the sun, working in harmony with the things of the earth, could produce.

With his back to the great stone house of three stories and sprawling extent, and unaware of the eyes upon him, Charles Rutherford stood gazing out across the countryside. He opened wide his nostrils and drew in a long sigh of pleasure. The earth spoke many things in the due course of its seasons. It was one of many things he had learned late in his life to care about. But after the great change which had taken place within the deep region of his heart, there were few things he loved so much as the smell of meadow grass after a rain.

Yet today a subtle disquiet accompanied the gentle wind-borne fragrances. Dissatisfaction with himself two years earlier had led him to contentment of soul and peace with his Creator. This morning's sense of unease, however, was altogether different and was one he did not understand.

It was time to visit the wood.

He had felt it ever since arising this morning, though the undefined promptings had not yet been given definite form and substance. No matter. Time in his natural sanctuary was never wasted, whether or not the specific purpose was known.

He struck out across the path through the semi-cultivated patch of heather not far from the house, then in a wide arc toward the meadow beyond.

Then he paused, prompted by some intuition to glance back.

In the third-floor window he saw the face of his daughter Amanda. That she was looking at him too he was sure enough.

Charles smiled and waved.

At the same instant, however, she retreated back into the room. Her form was lost to his view, and no answering greeting came in response. Maybe it was for *her* that today's urging to prayer had come.

It could not be denied that Amanda had changed. The changes had begun almost immediately after he and Jocelyn had given their hearts to the Lord. Why, neither father nor mother possessed so much as a clue. George had embraced the change in orientation with them, took his turn praying aloud at meals, and seemed to enjoy services at the village church in Milverscombe. Little Catharine had scarcely noticed that anything was different. But Amanda resisted from the start. The change of priorities seemed to confuse her.

Now, after two years, it was apparent that the discord had deepened between Amanda and the rest of the family. The once happy and spunky girl had become withdrawn and moody. Her father could not help being concerned.

Where did it originate? he wondered—this streak of sullenness that had come to define his daughter's personality in almost equal proportion with laughter? Why did she now find parental influence such an unwelcome burden, when previously she had apparently loved her parents with all her heart? And why did she seemingly resent the new spiritual dimension which had opened new worlds of understanding and peace within him?

In Charles Rutherford's mind the changes that had come to him and Jocelyn and their family were all for the better. But from Amanda's vantage point, did they perhaps represent restrictions she had never encountered until that time?

They had been such good friends when she was a younger child. He still recalled with fondness their laughter together on the trip to London for the queen's jubilee. Then had come the call upon his life—to give himself to a new Master. And that was when Amanda started pulling away. Did she somehow feel that God had taken him from her? He shook his head, worried and confused. How could she not see that now he loved her more than ever?

All these questions passed through his brain in a second, as they did frequently these days. But there were no more answers on this day than on any other. He turned and continued on his way, down a gentle grassy slope, across a level meadow, and toward the uncultivated heathland that lay between himself and his destination.

——————————— ♦ ♦ ♦ ———————————

Inside the house, nine-year-old Amanda cautiously approached the window again, peering tentatively around the wide ledge of stone enclosing it to see if her father was still there.

Why she jumped back when her father looked up, Amanda could not have explained. A sudden feeling of being caught at something she should not have been doing swept through her. So she pulled away, trying to hide from his gaze. She didn't want him to know she was watching.

Now, seeing her father striding away in the distance, Amanda brought her face close to the glass again. Silently she followed his retreating form.

Why does he always go out in that direction? she thought to herself. *What does he do out there?* If it was just for a leisurely stroll, why did he sometimes stay so long?

Suddenly an idea came to her.

She would *follow* him! She would see with her own eyes where he went . . . and why.

The next instant Amanda was bounding down the stairs two at a time, though quietly enough so that her mother would not hear, and out through a side door into the morning's sunshine. She knew well enough in what direction she was likely to find her father. She had seen him disappear across the heath many times. She therefore hurried out in a slightly different tack so she would not be visible should he look back again toward the house.

Thirty minutes later Amanda had reached her objective.

Carefully she made her way down toward the edge of the wood, then began walking as softly as she was able through the thin stands of birch and pine, careful not to snap a twig beneath her feet that might betray her approach.

It was not a thick wood, though it was some moments before she located her father. On she crept until a gradual clearing began to come into sight, a lovely meadow in the midst of which a small stream ran down from the surrounding hills.

On its bank, Amanda saw her father on his knees in the grass, utterly unaware of any other human presence. His back was turned and no sound came from his lips, but it was obvious he was praying.

She did not need to know more. Amanda was disgusted.

She should have suspected as much!

No sense rose within her that she was witnessing a holy exchange. Nor did it occur to her that she had secretly intruded upon a man's private closet without making herself known. Her only emotion was a quiet annoyance at the calmness of the activity.

Why had he changed?

All Amanda knew was that from the very beginning, she hadn't liked it.

As quietly as she had come, Amanda now withdrew from the wood. Then, rather than making her way back to the house, she struck out unseen in the general direction of the village.

40

A Lunch at the Cottage

*A*manda's present mood, after what she had witnessed, was a grouchy one.

She did not want to return home, yet as soon as she found herself on the edge of Milverscombe, with a few people about, she realized she did not want to see anybody there either. It was Saturday afternoon. The village school was out, and there would be too much activity to suit her irritable disposition. She had overheard her father mention the school to her mother recently, wondering if she and George were getting enough social education with their governess and tutor. The reminder made her all the less inclined to run into any of the village children on this day. She therefore turned toward the downs. She would take the northward path back home.

It was midway through a spectacular month of May. The glories of an unfolding springtime were abroad in the land. A light rain had fallen the night before, showering the trees and cleaning them off for the day's warm winds. Its remnants overspread the meadows and fields with ten million tiny droplets that the light would turn into radiant prisms of sparkling color. The rays of the sun now pierced them as invisible rainbow-making arrows, sending up from the blades of green a dazzling array of reds and golds and blues and yellows such as no diamonds around a woman's neck could hope to produce. The odors emanating upward from the sun-warmed ground, and spread throughout the region on the wings of the morning's breezes to gladden the hearts of men and women and turn their thoughts with thanksgiving toward their Creator, were the very fragrances of heaven itself to those nostrils who had learned to love the earth.

As young Amanda walked carelessly uphill and down, however, her thoughts occupied, she noticed neither springtime's glories nor earth's bounties. She was in general perturbed at the world, and wishing she were riding Red Lady now instead of walking on her own two hot and tired feet.

She went unseeing, an unfortunate thing to have to say about anyone, even one as young as she. Yet circumstances were already at work which would serve in time to open the very eyes now focused disinterestedly on the narrowing path in front of her.

She had entered a sparsely wooded area about a mile from the village. Her present course would take her in roundabout fashion back toward the Hall. She was in fact not far from the location where she had earlier observed her father. His prayer-wood lay at the extremity of the Heathersleigh estate, loosely joined to a lightly forested range of moderate hills north and west of Milverscombe. Into the outlying precincts of these hills Amanda had now wandered. She knew where she was and was by no means lost, though in her preoccupation with nothing in particular she had forgotten that human abode was nearer than she had desired.

"Good morning, Miss Amanda," said a cheery and oddly distinctive high-pitched voice. "What brings you so far from home?"

Amanda glanced toward the sound. Some thirty feet away among the trees stood Maggie McFee. A large basket of the twigs she had been gathering sat on the ground at her feet.

"Walking home," replied Amanda.

"From the village?"

Amanda nodded casually.

"I had only just this minute finished with my load," said Maggie, "and was thinking about lunch. How would you like to join me?"

Amanda considered the prospect momentarily. She was still not anxious to return home, and despite the woman's known peculiarities,

Amanda liked her. After a moment she nodded her assent, even allowing the hint of a smile to curl the edges of her lips.

"Good!" said the woman, "then come along."

Amanda turned off the path and followed her through the trees.

"I'll carry the basket for you," said Amanda, a moment of brightness in her disposition, like yellow winter's crocus, poking its head out of the ground toward the sunlight of the woman's friendliness.

"Thank you, dear!" replied the woman, stopping to set the basket down. "I'll just gather another armload myself."

She proceeded to pick up another small bundle as Amanda lifted the basket, and soon they were walking off together toward the woman's humble home.

"Come, Bobby," Maggie called out in the direction of the barn as she and Amanda emerged into a clearing at the edge of the wood and approached the cottage. "We've a guest for lunch!"

Immediately her husband's bald head popped out the top half of the rough-sawn double door.

"Why 'tis the daughter o' Master Charles!" he cried. "Welcome t' ye, Miss Amanda!"

The next instant the bottom half of the door swung open and he was striding forward to greet their guest. Already Amanda's spirits had perked up considerably. For odd as the man looked, and strange as sometimes were the things he said, even temperamental young Amanda Rutherford loved Bobby McFee.

He shook her hand enthusiastically, then returned briefly to the barn while Maggie led her into the cottage.

"Sit down, Miss Amanda," said Maggie as they walked inside.

The girl willingly complied. The cool darkness felt good, for the day had grown warm as she had walked, and she was more than a little fatigued.

Maggie began bustling about the small kitchen, and before many minutes had passed, a plate of thick-sliced dark brown bread appeared on the table. Another plate containing generous slabs of butter was set down beside it, followed by a cheese, a jug of cold milk, and all needful implements to consume the simple yet bountiful provision.

Bobby came through the door just as Maggie joined their guest at the table. He sat down, and without a word to either of the other two immediately began to pray.

"*Our Lord,*" he said, "*all the earth's bounty is yours, and we thank ye for*

*providing this small measure from yer abundance, not merely t' sustain and
strengthen us t' live the lives ye've called us t', but also that we might enjoy it.
With grateful hearts we thank ye that life is a good thing when we let ye direct
our paths through it. Thank ye for bringing young Miss Amanda's steps across
our path on this day, and may her life with ye be as rich as the one you have
given us, yer humble servants. Amen."*

Amanda scarcely heard the words. She had grown used to prayers
at mealtimes, for her father and mother had adopted the same custom.
It was a ritual, she assumed, which the whole world complied with as
some sort of requirement prior to the partaking of food but from
which she had been spared for the first seven years of her life. She never
gave the *content* of such prayers much thought.

"What brings ye out our way this fine morning?" asked Bobby Mc-
Fee as he passed the bread and cheese to their guest and poured out
three glasses of milk.

"I was walking home from the village."

"On some errand for your mother, no doubt?" said Maggie.

"No errand—only walking."

"We haven't seen ye in many a day," said Bobby. "And we haven't
really had much of a conversation in a month o' Sundays. Now, I hear
tell that ye've actually had words with the queen herself."

"I did!" replied Amanda brightly. "She was even older than you, Mr.
McFee."

Bobby threw back his bald head and roared with delight. "Was she
now? I don't doubt it. The good lady Victoria's been our queen many
a long year. Did she speak t' ye, lass?"

Amanda nodded, her mouth at the moment too full of a bite of
bread to reply.

"What did she say t' ye?"

"That I would turn the world on its ear when I was older," replied
Amanda as best she could amidst the bread.

"I see—and why did she say such a thing t' ye?"

"Because I told her I will be prime minister someday, just like my
father is going to be."

This time poor Bobby McFee did not know whether to let his laughter out again or keep it in. He chose the latter, though the matter required extraordinary strength of will to accomplish. He nodded his
head twice with a look of significance as if to say, *"Ah ha . . . I see every-*

thing clearly now!" and left Amanda free to interpret the expression however she chose.

"So your father is going to be prime minister, is he?" now asked Maggie. "Did he say so himself?"

Amanda shook her head.

"I said it for him," she answered.

"And how is yer father?" asked McFee.

Amanda shrugged, her expression suddenly changing.

"He never talks about London anymore," she said. "Or about Parliament or going to balls or being prime minister or anything!"

"He's a good and God-fearing man, yer father."

Amanda made no reply. Bobby's words may have been true, but what was that to her? She liked her father better before God was around. The wise old Irishman saw that their guest was thinking more than she was saying.

"Perhaps ye're not agreeing with me, eh, lass?" he suggested in a happy yet probing tone.

"Why should I? He was going to take me to London with him. He was going to take me to a ball when I was ten, and now everything is different," said Amanda. "And I'm tired of them telling me what to do all the time," she added, then closed her teeth around a large bite of bread and chewed it vigorously.

"Ah—ye don't think yer father ought t' tell ye what t' do?"

"I'm old enough to do what I want."

"How old are ye now?"

"Nine."

"Nine!" repeated Bobby expressively. "'Tis old indeed."

"Almost old enough to go to a ball! My father promised." Her lip jutted. "But that was before."

"Before what, Miss Amanda?"

"Before . . . before God."

There was a short silence around the table.

"Well, then, what do *you* think about God?" asked Maggie at length.

"I think everything was fine until Mum and Papa started talking about *him* all the time."

"What do they say about him?"

"That they have to do what he tells them."

"Oughtn't we do what God tells us?"

Amanda half nodded, half shrugged.

"What would ye do if he told ye t' do something?" asked Bobby.

"Oh, I'd probably do it," answered Amanda without much conviction.

"And you'll do what God tells you when you're older?" asked Maggie.

"I don't know."

"If you don't like your own father and mother telling you what to do, Amanda dear," the woman went on, "what are you going to think when you're older and God tries to tell you what to do?"

"Well—it's different with God," replied Amanda with confidence.

"*Is* it different?"

"If *he* ever told me to do something, I suppose maybe I would do it."

"But it bothers you that your parents try to do what he tells them?"

Amanda did not answer. Although adept at using logical arguments to get her way with her parents, she was not really interested in having logic applied to her own attitudes.

There was a brief silence.

"They let me do what I wanted before *he* was involved in everything. That's when everything changed. Now there are all sorts of new rules."

"Ah, so that's it—God made your father and mother change, and they began treating you differently and making more rules . . . and you don't like it?"

"No I don't."

"That's what yer father's there for," now said Bobby, "t' help teach ye t' do what ye're told, so that later ye'll be able t' do what *God* tells ye. How do ye expect t' be able t' do the one later if ye don't do the other now?"

"I don't like *anybody* to tell me what to do," said Amanda emphatically.

"Why?"

"I don't know," replied Amanda, squirming in her chair. "It doesn't feel good."

"No, I don't suppose it does. But, ye say," Bobby asked, "—if *God* told ye t' do something, then it would be different?"

Amanda nodded.

"Ye wouldn't mind how *that* felt?"

"It doesn't matter," said Amanda.

"Why's that?"

"God's never told *me* to do anything."

"Hasn't he now, lass!" exclaimed Bobby. "Why that will come as some news t' the old apostle Paul."

"Who's that?" said Amanda, though she had heard his name often enough in the village church during the last two years.

"Just the man who wrote some words in the Bible that were nothing more nor less than God speaking right t' young folks like yerself."

Again Amanda shrugged, not so sure she wanted to hear more.

"It was he who said *Children, obey yer parents.* So ye see, Amanda lass—God *has* told ye something t' do. And 'tis something ye're obliged t' do cheerfully and happily."

Amanda sat silently chewing the last of her bread, thinking to herself that maybe it hadn't been such a good idea to come here for lunch.

A moment later Maggie rose and walked across the room. From the open desk portion of a curiously ornate oak secretary, Amanda saw her pick something up. She returned holding what to all appearances was a Bible of exceeding age. Its black leather cover was well worn and beginning to crack and peel. She handled it with reverence, yet did not let admiration for the age and cover prevent her from appropriating what was far more important, even had the rare edition been worth a thousand pounds, the truth of its contents.

She sat down again at the table, opened the sacred book, and carefully turned through its thin, worn pages.

"This is my mother's Bible, Amanda," she said, "and my grandmother's before her. I was young when my grandmother died, probably not as old as you are now. But I can remember her telling me that if a body doesn't begin early in life to see the mysteries of the kingdom, they become harder and harder to see as ye get older. 'Margaret, my child,' she would say, 'a boy or girl's got to get their feet moving along the right road as soon as they can. Developing the kind of inner sight that makes you able to see what the people of the world're unable to see, that can't be gotten in a day or a week or a year. The high things of God take a lifetime to learn. That's why you must point your eyes toward them as early as you can. The Lord will take anybody, anytime, and will do his best with them. But whoever's got the chance ought to get their eyes open early, so that the Almighty has time to let his mysteries get down deep into their character.' "

The woman fell silent as she turned back several more pages.

"This was one of her favorite passages," she said after a moment.

"Unto you is given," she read, "to know the mystery of the kingdom of God, but unto them that are on the outside, all these things are said in parables."

Maggie paused again, then glanced across the table toward the girl.

"Do you hear, Amanda?" she said. "—*Mystery*. That is what the Lord calls life in the kingdom of God. It takes a special kind of eyes to see into it. Your father and mother have discovered that mystery. Bobby called your father a *good* man, and he is. He's always been kind to the people of the region. But now there's something more to him that many don't understand—just like it sounds to me that you yourself aren't understanding it. It's a mystery that's waiting for you to discover, lass, just like he did."

Maggie looked down once more at the page in front of her and read further: " 'That seeing they may see and not perceive, and hearing they may hear and not understand.' Do you hear the words, Amanda dear? 'Tis just what you're doing with your father—you're *seeing* him, but you're not understanding the mystery that's in him."

"What mystery?"

"The mystery of God, child. The old apostle said to young Timothy that *great was the mystery of godliness.* I'm thinking that same mystery's alive in your father ... and maybe God wants *you* to discover it."

Amanda was silent. She didn't like getting preached at any more than she liked being told what to do. She heard enough of this kind of thing at home, although her father didn't talk about mysteries—in fact, she had no notion what all the nonsense about mysteries was about. Bobby and Maggie had never talked like this to her before, and she didn't like it at all.

"No one ever finds that mystery, lass," said Bobby softly, "and lets it do its work of opening the eyes and ears, as long as the only person he wants t' please is himself. That's why 'tis important for young folks like yerself t' learn t' see the good, not the ill, in their fathers and mothers. 'Tis where learning t' see the mystery o' godliness starts. 'Tis why God tells young folk t' obey and please them."

Amanda had finally had enough. She got up from the table and walked out of the cottage. She didn't want to listen to any more of *this*.

It fell silent around the table. The old couple sat awhile, both praying inwardly for the daughter of the man and woman they had done so much to bring into the family of faith.

"Did we push the lass a bit far, Bobby?" said Maggie after a moment.

Her husband sighed. "I don't know, Maggie. We've been praying for her so long, and Master Charles and Lady Jocelyn have been praying, and I really thought she'd be ready t' be led along a wee bit more. But it doesn't seem that the humility o' the father and mother's yet found its way into the daughter."

"We must keep praying, just like Elijah under the juniper tree. The poor lass's mind isn't set on the high things yet. We must pray that the doors of her mind stay open enough for words of truth to get in."

Bobby rose slowly. "I'll wander out t' the barn. Perhaps she may yet be lingering nearby."

41

A Conversation in the Barn

*B*obby McFee emerged into the sunlight, shielded his eyes with his hand, and glanced about. The girl was nowhere to be seen.

He walked across the worn pathway and into the barn he had left twenty or thirty minutes earlier. Leaving the door opened, he resumed his work. Soon he was whacking away at a thick board with hammer and chisel.

A form darkened the doorway.

He glanced up. Amanda's silhouette stood in the sunlight shining in from outside.

"Come in, Miss Amanda," said Bobby. "I'm just needing an extra pair o' hands t' steady the end o' my lumber there."

Amanda came forward slowly through the door into the darkened building. The sights and smells of the barn and straw and animals and leather settled her agitated mood.

"Put your hands on the end o' it there," said Bobby. "Hold steady—"

The next instant a loud whack sounded, and a great chip of wood flew out from under his blade and to the ground.

"Perfect!" he exclaimed. "Thank ye, lass! Ye can relax now."

He eased the board back onto the center of his workbench, set down his hammer and chisel, and drew in a deep breath.

"Do ye not love the smell o' wood when a man's cutting at it and making things o' it?" he exclaimed.

"I never thought about wood having much of a smell," remarked Amanda, speaking now for the first time since leaving the table. Her tone was slightly peevish. Yet she was not inclined to bicker further.

"Ah, lass—wood's got the smell o' the earth in it, the smell o' growing things. And 'tis the smell the Master loved when he worked in his father's carpentry shop. That makes it all the more holy a smell t' this nose o' mine. *He* was one who learned t' do what his father wanted," McFee went on as he turned and ambled toward the back of the barn where a lone cow chewed lazily about with its nose in a trough of hay.

"That's why he was Savior o' the world, lass—because he did only what his Father in heaven wanted. *He* knew the mystery," he said, then stopped to chuckle to himself. "What am I saying?" he added, still chuckling, "—he *is* the mystery! And he learned the mystery first, I'm thinking, right in his earthly father's carpenter's shop, from chipping and sawing and planing and pounding away at wood just like this.— But come, Flora here needs some oats."

McFee led Amanda across the hard-packed dirt floor to a bin where two large filled burlap sacks stood on end, one of them open at the top.

"Here's ye a bucket, lass," said Bobby. "Fill it up and take Flora the rest o' her dinner."

Amanda looked up at Bobby with an uncertain expression, as if he must have been joking.

"Go on, lass—'tis perfectly safe."

Tentatively Amanda reached in and scooped handfuls of oats into the bucket. When it was full she carried it to the cow and dumped it into the trough alongside what was left of the hay. Flora's large wet nostrils immediately sent bits of the grain flying about with warm puffs of breathy anticipation. Then her long tongue reached out in a great curling motion to investigate the oats.

Amanda watched in fascination. At length curiosity overcame her. She sent out a hand with probing caution, and gently touched the rough wet thing with her finger. The next instant she drew it quickly back, laughing as she did.

"She won't hurt ye," chuckled Bobby.

"It felt funny!" giggled Amanda, the child-innocence surfacing from within her.

"The tongue's a curious device, all right," said Bobby. "But all she wants is her oats."

Bobby took a step or two back. Amanda continued to stand watching the cow scoop the grain she had provided into its mouth.

"What do you suppose Flora would do if I was t' tie a rope about her neck and lead her outside t' her pasture?" Bobby asked after a minute or two of silence. "Would she follow me out?"

"Yes," answered Amanda. She had seen McFee leading his cow in the fields more than once exactly as he described.

"Would she mind it?"

"No."

"Right ye are, lass. The animals don't mind being told what t' do. 'Tis because it's the most natural thing in the world. And Flora'd be out in the field today if she wasn't about t' give birth to a new wee calf. So I kept her in, and she obeys that just as well as if I'd led her outside. Why do you suppose humans, o' all the creatures, *don't* want someone else telling them what t' do?"

"I don't know. I only know I don't like it." The independent young woman suddenly replaced the child.

"Of course ye don't, lass. No one does. But there's nothing else that life's for than t' learn that one thing—how *not* t' do what ye yerself want. That's all this earth's for—t' teach us t' do what someone *else* wants."

"Who?"

"Who else? God himself. He's trying t' teach us that from the day we open our eyes."

"How? He never taught me anything."

"Hasn't he now!" said Bobby with an expression of grave astonishment.

"No," insisted Amanda.

"He'd no doubt be a mite surprised if ye told him so."

"Why?"

"Because the way he teaches us t' do what he wants is by our first learning t' do what those people around us want us t' do, those who are over us, our mothers and fathers first o' all. That's why Maggie and I said that doing what yer father and mother say is the best thing in all the world ye can do."

Amanda saw that she had been tricked. She promptly exited the barn without another word.

42

Paris in Spring

$\mathscr{A}$ lovelier city than Paris in midspring could not be imagined.

Up and down both sides of the great river Seine extended spectacular rows of blossoming ornamental cherry and other fruit trees. In the city's multitudinous parks a profusion of color from millions of flowers spread a gay atmosphere into every heart to whom nature was capable of speaking its living secrets. Along the Champ de Mars, under the shadow of the Eiffel Tower, built in 1889 to commemorate the hundredth anniversary of the French Revolution, tourists and lovers strolled happily amid the bright blossoms of God's handiwork and the fragrant aroma of freshly mown grass.

The secretive business being conducted over the table of a sidewalk cafe overlooking the Seine, however, had to do with neither flowers, nor monuments, nor love. The two had met here before, though the discussion now in progress concerned whether it would be prudent for them to do so again.

"I cannot come to France or Italy twice a year indefinitely," the one had just said, speaking in French so as to arouse no suspicion, but with an accent that would have curiously reminded an expert linguist of such distant outposts of Europe as London and Budapest. "This time it was especially difficult to get away by myself."

"Perhaps you are right," replied the other, in a French not so cultivated, and containing only the eastern influence. "I will look for some alternate method to get the information to you."

"Are there reliable possibilities?"

"We have many contacts throughout France and Italy."

"What about Germany?"

"Germany grows troublesome."

"You must find someone able to cross the Channel without being noticed. My husband suspects nothing. I want to keep it that way."

"We will locate the right person. Money is always a powerful inducement. In today's climate there are always those who can be persuaded to join nearly any cause."

"I must remain able to move about freely in England. Introducing an unknown could jeopardize the peaceful slumber of our associates there."

"What about . . . your son?"

"Hmm," murmured the woman thoughtfully. "An intriguing possibility. He is yet young. But the time may come."

"I will speak to the committee. We will proceed with caution. I will trust no untested newcomer with vital information. We will discuss further this possibility I have raised. In the meantime, you know what to do with this."

He slid a manila packet across the table.

"Borsheff will have it within the week."

"What do you have for me?"

Another envelope was exchanged.

Their business completed, there was little more to be said. The man stood first and left, followed at an appropriate interval by the woman, whose exit took her in the opposite direction.

As she went, she heeded neither pink clustered blooms on the trees nor the merry strains of the sidewalk accordionist. Flowers and springtime were for those with happy music in their souls. The footsteps of these two beat to the distant drum roll of revolution, not the harmonies of springtime dances.

43

The London Rutherfords

Several hours had passed by the time Amanda Rutherford again wandered back toward Heathersleigh Hall.

"Amanda . . . where *have* you been?" asked her mother as Amanda entered through the kitchen. "We've been looking everywhere for you."

Jocelyn Rutherford was just pouring boiling water from a kettle into two ornate silver teapots, while Sarah Minsterly set biscuits and assorted cakes onto a large tray.

"We have guests, remember, dear," Jocelyn went on. "Please wash up and then come to the east drawing room."

"Must I, Mother?—I'm really very tired," replied Amanda with the hint of a whine, her mood souring with the first claim made upon her obedience.

"I want you to see them, dear. Your father's cousin and his family don't visit very often."

Amanda's face knotted in irritation. It was not so much that she did not want to visit her relatives, just that she resented whatever might be requested of her. She was actually curious, for it had been some time since she had laid eyes on any of the London side of the clan.

Fortunately for the sake of family harmony, notwithstanding lunch at the cottage, the long walk had drained some of her physical energy toward open resistance. After another moment she left the kitchen for her room without further comment. She changed her dress and shoes, combed her hair, and five minutes later she entered the drawing room with a sulky look—more and more characteristic of the normal expression of her countenance.

Sir Charles' first cousin Gifford, though without title, had, like his own father before him, done well for himself in the business world and was of some repute in certain of London's financial circles. That he continued to enjoy the family name, in spite of the fact that the male line of inheritance had gone to Charles from their shared grandfather, was accounted for by the marriage of Gifford's mother to a distant cousin with no direct connection to the family other than his name. Her married name thus remained the same as her maiden. The two cousins were both now *Rutherfords* more by accident than reason of heritage, and notwithstanding the divergent destinies toward which both were bound.

Gifford was in fact not an unimportant man, quite well connected in governmental and financial circles. Though Charles' recently bestowed title and rising stature among London's political elite annoyed Gifford considerably, he was himself not without almost equal influence. But the fact that however wealthy he might become he could never hope to be addressed as lord, while his cousin was not only a lord of the manor but a knight as well, made him all the more determined to reach the pinnacle of worldly success in whatever avenues lay open to him.

His son Geoffrey, seated beside him with his tea laced with sugar and his mouth full of biscuits, was a notable example of that obnoxious breed of offspring who has been given everything money can buy and taught along with it that money can buy everything. The result was an eight-year-old character declining as rapidly in one direction as the body surrounding it was developing in the other, and giving every indication that he would grow even more self-indulgent and self-centered than his Mammon-worshiping father.

As heir to a fortune mounting higher by the day, the boy had had every advantage lavished upon him. He studied with the most expensive tutors, wore nothing but the finest clothes in the latest of fashion, and was already being groomed to follow a path that would lead from Eton to university and perhaps even to the House of Commons one day. He could carry on a conversation with adults as well as any twelve-year-old, and he knew more about compound interest even than did Amanda's father. His cheeks were pudgy, for he ate as well as he dressed. They were also pale, for he was indoors more than he was out. Whether he would be good-looking as the years advanced it was difficult to tell. Greed had early come to dominate the outlook of his eyes, a quality certain to ruin any countenance, however appealing otherwise might be its features.

Charles and Gifford Rutherford, as cousins, had spent a good deal of time together as youngsters, though the fact had done little to draw them closer then or now. The spirits of the two men, even prior to Charles' conversion and especially so now, were motivated by such opposite objectives that it could hardly be said that respect flowed between them. The pained compassion Charles felt for Cousin Gifford was met by a silent and disdainful tolerance from the latter toward the former.

Gifford's wife, Martha, in the midst of a monologue concerning a certain dress she had recently purchased for the Chelsea ball next month, had just taken a second tea cake when Amanda walked in. A new round of greetings were exchanged, to which Amanda replied with forced smiles.

"Is this my little Amanda?" Martha Rutherford enthused, the tea cake poised halfway to her mouth. "My, what a big girl you have become."

The following bite into the tea cake afforded Amanda opportunity to walk across the floor. She sat down in a chair some distance from the conversation which attempted now to continue. She gave but cursory glance of greeting to the other members of the visiting family. Her brother George, now eleven, sat in a chair beside her father, obviously uncomfortable in his stiff collar but managing to behave himself. Younger sister Catharine, grown now into a lively but sweetly behaved five-year-old, occupied Jocelyn's lap. "Amanda," said Charles, "you remember your cousin Geoffrey?"

Now Amanda glanced up. Of course she remembered Gifford's son, a year younger than she was. She also remembered she didn't like him!

Before she had a chance to think further, Geoffrey jumped from the chair he had been occupying.

"Show me the tower, Amanda," he said, walking over and standing in front of her. "Father said if I came you would show it to me."

"I don't want to go outside."

"Father *promised* I would be able to see it," whined the boy.

"Amanda, please," interposed Jocelyn with attempted calm. "Geoffrey and his parents have come a long way for a visit."

"Let George show him, then."

"I want *you* to take me there," insisted Geoffrey, who was every bit Amanda's match. Now that it was clear she did not want to take him, nothing would satisfy him short of gaining his will over hers.

As she was prepared to plant her feet in outright refusal, suddenly a new thought entered Amanda's brain. A bright expression came over her face.

"All right!" she said, smiling cheerily. "Come on, Geoffrey," she added in a friendly tone. She jumped up from her seat and walked quickly from the room. Geoffrey followed, happy in what he thought was his victory, while Jocelyn and Charles exchanged surprised glances at their daughter's sudden cooperativeness.

George, however, remained where he was. He had more reasons than interest in the adult discussion to avoid inclusion in the outing. He wanted no opportunity for questions that might reveal to their cousin what he had recently discovered.

After Amanda and Geoffrey had exited through the French doors into the garden, the conversation in the drawing room continued in much the same vein as previously.

"I say," remarked Gifford, "now that you're so interested in matters of religion, no doubt you often make use of the Hall's old family Bible."

"I don't think I know of it," said the lord of the manor.

"Come now, Charles—a lover of books like yourself! You must be having me on."

"It would take several lifetimes to know intimately every book in the library upstairs," answered Sir Charles. "I think I am at least familiar with most of them, and honestly, Gifford, I know of no family Bible."

"My mother used to talk of it. She said her father spoke of it as quite an unusual heirloom, which he misplaced and never was able to find."

Charles did not reply that while growing up he had heard similar rumors, passed down from his father, and different only in the conviction expressed by one or two on the Devon side of the family tree that the Bible had been stolen from the Hall by the London Rutherfords.

"Well, I shall keep my eyes open for it," said Charles.

"If you run across it, my good man, I should very much like to see it."

44

Amanda and Cousin Geoffrey

◆ ◆ ◆

Meanwhile, once outside, Amanda hurried along the back wall of the house toward the northeast tower. It was the highest portion of the structure, reachable by any number of interior corridors. Why Amanda chose this long way around was anyone's guess. No doubt her reasoning was based on the fact that the longer the distance they had to traverse, the more difficulty her chubby cousin was likely to have. Geoffrey tried his best to keep up with her, but soon he was breathing hard.

"Slow down, Amanda," he said.

She did not reply. Geoffrey spoke again.

"Father says Heathersleigh should belong to him, not your father," he said.

"That's a lie!" rejoined Amanda in as loud a voice as she dared, for they were not altogether out of earshot of the rest of their families.

"He says your father is just letting the property run down. He would buy back all the land that has been lost. My father says he would turn it into a fortune."

"What business is it of his anyway?" retorted Amanda, turning to face her cousin with a scowl.

"It's the family estate. We're just as much Rutherfords as you."

"My father's the lord of the manor of Heathersleigh," said Amanda.

"*My* father's not impressed."

"The title and the estate both belong to him!"

They were farther away now, and in consequence her voice grew louder and her tone more sassy.

"You shouldn't even be Rutherfords," Amanda taunted. "That's only your name because of some old cousin nobody cares about."

"Now you're the one who's lying!"

"No I'm not. Besides, my father knows the queen. Does yours?"

"Yes he does!"

"My father's in Parliament. He's going to be prime minister one day."

"My father's *rich*," declared Geoffrey smugly. "Everyone in London knows him."

"My father's a *knight*," rejoined Amanda.

"If my father had his way, he'd take Heathersleigh away from your father."

"He'll never do it. I won't let him."

"Ha—what can you do about it? You're just a girl!"

"I'm going to be in Parliament someday too. Then you won't talk to me like that."

"Ha and double ha! You make me laugh."

"Just you wait and see."

"My father thinks Heathersleigh should belong to the most important Rutherford in England, not a religious do-nothing like your father."

The words stung Amanda. They went all the deeper in that she harbored similar thoughts. But she would never admit her own annoyances to one so despicable as Geoffrey.

"How dare he say such a thing!" she cried.

"I never said my father *said* it!" said Geoffrey. Suddenly he realized he had given away too much about the nature of the conversation between his father and mother on their way to Heathersleigh an hour earlier.

"How else would you know he was thinking that!" snapped Amanda. "Your father will never own Heathersleigh!"

Geoffrey was already shrewd enough in the ways of the world to realize it best not to contest the point further, so he held his peace. He fell into step behind Amanda as she now led the way through the thick wooden doorway at which they had arrived. He continued to follow up a narrow circular flight of stairs.

Breathing heavily—Geoffrey more than Amanda, for his waist was as puffy as his cheeks, his legs were shorter, and his suit was tight-fitting about the neck—the two cousins at length reached the topmost point of Heathersleigh Hall.

A single room sat atop the cylindrical stone tower, from whose several windows one could look out upon marvelous vistas of the countryside in every direction. What had been the original purpose of the construction, no living person knew. It had been used through the years as lookout, as prayer chapel, as incarceration chamber, as secret place of play for servant children and their friends, and even as lodging quarters for a tutor who had been hired to teach the brother of Amanda's great-grandfather. What had been the latter's son's carpentry scheme, no one knew. Old Lord Henry Rutherford's fear of his wife's specter, coupled with his own insanity, had closed off any light he might have been able to shed on the Hall's history. If anyone was going to find out what had been in his mind when it was still functioning with clarity, George was at present the most likely candidate. He had little inkling yet, however, into what mysterious and spectral pathways his explorations had inadvertently stumbled. The tower was not currently utilized for other than an occasional visit to gaze out upon the Devonshire landscape.

"Here, you go in first," said Amanda, turning the key that stood in the lock, then swinging back the door, which ground on its metal hinges. "I'll let you have the first view."

Geoffrey crept through the door into the empty room.

Suddenly he felt a shove against his side. The next instant he heard the door slam behind him, and he was left alone within the round stone walls.

"Amanda, you let me out of here!" he cried.

"Not until you take back what you said about Heathersleigh running down."

"I will not—it's true!"

"Take it back, Geoffrey! Say that we're the only ones with a right to Heathersleigh."

"No, I won't! If Father says it should be his, I believe him."

"Liar!"

"Let me out of here . . . I'll tell Father!"

Amanda crept to the edge of the stairs and sat down.

"Amanda!" cried a voice behind her.

Amanda said nothing. She continued to sit silent and unmoving.

"Amanda . . . *please!*" Geoffrey's voice now contained a pleading tone. The eight-year-old was surfacing again, as the young man of the world retreated into the background, for he had begun to be afraid.

Several seconds of utter silence followed. Amanda held her breath, determined not to be heard. Neither could she detect the ear pressed tightly to the other side of the keyhole, where in fact another key should have been, straining for any sound of her breathing.

Another few moments passed, followed gradually by the whimpering sounds of the forlorn boy beginning at last to cry. She had conquered him. She continued to sit in the silence.

Presently it grew quiet on the other side of the door. Amanda listened intently. Geoffrey's crying ceased. Several long seconds of deathly silence passed.

Amanda thought she heard something, although what, she couldn't tell. It sounded like the scraping of stones followed a few moments later by a kind of faint jingling noise.

What was Geoffrey up to? Now it went silent again.

———————— ◆ ◆ ◆ ————————

Inside the room, Geoffrey had crept back to the door to listen. Suddenly a great metallic clank sounded against his ear as the bolt slipped back out of its slot. He leapt back a step, then stood upright and gave a shove at the door. It gave way and he found himself on the landing.

The only evidence of Amanda that remained was the sound of her quickly descending footsteps echoing back up the circular staircase.

45

Difference of Opinion

The day had already become a warm one, though the sun had not yet advanced more than two-thirds of the way to its zenith. The ground was moist and the grass green, lush, and growing rapidly from recent rains. Yet the work at which the men labored was as dry and dusty as had it been August instead of late May.

The season for sheep shearing had come, and though Gresham Mudgley could not have afforded to pay a single man to assist him, on this day he had four besides himself and his stout, hardworking wife, Betsy, engaged in the yearly ritual.

By midday, they were nearly done. Mudgley's flock of Wensleydales and Oxfords was not large, though most years it took him and Betsy all of two or three days to shed his several hundred animals of their winter coats.

A single-horse carriage approached. The workers paused and glanced up, amid tiny struggling hooves and legs and a cacophony of bleating.

"'Tis yer lady wife, Master Charles!" called out Bobby McFee, as he set a newly shorn animal upright on its feet, giving its white, woolless rump a slap and sending it scurrying off across the grass suddenly free from its burden.

Charles glanced up. "So it is, Bobby," he rejoined. "Perhaps she's come to lend us a hand."

"I agreed to accept yer kind offer, milord," said a third man, the owner of the sheep, who at the moment was clipping the last strands from the animal that lay under Charles Rutherford's restraining hands, "but I *won't* be letting your wife sully *her* fair hands in the coarse dirty hair of my darlings."

"Not to worry, Gresham. I think she's come on another errand."

Charles righted the animal he had held for the expert clipping of Mudgley's hand. Now he sent it on its way after Bobby McFee's.

"Jocelyn!" he said, rising from his knees and walking toward the head of the larger beast his wife had just reined to a stop. "To what do we owe this unexpected pleasure?" He took the reins while Jocelyn jumped to the ground. He gave her a kiss.

"The sheep all look so funny and small," she said, glancing around where some of the newly shorn animals grazed in the grass nearby. "I never accustom myself to how tiny the animals actually are that hide under all that wool."

"They do shrink considerably!"

"But, Charles—you said you would have the whole flock shorn in two hours with your new electrical device."

"What would you tell my wife, Gresham, in answer to her question?" said Charles with a smile, turning toward Mudgley.

"Meaning no disrespect, sir," answered the shepherd humbly, "but the old ways of doing things are usually the best ways of doing them."

Charles laughed. "In this case, Jocelyn, that is precisely the case. My contraption broke down within thirty minutes—just like all the others."

"How did it work until then?"

"Let me just say that Mudgley and his wife had five naked sheep on their way while George and I were still struggling with our first! *Some* day I will get the thing working properly. But for now, no modern device can keep pace with sharp clippers in the hand of an expert."

As they spoke, Mudgley took the brief lull as opportunity to send his sharpening stone scraping with a few quick deft strokes across the blades of his scissors.

"Well, I thought you all might be in need of refreshment," she said laughing. "I have lemonade and tea, depending on whether you want something cold or hot." She turned back to the carriage, and lifted a large basket out and onto the ground.

"Ah, the lady's an angel!" exclaimed McFee.

"No, Bobby," replied Jocelyn laughing, "only a wife who recognizes hard work and a hot sun.—Where is George, Charles?" she asked.

"In the pasture south of the house with Bloxholm and the dogs. They're rounding up the last of the herd."

"So, even without my husband's invention, do you mean you're almost finished?"

"That we are, milady," replied Mudgley, setting down stone and scissors and now approaching, wiping his forehead with the back of his hand. The gesture accomplished little, however, for his arm was sweating as profusely as was his face. "And I'm more indebted to yer husband and son, and McFee here and Bloxholm, than I can say."

She poured out a tall glass of lemonade from the canister, and handed it to the shepherd.

"Thank you, ma'am," he said, taking it and downing half its contents in a single swallow.

"Where is your wife, Mr. Mudgley?" asked Jocelyn.

"She just left for the cottage, milady," he replied, nodding his head toward the dwelling at the edge of the pasture, "to see what she can find for dinner for the lot of us."

"Then I am just in time. I have Sarah making dinner for you all right now over at the Hall. I'll just run after Mrs. Mudgley and tell her it's all taken care of, and that I shall expect her to join us.—Charles, how much longer do you think you shall be?"

"We will have the last of the sheep unclothed within the hour."

"Perfect," said Jocelyn, returning to the carriage, "—You'll bring everyone over?"

"Just leave the tea and lemonade!" he laughed. "This is hot work!" He handed her the reins.

"I'll ride over and fetch Mrs. Mudgley. I'll see you all at the Hall."

"Thank ye for the refreshment, ma'am!" called the shepherd after her.

He turned to pick up the blades of his trade. Already Charles had another animal in his grasp awaiting them.

It was but three or four minutes later when a commotion interrupted them from the general direction in which Jocelyn Rutherford had ridden. The sounds of galloping horses suddenly rose above the bleating of sheep. Even before Mudgley, McFee, and Charles could glance up from the work at which they were occupied, a small red fox darted past at a distance of twenty or thirty yards. Two or three yelping hounds came next, flying across the fields in a howling uproar, heedless of sheep and men alike.

Pursuing them at breakneck speed rode a young horseman. Only seconds before he had torn around the corner of the Mudgley cottage, sending sod and greenery into the air from Mrs. Mudgley's patch of vegetables. Her flock of chickens fled for their lives, scattering in a cackling frenzy in every direction. Behind the first rider, equally heedless of the damage being done by the hooves beneath them, galloped a band of a half-dozen or so riders doing their best to keep pace with the boy.

Observing the careless trespass against his home and garden, Mudgley dropped his scissors, leapt to his feet, and ran yelling in outrage toward the intruders. The same instant Charles let go of the half-naked sheep and likewise jumped up. He sprinted forward between the fox and its human pursuer, who was galloping straight into their midst. The whole fracas added to the considerable consternation of the sheep, who already were scurrying about in bleating dismay on account of the hounds who had just flown by.

"Whoa—hey there, young man!" cried Charles, running fearlessly in front of the horse with his hands in the air.

"What the . . . get out of—" cried the boy, as if he had not even seen the sheep-shearing crew until that very instant.

Whatever disrespect the lad was about to utter was cut short by the scrambling, skidding, rearing motion of his whinnying horse. Charles reached up and grabbed hold of the reins near its mouth. The rider nearly tumbled out of his saddle over the beast's head. Righting himself quickly, he tried to grab the reins and free himself from Charles' restraining grasp.

"Let go!" cried the lad angrily. He lifted his riding whip into the air. "You're letting the fox get away!"

"And you have no right to ride across this man's property so wildly," rejoined Charles, grabbing the whip out of his hand with a quick and unexpected move. "Now calm yourself or you'll only agitate your mount all the more."

By now the rest of the hunting party had ridden up in a noisy thunder of hooves over the turf, and gradually slowed. They were expensively outfitted in the most fashionable hunting attire, aristocrats every one.

"What do you think you're doing!" cried Mudgley, running toward them as they reined in. "You've ruined my garden. No doubt you've killed more than one of my laying hens with your madcap games!"

"Tut, tut, old man," said the leader of the party rudely. "Keep away, or you as well as your chickens shall feel my horse's feet. Now let us pass—our hounds are disappearing."

Still holding the reins of the young man's horse and leading it along behind him, Charles now approached the leader of the tense scene.

"I think the law would take Mr. Mudgley's side in the matter, Holsworthy," he said in a tone which was the last thing the marquess of Holsworthy anticipated.

An angry retort was about to escape the latter's mouth when he suddenly recognized the man who had spoken to him with such confidence. A humorous smile passed across his lips.

Furiously impotent, the boy, who appeared to be eleven or twelve, fumed in his saddle. "Father, the fox is getting farther away! Make this man let me go."

Ignoring his son, the marquess now led his horse a little away from the rest of the group. He motioned Charles aside. Charles handed the reins of the boy's horse to Bobby McFee—for he had already seen enough not to trust the lad not to bolt if given the chance—then followed.

As they went, the marquess's daughter, a girl one year older than her brother, impatiently glanced about for any temporary amusement which might be available. She spotted George some distance away, approaching with the sheep. Slowly she led her horse toward him. She knew who he was, and the fact that he was a boy of approximately her own age and station appealed to her newly developing feminine desire for conquest, however brief might be the encounter.

Meanwhile, the marquess leaned over in his saddle and spoke to Charles in a confidentially low tone.

"I must say, Rutherford," he said with a grin in which a condescending air was notably mingled, "I didn't know you at first, although the garb of a peasant becomes you. What's the game?"

"No game, Holsworthy," replied Charles. "I am helping Mr. Mudgley with his shearing."

"I can see that, my good man," laughed the marquess incredulously, "but *why*?"

"Because he is my neighbor. Now why don't you take your party in a direction that keeps to the fields and woods."

"What does it matter to you, Rutherford? It's only a few vegetables and chickens."

"Yes, and they are *his* very few vegetables and chickens."

"Tut, tut, Rutherford. What difference does it make? He is no more than a common shepherd."

"He is a man, exactly like you and me. There was no reason for you to ride straight through his garden."

An angry reply rose into the marquess's throat, and his eyes flashed briefly. He thought better of it, however, and swallowed his annoyance. He did not like to be challenged. At the same time he could not help but be cowed by the calm authority of Sir Charles' bearing. He had heard peculiar things about this near neighbor of his, the lord of the manor of Heathersleigh. Now he had seen evidence of the truthfulness of the rumors with his own eyes. Notwithstanding this ridiculous masquerade as a sheep farmer, however, the fellow was still an influential man in London. It would probably not do to anger him.

Without another word, the marquess reined his horse around and rejoined the others.

"Hubert . . . Gwen!" he cried to his offspring, "let's see if we can still pick up the scent of that fox!"

He dug his heels into the side of his horse, and led the way, galloping off toward a wooded region. The rest of the mounted party followed. They were soon out of sight.

46

Invitation to the Country
♦ ♦ ♦

*W*hen Charles Rutherford next called at the parsonage of New Hope Chapel in London, he was met at the door by the pastor's housekeeper.

"Mr. Diggorsfeld's gone to the midlands, sir," she replied to his request.

"For how long?"

"He's been gone more than a week now, Mr. Rutherford."

Charles could tell by the tone of her voice that the matter involved something more serious than a holiday.

"What is it?" he asked.

"It's his mum, sir. She was very ill."

"Was . . . ?"

"I received word yesterday that she passed on, sir. Mr. Diggorsfeld will be staying to conduct the funeral."

"Oh . . . oh, I see. The poor man—were he and his mother close?"

"Not that Mr. Diggorsfeld confided in me, sir," replied the woman, "but I would have to answer you no, sir, I don't think they were. Even as he was leaving, the strain showed on his face. I could tell he thought she was dying, and he didn't know what to do to help her."

"Help her—how do you mean?"

"She was an unbelieving woman, sir."

"Oh, I see."

"And she always resented his choice of profession," the housekeeper went on. "That's what she told me once when she was visiting. And none too kind she was to me either, sir, or to Mr. Diggorsfeld. A hard lady, she was, and now she's gone to see what the fire can make of her *there*, that she wouldn't let be done by more comfortable means down here."

"Oh . . . hmm, I see. Well . . . thank you, Mrs. Alvington. I shall see Mr. Diggorsfeld when he returns. Good day."

Charles turned and walked away pondering what the woman might mean by such a strange remark.

◆ ◆ ◆

The mail arriving at New Hope Chapel the day following his return from the north contained a most unexpected letter. Timothy Diggorsfeld opened it eagerly, for he had already grown extremely fond of Charles Rutherford. As yet, however, even after their many visits, he was not yet fully aware what an important man his occasional visitor was.

Dear Timothy, he read.

As you know I have often mentioned my desire that you and my wife Jocelyn have an opportunity to meet. Thus far, however, she has not been to London since my first visit to New Hope Chapel. Truthfully, she is not altogether fond of the city, and so no trips are planned in the near future. From your good Mrs. Alvington I learned of your recent grief in the matter of your mother, and it strikes me that a few days in the country away from your normal routine might do your spirits good. We are therefore hoping you might be able to visit us here at our home in the near future.

June is a lovely month in Devonshire. Might you be able to spend two or three days with us, a fortnight from now, coming down perhaps on Monday so as not to interfere with your Sunday services? If you can arrange it,

I will take the days absent from my duties at Westminster, and return to the city with you.

> *We hopefully await your reply.*
> *Yours sincerely,*
> *Charles Rutherford*
> *Heathersleigh Hall,*
> *Milverscombe, Devon*

Diggorsfeld put down the letter with a smile. Many times he had resolved to begin paying closer attention to current affairs, but he hardly ever even glanced at a paper. And now a Member of Parliament had been visiting him for two years and he hadn't been aware of it! He *had* known Charles Rutherford to be a sensitive and caring man, as his invitation clearly revealed.

Within ten minutes a reply was in an envelope and ready for that afternoon's post. He would happily accept Mr. Rutherford's kind invitation.

♦ ♦ ♦

When the pastor of New Hope Chapel arrived at Heathersleigh, the remnants of his ordeal still showed on his face. His countenance was haggard and his expression drawn.

Charles saw his approach and ran out the front door.

"Timothy!" he said, reaching his friend before he was halfway across the drive from the carriage. "I am so glad you have come."

The two men shook hands and gazed into one another's eyes like old friends, which in truth they were on their way to becoming.

"I appreciate your kindness more than you know," replied Diggorsfeld.

"I am deeply sorry about your mother."

"Thank you," smiled the pastor with a thin smile.

"You look tired," said Charles. "I hope we will be able to help you rest and regain your spirit.—But come, let us go inside. I want you to meet my family."

Jocelyn was already out the door after her husband, and now approached with a smile. "Welcome to Heathersleigh, Reverend Diggorsfeld!" she said warmly.

As they approached one another, the newcomer could not prevent his eyes from glancing toward the obvious red blemish on his hostess's face. Having seen her till then only through the loving mind's eye of her husband, he was momentarily surprised. He faltered for only the briefest of instants before returning her smile.

Jocelyn saw the response. Her eyes flitted away as Charles completed the introductions. But she recovered as quickly as had their guest, and the two shook hands.

"I am delighted to meet you, Lady Rutherford."

"And I you, Reverend Diggorsfeld. But please, call me Jocelyn. We are not particularly fond of the *sir* and *lady* around here."

"As I have come to realize," laughed Diggorsfeld, already feeling invigorated by the warmth of the company of friends. They all now began making their way back toward the house together.

"It was not until I received your husband's invitation," their guest went on, "that I began to grow curious. I investigated and what should I discover but that he was a Member of Parliament. That he is *Sir Charles* and lord of the manor are facts I found out this past week by even further sleuthing of my own."

"What!" Charles exclaimed in laughter as they entered the Hall. "You've been spying on me?"

"Only catching up on my reading in some past issues of the *Times*. You cannot imagine how woefully illiterate I am concerning the whole political sphere."

"Well, I hope you will forgive me," said Charles as they reached the main staircase and started up. "I meant no deceit. I only wanted to be no more nor less than just myself when I visited you. Surely you can understand."

"Of course. But I still feel taken in by a good joke. And you let me babble on in my office about political parties!"

Charles could not help laughing.

"In any event," said the minister, "knowing who you are only gives me all the more reason to respect you. Jocelyn, you will, I hope, do me the like courtesy of addressing me as Timothy. I'm probably less fond of the *Reverend* than you are the *lady*."

Jocelyn nodded her assent.

"Good—I am glad that is settled," laughed Charles, "and we all know who we are!"

"Well," said Jocelyn, "we have arrived at your room. We shall have your bag brought up. Shall we meet you downstairs in the drawing room in, say, five or ten minutes for tea?"

"That sounds wonderful," replied the pastor. "But how will I find my way?"

"I will send Sarah to fetch you. She is the closest thing we have to a butler around here, but don't let *her* know I said so," she added with a laugh.

"Agreed." Diggorsfeld paused, and his face became serious. "I really *very* much appreciate your invitation," he said after a moment, addressing both Charles and Jocelyn. "It has been an extremely difficult and draining month for me. Your kindness means a great deal."

47
The Other Side of the Door

❧he following afternoon Charles and the pastor, two men of divergent backgrounds but now common objectives in life, walked about north of the Hall on the grassy expanse of lawn stretching out toward the wooded slopes in the distance.

"As prepared for death as you try to be," Diggorsfeld was saying, "there is always an element of surprise in it when it comes at last."

"Is that because it is the one human experience a person can never truly prepare for, since it is so foreign to anything we know in life?" suggested Charles.

"Perhaps. Yet I consider it an enormously beneficial thing to *attempt* to prepare for it, both our own death and that of those we love. Death is the final culmination of life. It has always seemed to me that we ought to look it in the face rather than shy away from it."

"Look it in the face," repeated Charles. "How do you mean?"

"I mean confront it confidently, with an attitude something like, 'Death, you may be unpleasant, you may bring tears. But I know the Lord of death *and* life. Thus I shall do my best to rejoice in both in their turn, and not be alarmed when you visit me, as you surely shall, or when you take my loved ones from me. I know you are but a door into more life. I know the sadness I feel comes only because I do not see through to the other side. If I could, my tears would be those of happiness.'"

"What about your father?" asked Charles. "Is he still living?"

"No," replied Diggorsfeld, "he died when I was young. I was but five and have only scant memories of him. His passing did not affect me as deeply as that of my mother three weeks ago."

"Your housekeeper took the liberty of telling me that you and your mother were not close."

"It is a sad fact, but true," replied the pastor. "Neither of my parents were believers. Actually, that fact troubles me far less in regard to death than it does many Christians."

"In what way?"

"I do not believe that death suddenly slams an impenetrable door in the face of God's sovereignty over his children, nor shuts out his love and omnipotence altogether."

"His *children*," said Charles with puzzled tone. "I understood you to say that your mother was *not* a believer."

"You heard me correctly," rejoined Diggorsfeld. "There are obedient children and rebellious children, but God remains the Father of them all. He made *every* creature and thus is Father to all, whether certain ones acknowledge the relationship or not."

"That sounds like something the McFees might say!" laughed Charles.

"Ah, yes—your old friends who led you and Jocelyn to the Lord," said Diggorsfeld. "I do hope I shall have the opportunity to meet them."

"Indeed, you shall," rejoined Charles. "Bobby is fond of speaking of God's immediate family, on the one hand, and his distant relations who do not acknowledge the familial bond on the other."

"An excellent concept. I like it! Yes—I must meet this brother."

"When I told him you were coming, he had the same reaction. I have told him as much about you, as you know about him. We will go out to the cottage for a visit tomorrow."

"Excellent."

"But back to your comment about God's children. I remain curious how *you* meant the term."

"Will you object if I shock you?" asked Diggorsfeld.

"I don't know," laughed Charles. "Try me."

"All right. I will answer your question by saying that God is even the devil's Father."

"What!"

"I will admit it a theological conundrum inquiring more deeply into the extent of God's love than many individuals care to contemplate—and that I scarcely know what to make of myself!"

"I should say so!" laughed Charles. "I don't know where to pigeonhole such an outlandish statement as that!"

"That is one of Christendom's most glaring problems," rejoined the pastor, "—the great need its advocates seem to feel to pigeonhole truth. Please take no offense. I mean only that the principles of our faith are not always so easy to fit into compartments as our human brains would like."

"But the devil!" repeated Charles.

"God created him," said Diggorsfeld. "That fact can hardly be denied."

"I suppose not."

"To my thinking, that makes God his Father. But I suggest we leave it at that. It is a pointless issue to contend over if it troubles you."

"I must admit, it does," said Charles, still bewildered. "I've never heard the like before. I'm not sure I can go along with you on it."

"No matter. The only point I would try to make is that in my mother's case, or anyone's, unbelief is merely a testimony against their own foolishness and blindness. But it cannot undo the cord of fatherness between God's heart and their own existence. They may shut their eyes in denial of that central fact of the universe. However, the Father who begat them remains, and continues pulsating life into them regardless of their denial."

"You do have a way of explaining things that is somewhat out of the ordinary," laughed Charles.

"So I am told!"

48

The Mystery of Our Hope

A thoughtful silence followed. It was Charles who next spoke.

"That reminds me of something I had been meaning to ask you," he said. "Your housekeeper made a most curious statement when telling me about your mother—something I could not make heads or tails of. Perhaps you could illuminate me as to what she meant."

He now repeated that portion of his conversation with Mrs. Alvington.

The pastor smiled. "She is referring to perhaps *the* central mystery of the Christian faith," he said, "what Paul often refers to as our *hope*. It is a truth obscured from most eyes by God himself for reasons which I must admit I do not altogether understand."

"Will you explain it to me?"

"I think now is not the proper time," replied Diggorsfeld, "if you can trust me with such a reply. As in the question of what might be the extent of God's fatherhood over his unbelieving children, his distant family, as it were—such things are not matters to be spoken of lightly. I would not desire a dispute of theology to arise between us and cause us to digress too far afield from our present discussion. When the time is right."

"I *will* trust you with that reply," nodded Charles.

It fell silent for a few moments as they continued to walk.

"Yet you say your mother's death was hard for you," said Charles, returning to the previous thread of the conversation, "in spite of this more expansive view of death you hold."

"Very hard. I had hoped she would recognize the truth on this side of the door. It is always infinitely better that way. It grieved me that my mother's heart remained hard, not only against her God, but also against her son. I am a sensitive human being, Charles, no different than you or anyone. It *hurt* that she harbored much against me. It *pained* me that I was unable to love her with the love which lay in my heart, because of her bitterness toward life. The tears I wept at her grave were not because she was one of the *lost*, as some might say. They were simply the tears brought on by the pain of the unrightness of the human condition—*the unrightness between her and me*. She never forgave me for who and what I was. That is a burden of sorrow I will have to bear the rest of my own earthly life."

They walked for some time in silence.

"I am very sorry," said Charles at length.

"It is part of my own story," said Diggorsfeld softly. "God carries my sorrows in his heart with the rest, and all is well. He even has sorrows of his own. We must be willing to bear our own share."

"Sorrows—what sorrows could God have?"

"We killed his Son," replied the pastor.

"Ah, yes ... I see. Of course."

"What sorrow must that have brought to the heart of the Godhead. The rebellion of Satan has not made of the universe a happy place, for God or his creation. There is happiness within it, of course. It is a *good* creation. But not *everything* in it is happiness."

"Good ... but not happy—an interesting distinction," remarked Charles.

"A *vital* distinction for us to understand," rejoined the pastor, "if we are to walk in peace with our God. And all will yet come right in the end."

The silence which followed was lengthy. It was again Charles who broke it.

"You know," he mused, "since the Lord guided my steps to you, and *back*, I should say, to Maggie and Bobby, and since Jocelyn and I gave our hearts to him, everything really has changed. It has only been two short years. Yet my former life seems a century ago."

"That is often the way people feel following a conversion."

"I must admit I had not thought much about death before now. I had to face it, of course, when my own mother and father died. I loved my father and still miss him. But their passing did not contain, as it were, the dimension of spiritual pain you have spoken of. Now that I consider it, however, as you and I have been talking, I think that if the Lord told me I was going to die tomorrow, I would not grieve for myself. I would be content. That is not to say I do not love life, for I do, or that I would not weep to be temporarily parted from my Jocie and others I love. I only say I would not feel a sense of grief over not having accomplished what I hoped to in life. The fact that I now know my heavenly Father lends a great peaceful covering over it, such that death no longer seems a separation or an ending to what I hold dear."

He paused and laughed lightly. "I don't know exactly what it is I feel. Have I made sense?"

"You make perfect sense, Charles. I understand completely. You would not choose to die. At the same time, you trust your Father so completely that death seems no more fearsome. If it came you would meet it with a smile."

"Exactly."

Even as he said the word, however, the expression on Charles' face changed.

"There *is* one thing," he said, "wherein I am not ready to leave this world."

Diggorsfeld glanced toward him with inquisitive expression.

"That concerns my daughter."

"Which one?"

"The older of the two."

"Amanda?" said the pastor. "She seems a charming and delightful girl."

"Indeed, she can be that—and more. But a change seems coming over her which Jocelyn and I cannot help but be anxious about."

"She is becoming—what . . . disobedient?" asked Diggorsfeld.

"Not anything so stark as that exactly. It's just that an undercurrent of dissatisfaction seems gradually more evident in her countenance. We so badly want Amanda to become what God wants her to be. But I'm not sure *she* wants that."

"It is sad," remarked the pastor, "that so many young people grow dissatisfied. It is not something, I confess, I thoroughly understand, not having gone through such a stage myself. I took a different path from my mother by becoming a Christian and choosing the ministry for my profession, which irritated her greatly. But as to the rest, I do not find within my own history that which makes me understand the conflicts many young people have with their parents."

"I did not experience such with my father, either," added Charles. "I was always grateful for how he planted my feet and set my vision in life."

"Obedience and gratefulness have never seemed odious to me," Diggorsfeld went on. "I would say they even seem natural. Yet it must be admitted that many young people do not find it so. The first son to walk this earth was a murderer. Rebellion began in the garden and has been with us ever since. Our Lord's story of the prodigal would not have found such a wide hearing if it were not true to life."

"I am certain you are right. But it is painful to go through it on the side of the parent."

"It is indeed grievous that so many choose such a road. Yet God loves them and never stops wooing and seeking them. I have great faith for such ones. He promises that his words will not return void. And by none is this promise more to be prayerfully grasped than by the parent awaiting such a return in the heart of son or daughter. Have faith, my friend. The Father forgets *none* of his little ones."*

49

The Keys

───── ♦♦♦ ─────

$\mathscr{I}$t was several weeks after their visit to Devon that Gifford Rutherford became aware of what his son had discovered behind a loose wall-stone in the small tower room at Heathersleigh Hall.

"What did you and Amanda talk about when you were alone?" the father had just asked.

"Oh, nothing," replied Geoffrey. Immediately he began to sweat. But the boy needn't have worried. His father was after information, nothing more. "She said her father knew the queen," added Geoffrey quickly. "I said so did you, and that you were rich besides."

"Good boy," smiled Gifford with fatherly pride. "Nothing more? She said nothing about the estate or her father?"

Geoffrey squirmed slightly in his chair. This was the portion of the conversation with Amanda about which he would do just as well to keep quiet.

"No . . . nothing," he said. "She locked me in the tower."

─────────

* See the introduction for a longer explanation of the historical context for the theological issues raised in this discussion.

"What—in that little room on top?"

Geoffrey nodded.

"The impertinent little vixen! She's as high and mighty as her father," said Gifford.

"I found these when I was there," said Geoffrey. From his pocket he pulled out a brass ring with two keys around it—one large, one very small and ornate.

"Let me see those," said Gifford. He leaned forward in his chair with sudden interest.

Geoffrey handed them to his father.

Gifford took them and jingled them in his hand for a moment. His expression grew serious. "What do they belong to?"

"I don't know, Father. They were behind a rock in the wall."

"Behind a rock—what do you mean?"

"A loose rock. I was sitting on the floor after Amanda locked me in, and I felt that one of the stones was loose against my back. I fussed at it with my fingers and it came out."

"What was there?"

"A hole in the wall, with these keys in it."

"After you took them, then what?"

"I replaced the stone."

"Did Amanda know about the keys?"

"I don't know."

"I mean, did she know that you had them?"

"I never said a thing."

"Good fellow! Let's just continue to keep this our little secret, shall we?"

"Yes, Father."

"I shall keep the keys, my boy, and put them in a safe place."

This was indeed a stroke of brilliant luck, thought Gifford to himself. He knew what kind of keys they *appeared* to be. Only time, and the chance to find out for himself, would prove whether he was right. It would not do to seek such an opportunity immediately. If the keys were found to be missing, another visit too soon might give him away. He could afford to be patient. He was doing all this for his son anyway, and Geoffrey was yet young.

In the meantime, he would keep his own counsel.

50

New Values, Hard Questions

◆◆◆

*D*uring tea on the evening following his lengthy talk with Charles, their guest made greater efforts than he had made previously to engage himself in dialogue with George, Amanda, and Catharine.

In all three he discovered an intellectual maturity beyond what would be expected from their years. The positive fruit of the rigorous training early in their lives was as evident as the negative fruit brought about by the corresponding *absence* of disciplinary regulation.

"We sometimes don't know what to do, Timothy," Jocelyn said later that same evening when the three were alone together in the sitting room. "We realize now that we fed the sense within Amanda that she was the center of the world and need answer to no one. We too readily gave her her own way. There were few restrictions placed on all three of the children. We were loving parents, but we were not *thorough* parents."

"How do they now respond to the changes in your spiritual outlook?" he asked.

"Amanda seems to resent our intrusion, wouldn't you say, Charles?" replied Jocelyn, glancing toward her husband.

He nodded. "She still thinks she ought to be the center of the world."

"Hmm . . . I see."

"It is my own fault," Charles went on. "When I now look back, I see that she is simply being the person I taught her to be. In one way, perhaps, she is hardly to be blamed. I suppose we pulled the rug out from under her when we altered the entire perspective and priority structure here at Heathersleigh."

"We knew she was confused at first," put in Jocelyn.

"Then her confusion slowly gave way to the dissatisfaction of which I've spoken," added Charles.

"And the other two children?" asked Diggorsfeld.

"They've adapted a bit more smoothly," replied Charles.

"Life didn't change as much for them," added Jocelyn.

"It isn't as if there haven't been occasional stresses with them too," said Charles. "I've had to confront George with obedience a time or two when he walked off a little sulkily. But George is rather a steady young man," said Charles, "and so he didn't let it affect his attitude afterward. An hour later everything would be fine between us."

"And Catharine was so young," said Jocelyn. "I don't know if she was even aware of the change. But it seems we turned Amanda's world upside down. I'm at a loss as to how to correct the situation. We would be greatly in your debt, Timothy, for whatever advice you might be able to offer."

"I'm not at all certain I am the best person to ask," he replied.

"Why do you say that?"

"I am not married. I have never been a father. I have not occupied your shoes. Who am I to speak to such things?"

"Perhaps you're not in our exact shoes," said Jocelyn. "But simply *being* a parent in and of itself means nothing. Any two people can become parents. Knowing how to train children is another matter. *We* are parents. Yet we now realize how little we have known all these years— to Amanda's detriment. We honestly would like to hear whatever you have to tell us."

"And to answer your other question," put in Charles, "—who you are to speak to these things, is God's man. You may be younger than me by six or eight years, and you may not be a father. But you have been walking with God considerably longer than either of us. My wife and I ask for your help, not as a parent, but as a wise and experienced Christian man whom we trust to tell us the truth."

Diggorsfeld smiled. "If only my congregation was as hungry for my words as the two of you," he said with an ironic smile. "I pour my heart out to them week after week. Yet more than occasionally must pound on the pulpit during my closing remarks to wake some of them up."

Charles laughed. "I assure you, Timothy, we will not fall asleep on you."

"What about your friends, the old couple?"

"The McFees?"

Diggorsfeld nodded. "From what you have told me, they sound like wise children of God. Their counsel may be useful to seek as well."

"We have spoken with them about Amanda. Their insights are generally accurate. Yet as long as the new direction of our training annoys Amanda, what can we do?"

Diggorsfeld thought a moment.

"On my part," he began after a moment, "let me say first that I consider one of the greatest measures of maturity the capacity to receive advice from another, along with the desire to turn the light of truth upon one's *own* self first rather than upon others. The fact that you want another's help, and that you take your own share of responsibility in the matter of your daughter, blaming no one but yourselves—these things tell me that you are already well on the way toward receiving the truth you seek."

"But it seems our efforts with Amanda are of less than no use," said Jocelyn with a sigh.

"What efforts?"

"Our effort to make up for our laxity of the past by attempting to draw boundaries around her attitudes and behavior now."

Diggorsfeld sighed. "Perhaps, however," he said, "such is exactly what she needs. You cannot make up for the past. Those days are gone. But in the same way as a horse is trained, Amanda must learn to happily submit to authority or she will never know her heavenly Father with the intimacy he desires. Your responsibility is to help her begin moving toward that, however, much as she may resist it at first. She must know that authority exists and is the ruling foundation for all things."

"And if she resists more and more vigorously?"

"That is always the chance a parent takes."

They continued to discuss the practical implications of the matter. The minister shared a number of Scriptures with Charles and Jocelyn, encouraging them to stand firm in their resolve to apply their new values to the rearing of their children.

"I'll admit, however," he said, "that changing directions so radically once a family is well established—I don't envy you. It is a difficult undertaking. The shock to a young person's predictable world can be great. Especially in that you are attempting to impose a new set of values and a new outlook on life that *you* have adopted, but that one of your children in particular is not interested in."

"I thought I was being so modern, so contemporary," sighed Charles, "so in touch with the best new thinking of what children need. Now I wonder if I did more damage than good."

"You mustn't be too hard on yourself, Charles," said Timothy. "The Lord called you and gave you a new outlook toward life, at a certain time. He had a reason for that. Amanda, too, is bound up in that eternal plan. We might not see it at present. But you must simply go on, prayerfully do the best you can from this moment forward, and leave Amanda in God's hands. It may be she has a story to live out in that plan of which the timing of your own conversion is an intrinsic part."

"We know you are right, Timothy," said Jocelyn. "But it is so difficult not to look back and feel we are partly responsible for her present independent nature. We feel guilty at times for our past mistakes."

It fell silent, as the three considered Jocelyn's words. These were no easy matters to dismiss lightly.

51

A Prayer Garden

◆◆◆

*Y*ou know," said Diggorsfeld at length, "an analogy just struck me between your daughter and the heather garden you showed me this afternoon."

"We'd like to hear it," said Jocelyn.

"Heather has always been something of a favorite with me," he said. "Even amid the wildness of its nature, it *always* blooms. It cannot be prevented from blooming."

He paused and smiled. "Somehow I find myself wondering if such is not the way God occasionally views us," he went on. *"You are an unruly little thing, my child,* I can imagine our Father saying. *Yet still you bloom. You cannot help it, for the beauty of my life is in you. I placed it there, and nothing you can do to yourself can keep that life occasionally from exploding into flower. Ah, but my child, there is so much more you* could *be, so much more I want you to be. I want you to become not merely a thin little bush struggling for survival, with a single blossom appearing every so often, but a whole garden with flowers* constantly *in bloom, flowers that are expressions of my life and my love and my goodness bursting out from within you always."*

"You paint a lovely picture, Timothy," said Jocelyn softly.

"I suppose that is why I love heather," he went on. "So many varieties exist, so many shapes and sizes and colors of foliage and flower, exactly like the human plant it resembles."

"And like our Amanda," added Charles, "—a wild growing shrub at present, but one . . ."

His voice trailed off.

"One which *will* be brought into glorious bloom one day," said Diggorsfeld, completing the thought. "In the same way that the two of you, as you told me earlier today when we were walking there, began to cultivate and train your heather garden, our heavenly Father will tend the garden of your daughter's character."

"It is a beautiful image," said Jocelyn.

"There are many blooms upon her plant even now," continued the pastor. "When she smiles, the radiance lights up an entire room. She has such energy, such strength and determination. And from what you have told me, I believe she also has a passion for justice, a concern for the weak and downtrodden. Look to these blooms and take heart. Pray diligently. In his time God will cultivate the whole into a thing of even greater beauty as she grows."

"You are right," murmured Jocelyn. "I have been so vexed with Amanda, I have almost forgotten to see these beautiful things in her."

"But how can we pray with faith, Timothy?" said Charles. "We are still so new at praying. To pray and believe . . . the command sometimes seems impossible."

Diggorsfeld laughed. "Believe me, experience in the Christian life will not remove that particular challenge! It is *always* difficult to believe when we pray."

"Then what are we to do? Are not our prayers answered in proportion to our faith? How will *any* of them be answered?"

"I will admit, it is one of the paradoxes of being a Christian. We are told to pray believing. Yet because we are human creatures, doubt is part of our nature. I love the statement the man made to the Lord—*I believe, help my unbelief.* Somehow, Jesus took those words as a statement of faith rather than of unbelief. I think perhaps it is our example."

"In what way?" asked Charles.

"I think God takes the *willingness* to believe and the *desire* to believe and the *attempt* to believe almost as if they *were* belief themselves," replied the pastor.

He paused, then smiled.

"Why not let that special corner of your grounds—your heather garden—become a prayer garden on Amanda's behalf?" he said. "Walk its paths lifting up your daughter to the heart of her heavenly Father, who loves her even more than you do. As you walk there, remember how you have cultivated your garden into a quiet retreat that reflects God's creativity. I'm sure it has been hard work, has it not?"

Charles and Jocelyn both nodded.

"No doubt much pruning was required. You had to pull out many weeds, reestablish borders and pathways, shape those shrubs which had become overgrown and scraggly. The heather submitted to the work of your hand. But Amanda may not be so compliant. Your prayers will be like the sunshine, always shining down to encourage growth upward toward the Source of life. Believe in faith that God will accomplish in her life what you are doing for your garden. Let the heather be a faith-picture to remind you that you are *willing* to believe, that you *desire* to believe, and that you *choose* to believe that God *will* draw Amanda to himself, in his time and in his way. Say to the Father, 'Lord, we believe in you for our Amanda. Help our unbelief.' Let the heather remind you that he will one day transform even the wild human-heather into a gloriously cultivated and blooming one."

Charles said nothing. He glanced at his wife.

Jocelyn was silently weeping.

52

Why Must God Be Good?

◆◆◆

The evening was advancing toward night.

Outside, the still quiet of dusk deepened over the wooded countryside as the shadows cast by the trees lengthened over Maggie McFee's flower garden.

Inside the white thatched cottage, however, the conversation was spirited and the fellowship rich. Maggie had just poured water for a second pot of tea and placed before her guests another tray of scones, butter, thick Devonshire cream, and jam. Her husband and the pastor from London were engaged in vigorous dialogue.

"Ye see, Mr. Diggorsfeld," said Bobby, "I've always felt that if a thing can't be done, I don't consider it t' be a matter o' faith at all. Faith's the belief a man can *do,* and nothing else."

Jocelyn and Charles had been listening with great interest to the exchanges between their friends, who had known one another for less than two hours but who, despite some twenty-five years difference in their ages, gave every indication of having been friends most of their lives. They had never heard such a discussion between experienced Christians and were fascinated.

Before his conversion, Charles had been in the habit of considering Christianity a religion for nonthinkers. He had long since discovered that philosophical and rational thought was by no means limited to his colleagues in London. If any lingering doubts remained in that re-gard, they would be put all the more soundly to rest by the end of this evening. For Diggorsfeld and Bobby had taken so many thought-pro-voking side roads into theological matters Charles was but faintly fa-miliar with that half the time, to his ears, they could have been speak-ing a different language. Yet ever did a practical simplicity of faith run like an unbroken theme through their comments. On that single im-perative were the two men in absolute agreement, something Jocelyn and Charles had never encountered in the sophisticated circles of the world out of which they had come.

"I couldn't agree more, Mr. McFee," replied the pastor to the Irish-man's comment. "How it warms my heart to find kindred spirits such as yourself and your wife . . . and you too, Charles and Jocelyn," he added, turning toward them. "I think that if I could visit the warmth of your cottage and partake of your tea, Mrs. McFee, and engage in discussion over things of the faith such as we have here tonight—as I say, I think if I could do such a thing once a month, it would do much to prevent the discouragement of my pastorate and act as a spiritual restorative for my soul."

"Ye're more than welcome at our humble home as often as ye can come," rejoined Bobby. "We'd be honored t' have ye visit us *oftener* even than every month."

"Thank you!" laughed Diggorsfeld. "That is indeed a wonderful of-fer! Perhaps I shall move to Devon and see if I can find a small chapel down here in want of a pastor."

"But why do you get discouraged, Mr. Diggorsfeld?" asked Maggie.

The pastor sighed. "Please don't misunderstand me, Mrs. McFee," he said. "I consider the pastorate the highest of possible callings. I am greatly blessed to be entrusted with such a lofty responsibility and privilege as conveying the Gospel into the lives of men and women."

"But you spoke of discouragement."

"My people, God bless them, are goodhearted souls for the most part. But they are incapable at times of seeing this simple truth that your husband has spoken—that a practical *do* must be associated with belief. Without this *do*, it is impossible to live from moment to moment in the reality of the goodness of the Father. Some, as Sir Charles knows, try to live that *do* by passing out leaflets. Occasionally I join them, as I told you before, Charles, to show my support for their enthusiasm. But to move their vision beyond such a superficial level has proved a great challenge—one I do not feel I have met with much success."

"But ye're a shining light, Mr. Diggorsfeld," said Bobby, "a man o' uncommon insight and sensitivity."

"Thank you," smiled the pastor. "I feel the same about you. But I daresay not everyone in your community might recognize you as such."

"Ye're right there," laughed McFee. "Most o' the folks hereabouts think I'm a bit off my nut!"

"Not surprising. It takes commonality of heart to apprehend the true depth of another man or woman. Wouldn't you agree?"

"Aye, I would."

"Hence the discouragement I spoke of. When people are not dwelling in that vital center—the center of the Father's goodness—religion becomes a tedious affair. I'm afraid my words grow tedious in the ears of my parishioners as well. This is my fear and my heartache for my people—that many of them do not know that vital, pulsating foundation which is the mainstay of life—the center of the Father's goodness."

"Ah . . . I see it now."

"So they go about living a religion rather than a reality, more afraid of the Father than abiding in his love. They fear hell to a greater extent than they are convinced of his power to give life. They yet exist more in their negative and largely erroneous perceptions of God's nature than in the goodness and love which define his character."

There was a brief silence.

"I must confess," said Jocelyn at length, "that I struggle with how to do as you say. After what you say about the people of your congregation, I am hesitant to admit it. But it is very difficult for me to keep that goodness ever before me. The negative perceptions, as you call them, so easily intrude."

"Don't feel awkward to say it, Lady Jocelyn," said Maggie tenderly. "We all struggle with it."

"But you've been a Christian for years," said Jocelyn, turning toward her hostess.

"Yes. And the struggle to believe in God's goodness remains the hardest part of living as a Christian from day to day—even after a lifetime. Would you agree, Mr. Diggorsfeld?"

"It is a universal problem," acknowledged the pastor. "The human constitution seems to incline itself naturally downward and toward low interpretations. This tendency results in Christians basing their theologies more on hell than on God's redemptive power. It explains why his goodness is so quick to vanish from their considerations at the slightest bump in the road of life. It makes them believe so readily that God is responsible for cruelty, either to themselves or to others, though such a thing is a logical impossibility."

"You say it's impossible for God to be the initiator of something that's cruel?" repeated Maggie.

"O' course," put in her husband. "Cruelty and God are opposites. 'Tis impossible for them t' have dealings together."

"Well put, Mr. McFee!" rejoined Diggorsfeld.

"But how can we *know* God has to be good?" asked Jocelyn. "After Charles explained his prayer of acceptance to me two years ago, I eventually realized that I too wanted to give my heart to the Lord. But I did so on faith, not because I suddenly saw everything differently. I know God *is* good. I have accepted it. But that too I accepted on faith. When doubts come, that is the first point where my faith is attacked."

"Such is natural," replied the pastor, "exactly as Mrs. McFee has said. I face the struggle too."

"But I want to know that God *must* be good," Jocelyn went on, "—that there is no alternative, that it is impossible for him to be evil no matter what happens. Is it possible to know that? Can we know he is good no matter how bad things may seem, no matter how much suffering I or anyone faces?"

"I think you have said it most eloquently. I think it is indeed possible to know it."

"But I only expressed it as a point of puzzlement," rejoined Jocelyn. "I don't know if I could be victorious in the midst of a trial like Job's."

"Not many can do that, Lady Jocelyn," said Bobby.

"Then my question for you remains: how can we *know* God is good?" persisted Jocelyn. She paused and took a deep breath as if preparing to plunge into cold waters.

"Timothy, I know you must have noticed my face," she went on after a moment, "although you are kind enough to pretend not to. How could you not notice? Well, this . . . disfigurement . . . remains a struggle for me to understand. Charles has convinced me that I must learn to thank God for it, and I try, but half the time I must do so only out of obedience. That this mark could be a sign of God's goodness and trustworthiness . . . well, that still remains very difficult for me to grasp in a practical way."

Again she paused, then went on. "I do see his goodness around me," she said. "That Charles loves me, that I have a home and family and friends, that the downs and the woods are so beautiful—all this, as you have said, tell me of God's goodness. But I see things that confuse me too. Not just my birthmark, but the pain I have seen in the hospital where I worked, the poverty and sickness of the people in India, where I grew up. The cruelty one person shows to another.

"So you say we can *know* that God is good, all the time, and in all things. But my question to you is still *how?*"

"You've asked the question that has most puzzled both common men and women as well as theologians for millennia," replied Diggorsfeld thoughtfully. "I don't believe there are any easy answers."

"But you think there are answers?"

"I believe that answers exist for every conundrum it is possible for the human brain to pose."

"If I came to you, then, as an unbeliever, and asked this—*How can we know God is good? . . .* what would you tell me?"

53

Life—A Good Thing

———— ◆ ◆ ◆ ————

*D*iggorsfeld considered Jocelyn's question for several moments. No one else seemed inclined to speak. He knew this was no abstract point of theory for his friend's wife, but something her new faith hungered passionately to understand.

"That what is fundamentally evil cannot create out of nothing," Timothy answered at length.

"I'm sorry—I'm afraid I do not see the connection," said Jocelyn.

"Even atheists and pure chance evolutionists would generally agree that life is a good thing. Wouldn't you say so, Charles?" he added, turning toward Jocelyn's husband.

Charles thought a moment. "I'm afraid I'll have to reflect on that," he said. "It's not something I have really considered before now."

"Look at it this way, then," Diggorsfeld continued. "Evil could not have brought about life, because life is good. Whatever creative power exists in the universe, *somehow* life came about from original nothingness. For that to have happened, *good* must be at the root of it. Evil could not, by definition, have produced something as remarkable and inherently good as life itself."

"Why?"

"Because evil has no life of its own. It is only corrupted good."

"Might not someone argue," Charles asked carefully, "that life, rather than being inherently good, is simply *random*, good mixed with bad? I only raise the point because for so long I myself adhered to the theory of chance. So I pose the question to advocate for the devil, as it were."

"They could argue that," replied Diggorsfeld, "but only illogically. If you thought in such fashion at one time, Charles, then I would say you did so having abandoned logical reason."

Charles laughed. "I would not contest your assertion."

"Creation produces beauty—that is good," Diggorsfeld went on.

"Life sustains and reproduces itself—*that* is good. Love and compassion and kindness exist—*they* are all good. No theory of randomness can explain them. Any thorough observation of what we see around us—even a nonspiritual one—resoundingly validates good as being far more in evidence than evil."

"But you would agree that evil is present in the midst of the good?"

"Of course. But as a secondary thing. The good is foundational, the evil only a parasite living off the decaying fragments of its edges."

"What about death?" now asked Bobby.

"Death all the more proves the point that good is the foundation of all things."

"I'm afraid I do not follow you at all," laughed Charles. "Death seems to me the most compelling argument against a universal goodness."

"Quite the contrary," rejoined Diggorsfeld. "Death proves a foundation of goodness in the universe."

"What—how so?"

"Actually . . . I do not even believe in death."

"Because of eternal life, you mean?" said Maggie.

"There is that. But I mean that even were I not a Christian, I would still say death as a thing in and of itself does not exist at all."

"You say death does not exist!" exclaimed Charles.

"No—I said as a thing *in and of itself*, death does not exist."

"But death is all around us."

"I will respond to your perplexity by posing another question: What do *you* consider death to be?"

The others all thought a moment.

"Is it not merely the end o' life as we know it?" suggested Bobby.

The others thought and one by one nodded their heads.

"Exactly," said the pastor. "You see, death is not something that can exist on its own. To repeat my point from earlier—it is a parasite, a corruption. The very word signifies nothing as a thing you can isolate and look at. It only means the moment when *life* ends. Without life—which I still maintain is inherently a *good* thing—there is no death, no evil, no bad, no wickedness, nothing to go what we call *wrong*. Therefore, even death and evil and badness and wickedness all prove that a *good* foundation exists upholding the universe. Without that good foundation, none of the bad things could be there at all."

"More even than that," put in the Irishman, "—'tis a mysterious doorway into yet more and better life t' come. So what looks like a cruelty t' us, in reality is the best part o' life o' all."

"Bravo, McFee!" exclaimed Diggorsfeld. "Yes—that is the triumphant reality. Another reason not even to believe in death!"

"But if I may continue to ply the devil's counterargument," said Charles, "might I ask something further?"

"Of course."

"I still am uncertain how you can maintain that because life exists, it is good. I think many would disagree with you there."

"You are right. Many would. And I suppose that at some point one does have to take one's essential foundational beliefs on faith. And yet I believe that life itself must be seen by any rational, thinking, reasonable man or woman as essentially a good thing. Surely the existence of life implies—no, *necessitates*—a causative, foundational, creative *Good* at the back of it. People *can* say differently. Many modernists and humanists *do* say differently. But I contend that there is no evidence to back up their assertions. They have their conclusions formed and they express views based upon their backwards logic, without ever examining the real world in a truly rational manner. The evidence of life is all on my side of the argument—validating, everywhere you look, the existence of a *good* foundation in the universe."

"But what is that evidence?"

"Care to answer that, Mr. McFee? I think I detect a twinkle in your eye."

The Irishman chuckled. "It seems t' me," he replied, "that nothing more nor less than our rich fellowship here, and the bonding o' our hearts in brotherhood over tea and good talk together, offers the very proof we're looking for. When ye look at the thing reasonably—like ye yerself say, Mr. Diggorsfeld, with the logic o' the brain—wouldn't ye all say that when individuals get t' know one another in a right way, love is produced?"

He glanced about. Heads nodded.

"Are not our human hearts at this moment warm toward one another?" Bobby went on. "When we eat food, like my Maggie's scones with clotted cream that we had with our tea, not only 'tis the experience pleasurable, the food sustains life and makes us strong. What can that be but good? Food, fellowship, strong bodies, pleasure, beauty—there's the evidence o' goodness in front o' our eyes!"

Again he was greeted with nods of agreement.

"Ye see, food doesn't make us sick and weak. It *strengthens* these bodies o' ours. 'Tis a good thing."

"Exactly," said Diggorsfeld. "The created world may contain pain—indeed, we know it does!—but is not the world still more intrinsically beautiful than it is ugly? All these things, and ten thousand more, argue constantly that *good* is behind it."

Since posing her initial queries, Jocelyn had listened to the rest of the discussion intrigued. This was no abstract philosophical discussion to her ears, but the very breath of life. This was the question she had wrestled with all the days of her existence, it seemed—the question of how Goodness could have produced a face like hers.

If she could only get to the bottom of it, she thought, then all would be well. If she could only understand the mysterious relationship between good and evil and know beyond doubt that good was the supreme of the two—then truly could she give thanks for the fingerprint God had placed upon her, however much pain it brought with it. If she could but know that mark as coming from the hand of Good, she could rest and be grateful.

This evening's fellowship and discussion had begun to open the door into the revelation of that truth. It was one which would slowly and quietly change her life—even more than her conversion had. For as she began from this evening forward to take hold of the undeniable fact of the Father's goodness in a new way, the eyes of her understanding would open to much she had been unable to see before.

"But what about when something truly awful happens?" she now asked, "A child being taken in a cruel death, or an accident in a mine that kills hundreds of men . . . how does one believe in God's goodness at such times?"

"I think we may well ask why," replied Diggorsfeld. "Asking God why things happen is, it seems to me, an integral part of what it means for a mortal to walk in faith, for we wouldn't ask if we didn't have faith that God knows the answer! But we do not see as God does. Much appears evil and unfair to our obscured sight. But we are nevertheless commanded to walk in faith, trusting in his sight more than we trust in our own. We can and perhaps should ask him why, as long as we trust him even when answers may be slow to come."

"But how, in the midst of that, do we keep sight of the fact that he is good?"

"I do not think the question *Why?* necessitates doubting God's goodness. We may ask why. I think it is even good and appropriate to ask why, as a necessary part of our prayer-dialogue with God. But we must *not* doubt his goodness—that is, not without its eventually eroding our faith.

"God's goodness is and must remain the foundation. With the underpinnings of goodness and trustworthiness solid, any number of questions, even doubts, even crying angrily to God as Job did—all these are allowed.

"Job cried out *Why?* to God in a hundred ways. Yet he retained the foundational belief in God's sovereignty in the face of his whys and his doubts. His wife told him to curse God and die. Job replied, *No, God is good, though I do not understand his ways.* The two expressions of uncertainty are very different. Asking a good God *why* is a legitimate aspect of faith. We may question why to the depths of our beings, yet *without* questioning the Father's goodness. The foundation of goodness remains, even amid a sea of unanswered *whys.*"

While Mr. Diggorsfeld was speaking, Maggie had risen quietly to refill the kettle. Another round of tea and scones soon followed, and the discussion gradually drifted into other channels, though it continued to give all five much to think about.

As Charles, Jocelyn, and Timothy Diggorsfeld made their way back to Heathersleigh Hall in the small carriage in the moonlight two hours later, Diggorsfeld remarked, "You have extraordinary friends in those two. You are most fortunate."

54

Adventure in the Loft

❖❖❖

Young Catharine Rutherford enjoyed nothing more than an adventure with her older brother and sister. And for Catharine at five years of age, everything was an adventure.

From her very earliest years, even though George was a boy and the oldest, Catharine had recognized that when both brother and sister were present, *Amanda* was the acknowledged leader. On the present afternoon, however, George led the way as all three young Rutherfords found themselves exploring together in the stables. Such exploring was not one of Amanda's favorite pursuits. But on this day little in the house had amused her. So she and Catharine wandered out after lunch to join their brother.

The day was a warm one. An early morning fog had blown off, and now a gentle breeze wafted pleasant summer smells across the grassy downs. Cows and sheep grazed in the distant pastures. The air was cool and quiet inside the cobweb-filled stables. George had been attempting to drag an old rusting piece of machinery of unknown purpose into the light where he could see more clearly to tinker with it. By the time Amanda and Catharine joined him, he had succeeded in taking the thing more than half apart.

"What is it for?" asked Catharine.

"It's not for anything, silly," said Amanda. "It's just an old piece of rubbish."

"It's not rubbish," objected George, "—at least it won't be when I get through with it. I think I can make it into something that works!"

"I don't care about that old thing," she said, losing interest in George's project almost immediately. "I want an adventure."

"What kind of adventure?" asked Catharine eagerly.

"You know—like Gulliver or Robinson Crusoe."

"What's a Crusoe?"

"I'll *show* you. I'm going to climb up in the loft," announced Amanda.

"Me too!" exclaimed Catharine, following her toward the narrow stairway.

"Then let me go first," said George. "I know which boards to step on without falling through."

He jumped up from his project and ran after them, then squeezed past his two sisters. Soon all three were scrambling single-file from the steep darkened stairs out onto the floor of the loft. It was considerably darker here than below. Slanted shafts of light shone through cracks and knotholes of the walls to illuminate the place. One small window was situated high on the north wall. The silence was thick and muffled, insulated by stacks of baled straw and hay piled high against the north and east walls. Only a fourth of the year's supply now remained. It would be replenished in autumn for the Heathersleigh livestock. The fragrant grasses would then fill every square inch of the place all the way to the roof.

The darkness and quiet, the eerie light and hanging cobwebs, made it feel as if they had entered an altogether different world.

"It's dark," whispered Catharine with the slightest tremble in her voice, as if compelled to silence by something unseen. "Are there ghosts in the stables like in the house, George?"

"There are no ghosts either here or in the house," replied her brother.

"Amanda said Heathersleigh has ghosts."

"Well, it hasn't, Catharine."

"Oh, yes it does," now insisted Amanda. "I've heard them in the garret."

George knew better than to pursue the discussion.

The boards under their feet were not even visible, covered over with many years' accumulation of bits of straw and hay matted down to a thickness of two or three inches. As George walked cautiously across it, the surface appeared as one uniform soft-padded carpet, though he exhorted his sisters to follow exactly behind him.

"Oh, George, we're not going to fall through," said Amanda. "This floor's as strong as the ground."

"Hector told me," said George.

"Hector's only trying to scare you," insisted his sister, "—look!"

Amanda scampered off across the floor, jumping and skipping with carefree recklessness.

"See, I told you—it's strong as can be!"

George did not reply. He continued to walk with care, taking Catharine's hand as they went.

"I'm going to climb up on the stack and look out the window," said Amanda.

"Hector said we aren't supposed to climb up there," objected George.

"I'm tired of hearing what Hector said!" rejoined Amanda. Already she was scrambling up onto the third level of loosely rolled round bales and setting her sights still higher.

Reluctantly, George let go of Catharine and gingerly made his way after Amanda. Half his time it seemed he was following her for fear of what predicament she might get herself into.

"Can I come, George?" said Catharine from the floor.

"Why don't you climb up to about here," replied George, pointing out a sturdy platform of straw up about three bales off the loft floor. "Here, give me your hand."

Excitedly Catharine reached up as George stretched his hand back down to her.

"But no higher than this," he said. "It is tipsy up on top. I don't want all that straw falling down on top of you."

"All right, George."

In another moment Catharine had scrambled up to her seat. She was content. George turned and now climbed after the older of his two sisters. But already she had covered considerable distance into a higher region of cobwebs and rafters.

"Amanda, not so high!" cried George.

"I'm going to the top," returned Amanda. "I want to see out the window."

"You'll set it all tumbling. Come down, Amanda!" Hurriedly he scampered after her.

Amanda said nothing in return. Neither did she slow her attempt to get to the window before George could reach her.

The stacks remaining in the loft formed roughly a circular pattern around a three-foot square hole in the loft floor. Through this hole, during the winter and spring months, Hector Farnham would toss down to ground level whatever straw and hay was required. Over the months this process had hollowed out an upside-down conical cavity around the hole—a kind of hay funnel leading down to the opening.

As George and Amanda now made their way upward, they kept clear of the edge of this steep descent, for as George said, the bales nearest it were tipsy and unsteady. From the top of the bale-circle down to the loft floor and hole the distance was probably twelve or fifteen feet.

Amanda now reached the top of the circular mountain.

"I'm first!" she cried.

"Amanda, be careful up there!"

But Amanda was no more accustomed to heeding her brother's warnings than she was anyone else's.

She got to her feet, stood, then turned to peer out the window. But she could not quite get high enough. Grabbing the sill of the window ledge, she tiptoed with all her might. But the action succeeded only in shoving her feet all the harder against the bale of straw upon which she was standing. Already seriously unsteady, it now wobbled away from the wall.

Just as George reached her, suddenly Amanda's precarious footing gave way.

The roll of straw tumbled down, setting off an avalanche toward the hole in the floor, with Amanda toppling down head over heels in the middle of them.

Hearing his sister's scream, George leapt away from the hole to safety.

In only a few seconds the commotion was over. The slide seemed past, though dust and screams filled the air.

"George . . . George—help me!" came a muffled cry.

George peered in the direction of the sound. He could see nothing. Where the hole in the loft had been was now nothing but a pile of fallen hay and straw. And Amanda had fallen straight toward it!

In a single bound he was down onto the floor of the loft, grabbing Catharine as he flew past her.

"Catharine, run and bring Hector! Tell him to bring a ladder!"

Catharine followed him to the stairs. George flew down three at a time and onto the ground floor of the stables. He looked up behind him. There were Amanda's legs swinging from the ceiling.

"George!" she screamed. "I'm going to fall!"

How she had kept from falling through to the ground was a miracle in itself. Somehow she had managed to grab the ledge as she tumbled through. Now she clung by her fingers from the loft floor. Her feet dangled in midair high above the stable floor.

George glanced hurriedly around. He grabbed a fork and piled up the loose straw that had fallen through.

"Amanda . . . jump."

"I can't!"

"You'll land on straw. I made a pile under you. It won't hurt."

"I can't. It's too far!"

"The bales will cushion you."

"I won't, I tell you. Get me down!"

Again George glanced about. Frantically he looked for anything to reach high enough. If he could just get hold of her feet. . . .

He needed a ladder. But there wasn't one in the stables.

George ran to a stool across the floor and dragged it back. Now he scrambled onto the top of it. Carefully he stood.

"George!"

He stretched up his hands, though his legs wobbled. He could just reach Amanda's feet. With his palms upward, he exerted enough pressure so that she could continue holding herself by the ledge.

"Hang on," he said.

"How am I going to get down!" she yelled back.

"Hector will bring a ladder."

But already George's arms were beginning to tire.

"Get me down!" demanded Amanda. "I can't hang on here forever."

George did not reply. He knew better than to say anything to her at a time like this.

It became silent. Both were tired and breathing heavily. Even Amanda judged it prudent to put what remained of her strength to use with her hands, not her tongue.

Fifteen or twenty seconds later footsteps came running.

Hector appeared with Catharine on his heels. He ran inside and glanced quickly around.

"Why, Miss Amanda!" he exclaimed. "What on earth are you doing up there?"

"Get me down, Hector!"

Already he was setting down the two legs of the ladder that had come in on his shoulder. Resting it securely on the floor, he steadied it under Amanda.

The moment the ladder's two legs were in place, George guided one of Amanda's feet to the next highest rung with his hand. She felt the wood, tentatively probing it with her foot, then seeing if it would hold her weight. She let go her grip with one hand to grasp the ladder's rail. A second foot, then second hand, followed. Slowly she descended, then jumped from the ladder to the stable floor.

"This is all your fault, George," she said irritably.

"What are you talking about?" he said. He hadn't exactly expected thanks from Amanda's lips. But neither had he expected blame.

"You and that stupid piece of machinery," persisted his sister. "If it hadn't been for that, we would never have gone up in the loft."

Amanda now turned and hurried out into the bright sunlight without another word to anyone.

55

Unsought Advice

At tea that same evening, talkative young Catharine blurted out an excited and dramatized rendition of the affair in the loft. Following closer inquiry on Charles' part, the details were filled in by George. Amanda contributed little to the discussion. She had several nasty scrapes and bruises, and her arms hurt dreadfully. Her mood was not altogether a pleasant one.

"Well, Catharine, it seems you had an adventure indeed!" laughed Charles.

"I am only glad no one was hurt," added Jocelyn. "It sounds as though it could have been very dangerous."

"You know, Amanda," Charles went on a little more seriously, "I've been learning that everything that happens contains a lesson for us. There is a good one here for you: Listening to advice keeps you out of trouble—and sometimes out of what could be danger as well."

"There was no *real* danger, Papa," now replied Amanda. "George has exaggerated the whole thing."

"What if you had fallen through to the floor?"

"But I didn't."

"What if you had?"

"Then I might have hurt my feet," shrugged Amanda.

"You *might* have broken both your legs," added her father. "That ceiling is twelve, maybe fifteen feet above the ground. When Hector tosses the bales down from the loft, they land with quite a crash."

Amanda did not reply. She knew well enough that she had been in a dangerous situation. She had, in fact, been good and scared. But she wasn't about to admit it. Besides, at the moment she wasn't thinking about her legs at all. It was her *arms* that felt like they'd been broken!

Her father poured another cup of tea and slowly buttered a slice of bread. When he resumed, it was with thoughtful tone.

"You children know," he began, "that I have been discovering many new things recently. There is much that your mother and I still do not understand. We will do many things wrong as we try to apply these new principles of living as Christians. But one thing I have noticed is that the Bible speaks a great deal about foolishness and wisdom. It seems me that one of the key differences between the two is being able to listen to what other people tell you—especially when it goes against something you want to do yourself."

He paused and sipped at his tea.

"I don't yet know as much about wisdom as I would like to. But it strikes me, Amanda, that your brother was giving you sound advice up in the loft—and you would have done well to listen."

"Why should I have?" Amanda finally objected, now that her father's remarks had started to point in her direction.

"It would have been *wise* to listen to it. That is one of the marks of a wise person—listening to others."

"I don't see why I should have to listen to George. He's no more wise than I am."

"In this case he was. Listening to him could have kept you from falling and risking your neck."

"If you ask me, it was nothing but his own foolishness with that stupid machine that caused the whole thing."

Charles sighed but said no more. Their daughter would apparently have to learn through much more difficult circumstances the same lesson he had tried to give so gently today.

His years as an acknowledged son of God had been few. But Charles Rutherford was student enough of the human condition to know what likely faced his daughter in the years ahead. He recognized the principle that intensity of character pruning must increase throughout life to whatever extent it is not allowed to accomplish its purpose at less hurtful levels. How much better that relinquishment of self come of one's own volition.

The knife of the Spirit's surgery *will* penetrate to whatever extent it must. As deep into the parent trunk as self has ruled, though no deeper, must slice the knife of the master Husbandman. Only by such pruning will the plant of human character discover the freedom to develop and stretch high its branches and blossom with the fruit of its essential nature.

Most lessons come gently at first, whispering their truths softly into receptive hearts. Those who discern them gradually and steadily extend

their roots deeper into the well-nourished soils of knowledge, understanding, and wisdom. For those who refuse to heed these subtle Spirit-
promptings, however, corrections, warnings, and admonitions must be
sent from on high with increasing severity . . . until they are heeded.

Wisdom's voice will not be silenced.

Charles looked up and caught Jocelyn's eye. Her expression told
him she was thinking the same thing he was—that they must pray diligently for their daughter in the days to come.

56

A Puzzling Scripture

♦♦♦

---

*J*ocelyn Rutherford sat alone in her sitting room. It was midweek.
Charles was in London. The children were resting. The house was quiet,
and Jocelyn was in a prayerful and pensive mood.

Her mind had been preoccupied all day—active, thoughtful.

Good thoughtful. Anticipating. Something seemed at hand. Whatever she had stumbled onto, Jocelyn sensed that it had the potential to
affect her and Charles forever after.

She didn't know where today's reading would lead. Yet something
deep inside her pulsed with an excitement for what was coming . . . for
something God was about to show her.

At Timothy Diggorsfeld's suggestion, Jocelyn and Charles had been
reading regularly through the New Testament—both together and on
their own. In the several months that had passed since Timothy's visit
to Heathersleigh, she and Charles had worked their way through most
of the Gospels and Epistles and had even begun reading a few for the
second time.

For Jocelyn, this discipline of Bible reading had been a revelation.
So much that she read was new and alive, with a practical vitality she
had never dreamed possible. How could she ever have considered the
Bible a stale and old-fashioned book?

During her morning time alone with the Lord two days ago, for example, she had come upon a passage of Scripture that jolted her awake where she sat. Two or three times she read it through. Ever since, the puzzling words had continued to stir in her brain. She had hardly been able to think of anything else. And one of the marginal references in her Bible leading her back to the book of Genesis had further amplified her perplexity over the passage's meaning.

When instructing them about their New Testament study, Diggorsfeld had been extremely clear about one point. Over and over he had emphasized it: "Don't read the Bible if you're not going to do as I'm about to explain. Without this, reading and learning spiritual principles can do you more harm than good."

She and Charles had continued to listen attentively.

"There are two things you must do to make the Scriptures alive," the pastor went on. "The first is this: As you read, say to the Lord, 'How does this apply to *me*? Specifically. What does it have to do with *my* daily life and *my* relationships with others? What does it have to do with *my* attitudes, *my* outlook, *my* values, *my* priorities? What does it have to do with how I conduct myself and how I think?' These are questions you have to ask. Then you must say: 'Lord, what *changes* do you want to make in my life on the basis of this scriptural principle I am reading? What growth do you have for me here? What do you want me to *do* about it?'"

He paused and looked seriously at his new friends.

"Does this make sense?" he asked. "Have I been clear?"

"It seems clear enough to me," replied Charles.

Jocelyn nodded in agreement.

"I stress this so heavily," said Timothy, "because without this *how-does-it-apply-to-me* and *what-do-you-want-me-to-do* dialogue with the Lord, as I said, the Bible becomes a worthless book to you. Its principles are of no value whatever unless they are put into practice. It is this pragmatic obedience that forms the essence of living and growing as a Christian."

But these words! now thought Jocelyn, trying to reconcile this startling passage with Diggorsfeld's instructions. Were *they* to be put into practice in this modern day and age?

The words she had read that had set her mind in motion the day before yesterday were from the fifth chapter of Paul's letter to the Ephesians: "For the husband is the head of the wife, even as Christ is the head of the church. . . . Therefore as the church is subject unto Christ, so let the wives be subject to their own husbands in every thing."

The words had startled her. They seemed to go against everything her husband had fought for so long, that she herself had come to believe. After all, this was the year 1899. A new century would soon dawn. Men like her own husband were speaking of true equality between the sexes, and women were pushing for the vote. It seemed like such a positive direction for the world to go. Could God really want it to move *the other way*?

But there were those words again: women were to *be subject* to their husbands. To be subject to their husbands . . . *in every thing*. As if the husband were the absolute monarch and the wife had no say whatsoever. Why, even the queen of England no longer had that power over her subjects!

But as the words from the apostle Paul had circulated through her brain, so too had those of Timothy Diggorsfeld. She had prayed, "I truly don't understand this, Lord. It sounds like something from feudal times. I don't see how it can possibly apply to my life with Charles right now." But with this confession came the question the pastor had taught her to ask: "Lord, what changes do you want to make in *my* life? Do you want me to grow from this? *What do you want me to do?*"

Then this morning Jocelyn had come across another passage which, while not answering her questions about the first, showed her where to go for help. It was from Paul's letter to Titus. The words read, "The aged women, likewise, that they be in behaviour as becometh holiness . . . teachers of good things; that they may teach the young women to be sober, to love their husbands, to love their children, to be discreet, chaste, keepers at home, good, obedient to their own husbands, that the word of God be not blasphemed."

It was now midafternoon. Jocelyn set aside the copy of *Cornhill* magazine, in which she had been casually reading a profile of the suffragette leader Emmeline Pankhurst, and opened her Bible again to the book of Titus. She read through the words that had been with her all day.

What do you have for me here, Lord? What is it you want me to see?

Almost the same instant it became clear—*older* women, *younger* women . . . older women whose behavior is reverent should *teach* the younger women.

Older women should teach younger women how to *love* and be *obedient* to their husbands!

If she wanted to know what the verse in Ephesians meant about wives being subject to their husbands, she should ask an "older" and more mature Christian woman. The words from Titus could hardly be more clear.

That's what she would do, thought Jocelyn.

The next minute she had risen from her chair and was on her way downstairs. After making arrangements with the staff for the afternoon, she would pay a visit to Maggie McFee.

57

God's Daughters

♦ ♦ ♦

An hour later the two women of God were seated together at Maggie McFee's plain deal table in the kitchen of Heathersleigh Cottage. Light streamed through the window. A fragrant clump of colorful flowers from Maggie's garden sat in the center of the table in a slender earthenware vase.

Jocelyn and Charles had walked and ridden over to this warm and beloved home many times in the two years since the older couple had gently guided them into the family of faith. They had talked many things over with Bobby and Maggie. They had prayed together and read the Scriptures together and discussed dozens of questions.

But the walk to the McFee cottage on this particular day was one Jocelyn Rutherford had had to make alone. What was on her mind she had to resolve on her own, as a woman. She knew she could only do so in the presence of another woman who had journeyed the same road.

Much had changed during the two years since Bobby and Maggie had explained to them what it meant to become intimate members of God's family. *Everything* had changed.

But in her spirit Jocelyn sensed that perhaps another change was coming that would probe yet deeper into the marrow of her personal feminine identity.

As they sipped at their tea, Jocelyn explained why she had come. "You see, Maggie," she concluded, "the one Scripture explains why I am here to ask you about the other two—the one in Ephesians which started me thinking, and the verse in Genesis I ran across later."

"And they are hard for you to understand, is that it?"

"I don't suppose they are so difficult to *understand*," replied Jocelyn. "The words are straightforward enough. But do they really apply to-day? The one in Genesis three says husbands are to *rule* their wives. It's such a strong word, it startled me. I didn't know what to make of it. That's not really the way it's supposed to be, is it . . . not *now*?"

"And why not?"

"I don't know . . . it's so outdated. It sounds old-fashioned, from another time and culture. I didn't think of Christianity as such an archaic religion."

"It's not," replied Maggie, "and neither is it a religion. 'Tis a way of life."

"Husbands . . . *rule* their wives. I've never heard of such a thing—at least not among enlightened people. Why, men aren't better than women."

"Of course not, dear," laughed Maggie. "But what makes you say such words? You and Charles aren't . . . you aren't unhappy with your life?"

"Oh no. Charles has always been very gracious to me. He treats me entirely as an equal. These verses just confuse me!"

"Men aren't *better*," said Maggie. "They've just a different job to do. It has nothing to do with better or worse. 'Tis what God made them to be, and what he made us to be. He set in motion a plan for husbands and wives to work together in a way that is wonderful and full of harmony."

"But . . . *be subject in every thing?* That's so severe. It sounds almost . . . like slavery."

Maggie laughed.

"There is the word right there in Ephesians," Jocelyn went on. "It's hard to ignore it."

"Right you are. 'Tis *impossible* to ignore."

"I don't like the sound of it."

"Many women recoil from such a suggestion," said Maggie.

"Don't you?" asked Jocelyn in astonishment.

"Heavens no, dear. Haven't you learned yet that in the ways of God, everything is different than it seems through the world's eyes? It just may be that the kind of slavery the old apostle is describing here is really freedom. Besides, I love my Bobby, and my heavenly Father, enough to even be Bobby's slave if that's what God asks of me. I find nothing so terrible about slavery if it has a higher purpose, if it's part of God's plan. Didn't Paul talk about being a slave to Christ? No, dear, the evil's not in the slavery, so much as in our rebellious hearts."

Jocelyn had come here for instruction. But she found unexpected objections and annoyances rising up within her at this new idea of being told to occupy a role subordinate to her husband. The article she had just been reading had stressed that women would be asserting themselves more and more as the new century approached. She had read it casually, more from curiosity than anything, not feeling a great deal of sympathy for the women's causes being espoused. However, she now found many of its points coming back to her mind. They had struck deeper root than she'd realized.

Her natural servant's heart had led her into nursing. Yet it had been entirely her *own* decision. The same was true of her life with Charles—she *chose* to run his household and take care of his children.

Now here were hints in new and uncomfortable directions—toward relinquishing the right to make such choices and determinations for herself. Maggie hadn't said as much, it was true. But that was what Jocelyn felt was implied by the gist of the discussion—that Charles had the right to make her decisions for her and to tell her what to do.

Not that he showed any inclination to do so. Charles was too thoroughly a modern for that. But what if he did? How would she respond? What if he told her to do something she didn't *want* to do? What if he pointed out some aspect of her character or behavior that he wanted her to change?

Suddenly Jocelyn didn't like the sound of what Maggie was saying. She didn't particularly enjoy how it felt, and she wasn't sure she liked the implied consequences. It was fine when Charles built her up and helped her believe in herself. She appreciated his kind, gracious, loving side. But what if he suddenly decided to exercise this headship Maggie was talking about in *uncomfortable* directions? He had already shown himself capable of doing so when she had objected to his giving his heart to the Lord. Even then, however, his direct words to her had only been to convince her how much God loved her. What if he said or did something that *wasn't* so pleasant? Did she *want* such personal counsel from him, or did she want to be left alone to decide *herself* what was best for her life?

"I thought we were all equal," she said after a moment's pause. Maggie detected a slight edge creeping into her tone.

"Oh, we are, Jocelyn, dear," she replied. "*Equal*—we're all that, surely, in God's sight. But what's that got to do with a husband ruling over his wife?"

"If one person's ruling over the other, they can hardly be equal."

"Of course they can, dear."

"What gives Charles the right to rule over me?"

"Why, God does. And it's really *not* slavery, dear, but God's chosen method. 'Tis a relationship of equal partnership, where one person has been given the responsibility to lead, or rule, and the other has the responsibility of helping and following. 'Tis nothing more complicated than that."

"It hardly *sounds* like an equal arrangement—when one person is above another."

" 'Tis the common snag that untrusting wives insist on stumbling over. Not to say that you're untrusting, Jocelyn, dear—only that it's a common reaction of our kind."

Jocelyn was silent. She *was* stumbling over it.

"Then please, Maggie, explain it to me," she said. "I want to understand. And I want Charles and me to be like you and Bobby. I always feel such peace when we come here. But I have to admit that I've never thought of any of this before. How there can still be equality if a man's supposed to rule over a woman? I've never seen Bobby lording it over you."

Maggie laughed.

"Ruling over a wife doesn't mean lording it over her," she said. "God has just given us women and men different roles to live out, different ways to go about in life, that's all. We truly are equal in his sight. He loves every human creature as much as any other. Nobody's better or superior to anyone else. But we're not all to do the same thing. Women are supposed to trust men to look out for them, that's all. 'Tis the woman's job to trust her husband to make good decisions. Her belief in him gives them both the freedom to do what they do best, without the woman trying to take over a man's role or grasping to be something she's not intended to be."

"What *is* it a woman does best?" asked Jocelyn.

"To live as man's helper. 'Tis the woman who's to help the man and be part of *his* life, not have a life of her own. The man's not called the *woman's* helpmeet, but the woman's the man's."

It was quiet a moment. Jocelyn glanced down to the table, where her Bible sat open to the passage in Ephesians that had begun this new mental inquiry several days earlier. She drew in several deep breaths, trying to calm her inner protests and put herself back into a listening mentality.

"So how *do* you be subject to your husband?" she finally asked.

"'Tis an attitude," replied Maggie. "It's got more to do with a woman's outlook than with anything special to be done. . . ."

Even as Maggie said the words, Jocelyn understood what she meant. To all outward appearances, and probably in Charles' mind as well, she herself would have seemed to be a perfectly content, compliant, and submissive wife. Yet Maggie's words on this day had uncovered regions hidden deep in her own heart which squirmed at the thought of being ruled by someone else.

"—an outlook about herself as much as anything," Maggie added.

"*Herself* . . . rather than her husband?"

"Of course, dear. I'm sorry to say it, but it just comes so easy for us human folk to get grasping and independent—men as well as women, but women for certain. We listen to the world telling all sorts of lies about what it means to be a woman. The papers and magazines and streets of London are full of the cries of modern women these days. It's all about us—all this talk of women's rights. We can't help listening to it. Then we start worrying about everything around us, wanting what *we* want. And as soon as a woman starts down that pathway, the wife's natural calling begins to feel strange to her. If she listens to what everyone is saying, her *self* won't like what the Bible says."

"What natural calling do you mean?" asked Jocelyn.

"To fit under her husband's headship . . . to allow *him* to lead her. 'Tis an attitude, like I said, a nongrasping, nonindependent attitude. And that's why it's something we wives have to resolve ourselves. It's nothing anyone—not a man nor another woman either—can do for us. We each have to face it in our own heart."

"I see what you mean."

"I suppose what it comes down to is not insisting on ruling your own affairs. That's a struggle for most of us."

"Surely not for you, Maggie."

"I have my own struggles, like anyone else," replied the older woman thoughtfully. "We're all of different stations, and with different roads to walk, facing different things, and with different husbands ruling over us. But we're all women together. There are things we've all got to lay down and put to rest. God didn't place us on this earth to manage our own affairs. We all have to wrestle the Lord with that, like old Jacob."

Jocelyn considered her words. "I don't suppose that's easy," she said.

"*Easy!*" repeated Maggie with a tone between a *humph* and a laugh. "No it's not easy. Laying down your independence and saying you're not going to rule your own life is the hardest thing in the world. But then 'tis the only thing we're put on earth to learn. And men have to learn it just as well as women. 'Tis the human way to salvation, as I see it—laying down the right to self-rule."

"Men have to learn it too?"

"Of course. *All* human creatures have to learn it. 'Tis just that God gives men and women different ways to learn it. Women have to learn it by laying down their independence toward their husbands. Men have to learn it by laying down *their* independence toward themselves and toward God. But the lessons God is trying to teach us in our stubborn human hearts is the same lesson for everyone—*not to trust ourselves*, but to trust in our heavenly Father and those folks he places above us. Nothing could be simpler. But *easy*—no, Jocelyn, dear—'tis a hard lesson to learn. It takes us all our lives, and we barely begin to learn it then."

"So how can we learn the lesson?"

"For our kind—women, I mean—one of the first things is to recognize that being God's daughter changes everything about what it means to be a woman. We've got to get it into our heads that it's completely different than the grasping kind of thing the world encourages. 'Tis what it means to be *subject*—we must let men be our heads. 'Tis a change in the way we see ourselves. It might be something few people ever see. But in our hearts we, as wives, recognize that we are no longer independent agents. Everything about our lives goes through our husbands."

Jocelyn considered her words. A remnant of her independent self again flared up from the past, piqued by Maggie's words.

"But I don't know if I want what you say," she objected. "*I want* to be my own independent agent. I didn't get married to have someone else tell me what to do."

"Do you trust your husband?"

"Yes . . . I think so."

"Aren't you willing to take the difficult along with the pleasant?"

"What do you mean?"

"How fair is it of you," said Maggie pointedly, "if you want him to say only nice things to you, but you aren't willing to listen when he has a word of instruction or advice that may not be pleasant?"

Jocelyn stared down at the table. Maggie knew how to be direct.

"You took your husband's name," the older woman went on. "You allow him to support you. You became part of *him*, not him *you*. What did it mean that you took his name if it didn't imply relinquishing something of your identity and independence into him?"

"Yes, I took his name, but I didn't mean to relinquish who I am."

"This *is* the way to find who you are, Jocelyn dear. What looks like relinquishment is the doorway into discovering your complete self."

"How can that be?"

"You yourself have told me how Charles has already done that for you. You are walking in intimacy with God now because of Charles' very love for you."

Jocelyn nodded.

"I've heard Charles speak lovingly to you. You yourself told me how he helped you believe in your worth and accept your birthmark as a sign of God's love."

"Yes . . . he's helped me in a hundred ways. He's a very loving and caring man."

"One thing you will discover the longer you live and grow as a Christian is that most things are upside down from how they are in the world. Nowhere could it be more true than right here. Sometimes what looks like a giving up of freedom is actually the way to more blessing in the end. But it can't be seen until it is done in obedience. The dying has to come first. *Then* are the eyes open to behold the blessing that comes from it. But if you wait to obey *until* you understand what might be the result, it will never happen."

"It still doesn't look a fair arrangement, the way you describe it."

"You and I are women. We're only to concern ourselves with our half of it. *Fair* can't be in our minds. Because we're involved, we wouldn't know fair if it bit us in the face. That's why God just tells us what to do and expects us to do it ... and leave fair to him. And we have to remember that there's just as much dying that goes on for our husbands. *Both* sides have to relinquish. Both husband and wife give of themselves."

"What does a man have to give up?"

"The woman gives up her right to independence, allowing herself to flow through her husband, allowing him to be head, trusting him. But his headship means that he has to *serve* his wife. He has to look for *her* best interests ahead of his own. So he gives up his right to independence as well. You see—rule and submission are like the two blades of a pair of scissors. They *both* have to work at the same time."

Again it was silent. At length Maggie spoke again.

"In Ephesians," she said, "Paul was talking to men and women *together* when he told them what was expected of them. If you want it to be fair, Jocelyn, my dear, read what Paul told the husbands. I wouldn't want to be in their shoes!"

Maggie began to chuckle.

"What is it?" smiled Jocelyn.

"I was just thinking of the other side of it—though we're not supposed to do that. We've got enough trouble doing *our* half of the thing without craning out necks about to see if the men are holding up *their* end. But what I was thinking was that husbands stumble over the same snags as wives, because *they* don't understand the command to rule any better than we do."

Again she laughed. "Matter of fact, most men stumble over it even worse."

"How?" asked Jocelyn.

"They also think *rule* means they're to lord it over their wives. So they strut about like roosters in a henhouse thinking that's what the Scripture means. And they miss the mark further than their untrusting wives."

"At least Charles doesn't do that."

Maggie nodded. "You're a fortunate woman, as am I. Ah but, Jocelyn, dear, these are mixed-up times we're living in, with everyone trying to be equal and get their rights. Men are mixed up. Women are mixed up. And we're all getting further and further away from the way the Bible tells us to live. That's why we wives have to be diligent to obey our half of the thing, to help our husbands serve and lay down their lives for us."

"So *rule* really means . . . to serve?"

The old woman's eyes twinkled as if she understood a joke the whole world was blind to. "Of course, dear. That's how my Bobby rules over me, by loving me and serving me. That's what your Charles does to you too. I've seen him. That's why you can trust him, because he loves you. Isn't that what Paul told the Ephesian men along with what he said to their wives? He said, *Husbands, love your wives, even as Christ also loved the church, and gave himself for it.* What else is that but laying down their lives for their women?"

Jocelyn pondered her words.

"If you ask me," Maggie went on, "the men have the harder time of it. We only have to be subject to our husbands. But they've got to give themselves *completely* for us, even die if need be, like Jesus did. Women who complain about a marriage not being equal don't see that the husband's given the harder job of the two. We get security and protection while we build a home. Our husbands have to give up their whole lives for our sake."

58

What Would Happen If We Trusted Men?

---◆◆◆---

$\mathcal{B}$ut what about the women's movement to have more rights?" asked Jocelyn after the two women had sat for several minutes in silence. "Especially the right to vote. Isn't that good? I think it is. But how does that reconcile with a man being a woman's head? Should women leave *everything* to men? Are women to be nobodies in the world?"

Maggie contemplated her answer. She took a sip of her tea and swallowed slowly. Jocelyn had by now learned to be patient. She knew that Maggie's wisdom in viewing life's complexities was not to be rushed.

"You ask many questions," she said at length. "The old queen would enjoy talking over the world's affairs with you, I think!"

The words brought a pleasant remembrance of Victoria to Jocelyn's mind, and she smiled.

"I believe 'tis good for women to be able to vote," Maggie went on. "I hope it happens in my lifetime. I look forward to the privilege. God has given women a measure of wisdom to balance the leadership of men. And I believe women should be aware what is going on around them. World events don't always concern the likes of an old peasant woman like me. But they often affect my man or people I care about. Some of the points being talked about by your Charles and the others in Parliament I'm in agreement with."

Jocelyn stared to hear Maggie speak so knowledgeably about the issues.

"You look surprised," laughed Maggie. "Did you think I would say that women should do nothing but tend their flowers, like I do, and shouldn't be up on what the world's about, or never voice their opinions?"

"I don't know. But I didn't expect you to have sympathies with the suffragettes."

"There is no approval within me for the women in London throwing eggs at the prime minister's carriage. Those women will get no sympathy from me."

"Now I'm confused, Maggie."

"I expect Bobby and me do occasionally take the long way around the barn in what we're trying to say. I suppose that comes from not being in much of a hurry. But sometimes the world *does* need to change. Young Master Charles used to come 'round quite often to tell us we needed to change with it."

It was Maggie's turn to smile—at the remembrance of Charles Rutherford's attempts to get her and her husband in step with progress.

"And the world you two grew up in was different from ours," she added. "Look how things were different in Bible times than they are now. God is always doing new things with his people. I think 'tis a good thing these days for women's voices to be heard in the world. 'Tis the way they're going about it that's all wrong. They're not letting men lead. They're forgetting the roles God gave us all. The glory of a woman is in service, not seizing rights. 'Tis the same as a man's glory—laying down his life for others."

"But how can women get the vote and make their voices heard without the work of the suffragettes, without insisting on it?"

"Maybe it will help to tell you a little game I play with myself when I'm wanting something or the other. I say—what might be the good to come of trusting my Bobby to see to it?"

"What does that have to do with women's rights?"

"How do you think those uppity suffragette women with their obsession with women's rights would react to the Scripture verses we've been talking about?"

Jocelyn smiled at the very idea. "I doubt they would pay the slightest attention to them."

"Or they'd be offended by the suggestion that they mean anything at all," rejoined Maggie. "They would either ignore them or say they mean something different than what they say. People are so hasty to rewrite the Bible when they don't like what it says."

"But I want to hear about your mental game."

"All right, dear—what might happen if women in England asked what might be the good to come of this situation if they trusted the men to see to it? What if they said, 'Men, do what is best. Not only that—do what is best *for us* . . . for women. We place ourselves in your hands. We will trust you. If you want us to vote, we'll vote. If you don't want us to vote, we'll be content.'"

"The suffragettes wouldn't go along with that for a second!" laughed Jocelyn. "It would sound like nonsense to them."

"But what if they did?" persisted Maggie. "Might it not all turn out for the best in the end? Don't you think men would get around eventually to seeing the wisdom of women voting, just as they gave laborers the vote?"

"I don't know," said Jocelyn thoughtfully. "It's not a thing I've ever considered. Your game comes at the situation from such an opposite angle than most people do. Rather than insisting on having something your way, you leave the decision in somebody else's hands."

She paused, still turning the notion over in her brain. "Do you really think it would happen?" she said. "Do you really think Parliament might end up giving women the vote without the suffragettes at all?"

"I do," nodded Maggie. "Perhaps even sooner than with the women causing such a fuss. But even if not, might we not gain more by trust than the vote is worth anyway, by living as the Bible says? All this grasping these women like the Pankhursts are doing—it's just wrong."

"And you think that can be brought into a marriage too?"

"'Tis the same principle between a man and a wife. *Husband, do what you think is best for me.*"

"What if a man is selfish and *doesn't* do what is best for the woman, or doesn't even try?"

"Surely, your Charles—"

"Of course. My Charles is always thinking of me. But in trying to understand this, I only wonder what women are supposed to do who *don't* have husbands like Charles, or like your Bobby. What about poor Mrs. Blakeley in the village who is married to a drunk? I can't imagine that God expects her to do whatever Rune Blakeley says."

"Instead of doing what the Bible says, a lot of folks look around to see why *other* people should or shouldn't be doing something. That keeps them from thinking about their own responsibility. Each person has their own story and their own life to live. I can't say what God might be wanting Mrs. Blakeley to do. 'Tis a hard question. But I'm sure God will bless her if she finds what she can trust even in such a man as that."

"It's hard to think there could be anything."

"Even the worst of men are still created in God's image. Such a wife has the opportunity to trust God's wisdom to work good out of what she *does* find to trust in her husband. Maybe the man doesn't yet see his role properly. Maybe it will be her quiet trust that will help him see that strutting about like a rooster isn't what God wants. Perhaps her trust can help him see that he's to be a servant to his family."

"I'm not sure I could trust that much," admitted Jocelyn. "I can't imagine how hard it would be to live with a man like Rune Blakeley."

Maggie smiled as if she knew more than she was telling.

"'Tis easy to find reasons *not* to trust men. Any crabby, critical woman without an ounce of sense can do that. But it takes a woman of insight and maturity to trust a man even when his trustworthiness may be hard to see. I don't know about you, Jocelyn, dear, but I want to be a wise daughter of God, not a grumpy one. If men have faults, and they all do, it's God's job to change them, not ours. In truth, 'tis more a question of trusting God to work through the man than trusting the man himself. People will always let us down, but God never will. So we can always trust God to work through our husbands for us, faults and all."

"The suffragettes wouldn't like that statement much either," laughed Jocelyn.

"No doubt. But how many of them are trying to become quiet, humble daughters of God?"

A lengthy silence followed. The afternoon's shadows had begun to fall over the cottage. No more rays from the sun shone through into Maggie's kitchen.

"Then what am I to do?" asked Jocelyn at length.

"If your heart is open, God will lead you right. You can trust him. When God said that man was to be woman's head and that a wife would be subject to her husband, he was laying out the easiest path for the two of them to walk. It takes both of them to walk it together. You're doing the right thing looking in the holy book to find out what *you're* supposed to do. That's part of this road you and your dear husband are now on. When you come across something you don't understand, you ask, 'What is there here for me? Do I need to do some changing?' "

"That's exactly what Timothy Diggorsfeld says."

"A good man," Maggie said. "Now, dear, you just keep reading, looking into the Proverbs to remind yourself how to behave every day and into the Gospels to see how Jesus told us to live and be. And look to what Paul wrote to the churches to see the advice he gave to new Christians with questions."

Jocelyn smiled with admiration for this woman. Maggie had such wisdom and peace.

"The day is drawing down upon us," Jocelyn said. "My three young ones, especially Catharine, will be frantic for my presence. It is time for me to get back to the Hall."

Jocelyn stood and hugged the old woman. "Thank you so much. I will think and pray about everything you've told me."

She paused, then smiled as a memory suddenly returned to her from two weeks earlier.

"I had a dream about you, Maggie," she said. "It just came back to me. I was in school, and you were my teacher. It was just like today."

Maggie smiled. She was content in her life. She had been for years. But it was especially wonderful to be able to be part of this younger woman's growth.

A few minutes later, Maggie stood watching at the door of the cottage as Jocelyn disappeared through the forest. Bobby approached quietly. He drew alongside her and placed his arm about her.

"'Tis a blessing, indeed, eh, Maggie," he said. "'Tis glad I am that we lived long enough t' be able t' watch this new life growing inside the two o' them."

59

Husband and Wife

◆◆◆

*T*hree weeks had passed since Jocelyn's visit to the cottage. Now Charles and Jocelyn were both on their knees in their heather garden, setting in several new small plants. It was late on a Saturday afternoon.

"There," Charles said with satisfaction as he scooped in the last of the dirt around the small bush and patted it snugly down. "Next July we shall see the flowers of our labor."

Both fell silent.

"*Lord*," he began to pray softly, as had become their custom whenever they were here, "*once again we lift up our three dear young ones to you. Draw them all in their own unique way, to your heart. Especially do we pray for Amanda. Continue to nurture the garden of her character, that the seeds of your truth will one day germinate within her. Nourish her soil, that when they do, they will sprout strong and take deep root. May they grow and flourish and bear fruit as she comes to know you as we have come to know you. Keep her in your care, Lord. Protect her. Be a Father to her.*"

He stopped. Jocelyn murmured a quiet *amen* but did not pray further.

Slowly they slipped back from their knees into a sitting position and remained seated for a while, contemplating their day's efforts.

"Actually," said Jocelyn at length, "I've been thinking more about *us* lately than I have about Amanda."

"Why us?"

"I came across an interesting verse in my Bible reading a couple of weeks ago that started me thinking about many new things."

"I am immediately curious," said Charles.

"I went and talked to Maggie about it."

Again it was silent. Charles could tell Jocelyn's mind was heavy with something she wanted to say, but she seemed to have difficulty expressing it. He waited patiently.

"You know, Charles," she said at length, "as good a marriage as we have, we're not really functioning in all ways like a husband and wife are supposed to—a Christian husband and wife."

"How do you mean?"

"We're too much in step with the times in which we live."

"I don't see what the problem is with that."

"Our being modern individuals, and more or less progressive in our outlook, has caused us to think of ourselves too much as equals, as if the marriage is a partnership, a democracy."

"Isn't it?"

"That's not the biblical pattern."

"What?"

Jocelyn quoted the verse from Ephesians, which by now she knew from memory.

"So you see," she concluded, "—you're supposed to be my *head*. I'm to be *subject* to you. You're to rule, to be the head of the marriage and family. You'll have to admit, it's not a very reformist-sounding arrangement."

"I *am* head of this family," he said.

"Of course you are. But I think there's more that's called for from you."

"Such as?"

"Perhaps . . . more assertive headship."

"But I don't want to *rule* you."

"Even if God wants you to?"

"You can't really want me to do that."

"Yes, I really think I do."

"What woman would want that?"

"I do."

"But, Jocelyn, I've given my professional life fighting against this very sort of thing—one person being over another. Now you're suggesting such an arrangement in my own home. What would my colleagues in Parliament think!" Charles could not help laughing.

"But it's there in black and white," rejoined Jocelyn, pulling herself to her feet and walking over to the small bench where her Bible lay. Opening it to the passage she'd marked, she handed it to Charles. "See, it's right there. So I think we have no choice but to want it, if we want to obey God. Besides, I trust you. I know you will only do what you think is in my best interest."

"But why do we need any change?" Charles continued to protest. "You and I've always had a totally agreeable relationship. When questions come up, we talk and arrive at a consensus. I have no complaints. I like you just as you are. I like our marriage the way it is."

"Maybe on the outside I've been compliant, Charles," said Jocelyn, more seriously this time. "I never knew there was anything missing. But talking with Maggie revealed to me that some of my attitudes haven't been all they should be. You should have heard me, talking to her! I flared up and said I wanted to rule my own life. I surprised myself, Charles. I *have* harbored an independent streak without even knowing it. And this week, praying about it, I've realized I don't want that for our life together."

"Surely it's not as serious as all that."

"I don't want to be an independent woman, Charles," she persisted, "even if it's only silently and invisibly. I *want* you to be my head. I want you to seek God for me. I want you to tell me what you want me to do. I want you to help me, lead me, guide me, as a pastor or priest would do."

Charles sat dumbfounded, trying to take in this new relational twist his wife had thrown at him.

"Let me see if I understand you," he said after a moment. "What you're saying is that marriage isn't *supposed* to be a partnership between equals—"

"I didn't say that, exactly. Equal in *worth*, yes . . . but with different roles to occupy. And I'm not sure you and I have seen those roles very clearly up until now."

She went on to explain the distinction as Maggie had explained it to her.

"What if I do something selfish?" he asked after a few minutes.

"I trust you anyway, even though you'll make mistakes," she said.

"Then as the first act of this newly appointed head of the Rutherford home, I shall pray about all this we've talked about and see what our Father would have me . . . that is, have *us* do."

Jocelyn smiled. "I knew I could trust you," she said.

"What do you mean?"

"Maggie said that was the sign whether a man truly understood what rule in the home meant—if he asked *God* what to do rather than make every decision on the basis of what he himself might want."

"So you mean I passed my first test?" smiled Charles.

"With flying colors!" laughed Jocelyn. "The truest sign of godly manhood, Maggie said, is when a man realizes that headship doesn't originate with him at all, but flows through him from God."

60

Wintry Surprise

◆ ◆ ◆

*C*he rest of the summer passed uneventfully. Charles and Jocelyn Rutherford continued to accustom themselves to the many changes in outlook their new faith gradually brought them. Charles stopped in on Timothy Diggorsfeld in London as he had opportunity, and the minister paid another visit to Heathersleigh in mid-September.

The leaves turned. The harvest was brought in. Gradually a nip crept into the air, that hint of sharpness which said winter had probably arrived in Scotland and was headed toward more southern climes as well.

Black clouds gathered on the horizon one day toward the end of the first week of December as afternoon gave way to evening. But owing to the mild temperature and relative stillness of the air, Jocelyn Rutherford suspected nothing. It is true that she woke chilled some time after midnight and sought another blanket for their bed. But still she had no idea just how rapidly and how far the temperature was falling.

When Jocelyn awoke in the morning and walked sleepily to the window, to her surprise she saw the fields and forests of Devonshire lying buried beneath a quiet and wintry blanket of purest white.

"Charles . . . Charles, get up!" she exclaimed in delight. "It snowed."

"What are you talking about?" asked Charles, rolling lazily over in bed to face her.

"It snowed last night!"

"It hardly ever snows in Devon and Cornwall."

"But it *did*, Charles—come look! Oh, it's beautiful."

Already Jocelyn was dressing as if she were a child again and couldn't wait to get out in it. Never having lived where snow fell with regularity, it would always be new to her.

By the time Charles got to the window and beheld the sight, already Jocelyn was scurrying downstairs. Charles dressed and hurried after her. He found his wife standing in front of the open kitchen door, frigid air streaming in, beholding the sight.

"I just love it!" she said.

"From the looks of those footprints," said Charles, pointing to the trail that led from the side door across to the stables, "you're not the only one anxious to get your feet cold and wet. Hector must have already made it out to tend the horses."

"I'm not so sure it was Hector," replied Jocelyn. "They look like smaller feet than his."

"Only one way to find out!" Suddenly Charles had charged past her and out into the three-inch blanket.

"Charles . . . come back!" she laughed. "Your boots . . . you'll freeze!"

But he was already tromping across the buried lawn, kicking up great sprays of fluffy powder in all directions and laughing like a boy.

"Wait for me!" cried Jocelyn, running after him with as little thought for her feet as he had shown for his. Before she had taken three or four steps, suddenly a hastily assembled snowball flew past her head.

"Charles—you stop that!" she laughed. "Two can play that game, you know!" Jocelyn bent down and quickly formed a ball of her own which, three seconds later, exploded in the middle of Charles' back. He tossed two or three more in his wife's direction, then turned and made for the stables. Several more snowballs flew past him, and he ducked out of their path.

"George, my boy—it's you," he exclaimed, running inside as a frozen clump smacked against the wall beside the door with a dull thud.

The next moment Jocelyn ran inside.

"My hands are frozen!" she exclaimed. "George—what are you doing out here?"

"It snowed," George replied matter-of-factly, continuing on with his project, thinking nothing out of the ordinary about his father and mother engaging in a snowball fight at half-past seven in the morning. He was well used to their playful antics.

"We know!" laughed both Charles and Jocelyn in unison.

"I'm making a sled, Papa," said the boy. "I'm going to take it up onto the hill and slide down."

"Good for you, George—how will you do it?" asked Charles, rubbing his hands together as he approached George's workbench.

"I found these two long pieces of metal—"

"You two go on with your sled," interrupted Jocelyn. "I'm going back inside to warm up and put on some dry shoes!"

——————— ◆ ◆ ◆ ———————

An hour later, the family was seated around the breakfast table, all five faces red from the cold and aglow with excitement as everyone spoke enthusiastically. Even Sarah and Hector seemed to have been injected with the festive spirit brought on by the snowfall. Amanda and Catharine had already been outside long enough to get thoroughly cold and wet and were dressed in the second of what would be numerous changes of clothing before the day was over. Everyone shouted out their plans and ideas for the day all at once.

"Can we build a snowman, Papa?" said five-year-old Catharine.

"Of course you can, my dear, just so long as you wear your mittens. Snow can be very dangerous for little fingers, you know."

"I want to go sliding on George's sled," said Amanda. "Will you make one for all of us, Papa?"

"We'll see what we can do. If not, I'm sure George won't mind sharing. We'll all go out to the hill together. I might try it myself! How about you, Jocie?"

"I'll try. But I've never been on a sled in my life. We didn't have snow in India when I was a girl. The only thing I ever did with snow is eat it—and my London friends taught me that one holiday in the Lake District."

Suddenly a look of inspiration came over Charles' face.

"I've got it!" he said. "George, my boy, let's take your engineering design a step further. What do you say to you and me making some iron rails to attach to the wheels of one of the carriages? We'll immobilize the axles so that when it's pulled it has to slide along the ground—we'll turn it into a sleigh! Then we'll hitch it up to Red Lady and take a ride."

"A sleigh ride—how wonderful!" exclaimed Jocelyn. "Oh, Charles, when will it be ready?"

"What do you say, George—shall you and I get working on it right after breakfast?"

At the moment George had a piece of toast in his mouth, but he nodded eagerly.

"Then a sleigh ride after lunch it shall be!" announced Charles. "We'll go cut a Christmas tree in the woods."

"And visit the McFees," said Jocelyn, "—oh, and I'll show the children how to make sugar snow the way we did in Keswick! It will be so much fun."

"I still want to make a snowman," said Catharine.

"You shall have all morning, while George and I are busy with the sleigh."

"And I still want to go sledding," said Amanda.

"We'll take the sled along and go sledding, and we'll make sugar snow and visit the McFees and cut a Christmas tree. We'll just have a regular adventure all afternoon!"

61

The Sleigh Ride

◆◆◆

*F*our hours later the family Rutherford set out for their ride in the sleigh, newly fabricated by father and son.

"Just think, children," said Charles as he gave Red Lady the rein and the sleigh started on its way, its makeshift runners jerking only a little before gaining momentum, "in a little less than three weeks it will be Christmas, our third holy season as a Christian family. Everything about Christmas is so much more meaningful now, isn't it?"

"Did it snow in Bethlehem, Papa?" asked Catharine.

"I don't know, dear. I doubt it."

"Why?"

"It's warmer there than here. And the Bible says the shepherds were out in their fields. I don't think they would have been out had it been snowing."

"Oh."

"What's the best part of Christmas, do you think? What's the most special of all?"

"Presents!" said Catharine and Amanda at once.

"No doubt, no doubt!" laughed Charles. "But what's the most *significant* about Christmas?"

"The baby Jesus," suggested George.

"That's probably what most people would say. What else? What's the greatest gift at Christmas?"

Now it was quiet for some time as they whisked along.

"Jesus himself, don't you mean?" asked Jocelyn at length. "That's what Christmas means, that Jesus was born."

"That is surely why we celebrate Christmas," rejoined Charles. "So what is God's greatest gift to us?"

"Jesus," repeated Jocelyn.

"What did Jesus bring us?"

"Salvation."

"How did he do that? How could he do that?"

Jocelyn thought for a moment. The children listened to varying degrees as they watched the snowy countryside glide along beside them. They were used to their father's way of teaching and trying to get them to think about things in new ways—questioning, discussing, and sharing his own observations.

"Because Jesus is God," suggested Jocelyn.

"Right. So what was his gift?"

"I think I finally see what you're getting at," she said at length. "God gave us himself."

"Exactly," rejoined Charles. "I was turning it over in my mind the whole time George and I were working this morning. Suddenly it dawned on me that God himself is the wonderful message of Christmas. He sent Jesus to us so that he could show us himself as our loving Father. That's what he was giving us—himself."

"But they're one, aren't they?"

"Of course. It's impossible to separate them. But his fatherhood was God's most precious gift to mankind. And he sent Jesus to earth to give it to us. Jesus is not the gift in himself, but the bearer of the gift. The gift is the good news that we have a Father in heaven who loves us and whom we can trust."

"It makes so much sense now that you say it," replied Jocelyn thoughtfully. "Of course that was the reason Jesus came, wasn't it, because he said so himself—to tell us about the Father. He said it over and over."

"Timothy is constantly stressing that," said Charles, "—that Jesus came to let men and women know the wonderful and amazing truth that had been kept obscured through Old Testament times."

"In other words, Jesus' birth means that the Son has a Father."

Charles nodded. "It was about more than a baby being born. It was that the baby had been sent by his Father, the Father of all mankind."

"I thought Jesus came to bring salvation, Papa," said George.

"He did, my boy. Jesus came to provide the way to salvation, which exists nowhere else but in the Father's loving and forgiving heart. Without God's fatherhood there is no salvation. It is because he loves us with a father's unconditional love that he—the Father—saves us. Such was Jesus' purpose for living here on earth, to take us by the hand and bring us to the Father's heart of love. That was the purpose of his dying too, the whole purpose of the cross—reconciliation with our forgiving Father."

"Everything you've been saying makes Christmas suddenly seem so much larger," said Jocelyn.

"Timothy often says that *everything* of God's is so much larger than *we* think," said Charles thoughtfully, "—especially his salvation."

"Why did it take us so long to see the largeness of God's ways?"

"Spiritual insight is such a curious thing, Jocie," sighed Charles. "Timothy says that small-minded men are forever eager to place boundaries around what God does, or can do, or *might* do, so that they can explain his ways and means to the satisfaction of their finite intellects."

"Are such boundaries a bad thing?"

"I don't know," replied Charles slowly.

He paused, and gradually a smile spread over his face. "I think I know what Timothy might say in response."

"What?"

"That some of them might be necessary to help us understand what might not otherwise be understandable to our earthly minds. But he would probably be quick to add that God's work among men has fewer boundaries than we generally think."

"I'm not sure I understand what you mean."

"Boundaries and limitations speak of finiteness," Charles went on, "and by definition God is infinite. Especially must God's love and salvation not be limited by man's interpretations—and by the boundaries man would attempt to set for the extent of their reach."

Jocelyn nodded as she contemplated the implications of what her husband had just said.

They had by now left the Hall out of sight and entered a wooded region about a mile west of the McFee cottage. As the day was cold and still, the fluffy powder yet clung to every limb and branch, transforming the entire landscape into a white, sparkling wonderland.

"It is so beautiful!" exclaimed Jocelyn for the twentieth time that day.

"Keep your eyes on the lookout for a Christmas tree, children," said Charles. "We want one as beautiful as the queen's!"

"Could we cut two trees, Charles?" said Jocelyn. "I've been wanting to do something this Christmas for poor Mrs. Blakeley down in the village."

"A good idea, Jocie. I'll take it over to Rune myself. Might give me a chance to talk to him."

"Then I'll bake them a ham and give it to his wife later.—Oh, there's a good spot of thick snow. Could we stop, Charles? It's perfect for sugar snow."

He reined in Red Lady. In an instant George, Amanda, and Catharine were over the sides of the temporary sleigh and tearing off through the snow.

"Children, come back! I've a treat for you," called Jocelyn after them.

But already snowballs were flying. Luckily Catharine was well bundled, her head protected by a white fleecy hat tied securely in place down over her ears, for she quickly had the worst of the battle. Giggling with delight, she tried in vain to return the volleys from her brother and sister.

"George, stop that!" yelled Amanda. A white blob had just smacked the side of her head.

"George, not in the face or head," said Charles.

"I didn't mean to, Amanda," said George.

"You did too!" she shot back. "You've just been waiting to throw one right at me."

"I wasn't aiming for your head."

"You were too!"

"Children, please," said Jocelyn, "I brought sugar and some cream and vanilla. If we mix them with the soft snow we can make ice cream. Here are cups for you all—go fill them with snow. Then bring them here, and I'll pour cream and vanilla and sprinkle sugar over them."

The three scampered off.

"Always the activity director," laughed Charles.

"I never did things like this when I was a girl. So I'm enjoying it now!"

"You're quite a mother, do you know? Our three children are the luckiest children in all the world."

"Stop, Charles—you'll embarrass me."

"I am perfectly serious. You always make things fun for the children. I don't know how you always come up with such ideas."

Husband and wife were interrupted by the sounds of argument.

"Find your own snow, Amanda," George was saying.

"You took the best place. Give me some of it!" As she spoke, Amanda scooped up a handful in front of George, knocking over the cup he had been packing.

"Children, for heaven's sake," called their father good-humoredly. "The whole forest is full of snow. There's enough for ten thousand cupsful. Surely you don't have to both take it from the exact same spot."

"George took the best place," insisted Amanda.

"I did not!"

"The snow's all dirty everywhere else."

"You'd just want mine wherever I went."

"Please, children, can't one of you move to somewhere else? There's a whole world of snow!"

With resignation, George stood and began to move away. As he did, he gave a kick of snow in his sister's direction.

"George kicked me!" she cried.

"I did not. It was only a little snow. Don't be such a baby."

"George, Amanda, stop arguing this minute," said Charles, at last losing his patience.

"I found some snow for my cup!" cried out Catharine, who had wandered away on the other side of the carriage.

Suddenly Amanda was off like a shot toward her little sister, deserting the prized territory so recently disputed with her brother.

"Amanda, leave Catharine alone," said Jocelyn, climbing down onto the ground as Amanda ran past. "Find your own place."

"It's not fair. Everyone else gets clean snow, but there's none for me."

"Good heavens, Amanda!" laughed Charles in disbelief. "Don't be ridiculous. Open your eyes."

"Come over here, Amanda," said Jocelyn. "I'll help you find a perfect spot."

Reluctantly Amanda complied. A few minutes later everyone had their cups in hand and stood beside the sleigh.

"And do you have *your* cup, Charles?" said Jocelyn.

"Of course. I wouldn't miss this."

"All right, then. Everyone, get your spoons ready, and hold out your cups. I'll pour on the cream and vanilla . . . then sprinkle on the sugar."

"This is good!" said George, sampling the concoction.

"It just tastes like sweet water," said Amanda.

"I like it!" said Catharine.

"The whole thing seems rather stupid to me," insisted Amanda. "The ice cream we had when we were in London was so much better."

"But it's fun to make it," said Charles. "Amanda, your mother has planned a pleasant activity for us here. Can't you enjoy it without complaining?"

"I don't think it's fun."

"Your mother made an effort to do something special and you—"

"It's all right, Charles," said Jocelyn softly. "I don't mind."

"But I do. I get tired of her not appreciating all you do for her."

"Please, it's not so important. The rest of us are enjoying it."

George glanced up and saw his mother sigh with disappointment. He had seen the look many times before. He gave Amanda a sharp poke in the ribs.

"George, stop it. George hit me!"

"You always spoil everything," he returned.

"I do not. It was all your fault."

"George, that wasn't a very kind thing to say to your sister," said Charles. "I want you to apologize."

"Why do I always have to apologize? Besides, what I said was true."

"You were unkind. That deserves an apology."

"Why don't you make Amanda apologize?"

Before Charles had a chance to say anything further, Catharine began to cry. Jocelyn gathered up the cups and supplies and climbed back up into the carriage.

"Let's just go back to the house, Charles," she said. "I think that would be best."

"Nonsense—come on, everyone," said Charles, doing his best to regain a cheerful spirit, "let's go get those trees!"

"Who cares about Christmas trees anyway?" groused Amanda.

Charles sighed with frustration and glanced toward Jocelyn. This was not how they had hoped the day would turn out.

"*I* care about them," he said. "We're going to get those trees, and this *is* going to be a pleasant outing. Come on, everyone—load back into the sleigh."

Charles urged Red Lady forward, and again the sleigh whisked off through the woods, though their surroundings did not seem nearly so magical as they had fifteen minutes earlier. The mood remained subdued, and they rode along for some distance in relative silence.

"It's the Christmas season," said Charles at length. "It's a wonderfully beautiful day. Let's not let a little argument spoil it. We'll go cut a couple of trees. We'll find a good steep hill and try out George's sled. We'll go pay a visit to Bobby and Maggie McFee. Then we'll go home and set up the tree in the entryway—what do you all say!"

Jocelyn glanced at her husband and forced a smile, then gave Catharine, who sat on her lap still whimpering, a tight squeeze. She just hoped there would be no more incidents today. If they hadn't been able to get along over the snow, she couldn't imagine how they would be able to share a single sled.

PART V

---◆◆◆---

Challenge and Decision
1904

62

New Challenges, New Opportunities

———————— ◆ ◆ ◆ ————————

𝒯he new century came, and the future accompanying it was now in full stride.

King Edward VII shared the throne of Great Britain with the memory of his mother, dead for three years. Many and strong continued the forces for social and political change. The new century, however, would bring with it a future far different from what most English citizens would have predicted.

On the horizon, not nearly so distant as one might imagine, already sounded the faint drumbeats of approaching conflict. Accompanying them, for those with ears to hear, were dissonant tones of strife, a global symphony in minor key whose movements were titled unrest, revolution, and change.

This music, if such it could be called, originated in the east. From Russia especially it came, where the communist movement, spawned by the German Karl Marx during his sojourn in England, took deeper root with every passing year. The turbulent lands of Serbia and Austria-Hungary added their strident treble to the ominous bass of the crumbling Ottoman Empire. In the midst of it all sounded the sinister beginnings of a dangerous nationalistic march from a newly unified and increasingly powerful German empire.

To the discordant strains of this confusing cacophony, old alliances were shifting, new ones forming. The power structure of the globe was being shaken as the music of change continued to swell, its drums beating with the cadence of foot soldiers striding unmistakably toward war.

But few west of the Rhine as yet detected the faint strains of coming discord. Though the majority of English men and women knew change to be inevitable, they still harbored the illusion that the change would be peaceful and progressive, that the greatest of the world's powers would continue to enjoy peace and prosperity, happiness and tranquility, for many decades to come. They read in their newspapers of developments on the Continent almost as if reading a novel, secure in the belief that the channel between the French coast and Dover would prevent aggression from intruding upon their hallowed shores.

There were those, however, who understood that the alliances that had maintained Europe's peace since German and Italian unification in 1871 were inevitably shifting and fracturing with the passage of time and in some cases eroding altogether.

Thus far had diplomacy carried the day.

But perilous times lay ahead.

The request for a meeting with prime minister A.J. Balfour took Charles Rutherford completely by surprise. It was not merely that the two men represented opposing parties in Parliament. They were also relative strangers, despite many years across the aisle from one another.

"Sit down . . . sit down, Sir Charles," said the prime minister, closing the door behind him that their meeting might be private. "Would you care for something . . . brandy, Scotch?"

"Tea will be fine, Prime Minister," replied Charles.

"I'll ring for a pot."

Taking his own seat a moment later, Prime Minister Balfour's face grew serious. He went straight to the point.

"You are no doubt perplexed about my calling you in like this," he said.

"I confess—yes, I am, Prime Minister. I don't believe the Conservatives need our Liberal bloc of votes just yet. Besides," he added with a smile, "I doubt my colleagues would agree to a coalition."

"I have no doubt of that," returned Balfour, also smiling shrewdly. "No, I have called you here on another errand altogether. One that I consider—and I hope you also will see it as such—nonpolitical."

He paused. As if he had anticipated it, a knock sounded on the door. His secretary entered bearing a tea tray. It was two or three minutes before he resumed.

"The Continent grows steadily more worrisome," the prime minister said at length. "That fact will come as no surprise to you or anyone in either the House of Commons or the House of Lords. We have been debating and discussing the various trouble spots for years. But I fear for the stability of Europe, Sir Charles. We must be prepared, whatever direction events take. The Germans and Russians are entirely unpredictable. Their histories are rife with violence—and I fear we have not seen the last of their warmongering."

Charles Rutherford listened respectfully, sipping at his tea. Many in Parliament were voicing similar sentiments, despite general public complacency.

"Well, sir, I have decided to do something about it," Balfour went on. "Whether it will help, who can tell? But we mustn't sit idly by. I have, therefore, decided to sponsor an inquiry into the likelihood of war and England's preparedness for it."

"Are you not concerned about raising public alarm?" now asked Charles.

"It will be done quietly," rejoined the prime minister. "For this Commission on Preparedness, it is my hope to enlist the support of all parties, thus making the venture truly apolitical."

"I see."

"There are times when politics must subserve the greater national good, and this is such a time. We will not make a display of the Commission's findings. I would hope we could keep the *Times* off our backs for a while, though I have no objection to your talking the matter over with your colleagues. We must all lay aside partisanship for the good of England."

The prime minister paused.

"Talking over . . . *what* matter, sir?"

Balfour eyed Charles carefully.

"It is my hope," he went on after a moment, "that *you* will agree to head the Commission."

Charles returned his gaze with an expression between surprise and incredulity.

"Me," he said in astonishment. "Why me? Why not a member of your own party?"

"Precisely because you are *not* a Tory, Sir Charles. It is my hope that my appointing a Liberal to head a broad-based effort will demonstrate my good faith in keeping the matter free from political controversy. You are one of the most respected men in the Commons. You are recognized as one of Parliament's rising stars, and you are well thought of among your own colleagues. Simply put—I consider you the best man for the job."

"You are most kind, sir. I am flattered and honored."

"Then you accept?"

"I must, of course, take time to think the matter over . . . and talk with my wife."

"Ah, yes, I understand. But as you do, Sir Charles, bear in mind that there may be more than the future of your nation at stake. This may also be an important opportunity for you."

"In what way, Prime Minister?"

"To put your stamp on history, Sir Charles," Balfour told him as he rose from his chair. "To make an enduring mark for which you will be remembered . . . to establish your political legacy."

63

The Boy With the Withered Leg

♦♦♦

*W*alking in Milverscombe with her mother, Amanda Rutherford heard rude sounds as they approached the entrance of a side street.

Amanda glanced up. A boy who looked to be a year or two younger than her own fourteen years, though his condition made age difficult to estimate, struggled across their path. He limped decrepitly in the vain attempt to keep up with his father. The man had hold of the lad's hand and was half dragging, half yanking him into the street. The boy, whose right leg was withered to only about half the thickness of the other, could scarcely walk upright. Yet his father, clearly under the influence of strong drink, pressed forward with great strides.

"Keep up with me, you good-for-nothing cur!" growled the man. He gave him a cruel tug that now pulled the strong leg out from under his son. Released from the supporting hand of his father, the boy sprawled on his face in the dirt of the street.

"Get up, you fool!" cried the man. He stopped, turned, and gave the boy a kick in the ribs.

Whimpering in pain, the lad struggled to his knees, then fell back unsuccessfully. His father was about to strike again when Amanda broke from her mother's side. She ran forward into the middle of the street. She stooped down and helped the boy to his feet.

The eyes of the two met for the briefest of seconds—the young cripple and his pretty young champion—but there was no time for words between them. The next instant Amanda felt a vise-grip on her shoulder. A great man's hand pulled her forcefully back.

"If you know what's good for you, Lady Rutherford," the man said menacingly to Amanda's mother, "you'll keep this daughter of yours from meddling in other folks' affairs! And I'll thank you to keep away from my wife. We need no charity from the likes of you."

The man yanked Amanda back to her feet and shoved her toward her mother, nearly throwing her to the ground as he did. He grabbed the boy's hand once more, sent the back of his free hand against the youngster's face with a wicked slap, then twisted the thin arm viciously. He now pulled the boy up behind him and once again continued on his way.

Seething indignation rose up in Amanda's heart. For a moment she stood as if paralyzed while, behind her, tears quietly filled Jocelyn Rutherford's eyes. Only a moment more did Amanda's silence last.

"We have to *do* something," she said through clenched teeth. Her tone was one of quiet wrath.

"There is nothing we can do," replied her mother softly. "Not here. Not now."

"Father's a knight and an important man!" rejoined the fourteen-year-old zealot, as if the fact of her father's position both in the village and in London could of itself right any wrong.

"Your father is not here. And I am a woman," replied Jocelyn with no less pity in her heart than Amanda felt. The wisdom of her years, however, had tempered her compassion with caution.

"What difference does that make?" demanded Amanda.

"There is nothing I can possibly do. And even if there were, I would not do it without speaking with your father."

"Why? He's not here."

"He is my spiritual head, Amanda—at all times, not just when we are together."

Amanda rolled her eyes. This was another of her mother's sermons about a woman's place. She made it sound as if Father were a god or something. Couldn't she think for herself anymore?

"Any interference from us," Jocelyn went on, "would not only place us in danger, but make things worse for the boy."

"That man wouldn't dare hurt you, Mother. If he touched you, he would be put in jail."

"Perhaps," replied Jocelyn, "which is yet another reason I mustn't interfere."

"Why?" asked Amanda, unable to grasp her mother's reluctance.

"His being in jail would do the boy no good."

"He would be better off than he is now!"

"Not without a father, Amanda."

"But he's a bad man. Didn't you see him, Mother? He was drunk! He hit him."

"He is still the boy's father. That must always count for more than we might be able presently to see."

"Why?"

"A bad father is better than no father at all, because you never know what healing God might intend in a family."

Amanda could find no trace of her mother's reasoning to agree with. To her youthful ears, it sounded more than ridiculous.

"Rune Blakeley is a heartless father; everyone knows it," Jocelyn went on. "The poor boy's situation is sad, but I fear you and I cannot change it today. I will continue to do what I can for his mother, and your father has long been trying to have an influence with Mr. Blakeley, but—"

"He's a drunk and a wicked man!" insisted Amanda.

"We cannot change that, Amanda. Your helping young Stirling just now only made his problems worse. He will probably be whipped mercilessly when they reach home."

◆ ◆ ◆

The incident was suddenly as vivid as yesterday. Eight-year-old Jocelyn Wildecott struggled to climb down from the carriage after her mother. The Bombay street was wet and slippery from recent rains. So too were the carriage steps.

Mrs. Wildecott, stepping carefully herself to avoid the wet patches in the street, did not have hold of her daughter's hand. The tiny white thing repulsed her, and she would touch it only if absolutely compelled to do so. Such occasions were extremely rare.

On the bottom step young Jocelyn slipped, stumbling to the ground and onto her knees in the mud.

A cry escaped her lips.

"Shh!" sounded the stern voice of her mother towering above

her. "Get up—do you want everyone to see? And keep your feet out of the puddles!"

The girl glanced up, where a small crowd of women stood in front of the church. A few heads had turned toward them. She was agonizingly aware that eyes now watched her and her mother. Small wonder that as she grew, the place had never become for her a symbol of life, but only one of pain and humiliation.

Mrs. Wildecott stooped down, pretending for the sake of the onlookers to help her daughter up, but in fact lending no hand of support.

"Stand up!" she whispered to Jocelyn. "As if your face isn't enough, you have to find other ways to embarrass me in front of my friends."

Jocelyn managed to regain her feet, tears rising in her eyes. They were more from her mother's cruel words than the stinging of her knees. But she would blink back the tears until they were dry. She could not let her mother see them.

Mrs. Wildecott took a handkerchief, brushed it roughly against the two thin knees, succeeding in removing most of the stain, then tossed the muddy cloth onto the floor of the carriage. With her daughter again halfway presentable, which was the most the lady ever hoped for, Mrs. Wildecott stood again to her full height, turned, and walked smiling toward the gathering at the church steps.

Doing her best to keep her head tilted slightly downward, and the side of her birthmark turned away from view, Jocelyn silently followed.

———— ♦ ♦ ♦ ————

Jocelyn Rutherford shook her head, trying to rid herself of the painful memory of childhood. She had felt the sting of a parent's rejection no less than Stirling Blakeley. She had had to learn both to forgive and to discover what good there was to glean from it.

As they walked away, Amanda knew her mother was murmuring a prayer for the poor boy whose plight they had just witnessed. The fact did nothing to soften Amanda's heart. She *hated* Rune Blakeley. If she were older *she* would see that he was punished for his brutality.

How dare he treat her as he had—and talk rudely to her and her mother!

She glanced back for one last look over her shoulder, then turned and continued at her mother's side. As the day progressed, the injustice she felt for lame young Stirling, and her hatred of his father, gathered to itself a smoldering irritation against her mother for being so unconcerned, as Amanda judged it, in the face of the horrible encounter. How *could* she just walk off as if nothing had happened?

A determination rose up within the young daughter of Sir Charles and Lady Jocelyn Rutherford that day. She resolved to do more than just *pray* for things like her parents did or take people an occasional ham. When opportunities were presented her she would *do* something that made a difference.

Praying—what did that ever accomplish!

Her mother's words repeated themselves over and over in her mind throughout the afternoon: *I am a woman. There is nothing I can possibly do.*

She would be different, Amanda determined. She would not let indifference dominate *her* life as it had that of her parents ever since they had become so religious! And she would never let being a woman hold her back. After all, Queen Victoria had influenced the entire world for more than half a century—more than any *man*.

Amanda still recalled the late queen's eyes and gentle voice as she looked into her face. *I am sure you will turn the world on its ear when your time comes, won't you, dear?* the soft voice sounded in her memory.

"Yes, I will," whispered Amanda as they rode silently home from the village that day. *"Yes . . . I will!"*

They called this the Edwardian era, the age of men. But women were making their mark everywhere too. Not all women were like her mother, timidly following behind their husbands and never doing anything for themselves.

Amanda certainly had no intention of living such a passive life. She would assert herself. Maybe she could never be queen. But she would make her mark, just as she and her father used to talk about before . . . before he had changed, and become so complacent to everything around him, and her mother along with him.

When she was older, she would come find Rune Blakeley if it lay within her power; then she would give him what he deserved!

64
Opportunity and Adventure

♦♦♦

*T*he dimly lit coffeehouse in Vienna, situated as it was so near the university, had been a center for student debate, discussion, and political dialogue since the days of Napoleon.

Now in the heady days of the first decade of the twentieth century, with socialism in vogue throughout Europe's centers of learning, it was a popular gathering spot for those who considered themselves singularly capable of changing history. Not an evening went by in the Vienna *Kaffe Kellar* that discussion did not range from democracy to revolution. In the process it covered nearly everything between.

"What do you think?" said a young man at a corner table, apparently in his mid-twenties. He took a tentative sip from his steaming cup of strong coffee. "Will it come to revolution in Russia?"

"It appears likely," answered the other, a twenty-year-old student from England visiting the city for the first time, "if the reports are true."

"Oh, but they *are* true," rejoined his companion. "I was in Moscow last year. Russia's war with Japan has weakened the government, and the student movement remains strong. There will be revolution within the year—depend upon it."

"You sound enthusiastic," remarked the young visitor. His tone was uncertain, yet curious.

"But of course. The possibilities for changing the social fabric of Europe have never been greater. Revolution is the answer to our dreams. You told me you are a socialist."

"I am, but—"

"But what? Our time has come—the moment when history takes its new course. It is those such as you and I who will bring it about."

"You really think it is possible?"

"Only for those who are not afraid of the adventure—those who are willing to seize the chance when it comes to them."

It fell silent a moment. The younger of the two sipped from his cup of weak tea and grimaced slightly. If it were true, as many of his friends on the Continent claimed, that the English were incapable of making good coffee, it was equally axiomatic that the rest of Europe could not brew an acceptable pot of tea.

"What kind are you, my friend?" asked the coffee drinker at length. His voice contained, as he intended, a tone of significance and intrigue.

"How do you mean?" asked the student.

"Are you one of the few? Do you possess courage for the adventure ahead?"

"I've always considered myself unafraid to face new challenges," answered the youth.

"Even in the face of opposition and persecution?"

"What persecution?"

"Some would consider those of our outlook a devilish cult. But they are merely those who have not seen the light of revelation."

"What revelation?"

"The fountain of truth."

The student's eyebrows lifted at the cryptic statement, but he decided for the present not to inquire further into its meaning. "What are you called?" he asked.

"We go by no name. We know ourselves. The source of the fountain's light must remain hidden for now."

They drank again from their respective brews.

"So, my friend . . . are *you* eager to seize the opportunity?" asked the drinker of strong coffee.

"What opportunity? Be more specific," said the drinker of weak tea.

"To join our number, to become one of the enlightened, to be one of the fountain's chosen when the new era dawns. There are always opportunities in times of change, opportunities which can involve making a great deal of money very easily."

"Money means little to me. I am well provided for."

"Is that why you travel?"

"One of the reasons. It relieves the boredom."

"If money means little to you, does the cause?"

"Perhaps."

The two continued to speak in low tones.

"There is someone I want you to meet," said the native of the Continent. "He has been looking for one like you who is able to travel freely."

"To do what?"

"Nothing strenuous, I assure you. At first, only to take an occasional small package past your own border officials."

The student laughed. "Nothing could be easier!" he said.

"Ah, now it is *you* who sound enthusiastic."

"Just the sort of prank I would enjoy!"

"Then come," said the other, rising, "I will take you to meet my friend tonight."

65
The Place of Heather

*C*harles Rutherford arrived back from London late that afternoon. His day had been eventful enough in its own right. After his meeting with Prime Minister Balfour in the morning, he had met later in the day with the leadership of his own Liberal party.

These were momentous times, and the lord of the manor of Heathersleigh was squarely in the thick of them. His heart, however, was heavy rather than enthusiastic about the prospects that faced him, and he greeted his wife with a preoccupied smile.

Jocelyn's welcome was subdued as well, her mind still troubled by the incident in the village that day. Both husband and wife knew their ears were needed for one another, so they left the house together immediately after tea. Hand in hand they walked across the entryway and down to the heather garden they had together reclaimed from the encroaching woods and begun cultivating some years ago.

Their talk with Timothy Diggorsfeld during his first of many visits to Heathersleigh five years earlier had sparked a new round of horticultural creativity. Since then, they had worked tirelessly among the heather plants, praying as they worked for Amanda and the similar work the hands of the Lord would perform in the soil of *her* garden when she at last relinquished the tools of it into his care. As a result of their efforts, several new paths, a stream, and a small wooden bridge had been added to the garden, all the labor of Charles' and Jocelyn's own hands.

The heather garden was now their favorite haunt about the place. Especially on such a warm autumn evening as this, when probably half the various species were in bloom, it was peaceful and lovely.

They followed the brick-lined path into the garden, strolling casually and aimlessly through its winding depths, passing between hedges and single shrubs and beside rock gardens. They crossed the small winding stream in several places, here by bridge, now by large rocks in its midst. Except for a few species of dwarfed pine, nothing grew here but heather blooming in variegated shades of white, pink, and purple. As was now their custom, husband and wife prayed silently as they went.

"It is an unlikely plant to be capable of such beauty, is it not, Jocelyn?" finally remarked Charles as they ambled along.

Jocelyn smiled in acknowledgment. "Just like this face of mine," she said, "which you always insist you see beauty in, however unlikely that is. I must admit I still have a difficult time believing you."

"You *are* beautiful, Jocie, and I will keep telling you, until you believe it. Even then, I will not stop."

"There are times when even a simple *I love you* from your lips sends me into a fresh round of doubts about myself. Even after so many years, I find it hard to believe someone could love me as you do."

"I know," replied Charles with a serious face. "Such is your path to walk. But you must walk it, Jocie. You must keep moving forward, reminding yourself that even these stem from the Father's love for you, for the deepening of your character and your trust in him. You must keep telling yourself that you are his handiwork . . . and you have his fingerprint to prove it."

She sighed. "I *do* know that, Charles. I even believe that the Lord gave me you to help me know what his love is like. It's just so . . . well, it's still so difficult to see this *thing* as a mark of God's love. You say I am beautiful. But sometimes I wonder if I shall ever believe it . . . truly believe it in the depths of my heart. . . ."

"There is a mystery in all lovely things," he mused. "Beauty has so many facets. The beauty in one human face, especially, may be more difficult to find than in another. There is a beauty that presents itself to the first glance. But there is a deeper radiance that takes time to see.

This deeper beauty is all the more special in that it is reserved for the eyes of the truly discerning. Heather is just the same. Its beauty is perhaps not for all to see."

It was quiet a moment or two.

"There is indeed a quality of mystery about heather," added Charles, bending over to check on a plant, "altogether unlike the beauty of rose or the orchid or the tulip. Nor does it contain the fragrance of a hyacinth."

"The plant itself is really quite ordinary," said Jocelyn.

"Even ugly," rejoined Charles. "In many parts of the world, at most times of the year, it is considered little more than a weed that grows where little else will survive—a wiry little annoyance even sheep and goats are reluctant to eat. And yet..."

Charles paused and gazed about him, gesturing with his arm.

"—and yet all together, the infinite variations of hue, when the colors mix and flow into one another like this—there is such an inexplicable and subtle beauty to it. I have grown to love it like few other growing things. I cannot imagine how I could have been so unseeing all those years."

"We were unseeing of many things," said Jocelyn with a sad smile. "Thankfully we are learning to appreciate them at last."

"But I grew up here, Jocelyn! Overgrown as this place was, the heather must still have bloomed. Of course it bloomed. Remember what Timothy said—heather is so rugged it blooms *whatever* its surroundings. So it must have flowered here all year round, every day of my boyhood and youth, and after I was grown. But until the Lord began opening my eyes to his world and his work in it, I never saw its beauty."

He paused a moment, gazing at the shrubbery around him.

"Have you noticed," Charles went on, "how the heather even changes shades—or seems to—depending on the light, appearing different in a morning sun than at evening's dusk?"

"I have noticed," said Jocelyn.

"The yellow or blue of the primrose or the purple of the viola is the same yellow or blue or purple in every setting. But heather always seems to summon a slightly different hue to show its admirer."

"Like the infinite expressions of the human face?" suggested Jocelyn with a small smile.

"It does make you think that God created each face and flower and placed a different message inside each one for us to discover as we gaze upon them . . . and ponder the One who made them."

"I do love the way everything that bears God's image is a little different than everything else."

"Do you see why I am so fond of Timothy's analogy of God's fingerprint—because all fingerprints are different and personal? *Everything* God made is so wonderfully unique. And unlike the rose or the tulip," Charles went on enthusiastically, "which are so regal they cannot help but be stunning, heather is beautiful only to those eyes to whom it reveals its subtle secrets."

"A revealer of moods and subtleties?"

"Exactly—it speaks as much to the imagination as it does to the senses . . . like my beautiful wife!"

"Charles!"

"It's true."

He paused as a thoughtful expression came over his face.

"—yet for so long," he added, "I was unable to see the heather's nuances, though they were right in front of me. I was able somehow to recognize the principle when it came to human beings. But I was slower to awaken to the secrets of nature."

"Perhaps because during those years your intellect predominated over your imagination," commented Jocelyn. "You only beheld what your intellect saw."

"You are a shrewd one—you have me all figured out!" laughed her husband. "We'll have Professor Freud paying a visit to Heathersleigh before long to consult with you and garner your opinions!"

Jocelyn paused, stooped down, and plucked a blooming purple tip off one of the knee-high shrubs. She stood and held the flowery twig to her eyes for closer examination.

"Its intrigue must be why heather is legendary in Scotland and Germany and other places," she said as they continued on. "*Someone* in your family back in ancient times must have understood its complexities and loved it. Otherwise why would they have named the estate Heathersleigh?"

"I've never heard how the place came by the name," replied Charles thoughtfully.

"Heathersleigh—*place of the heather?*" mused Jocelyn. "Whoever named it, it's beautiful. Maybe there's a clue to the name somewhere in that Bible Gifford was asking about," laughed Jocelyn. "Do you think it will ever turn up?"

"We'll turn George loose on it," rejoined Charles. "After the connections he found between that locked old basement room and the garret, perhaps there are others. Perhaps some yet undiscovered chamber may contain family secrets."

"George was poking around up in the attic of the west wing the other day. He still insists there is a whole network of hidden corridors up there. That boy's curiosity is remarkable!"

"And his imagination!" laughed Charles. "He reminds me of myself at his age," he added, "—always tinkering and fiddling with something. Although I never undertook to explore the Hall the way he has."

66

Different Human Plants

◆◆◆

The conversation about their children reminded Jocelyn of the day's incident in the village, which in the course of their walk she had almost forgotten. Now she related it in detail to her husband.

"All three are different," sighed Charles, shaking his head, "but especially George and Amanda—they're like night and day. It's so much more than can be explained by the fact that George is a boy and Amanda a girl."

"They're like different human plants," sighed Jocelyn, twirling her little branch of heather. "That much is easy to see—and they're growing in such different directions."

"What have we done wrong, Jocelyn," asked Charles, "that Amanda seems so resentful of the perspectives we are trying to bring to our family? And why have George and Catharine, on the other hand, fallen in so naturally with them?"

"I thought we had done with blaming ourselves after talking and praying with Timothy," said Jocelyn.

"It's difficult not to place a burden of guilt upon myself when one of my own children seems to despise what I stand for. And look, Jocie—

Amanda's attitude has only soured since then, not improved."

"We mustn't measure the answers to prayer by our own timetable, Charles. You know that."

He nodded. "Yet how can a man help but feel he's done something wrong?"

"Amanda is fourteen years old, and she has been a strong and independent thinker for years. You can hardly blame yourself for that."

"Unless she came by her independent streak from me," he smiled.

"Independence can be a virtue or a vice, depending on whether it is used to *do* God's will or *resist* it."

"But it can hardly be denied that for the first years of her life I encouraged her to make up her mind for herself, to question and even to disagree with me if she was so inclined. I thought I was doing her such a service—expanding her mind, teaching her to think. Now I feel I overdid it. Not that I don't want all three, Catharine and George included, to think. What parent doesn't want that for his child? It's the resentment of rules, which I feel my training somehow fostered, that concerns me. I certainly never intended to encourage that. How can I not feel that I contributed to her present hostile attitudes?"

"Even if she acquired her spunk from you, *she* is still the one who must choose what she does with it."

Charles nodded. "She has *never* done well with restrictions," he said.

"Amanda's own motivations and choices in the matter must be taken into account," rejoined Jocelyn, "just like George's and Catharine's—and they are responding entirely positively to our becoming a Christian family together. George loves the Lord and is devoted to you. His garden *is* blooming. We must just wait longer for Amanda's, that's all."

Charles nodded thoughtfully. "A man can't help wondering, however, about his own role in those choices. What if I had not been away in London so much of the time? What if I had been more assertive in conveying my spiritual perspectives right when the change came?"

"We were struggling to understand everything ourselves," reminded Jocelyn. "We didn't speak out so much to the children initially because we were talking so much over between ourselves, trying to come to terms with a whole new way of looking at life. And then you and I had to learn a whole new way of being together as husband and wife. That wasn't easy—telling you to be more assertive!"

"It wasn't easy for me to do, either. I couldn't have done it without your prodding," he added, laughing. "You had to *make* me lead."

"I was happy to help," laughed Jocelyn.

"It remains difficult," said Charles, pensive again. "For so long I believed in equality all the way around. I was extremely uncomfortable trying to think of myself as the so-called authority of the family."

"But you saw the scriptural necessity of it. And you've stepped into your role as head of the home naturally and wonderfully."

Charles nodded. "Only with your help and encouragement," he said. "I didn't particularly like doing it. Temperamentally I would still prefer a more liberal, egalitarian approach. But if God tells me that I must be the head of the family, I really don't have any choice but to do my best at it. Perhaps my struggle in this area has also contributed to Amanda's difficulty in accepting our changed priorities. I have to admit that even as her father I was occasionally intimidated by Amanda, which added to that difficulty. It was far easier to be *your* spiritual head, because you welcomed it, than to be Amanda's."

"Amanda intimidated us both," sighed Jocelyn.

"That feeling is still there. More than ever, she resists all mention of spiritual matters."

"Your character is what must speak louder in the end than all the rest," reassured Jocelyn.

"I do hope it will," Charles replied with a sigh. "But I must admit, I see little that my character has caused in Amanda's heart other than annoyance, even bitterness."

"Remember the lesson of the heather," Jocelyn urged, "and what Timothy told us to do—*pray for her*. We must give God time to perfect his work in Amanda, Charles. Look how long it took for him to break through *our* outer shells."

They walked on several moments in silence. Charles was the first to break it.

"Even after seven years of trying to fall in with God's designs," he said, "there is still so much I find difficult to understand—such as the effect of spiritual values on children growing into adulthood."

"I know. It is hard to watch them, now that they are having to make determinations of belief for themselves."

"Do you ever wonder, Jocie, how it might have been different had we been Christians from the start? Different for George and Amanda and Catharine, I mean."

"Of course I wonder. How can I not? But I don't know, Charles—

would it have been different? It seems to me that one has to take life as it comes. When the Lord spoke, you listened. You gave your heart to him. You told me what you had done, and after a struggle, and your help, my heart responded as well. Since then I think we have honestly *tried* to obey him. We haven't done so perfectly. But whatever mistakes we've made, our *desire* and *prayer* has been to do as he wants us. George sees the man you have become as a result, and he honors it. He wants to be the same kind of man. Amanda *doesn't* see it in either of us. She resents me as much as she does you—resents my going along with you in everything, as she sees it. She is blind to the kind of sharing give-and-take and prayerful dialogue we constantly engage in. She has no idea how much freedom and latitude your loving headship allows me, nor how much trust you place in me. She doesn't have eyes to see any of those things yet. Opening her eyes is not something you or I can force her to do."

Charles sighed. "I continually pray exactly that for Amanda," he said, "that she will allow the Lord to open her eyes. But I cannot help wondering if there is something more we should do."

"What can we do but live faithfully? We must pray the day comes when she will see the Spirit at work both in us and in her own heart. It is *the Lord* who must cause Amanda's garden to bloom. At present she hasn't given us the option to actively cultivate her soil, so we must pray and leave it to him."

They had worked their way around in a circuitous loop that brought them back to the path by which they had entered the garden. Along this walk they now saw Sarah making her way with a tray.

"Thought you two might enjoy another cup o' tea before we all settled in for the night," she said.

"Ah, Sarah, you are a dear!" exclaimed Charles. "Thank you!"

"You are most welcome, sir."

"Will you join us?"

"Oh no, sir. I've the kitchen to tidy up. And you both looked so peaceful together as I came, I thought I had never seen such a couple as the two of you.—I could not intrude in *that*, now could I?"

Charles laughed.

"Well, Sarah, you are very kind . . . but we would be delighted to share our tea with you."

"Thank you just the same, sir."

She turned and walked back to the house. Charles and Jocelyn sat down on a flat stone bench with the tray of tea things between them. Jocelyn poured out two cups, which they sipped at for several minutes in silence.

67

Happy Evening

I wondered if we would ever have children," smiled Jocelyn. "Now we have three. And two are on the threshold of growing up."

"Time races by. Do you remember the evening I asked you to marry me?"

"What kind of a question is that!" laughed Jocelyn. "Of course I remember. How could I forget? You were so regal in your dress uniform."

"I almost had to drag you there."

"Not exactly *drag* me . . . but I'll admit I was apprehensive at first. When we walked in, and I saw all those people in their gowns and uniforms—I thought I would die of embarrassment."

"You did splendidly. No one would have known."

"Right at first—I don't know if I've ever told you this—I was angry with you. I almost turned and walked out."

"Angry," laughed Charles, "—why?"

"I thought you'd lied to me."

"Lied!"

"Well, all right—maybe that's too strong. Fibbed, then."

"About what? I would never lie to you, or fib either."

"I know that. And I knew it then too. But you had talked me into accompanying you to that affair by saying it was nothing out of the ordinary, nothing that would make me feel uncomfortable. And then we walked in, and—"

"It wasn't *that* big an event. Why, Jocelyn, you've mingled with M.P.s and spoken with Queen Victoria. That was just a little military soirée."

"I met Victoria *after* you taught me to believe in myself—and even that was difficult. But back then—Charles, those were not the kind of events I was accustomed to. I was mortified when we arrived. I wanted to shrivel up and hide. Will you never understand what it's like to feel self-conscious about everything? I didn't want anyone to see me . . . especially with you."

The festive sounds of music, celebration, and voices faded behind them as twenty-three-year-old Jocelyn Wildecott followed her escort out of the grand ballroom into the moonlit gardens adjacent to the seventeenth-century mansion where the gala event was being held.

She let out a quiet sigh of relief. It was good to be out of there! Too many people. Every one of them beautiful . . . perfect . . . with every hair in place. What was she doing here? How had she let Charles talk her into it!

The cool evening breeze felt good on her face.

Charles had insisted that she must be with him when he received his honor on this night. She had reluctantly agreed. And thus far, after she had recovered from her initial fear and anger, he had succeeded in putting her somewhat at ease. There had even been a few times, as they danced together, when she had almost forgotten her face, forgotten that they were in the midst of a crowd, and been swept up in the happiness of the moment.

They were only moments—brief respites in an evening of all-too-familiar anxiety—but they were real. Somehow, Charles was able to make her forget more than anyone ever had. Even then, it was hard to believe, even though he said her red scar meant nothing to him—that he cared about her because of the person inside.

The setting out here, away from the crowd, was one for leisurely strolling. Yet the instant they left the ballroom, Charles' steps took on uncharacteristic vigor. He grew silent. After several long minutes, he spoke.

"Thank you for coming tonight, Jocelyn," he said. "It would not have been the same without you."

She did not reply. She had not quite put all her nervousness to rest. But as she quietly followed his meandering through the grounds, she could feel her hand on his arm gradually relax. The sounds from inside faded further behind them. A full moon and abundant garden lanterns lit the hedge-lined walkways under their feet.

"In fact," Charles went on, "I never want to go anywhere without you again."

"I enjoy being with you too, Charles," replied Jocelyn, at last finding her voice.

"I'm not sure you know what I am saying."

A look of question passed across Jocelyn's face. She glanced up toward him, then quickly back down at the ground. Suddenly her cheeks were very hot. The feeling was not from the red of her birthmark.

"I had . . . there were two reasons I had for wanting you to come here this evening. . . ."

Charles paused briefly.

"I wanted to bring you, not only to accompany me to the ball . . . I also had something I wanted to ask you."

"Of course, Charles, what is it?" said Jocelyn softly. Her cheeks burned.

"It's just that—well, you see, I'm getting a new post. I've been assigned to Manchester."

"Oh . . . oh, I see."

"No—it's not what you think. It's not that I'm trying to soften my good-bye. What it is . . . well, I don't want to say good-bye at all. I can't go north alone, don't you see? I can't make such a change without knowing that you will be there with me."

"I . . . I don't . . ." Jocelyn faltered.

"Jocelyn, what I want to ask you . . . is . . . will you be my wife?"

The words fell like bricks crashing onto her head. She must have misheard! Did he say . . . wife? It could not be . . . he could not have said such a thing to her!

She stopped and looked up. Charles was gazing into her face, a smile on his lips. Jocelyn stared at him in disbelief, her eyes wide, mouth half open.

"Jocelyn Wildecott," he said softly, "will you marry me?"

Still she stared. Her heart pounded.

"But . . . but, Charles . . . I couldn't . . ."

Again words failed her.

"I mean it, Jocelyn. I love you. I want to spend the rest of my life with you."

Already she had begun quietly to weep. She turned away. She could not return his earnest gaze. It was too wonderful, yet too awful! She had never dared dream such a moment would come. But she could not marry someone like Charles . . . someone like Charles Rutherford!

An awkward silence followed.

"But . . . but, Charles . . . you can't marry me," she said at length.

"I've talked to your father. He's given his blessing."

"But you need someone who can stand proud beside you . . . you . . . you need someone who can be with you at social events . . . someone who . . . don't you know how people—"

His finger on her lips silenced her objections.

"I need someone like you, Jocelyn," he said.

"No . . . you need . . . oh, Charles—how can—"

Tears now began to flow in earnest.

"Don't you know that I am proud to be seen with you, proud to have you stand beside me?" said Charles softly. "Jocelyn Wildecott, you are the most beautiful person in the world to me."

"But—"

Gently Charles took her in his arms and drew her close.

"I want no one beside me," he said into her ear, "but you. And I want you there forever."

And then he was saying it again, his voice strong and tender in the balmy night. "I love you, Jocelyn."

When Charles and Jocelyn reentered the ballroom thirty minutes later, the music and dancing had stopped. It was time for the presentations to begin. Jocelyn's eyes were still red, along with her face. But a contented smile of joy shone through the remnants of her drying tears. She and Charles stood at the back of the ballroom, content in one another's presence, for the first of the brief speeches that followed.

"Finally," announced the admiral at the podium, "we have a special honor to be presented to Commander Charles Rutherford—is Charles . . . Charles, where did you get off to?" he added, glancing about.

With a last smile of reassurance, Charles left Jocelyn's side. He strode forward through the crowd, amid enthusiastic applause.

A brief speech by the admiral followed.

After ribbon and medal had been pinned to Charles' dress naval uniform, he and the admiral exchanged salutes.

"I have a feeling this young man may replace me one day," laughed the admiral to the approving gathering as he stepped away to allow Charles center stage. "He will be eligible for a rear-admiralty next year!"

Cheers and more clapping gave evidence that many agreed with his assessment of young Rutherford's future.

"Commander Rutherford," he added, "would you care to say a few words?"

"Only briefly, Admiral," replied Charles. "Thank you very much. Thank you all. There is one presentation I would myself like to make."

The crowd quieted. Charles' hand crept toward one of his pockets.

"I have something here which, I am delighted to announce, has as of just a few moments ago found a new home."

Out from his pocket came his hand, which he now held aloft. Between thumb and forefinger glistened an unmistakably beautiful ring.

"I would like to introduce you all to the young lady who, out in the garden during your last two dances, has graciously consented to become the future Mrs. Charles Rutherford—"

Oohs and sighs spread through the women in attendance. Heads quickly turned this way and that.

"—ladies and gentlemen," Charles continued, "may I present to you Miss Jocelyn Wildecott, a young lady whom I love with all my heart, and whom I will be privileged to make my wife.—Jocelyn, will you come up and join me?"

Face burning, and hardly feeling her legs and feet as she went, Jocelyn now made her way forward. Clapping and cheering sounded around her, but she scarcely heard it. There was Charles. She was drawing closer. He took her hand. She felt him slip the ring onto her finger.

Suddenly she was in his arms, clinging to him as if for dear life. For a few moments the clapping continued. Then the music began again. Slowly Charles led her as they began to dance. Gradually the crowd filled in around them. Jocelyn hardly dared look up, but kept her face pressed to his shoulder.

"I don't deserve you," she whispered at length. "You are so good to me."

"Love isn't about deserving each other," he replied, "it's about loving each other. After that—what else is there?"

"How long have you had this planned?" she asked.

"A while," Charles answered. "Long enough to buy a ring." She could feel him smiling as he said the words.

"How did you know I would say yes?"

"Because our hearts were already knit together. I could not imagine any other future either of us could have . . . except with one another."

❖ ❖ ❖

The happy memory of their engagement faded back to the present. Charles and Jocelyn Rutherford sat for some time in silence after their tea, almost as if reliving that memorable evening from sixteen years earlier. Gradually their thoughts returned to what had brought them to the garden in the first place.

68
The Mystery of the Heather Garden

"You know," mused Charles at length, "our talk about the difference between George and Amanda and Catharine—and your calling them different human plants—reminds me of what the Lord said about the seed scattered on different kinds of ground. It was the same seed, but it grew differently."

"I was thinking about that too," replied Jocelyn with a smile. "Although my reflections had gone along different lines."

"Tell me."

"I was reflecting on the similarity between Amanda's not seeing our spiritual priorities at present, and what you said about the heather garden."

Charles laughed. "I'm afraid your analogy's lost me."

"You were saying that it takes a certain kind of eyes to see the secrets of the heather in the midst of what at first glance appears so common."

"And what, pray tell, does *that* have to do with our daughter!"

"Just this—that sometimes eyes can see, but yet *not* see at the same time. You yourself said this very heather has been blooming in front of you all your life, yet it is only recently that your eyes have been opened to see the subtleties of its beauty. Perhaps God's working in our lives will be the same for Amanda."

"Ah, I see," said Charles, nodding his head as he grasped his wife's meaning. "We are right in front of her, as the heather was there for me to see, if only I had looked."

"You and I, and even George," Jocelyn went on, "—I suppose Catharine is a little young for it to be said of her, but the rest of us are all so changed by what the Lord has done, and to us the change is nothing but good. Yet Amanda remains, at least so far as we can tell, completely oblivious to its beauty. To her, it seems, our conversion has been a negative rather than a positive in our family's history."

"I am constantly conscious of something like the same principle when I am in London," said Charles. "Most of my colleagues shake my hand and talk and joke and carry on as always. The issues change, of course, but the political discourse and repartee all continue year after year. Sometimes I want to stand up in Parliament and shout out, 'Hallo, all of you—don't you realize I'm different? Aren't you aware that my life has changed, that the Lord Jesus Christ has changed me? I'm a completely new man ... don't you *see* it?'"

"It would be of no use," murmured Jocelyn. "Perhaps it is as the Lord said—that they don't have eyes to see."

"There are a few who understand," he continued, "but then they are generally looked upon as peculiar as well. Even though I, in my own way, try to speak spiritual perspectives into the discussions if an opportunity presents itself, most don't really grasp what I'm talking about. Most of my close colleagues are so progressive in their views— exactly as I was myself for so long—that the spiritual dimension altogether eludes them. Yet now that I see things from an eternal rather than a worldly vantage point, I can't avoid seeing God's principles everywhere!"

"If you're not focusing your eyes otherwise, it is natural to look only on the surface. It takes a different kind of eyes to see what's hidden."

"Like the nuances of the heather. One has to train oneself to see it. Otherwise, one will never see the subtle mystery."

"Not only do you have to train yourself to see it," suggested Jocelyn, "don't you think that perhaps you must *love* something before your eyes are opened to the secrets it has to reveal?"

Charles thought a moment, then began slowly to nod his head.

"You're right," he said. "I realize that I did begin to love this garden before I became aware of all its intricacies. Even before our talk with Timothy and all the work we began to do here, something prompted love to begin growing in my heart."

He paused a moment, then a smile broke across his face. "In fact," he said, "do you remember that day—it couldn't have been more than a month or two after the queen's Jubilee—when I came excitedly to find you?"

Now Jocelyn joined in his laughter.

"I remember," she replied. "You said you had something wonderful to show me—I thought you'd discovered a buried treasure or something! And it was only a patch of scruffy little bushes out near the woods with tiny little purple and white bells all over them. I wondered what the fuss was about."

"But that was the beginning of everything we've done here since. Once I fell in love with the heather garden, it began to reveal the subtleties of itself to my heart."

"Because now you were *seeing* it differently, through eyes of love."

"Perhaps *love* is indeed the eye-opening ingredient, just as you say."

"Jesus called the kingdom of God a mystery."

"As Paul called the life of the Spirit of God within us," added Charles. "How he accomplishes this nurturing work in the human character is indeed a mystery."

Jocelyn glanced back at the ancient house which was her home, its grey walls now soft in the last glow of the sunset. A smile came over her face.

"Let me in on your secret!" said Charles.

"It's silly," said his wife.

"I want to hear it anyway."

"Your talking of the mystery of the kingdom sent my mind spinning off and thinking of what *mystery* means when most people hear it. Then I found myself wondering about this old Hall with all its doors that have rusted shut and its rooms we haven't even explored. George seems to think it's all very mysterious indeed. But what we're talking about is something even greater, isn't it? It is a mystery of *character*, not rusty doors and dusty garret rooms."

"It is *the* human drama," added Charles, "unfolded within the heart of every man and woman—the mystery of God's life. It is a mystery waiting for every man and woman to uncover within his or her own heart, as his or her own character unfolds—the mystery of what God is making . . . *of me!*"

"However many so-called mysteries an old place like Heathersleigh might contain—whatever our George might stumble upon in all his exploring, though I doubt he'll discover much—they are all nothing compared to the mysteries of the human spirit."

"I suppose it is no wonder that such mysteries are hidden from the eyes of many," said Charles, "—sadly, like our own Amanda at present."

"Is that perhaps why the Lord said that for those who do *not* see, everything is in parables—in other words, shadowy and confusing?"

"No doubt. But it is agonizing for me to have our own daughter be one of the unseeing. It absolutely defies my brain to ponder how, after the way we've taught her, she can be so thoroughly blind to the realities we've discovered. I used to believe in a strong cause-and-effect relationship between a person's training and that person's later outlook. I am gradually coming to see, painful though it is, that such a theory fails to account for personal choice and motive of heart, which are aspects of temperament which I don't suppose *can* be taught. I love Amanda so much. Yet she is unaware of the foundation of that love."

Jocelyn sighed. Her mother's heart knew the same pain. She had wanted so much to give Amanda a wonderfully happy childhood that would progress into an adult relationship of deep friendship and mutual respect between mother and daughter. But her relationship with Amanda was turning out so differently than she'd hoped. Despite her most strenuous efforts to do otherwise, Amanda was being hurt . . . just as she had been.

♦ ♦ ♦

The memory was only a feeling.

No event, no image, no specific picture came to Jocelyn's mind. Only a dull ache in some deep corner of her heart where the little girl she had once been still lived.

She was walking . . . walking along an unknown path, alone. She could feel hot tears in her eyes. What had caused them, she didn't know. Had something happened? Had she done something bad, naughty, disobedient? Had she accidentally broken something? In a way, that would have been easier. But she rarely remembered being naughty or bad. She was too afraid of what her mother might say to misbehave.

Except for unintentional actions, such as when she'd slipped on the carriage step, it was not what she did that aroused her mother's biting disapproval. Rather it was simply who she was. That made it hurt all the more. Her mother simply didn't like her. She had known that anguishing truth from earliest memory. Her mother disapproved of her very existence. There was nothing she could ever do to win the stern woman's acceptance.

And now as she walked, the last words she had heard still echoed in her ears. They sounded out like a curse against her that would follow her the rest of her days:

"I only hope when you grow up, Jocelyn," said the voice she knew only too well, "that you feel the pain of motherhood that I have known . . . and that your children cause you as much trouble as you've given me."

◆◆◆

Jocelyn shook the memory away.

She would not let discouragement from the past gain a foothold in the present. Her life was good now, she reminded herself. God loved her. Charles loved her. And he had helped her love herself.

She was God's daughter. There was no moment when she did not exist within the tender care of his love. When he looked upon her in his heart, he smiled. She must focus on that truth and not allow herself to lose sight of it!

Biting her lip, she forced her thoughts to the present. Charles' words still sounded in her ear: *She is unaware of the foundation of that love.*

"It is such a difficult line to walk," he now went on. "You love your son or daughter and want them to be happy. So you want to give them what they want. At the same time, when you set out to live by certain principles, you run the risk that they will *not* understand, that they may resist or even turn away when you *can't* give what they want."

"I really think it is more difficult being a mother now—as a Christian, I mean—than it was before . . . before I was thinking about what sort of mother *God* wants me to be. Sometimes I get so discouraged when Amanda looks at me the way she does. It is so defeating. It is—"

She looked away and began to cry softly, her determination crumbling.

"—it's like my mother is coming back to haunt me," she added through her tears, "through my own daughter."

Charles put his arm around her shoulder to comfort her.

"I think we need to ask," he suggested gently, "whether children who get everything they want are truly happy. My nephew Geoffrey has been indulged from the cradle and is terribly spoiled, yet he seems to have a perpetual frown on his face and a whine in his voice. No, I think Timothy was right in the counsel he gave us. As hard as it is, we must keep our priorities firm and our authority in Amanda's life clearly established . . . whether she is grateful for it at present or not. Amanda's choices are going to be her own to make. We cannot assume the burden of guilt for what she brings upon herself. And, Jocelyn, you must not let yourself compare what we are doing with what your mother did. She was cruel and selfish. You *love* Amanda and are truly trying to do what is best for her. You *must* keep telling yourself that!"

She could only nod through her now-diminishing tears. He pulled her closer and held her tightly.

"Amanda will see deeper into the Lord's purposes in time," he murmured. "We have to believe that. If we learned to revere the hidden hues of the heather, surely the Lord will open her eyes one day to the spiritual hues around her. Maybe that is one of the reasons he gave us the heather—to remind us of that promise."

Jocelyn nodded.

"Perhaps we should think of Heathersleigh not only as the place of heather," she said with a sniffle, "but also as the place of the promise."

"Learning to appreciate blooming flowers is one thing," Charles said, "learning to apprehend the mysteries of God's kingdom and view one's parents in a more eternal light—those are more difficult truths to see."

"In time she will see the heather for what *it* is, you and me for the people *we* are in the Lord, and the truth of God's love for *her*. We are praying. The scales will fall from her inner eyes sooner than they did from ours. We must always remember the promise and the secret of the heather."

"Would you like more tea?" Jocelyn asked after both had quietly contemplated the implications of their discussion.

"Is there any left in the pot?"

Jocelyn opened the lid and peered inside. "About half a cup. I think it's still hot."

"I'll finish it then," said Charles.

His wife emptied the contents into his cup, added a bit of milk, and he drank it in one swallow.

"It's getting dark," he said as he set down his cup. "What would you say to our finishing this conversation in the library? Somehow I find myself in the mood for the companionship of books and mysteries out of the literary past."

She had already risen and picked up the tray. "I would say let us do exactly that."

69

Exploration

◆◆◆

The flickering of a single candle sent shadows dancing upon stone walls that perhaps had not seen light for more than a century. George shivered, more from excitement than fear, as he held the candle high, illuminating yet another turn in the dark, close passageway. Where would its meandering take him?

While his parents had been occupied in the heather garden, George had begun rummaging in one of the little-used storerooms on the second floor of the north wing. He had originally wandered there for no reason other than curiosity, drawn by doors behind which one could never tell what might be found. Old books, chests, ancient tools, contraptions, and devices from ages long past, anything and everything intrigued young George Rutherford. He had spent his short lifetime finding interest in other people's castoffs—and more often than not, some use as well.

An old wooden chest in one corner of a large closet in the storeroom had caught his attention, primarily from the carving upon its sides. Testing it, he found the latch unlocked and carefully lifted back the heavy top. Within minutes he was elbow deep in what he found inside—records, receipts, journals, and logs of some kind that seemed to have to do with ships and the sea. But the chest was not the discovery for which he would remember this day. The real find was what lay underneath it.

Seeking better light with which to examine the chest's contents, George had closed the lid and dragged the box out of the corner and toward a window where the last rays of sunlight still streamed in. No sooner had he moved it five or six feet than his interest in the old chest suddenly vanished.

The movement across the floor had dislodged several loose floorboards. His curiosity aroused yet further, George easily removed the unattached boards. Within moments he found himself staring down into a blackness that resembled an indoor well.

The next instant he was running back through the corridors of the house at full speed to fetch candle and matches. Ten minutes after the discovery, with mingled fear and awe and an explorer's excitement, George lowered himself down into the blackness.

What his feet discovered was not exactly the yawning pit of some long-forgotten dungeon—as his imagination had already made of the darkness—but the crude stone steps of a narrow circular stairway leading downward from the room where the chest had been stored. Once he saw what manner of construction lay beneath him, George cautiously descended into the darkness with candle in hand. Presently he found himself standing in a narrow stone corridor, wide enough only for a single person to pass and of a height equal to the distance between floors in the main portion of the house. The passageway had clearly been fabricated between the walls of various of the rooms or wings of the place, though for what purpose George hadn't an idea. Neither could he guess where it might lead.

Feeling no small sense of trepidation, yet nearly beside himself with curiosity and the thrill of discovery only an adventurous youth can know, he crept forward, checking his pocket to make sure he had an ample supply of matches in case some sudden gust should extinguish his candle.

He lost all sense of direction after three or four turns. After ascending one more circular staircase like the one he had crept down, George slowly made his way yet more deeply into the central regions of the great and ancient Hall.

70

Pinnacle of Success

*M*eanwhile, in the library of Heathersleigh Hall, the explorer's two parents had each taken a book and sat down together, intending to spend a quiet evening reading. Almost immediately, however, their conversation resumed and the two books remained closed.

"But what of *your* day?" Jocelyn said. "I told you of the incident with the Blakeleys in the village. You said when you arrived home that there were developments in London."

"That there were," sighed Charles. "My quandary over the future has suddenly increased many times over."

He set the book down on his lap and glanced about pensively.

"Eight years ago," he said, "I would have been thrilled by today's events."

"What events?—it sounds exciting."

"I had a couple of rather significant meetings this morning. In the first, Prime Minister Balfour offered me the chair of a new Commission on Preparedness."

"He offered a chairmanship . . . to *you*?" said Jocelyn in surprise.

Charles nodded.

"But . . . *preparedness*—for what?"

"For war."

"War," repeated Jocelyn in alarm.

"I'm afraid so. Not imminent, of course, but in the event that the unrest of the Continent should spread."

"But why did he not choose someone from his own party?"

"Balfour's Conservative majority is weakening. The Boer War threw everything into flux, and the labour movement continues to grow. Sentiment for the new socialist Labour party is gathering momentum. I think Balfour knows he has to reach out beyond strict Tory boundaries to maintain his grip on power. It's not so much that this commission is politically significant in itself—aside from the gravity of the world situation, of course. But the offer does symbolize a reaching out between parties. And in all candor, Jocie, I think some people have their eyes on me for the future."

"Do you think the Conservatives will manage to hold the government together?" she asked.

"It begins to seem unlikely."

"So you anticipate an election?"

"Mark my words, Jocelyn," Charles replied, "unless I misread the political signs completely, there will indeed be elections within two years."

"And then?"

"Unless I am again badly mistaken, we will be back in power, and could remain in control of the government for some time. I truly think the age of liberalism has arrived."

"But you said you had *two* meetings," she said, prompting him for more.

"Yes," replied Charles, "the other was with the leaders of my own party."

"Is it the moment you thought might come?" she asked quietly, drawing closer and slipping her hand through his arm.

"You are a more astute politician than you let on," smiled Charles.

"I am interested for your sake."

"To answer your question—yes ... the moment of truth has arrived."

Again he drew in a deep breath and let it out slowly. "It's ironic," he said. "Something I anticipated for so long, and which seven or eight years ago represented the very pinnacle of power and success in my ambitious imagination—now it has come." He paused and smiled almost sadly. "And yet rather than elation, my mood is one of melancholy."

"Were you actually offered the leadership of the Liberal party?" asked his wife.

"No, that must be done by vote. But the matter of our future leadership and my place in it *was* discussed. As Balfour's power diminishes, the likelihood of another Liberal government grows. So we must make plans."

"Who else is in contention?"

"It is clearly a contest between myself and Campbell-Bannerman."

"And how does it look?"

"Henry is sixty-eight. Notwithstanding his vast experience, there is concern about his age. If a vote were taken today, I would no doubt be elected."

"But, Charles, that means—" She paused and glanced sideways up into her husband's face.

Charles nodded knowingly.

"—it means," Jocelyn continued, "that within two years ... you could be the prime minister of England!"

Husband and wife sat in silence, neither knowing quite what to say in light of the enormity of the words that had just fallen from Jocelyn's lips. Outside the library windows, darkness continued its gradual descent, although a three-quarter moon came out to add a bright luster to the evening and prolong yet a while longer the lingering brightness of day.

"Life is full of such paradoxical twists of fate, is it not, Jocie?" said Charles at length. "What ambitious man in all the empire wouldn't trade his soul to achieve such heights? Imagine it, Jocelyn—your husband ... one of the most important men in all the world, the leader of the British Empire, more influential than the king himself!"

"I am so proud of you, Charles," said Jocelyn softly.

"But don't you see?—there's the rub. It's all changed now. *I've* changed. The socialists and the Fabians and the Labourites have become more vocal and influential. They all look to *me* as a spokesman for the new progressivism. Yet I actually find myself growing gradually more in tune with the conservatism I used to despise. How much of the Liberal program—half of which I helped write—can I still in good conscience endorse? It is a significant question I must face."

He paused, then laughed lightly. "What am I going to do, change parties just when the Tories are going under and the Liberals are on the rise! Young Churchill deserted the Tories for our Liberal party last year. He's now one of us. Perhaps I shall be making the opposite switch and leaving the future Liberal leadership to young Winston. He has considerable more political savvy, in my opinion, than did his father, Lord Randolph."

He continued to chuckle at the thought.

"If I did that, the whole country would call me the political dunce of the decade!"

"No one would call you that."

"Oh, wouldn't they! Men are called a hundred equivalents of that in the House daily—in the most civilized of terms, of course. We *are* Englishmen, you know! We must behave with decorum even when we lambaste the foe. I would be called the *honorable gentleman dunce.*"

Jocelyn laughed at her husband's comic representation of the parliamentary double standard.

"It's really not even a question of the politics involved," Charles went on, "—conservatism versus liberalism and all that. Rising to the heights of the political world no longer even represents what I want. I stopped seeking that level of acclaim seven years ago. And yet—there's the irony again!—now here it is staring me in the face!"

"What *do* you want, Charles?"

"You know the answer to that question—I want to be God's man."

"But can't you be both?"

"God's man and the world's?"

Jocelyn nodded.

"I hope I can be . . . I hope I *am.* But the question insofar as politics is concerned is—what does *he* want me to do? It ceased being a matter of what I *myself* wanted seven years ago. And now I begin to wonder whether he wants me in politics."

"Then what will you do?"

Charles shook his head. "I must find out what the Lord wants," he said. "At this point, I am not sure it is from Number Ten Downing Street that he wants me attempting to change the world."

"You still want to change it?"

"Of course. What man doesn't?"

"How, then?"

"Perhaps in more subtle ways. By methods not as easily seen by men."

"Subtle . . . like the heather?"

"Like the heather," he repeated.

71
Surprise Discovery

◆◆◆

$\mathcal{A}$s it fell silent between them, both Charles and Jocelyn Rutherford opened their books again and began to read.

The silence in the library, however, did not last for long.

"What is that noise?" asked Charles, looking up. "Did you hear it?—listen."

Jocelyn now listened. A dull tapping sound met their ears. Charles set down his book, rose, and began to wander about the library.

"It's nearby," he said. Slowly he approached the wall where he thought he heard the sound most loudly. He leaned the side of his head between a row of books.

"It sounds as if it is coming from behind the walls," he said, "but—"

Suddenly, without warning, the bookcase against which he had been standing moved slightly.

"What!" he exclaimed, jumping back.

With slow, jerky motion the bookcase continued swinging out from the wall on some kind of hidden pivoting device.

"George!" Charles cried. There stood his son inside a darkened cavity behind the library wall. He held a candle, which flickered rapidly from the influx of warm air from the library. The expression on George's face showed astonishment equal to his father's.

"Look what I discovered, Father—a passageway leading to the library!"

"I can see that, my boy! Where in the world did you come from?"

"The north wing."

"But ... I knew nothing of this! Come, George—show me what you've found!"

George turned and led his father back the way he had come. Suddenly Charles was a schoolboy again and could hardly contain his own enthusiasm. Father and son disappeared, leaving Jocelyn staring incredulously after them into a yawning hole in the library wall. She continued to hear faint echoes through it for some time. Gradually the muffled voices gave way to silence.

They were gone perhaps fifteen minutes. Suddenly Charles reappeared, this time alone.

"It is absolutely amazing what George has discovered, Jocelyn," he said. "It's a positive labyrinth of hidden corridors!"

He sat down, shaking his head. "This is going to take some major exploration." He began chuckling to himself. "George is in positive heaven!"

It took five or ten minutes for him to settle his spinning brain.

"You'll never believe what I had just been reading when George interrupted us," said Charles, at length settling back into his chair and opening again his copy of the Scottish title *Robert Falconer* by George MacDonald, the volume the queen had given him on the occasion of his knighting. In the seven years that had passed since that day, it had become one of his favorites.

Jocelyn, of course, had read it as well. "Judging from where you are in the book," she now said, "I would say it must be the passage where they find the secret door between the two houses."

"Exactly—I see you know the spot."

Charles turned several more pages, found his place, then began reading aloud.

It is perhaps necessary to explain Robert's vision. The angel was the owner of the boxes at the Boar's Head. Looking around her room before going to bed, she had seen a trap in the floor near the wall, and, raising it, had discovered a few steps of a stair leading down to a door. Curiosity naturally led her to examine it. The key was in the lock. It opened outwards, and there she found herself, to her surprise, in the heart of another dwelling, of lowlier aspect. She never saw Robert; for while he approached with shoeless feet, she had been glancing through the open door of the gable-room, and when he knelt, the light which she held in her hand had, I presume, hidden him from her. He, on his part, had not observed that the moveless door stood open at last.

I have already said that the house adjoining had been built by Robert's father. The lady's room was that which he had occupied with his wife, and in it Robert had been born. The door, with its trap-stairs, was a natural invention for uniting the levels of the two houses, and a desirable one in not a few of the forms which the weather assumed in that region. When the larger house passed into other hands, it had never entered the minds of the simple people who occupied the contiguous dwellings to build up the door-way between.

He glanced up. "I *am* extraordinarily fond of this book," he mused. "I wonder if the good queen's grandchildren have benefited from it as much as I have."

"Do you suppose our *own* George has made such a discovery in our old Hall?" said Jocelyn.

"Quite obviously he has," laughed Charles. "Ancient places like this usually contain more mysteries than any single one of their residents knows. I'm certain many such died with my grandfather, who was never one for passing on his secrets. After this evening's discovery, my brain is full of old stories I faintly recall from my boyhood, about which I never paid much attention ... until now."

"You sound as excited about the prospects as George," laughed Jocelyn.

"I am!" replied Charles. "Perhaps there is more to some of the old tales than I realized. I think it's time I tried dusting off my memory."

"What do you mean?"

"Old Henry Rutherford," said Charles. "I was afraid of my grandfather. There were strange tales told of him. I think that's where the ghost stories began."

72

In the Stables

*A*manda's face was hot as she walked outside in no particular direction.

It was not the out-of-doors that drew her so much as the fact that sometimes she just had to escape the confining walls of the house.

In a few minutes she found herself approaching the stables. She had not planned to do so, but she wandered inside. The cool, still, dark atmosphere felt good against her skin and suited her mood. She wanted to be alone, and did not consider the three or four horses who were present an intrusion upon that desire. They shuffled about as she entered. One or two stretched their long necks over the doors of their stalls to see whose footsteps sounded softly against the hard-packed dirt floor.

A strange sensation pricked at Amanda's conscience. She didn't like it. It was comfortable for her to nurse an irritation. But having to share the feeling with a gnawing sense that perhaps she might have done something wrong—that definitely detracted from the pleasure.

Her annoyance only increased as the incident played itself out again in her memory. It had only happened ten minutes ago.

———————— ♦ ♦ ♦ ————————

Jocelyn Rutherford walked along the first floor corridor of the east wing toward her daughter's room. She heard a loud and distinctly unkind tone ahead.

"These are all wrinkled! What were you thinking, bringing them to me like this?"

There could be no mistaking Amanda's voice.

Jocelyn increased her pace but was still too far away to hear anything but the last portion of a reply through the partially opened door.

" . . . as I always do, miss. I am sorry, Miss Amanda."

"Do you call this ironing?" retorted Amanda. "Look at these tucks and pleats—they've hardly been touched! Now take them back downstairs. I want you to do them all again. And bring them back the minute you are finished!"

As Jocelyn approached, the door to Amanda's room opened further, and a young maid of eighteen hurried out carrying three dresses and two white shirtwaists. Her face was flushed, and she was clearly struggling not to cry.

The girl glanced up when she saw Jocelyn and tried in vain to stretch the muscles of her face into an embarrassed smile. She nodded to her mistress, then continued on along the corridor, wiping at her eyes once or twice with her hand.

Her own face now flushed, though not from embarrassment,

Jocelyn continued straight through the open door.

"Amanda," she said, "wherever did such haughtiness come from?"

Amanda looked up. "What do you mean?" she asked.

"I mean the way you were talking to poor Eunice."

"The clothes weren't ironed properly."

"That gives you no right to be rude to her."

"Rude? I wasn't rude," rejoined Amanda. "I just told her to take them back and do them again."

"I heard every word. It was indeed rude the way you spoke to her. If you can't be gracious to your father and me, at least be kind to the servants. I don't know where you ever learned such an attitude."

"What attitude? Mother, you're being completely unreasonable."

"Eunice is older than you, besides. Does that count for nothing? How could you speak to her so!"

"What does her age have to do with it? She is still just a servant."

"The Lord was a servant, Amanda. He said we are all supposed to be servants. To say someone is only a servant is to pay the highest compliment in the world."

Amanda sighed. Now her mother was preaching at her again!

"I want you to apologize to her, Amanda," Jocelyn concluded.

"What—apologize to Eunice?"

"Yes. She deserves an apology."

"I will do no such thing!"

"I insist, Amanda. You will be mistress of your own home one day. You need to learn to express respect and compassion for those who are in your employ. I want you to apologize."

"I will not!"

For a brief moment mother and daughter stood glaring at one another. Then Jocelyn spun around and left the room, mortified to hear this complete stranger speaking to her from out of her own daughter's mouth. She was both angry at Amanda's presumption and heartbroken that she had so little influence left. At just fourteen, the daughter defied any efforts her mother made to compel obedience.

Amanda had defied her and won the encounter. What was left

now, thought Jocelyn, if guiding, correcting, exhorting motherhood was taken from her? How could she train and nurture a daughter who wrested that role out of her hand?

The weeping and forlorn mother hurried away from the encounter, praying with tear-filled eyes—and, if truth be told, without much faith—for the girl who had grown so proud.

But where she thought she had failed, influences beyond Jocelyn Rutherford's awareness were at work. For her prayers—given energy in deep realms by God's Spirit—were even now serving to poke and goad unpleasantly within the daughter for whom she was so concerned.

♦ ♦ ♦

In the stables, Amanda walked about uneasily. She was thinking with less than a comfortable heart about what had happened. Without even knowing it, she began to talk softly to the gentle old mare called Celtic Star.

"I'm not really haughty and rude, am I—as Mother says?" she said. "I don't think I am. I don't mean to be. I want to be good, and I try to be. Sometimes I even wish I could be like George and Catharine, but I can't. I'm not them, I'm just me. I can't help it. Why do they always want me to be someone else? Why does Mother say such awful things to me recently? She never used to talk to me like that."

She stopped and wiped unconsciously at her nose and eyes, both of which were beginning to run. She sniffed and tried to shake away the melancholy mood.

"I can't help it," she repeated, now stroking the horse's long grey nose. "And besides, the clothes *were* wrinkled. What was I to do? Mother would have done the same had they been hers."

Suddenly the face of the maid came into the eye of Amanda's mind in a new way. She saw poor Eunice tremble and step back, shocked at the harsh words of her own rebuke, as her eyes filled with tears.

The sudden realization struck deeply into Amanda's soul—*She had herself caused Eunice's pain!* She had hurt the girl, wounded her.

She had never before had such a realization. A stab pierced her heart in the awareness that she had caused another human individual to suffer.

Amanda sniffed again and turned away from Celtic Star as if mere motion would take away the unpleasantness. But it could not. Her mother was right. She had been cruel.

No! Amanda told herself, trying to shake away the pang of conscience. *The clothes were wrinkled and needed to be ironed again!* What was it to her if Eunice was such a frail thing that she got her feelings hurt by a few insignificant words?

Try as she might, however, the unpleasantness of the memory grew.

73

Unfamiliar Ground

◆◆◆

Amanda crept into the house through one of the seldom-used back doors. She would make her way to the servants' quarters unseen if possible. And she would never admit to her mother what she was about to do. To obey was distasteful enough.

She would probably find Eunice in the ironing room upstairs, working on her dresses. Amanda hoped the girl was alone.

Feeling strangely like an intruder in the very house she had always ruled, Amanda stole quietly along the wide empty corridor. She was relieved to hear no sounds. She encountered no one.

She reached the ironing room.

Amanda hesitated at the door and stood several moments with her hand on the latch. As she debated within herself, the thought crossed her mind that she *could* turn back. No one would ever know. Why was she doing this anyway?

Oh, well, her mother was right about one thing. She would eventually have to know how to handle servants of her own.

She made up her mind to do it. And she might as well get it over with.

She drew in a deep breath, then opened the door and walked inside—not quite with determination, for this *was* mortifyingly unpleasant, but with a sense of stubborn resignation. It must be done. She could not shrink back now. So Amanda attempted to draw herself up, as much as she was able under the circumstances, to her full aristo-cratic stature.

The room lay on the west side of the house. Light through one win-dow illuminated stacks of table linens, shirts, and dresses waiting to be stretched and ironed. It was warm inside and stuffy, not only from the afternoon sun streaming in, but from the heat generated by the small woodstove where Eunice heated the heavy irons to apply to the dampened garments.

As Amanda had hoped, Eunice was alone. One of the dresses that had fueled the whole controversy was spread out on the ironing table before her.

The girl glanced up. Her face filled with fearful anxiety, and un-consciously she drew back. Amanda saw the expression and was stung with much the same feeling as that which had driven her here. But she tried not to reveal it.

The iron fell from Eunice's hand onto the board. She stood with pale face and wide eyes as one awaiting her doom.

"I . . . don't be—that is, there is nothing to be afraid of, Eunice," said Amanda haltingly. She could not quite look into the poor girl's face, but stood with her body pointing in the general direction. "I want to say, well . . . you see, it *is* important that you learn to properly prepare the garments and linens before—"

She faltered, unable to continue with the lecture. She had not come to criticize the girl further, and in her heart she knew it.

She glanced momentarily toward the floor.

"I . . . that is, what I actually came here to tell you . . ." she tried to begin again, her tone now altered. It was difficult to keep her head held high when speaking like this, for even a poor attempt in the direction of humility will do much to drive away condescension and pride.

"I . . . I only came," Amanda went on, having more difficulty getting these words out of her mouth than any she had ever uttered in her life. "I just came here . . . well—I came to apologize . . . for speaking rudely to you a while ago."

She exhaled largely at the herculean effort of will that had been expended to do the thing.

"There—that's all I wanted to say," she added hastily. "You don't have to iron the dresses again if you don't want to."

Without additional fanfare, Amanda turned and left the room. She had never once actually looked Eunice in the eyes. Yet the deed was done, and she was glad to have it behind her.

In a stupor of perplexity, Eunice stared at the closing door beyond which Amanda's retreating form was rapidly becoming invisible.

"Thank you, miss," she said in something like a relieved and bewildered whimper. For the second time that day her eyes filled with tears prompted by unexpected words from her mistress.

74

Far-Reaching Questions

Little did Charles Rutherford realize the painful and far-reaching consequences the decision facing him was destined to have.

For the following week he contemplated and prayed, thinking it was chiefly his own future that was at stake. It would be his daughter Amanda, however, whose life would feel the impact perhaps in greater ways even than his own.

The decision cost him no little time on his knees. The new decade was fraught with every political opportunity he had ever dreamed of. He could well lead a victorious Liberal party to victory in the next elections and himself emerge at its very apex, as the prime minister of the Commonwealth of Great Britain.

But *ethically* speaking, could he remain a Liberal when his views were moving more toward those of the other party? And *spiritually*, how much longer could he remain in politics at all? Was this the arena in which the Lord would have him focus his energies for however many years he had left on this earth?

These extensive personal dilemmas now consumed the mind and heart and soul of the lord of the manor of Heathersleigh. Frequent were his visits to the prayer wood, where he sought the guidance of his Master.

Meanwhile, though the news of the prime minister's offer was not supposed to be public, it quickly reached the ears of Charles' cousin, Gifford . . . and it galled the banker nearly as greatly as did his cousin's steadily rising reputation. Had it not been *he* who introduced Balfour and Charles at a social gathering years ago, before his cousin had risen so high in the political arena? And had he not since done everything in his power to secure a political appointment for *himself*? Was he not one of London's leading financiers, risen to a vice-presidency in the Bank of England, and clearly eligible for a prestigious position? Yet the choicest plums seemed instead to fall regularly into the lap of his religious lamebrain of a cousin, who was being spoken of as one of the leading men in the Commons! It was all Gifford could do to carry out his duties at the bank without letting his seething resentment boil over into outbursts.

After ten days of serious thought and prayer and discussion with Jocelyn, Charles took the train back into the city with his answer. He requested a private interview with Balfour.

When Charles entered the prime minister's office, Balfour was seated behind his desk. He rose and shook hands with the Liberal leader.

"Hello, Sir Charles—please, sit down."

"I cannot tell you how much your offer means to me, Prime Minister," said Charles after a few minutes of small talk. "I applaud you for looking outside your own party. I think it is just such a spirit of cooperation as you have demonstrated that Parliament needs. I am humbled that you thought of me among so many other qualified men."

"You were my first choice, Sir Charles. I believe you to be the most qualified."

"You are most gracious. However, I find that I must respectfully decline your offer."

"Whatever for? I assumed—"

"I cannot give you a clear answer in political terms, Prime Minister. For me this is a spiritual question."

"Then I will take your explanation in spiritual terms, if that is all I can get."

"I will tell you then very simply," replied Charles. "I prayed for more than a week, both about my own and our nation's future. After that time the sense had grown upon me that it was not the Lord's will for me to accept."

"The Lord's will . . ." flustered Balfour, shifting in his chair, "—The Lord's will, indeed . . . I've never encountered that as a reason to turn down a political post, especially such an important one."

"As I said, sir, it is not something I can explain in political terms."

"Well, Sir Charles, as ... as out of the ordinary as this is—what might I do to change your mind?"

"I am afraid there is nothing you can do, sir. With all due respect, I am answerable to One higher, and I believe he has spoken on the matter."

"One higher? Who—oh, yes, you mean Campbell-Bannerman. But surely he does not object to—"

"You misunderstand me, sir," interrupted Charles. "I mean the Lord Jesus."

"Oh ... oh, yes ... of course ..."

The poor prime minister was quite beside himself with how to reply. A few more pleasantries were exchanged, after which the awkward interview drew to a timely end.

When Gifford heard that his cousin had turned down the post, he burst into a bitter laugh of contempt. The denial of such a position only deepened the banker's disdain. Charles was even more a fool than he had taken him for!

Gifford could not know what thoughts the offer had stimulated in the mind of his cousin. For as Charles had prayed regarding the prime minister's offer, the sense grew upon him that this decision on the Commission on Preparedness involved his entire political future.

Declining the chair had in no wise settled his mind. He was now more conscious than ever of yet *another* decision—and this a more far-reaching one—that could influence the entire nation.

All week he battled within himself to remain focused on his parliamentary activities. It was only with extreme difficulty that he managed to endure the rigorous schedule.

75

The Future of Liberal Leadership

♦♦♦

*W*hen Sir Charles Rutherford entered the club room of Brown's Hotel on Thursday for luncheon with his Liberal colleagues, none of his friends and associates suspected the surprising direction the conversation would take.

This informal meeting prior to that day's parliamentary session had been scheduled to discuss further what ought to be their strategy for the election, which more and more appeared inevitable. The discussion quickly turned, however, as it usually did these days, to events on the Continent.

"The situation is not good," commented Harry Cuxton in his thick Welsh accent. "They've assassinated von Plehve in Russia, and the whole country could blow apart if a spark were thrown in the right place."

"Between the Russians and the Turks and the French, I see little hope for peace continuing," remarked William Petworth, a Lincolnshire native.

"Yes, but not a soul in England seems to know it," rejoined James Beckenham, an outspoken progressive from Hythe. "The people are asleep. They think this peace will last indefinitely."

"Morocco is the tinderbox," observed the earl of Westcott.

"Perhaps," remarked Winston Churchill, the youngest and newest member of the Liberal inner circle. "But none of these represent *our* most critical danger."

"What do you mean, Winston?" asked Arthur Alfington, who, like the son of Lord Randolph, was a former Tory.

"It is the *sleepers*," Churchill replied in significant tone, "who most seriously threaten England's security."

"What—you mean the masses who are unaware of the continental situation?"

"I mean the sleepers who are already, even as we speak, infiltrating

England—spies from Prussia and Germany and Austria, sympathizers of the revolutionaries in Russia. I tell you, gentlemen, we are in graver danger of invasion than most of England's leaders recognize. But it is a silent, invisible invasion."

"Come, Winston," laughed Westcott, "are you not overstating the case?"

"Not at all, Westcott. The threat is real. Already secret networks of Prussians, Austrians, and Russians are developing throughout England."

"How do you know?" asked Petworth.

"I make it my business to know," replied Churchill. "The more I have traveled and the longer I am in politics, the greater becomes my distrust of the eastern element in European affairs."

"Surely you dramatize the problem."

"I tell you, gentlemen," Churchill went on, "the wall between East and West is widening even as we speak. It is almost as if a great . . . curtain . . . is hung down the middle of the Continent. At the one extreme you have the Russians, at the other extreme the English. At present we are what are called allies. But I am not for an instant misled by that word. We English remain as different from the Russians as night and day—as different as East is from West."

"That may be, but that does not render war inevitable. And since Peter the Great, the Russians have adopted more and more of our Western ways."

"You are right. But notwithstanding progress, William, war may yet be more likely than you know. Believe me, the day will come when this difference I speak of will be manifest for all the world to see. Until then, I say we must be alert and vigilant. Revolution will come to Russia— whether it happens next year or in ten years—and it will change all of Europe when it does. There are many already who are secretly working toward such an end. I tell you, there are sleepers in our midst who do not seek the good of England."

A lengthy silence ensued.

"Well, I doubt that we six are going to solve the problems of the Turks, the French, or the communist revolutionaries," said Sir Charles, who till then had remained mostly silent. "But there is another matter about which I must communicate my mind to you on this particular day."

From his somber tone and expression the others around the table realized the matter was serious and quickly gave him their attention.

"There are implications in this for the election, as well," continued Charles. "I feel it imperative, therefore, that you know what I am thinking regarding the future of our party. Without drawing the matter out, let me simply say this: I believe it is important that you consider *all* the options with regard to the leadership of the Liberal party in the House of Commons."

A moment of silence followed.

"I'm not altogether sure I understand you, Charles," said Beckenham at length. "I thought it was understood that all of us here planned to support *you* for the position."

"Right," rejoined Charles. "But I am now telling you that perhaps you should explore other options."

"But . . . but why, Charles?" now asked the earl of Westcott. "You are clearly the best man for the position."

"Because I may not be available, Max."

The silence that now followed was brought about more by bewilderment than disagreement.

"*Not available?*" repeated Alfington. "Whatever can you mean, my good man?"

"I am telling you that I have not decided whether I will run for Liberal leader. Surely, Arthur, there is nothing so odd about that."

"Well . . . but—I must say, Charles, this is a trifle unexpected," said Petworth. "Especially with our being in such a strong position to win the general election. I hardly need tell you what *that* means."

"I understand the parliamentary system well enough, William," smiled Charles. "But Henry has long wanted to be prime minister."

"And Henry is sixty-eight years old," remarked the earl.

"Campbell-Bannerman is not the leader for our future, Rutherford—you know that fact as well as any of us," objected Beckenham.

"James is right. Why do you think Henry is not here with us today? He is of the past. We all respect him. Henry has been a worthy and influential Liberal leader. But the twentieth century must look *ahead*, Charles."

Charles sighed. How could he possibly make them understand?

"And if what Winston says is accurate, Charles," persisted Westcott, "then we must have the best leadership possible. The world situation needs your leadership, Charles—your clear thinking, your perspective.

Our party could elect the next prime minister. Good heavens, man—I'm talking about you!"

"Perhaps Winston would like the job," smiled Charles.

"I am flattered, Sir Charles," rejoined Churchill with a laugh, "but I fear I am yet a little green for the country. Someday, perhaps, when I am older and wiser like the rest of you!"

Charles was glad for the laughter that followed. The discussion now rambled off in the direction of assessing the party's prospects if Prime Minister Balfour either resigned or called for new elections. Rutherford's hesitations about his continuing role in the future government were easily dismissed by his colleagues, who seemed not to apprehend how serious and important the quandary was in his mind.

It was by now clear enough to Charles that whatever decision lay before him, he would have to make it at Heathersleigh, not in London.

76

In What Arena Change?

*C*harles Rutherford was on the train bound for Devon ten minutes after Friday's adjournment.

The city had become foreign to him. He had to get home to Heathersleigh!

The four-hour ride settled him somewhat, though his thoughts on the journey raised as many questions as they resolved. As soon as the late supper was over, he and Jocelyn walked outside together into the twilight.

"I don't know, Jocelyn," Charles sighed once they were alone. "I just don't know what to do."

"It was a difficult week, wasn't it? I could see it on your face the moment you arrived home."

"Not as much for what happened in London," replied Charles, "but rather for the turmoil inside my own soul."

He paused and smiled ironically. "Well," he added, "I did have two rather interesting conversations, one with the P.M. and the other with my colleagues."

As they walked toward the heather garden, he recounted both briefly.

"You know," he said at length as they entered the narrow pathways and continued slowly on, "at first, becoming a Christian answered many questions and put many things into perspective. Yet as time has gone on, more situations have arisen that are not easy to sort through one-dimensionally. Living as a serious and thoughtful Christian is no simple matter."

"What does that have to do with your week in Parliament?"

"For instance," replied Charles, continuing his train of thought, "ought I to be in politics at all?—that is my struggle at present. If my life continues as before—before our conversion, I mean—and nothing *changes*, what difference has my faith really made?"

"But *you* are different, Charles. You are a different man. You live by entirely different principles and have a whole different outlook now."

"Granted. But am I not still attempting to influence my surroundings just as before? Am I not still as involved in man's kingdom as when I believed that was the only kingdom? What has really changed?"

"*You* have changed," repeated Jocelyn. "You are a new man inside."

"But is that enough?"

He paused and chuckled.

"Do you remember how Amanda and I used to talk about changing the world together?"

"I remember," replied Jocelyn, smiling.

"I wonder what she thinks about that now," mused Charles, "or if she even remembers. . . ."

His voice trailed off as he remembered with sadness the fun he and his daughter used to have together.

"—In any event," he went on in a moment, "after talking to the P.M., rather than the relief I expected to feel from my decision about the Commission, I found instead whole new quandaries rising within me. I wondered all week if there wasn't some obligation upon me to try to change the world *as Jesus did*, rather than as politicians and parliamentarians and presidents and prime ministers do. Is there a difference?"

"Jesus *had* to be different. He was God's Son."

"But aren't we to be different too? Isn't he our example? If Jesus were alive today—of course, he *is* alive, but I mean if he were in my shoes at this moment of time, what would *he* do? Would he sit in the House of Commons, or would he seek to influence hearts by some other means? Would the change he sought to bring into people's lives perhaps exist in another arena than the political one? Would his agenda be national or personal? Would it be social and societal ... or spiritual?"

"I have a feeling," said Jocelyn with a smile, "that you already know the answers."

"Of course. That's what I've been pondering during the whole trip home. He *didn't* work through politics. God was concerned for nations in the Old Testament, but not Jesus in the New. His agenda was *entirely* personal. It wasn't societal in the least."

"I see what you mean."

"That is the whole point. Jesus eschewed the world's systems altogether. The change he sought was eternal—change in people's hearts. He did not attempt to set right all the world's ills. In fact, that was one of Satan's temptations—showing Jesus that he *could* have changed the world for good. But the Lord said, 'Satan, I will not try to change the world by your methods!' Surely there was drunkenness in his day. But Jesus did not set up a Temperance Commission. War would come with the Romans, but he set up no Commission on Preparedness. He knew that solutions of man's devising were temporal and incomplete. Is there drunkenness and war in the world? To address it, Jesus would say, *Your Father loves you ... give him your heart and turn from your sin.* There is no other solution to man's need than that."

"Are you saying there should not be such things as commissions and parliaments, or that we should not seek to do good and make change in the world?"

"Of course not. Good must be done. Worthy men must rule the nations of the world as wisely and as compassionately as they can. Society *ought* to be changed for the better. I am proud of our English heritage, which has led every nation on earth in human compassion. But is that how God wants *me* expending *my* efforts?—that is the question."

"What do you think?"

"I am no longer certain it is."

"In other words, different kinds of good must be done, and it takes different men to do them," suggested Jocelyn.

"I might not have put it exactly like that," rejoined her husband, "but that is something like it. The world will always be the way it is. There will always be problems to overcome. I want to give the rest of *my* particular life to the kind of change that *Jesus* brought into men's and women's lives rather than to political change. I am not certain I can accomplish that in Parliament. If the Lord is my example, and if he would not sit in the House of Commons or seek the prime ministership, what does that indicate *to me*?"

"Can politicians follow such a high example as the Lord's life?"

"If not, then politics is no life for me," replied Charles. "I *have* to make the Lord my example to whatever extent I am able. What other model is worthy to be followed?"

"There are godly men who have been politically and socially active."

"Of course, because that was how God led them. But can the kingdom of God be brought to the world through political maneuvering? That is the issue, Jocelyn. I do not want to look back on my life one day and realize I did not follow the Lord's example in *every* area I might have. So now, for me, it has come down to this one area—the most important area of my life . . . my whole career."

It was quiet for a few moments.

"Do you want to be prime minister?" asked Jocelyn at length.

A moaning half-laugh followed. Jocelyn turned and gazed into her husband's face. His expression was one of deep and ironic anguish.

"Jocelyn," he said, "don't you understand? I have never wanted anything so much! Being prime minister is what every M.P. dreams of. It has been my silent hope for years. Want it? I desperately long to be prime minister."

The silence that followed this time was even longer.

"What are you going to do?" asked Jocelyn finally.

"I don't know," Charles sighed. "Times and circumstances change. I have been happy in politics, and I like to think I have done some good. It would be very difficult not to be involved. But might not this present unrest signal that God is speaking to me of a new season where he will give me other things to do?"

Charles laughed softly, though there was not much humor in his tone.

"You know, *you* are the one who made me start thinking of being more decisive as a spiritual man," he said. "It's all your fault, for getting me to think as a spiritual leader."

"I hope you don't regret my doing so."

"No, you were right," smiled Charles. "But if this decision were to be arrived at by consensus, I would make no change. My colleagues are all against it. I'm not sure how you would vote.—What do you suppose Amanda and George would say?"

"I never know what Amanda is thinking anymore," sighed Jocelyn.

"Yet here I am facing a major decision as a minority of one. The decision is no one's but mine."

"I will pray that the Lord will show you his will," said Jocelyn. "And I will support you in whatever you decide."

77

The Decision

❖❖❖

The following morning, Saturday, Sir Charles awoke shortly after dawn.

He sensed immediately that a turning point had come, that he was about to cross a Rubicon of some kind. He knew the Spirit was drawing him.

He rose, dressed, and went outside.

It was a chilly day in early autumn. A light rain had fallen during the night, and the ground was wet. The thermometer had dropped more than several degrees since the previous afternoon, and even with a thick overcoat he felt the nip of winter's approach. A light breeze met his face. He breathed in deeply, pulled his coat tightly around him, and struck off northward toward the hills and forest.

His heart was full of what he sensed was coming. He could not be said to relish it, for relinquishment of ambitions long cherished is among the most agonizing of privileges known to a few of God's sons and daughters. He did not relish it, yet neither would he shrink from it. He would obey, however painful, whatever it cost his flesh, whatever worldly aspirations he must lay on the altar of denial.

He had a vague idea of working his way around eastward in a large circle through the forested hills to his prayer wood. But he had scarcely reached the first of the trees when a great impulse seized him.

He fell on his knees, heedless of the soggy ground, lifted his hands to the sky, and cried out in a loud voice,

"*Oh God—what do you want me to do!*"

Then followed silence.

The hour was early. The place his footsteps had led him was the loneliest and most barren for miles. No daughter followed here on this day. Charles Rutherford was utterly alone, except for the One who had awakened him and drawn him out into the world of his home.

Charles dropped his hands, then fell forward onto his knees and elbows, his face bent to the damp earth.

"Oh, my Lord," he sighed softly, "*I am willing to follow wherever you lead me and do whatever you ask me. Help me, my Father—give me strength to obey.*"

And there, unseen by any eyes save those of him who never sleeps, the man who for the asking could become the most important politician in the empire quietly wept. For even as the voice of his loud cry died away in the chill morning air, Charles knew the answer to his prayer.

Some minutes later he rose, breathed in deeply, wiped away with his bare hands what remained of his tears, then continued on into the forest.

Gradually he made his way to his prayer wood. Receiving a healthy dousing from the remnants of the night's rain from the pine needles and branches as he entered, he slowly walked about the peaceful closet of the private sanctuary where he had conducted so much high business during the last seven years.

The day's crisis was past and its prayers mostly accomplished. All that remained was the one great prayer, which was a continual opening of his heart upward. His soul was calm, though heavy. Laying down one's life rarely brings exuberant joy. Yet it brings a quiet peace of cleansing. Charles was subdued and content.

"Thank you, Father," he whispered, "*for calling me to be your son. Help me now, with this change, to serve you with yet greater humility. Show me what it is that you want me to do next.*"

The sighs that emerged from his depths were groans of the Spirit. It was no easy thing, this that he had done, and he was spent. The battle was done. Now its victory must be carried out.

With slow and deliberate step, Charles Rutherford made his way back to Heathersleigh Hall. He would talk with his family at breakfast.

They must know of the decision that had been made.

78
What Came of It

$\mathcal{H}$e walked into the breakfast room to find Jocelyn, George, and Catharine awaiting him.

"Where is Amanda?" he asked.

"In her room," replied Jocelyn. "She said she wasn't hungry."

"I need to talk to the whole family. I'll get her."

Charles turned, left the room, and ran upstairs.

He knocked quietly on her door. "Amanda," he said softly. "I would like for you to please join the rest of us for breakfast."

"I'm not hungry," came the reply from behind her closed door.

"Nevertheless, I would appreciate your coming down. Just have some tea if you like."

"I'm not thirsty."

"Please, Amanda, dear . . . I have something I need to talk to everyone about."

"I don't want any breakfast or tea."

"Then just sit with us if you like. I would like all of us to be together."

"I have no interest in what you might have to say."

A slight pause followed. Charles drew in a deep breath of resolve.

"Amanda, I want you to come down to the breakfast room," he said. There was now no mistaking the tone of command in his voice.

Inside the room was only silence. He waited.

About thirty seconds later the latch turned, the door opened, and Amanda walked out. She gave no look in her father's direction, nor any hint that she was aware of his standing in front of the door. Her face wore a cloud black as any winter's storm.

She brushed by her father with cold disregard for his presence and walked down the corridor toward the stairs.

The natural tendency of her will, strengthened now by years of practice, pointed in the opposite direction from any outside force coming to bear upon it. She was a human magnet turned the wrong direction, resisting any and all things but that which *she* willed. Even had she been famished with hunger at the moment of her father's knock, the result would have been the same. He could lead her downstairs to a table laden with every one of her favorite foods. But let him say, in a voice that hinted at command, "Amanda, have something to eat," such in itself would be sufficient to rouse the spirit of resistance in the girl, cause her to plant her feet, and declare, "I won't!" Much rather would she go hungry than budge from her resolve. But let the injunction of obedience be removed, and give Amanda the free choice to determine a course of action for *herself*, and instantly would she flash a smile of conquest and proceed to do what was in her mind to do.

Charles followed his daughter downstairs. The family gathered around the table.

Amanda sat silent with her arms crossed. She touched neither utensil nor cup, but stared straight ahead through the meal, scarcely allowing an eyelash to flutter.

Charles prayed. The others began their breakfast.

"I have reached a decision I want you all to know about," he began, trying his best to disregard Amanda's cold stare. "I have been praying and your mother and I—" he said, turning toward each of the children, though avoiding Amanda's face, "—we have been discussing this for some time. It is not *my* decision, exactly. We committed it into God's care and asked what he would have us do. As always, of course, your mother is entirely supportive of me. I have asked her counsel and advice, but the decision has been mine."

He drew in a deep breath, conscious of Amanda's censuring silent rebuke of all he was now trying to be as a man.

"There is little else to say other than this," Charles went on. "I will return to London next week and tell the leaders of my party to withdraw my name from consideration for the party leadership. Following that, as soon as I feel I can effectively carry it out and still remain faithful to my commitments, I intend to submit to the Speaker my resignation from the House of Commons."

The words fell like a silent bombshell.

Jocelyn had known it was coming, for as Charles said they had discussed it together. The faces of George and Catharine displayed initial surprise, then, after a few seconds, enthusiasm. Almost immediately it dawned upon their understandings that this would mean their father would remain home with them all week. Nothing could have delighted them more, for they loved him. George realized instantly that he could have his father for a cohort for more of his explorations about the place. Catharine, who liked nothing better than to sit with her papa in the afternoon while he read the newspaper on weekends, realized she would be able to enjoy many more such days during the week.

Amanda, however, had been nursing a mounting irritation against her mother ever since the incident in the village two and a half weeks earlier. Her father's having made her come down to breakfast against her will had only made things worse. Now the fuse of her resentment finally burst into flame and ignited the dynamite which had been waiting to explode.

"This is simply wonderful!" she cried in a tone of mocking disgust. "I can hardly believe what I am hearing."

In truth, her vexation was not a mere few minutes, nor even two weeks old, but had been seven years in the making. Now erupted years of resentments, a torrent of bewildering accusations so contorted that they left Charles and Jocelyn emotionally staggered and helpless to respond.

"I've never heard anything so unbelievable! To resign from Parliament—how could you be so irresponsible?"

A long, heavy silence followed.

"Amanda, what do you mean?" said her father at length in a soft voice. He glanced toward his daughter in bewilderment, yet was almost afraid to look into her eyes.

"It's just the perfect ending to this ridiculous Christian charade the two of you have been playing, with us three as your pawns!"

"Who?"

"George and Catharine and me. Maybe they don't feel as I do, but *I* feel like a piece on your gameboard that you move around however it suits you!"

"Whatever can you mean? There has been no game." Charles' face was grief-stricken and white.

"What would you call it? Everything was fine until you had to go and get religious about everything. First you took it out on me—do this, don't do that! How could I possibly have known what you wanted? You turned this whole stupid house into a church! Now you're going to make the whole country pay for it. How could you be so self-ish!"

"Took *what* out on you? Amanda, dear? What have I done to cause this outburst?"

"No more trips to London, no fun, no parties, no anything—just church and lectures and walks in the country! You thought I ought to be glad to go along with everything just because George and Catharine did. Well, I wasn't! I hated all the changes you forced on us. I hate it. I hate it, I tell you!"

"We have been trying to behave as Christians."

"Well *I'm* not a Christian!"

"Amanda!" exclaimed Jocelyn.

"Does your behaving as a Christian include breaking promises?"

"What promises?"

"You promised to take me to London and to a ball when I was ten."

"We were just talking in fun."

"Oh, it was just a joke to you!"

"Not a *joke*, Amanda . . . but neither was it a hard and fast promise. Is that why you resented our trying to live as Christians?"

"You never asked me what I thought, never asked if I might *not* want to live that way."

"We can understand that it might have been hard for you to adjust to the changes, but—" said her mother.

"You *never* understood," interrupted Amanda. "You never even tried to understand! You just told me the way it was going to be, and if I didn't like it, it was just too bad. Of course I resented the changes! You taught me to make a difference. You said we would make a difference in the world. But now look at you. I hate the whole bloody thing!"

"Amanda—where did you learn to say such things!" said Jocelyn, halfway between shock and anger.

Amanda's brother and sister sat stunned, listening in silent horror. Catharine's mouth hung open to hear her sister so brazenly raise her voice to their parents. George had received more than one tongue-lashing from Amanda himself. In his own youthful way at sixteen, he knew something of what his father was feeling, for Amanda showed no more respect for him than she did for their parents.

"But Amanda, we didn't—"

"And then you made me go along with all your new rules," Amanda interrupted again, face red, "and started talking about how you wanted me to obey. Ha! Well, maybe I didn't want to. Maybe I didn't *want* to be unselfish and nice like George and Catharine. Did you ever think of that?"

"Amanda—"

"I liked it the way it was before," she said, turning now again toward Charles. "You were a man people looked up to. *I* looked up to you. But then you stopped being that kind of man. How can I look up to you now? I *don't* look up to you anymore! Just look at you. On the few days that you're home, you spend all the time wandering around the grounds and digging in the dirt somewhere outside . . . what are you, a gardener?"

"I happen to enjoy things of the earth. God has made—"

"You've become a commoner! You never do anything important. You walk around with dirt on your hands and trowsers. Your life doesn't mean anything!"

"I know we made mistakes," Charles tried to reply. "I'm sorry, Amanda—truly sorry. We honestly tried—"

"Tried what! Tried to think about me? Did you care about *my* feelings, *my* thoughts! Did you ever stop to consider *me*? Not that I could see!"

"We have been praying—"

"Praying! I'm sick of all that. You probably *did* pray for me—wonderful! Ha, ha, ha!" she laughed with derision. "Prayed!—and then tried to force me to accept everything just because you thought I ought to!"

"It wasn't easy, Amanda," said Jocelyn. "We were new at trying to live as Christians. We didn't know what to do, either with ourselves or with you children. We did the best we could. We made mistakes—we admit that. Surely you can forgive us that. Did you expect us to be perfect parents in everything we did?"

Momentarily Amanda was silenced, not because she had *heard* her mother's question, but because her anger needed a breath before continuing its rampage.

"Amanda," said Charles, his voice subdued, trying to find some way to express himself to her with loving tone, "I am so deeply sorry for the pain I have caused you in the past. You must believe me. I love you so much, and I would never intentionally hurt you. I can understand your anger toward me. Yet I do not see why my decision to resign from the Commons should add to it, or why you would think it has anything to do with you."

"Of course, it had everything to do with me," she spat. "I have the chance to be the daughter of a prime minister instead of wasting away here on the outskirts of nothing, and you want to take that away from me. But even without that, Father, it is still a horrible thing. I don't believe you're really going to do it. What about making a difference, about changing the world?"

"I do not feel that being involved in politics is how the Lord would have me change the world, Amanda."

"What other way is there?"

"The way Jesus did—by prayer, by ministering to the needs of individual men and women."

"The way Jesus did!" laughed Amanda. *"Jesus, Jesus* . . . ha, ha! Can you imagine how stupid that sounds! As if a dead man has anything to do with anything!"

"Amanda!"

"I'm sick to death of all that religious talk," the girl shot back, her anger rising again. "What you really mean is that you're not going to do what you said. It's just one more promise you do not intend to keep."

Charles sighed in great pain.

"People change, Amanda," he said. "Circumstances change. *I* have changed."

"I saw that a long time ago!" rejoined Amanda in a biting tone. "You used to be so concerned with what is wrong with the world. Now you just don't care."

"Your father is not unconcerned, Amanda," said Jocelyn. "How can you say such a thing?"

"What would you call it then? He has the chance to influence the course of nations, and he isn't going to take it."

"As I said, I sought the Lord's will, Amanda," began Charles, attempting yet again to explain. "I no longer think the Commons to be the most effective way—"

"It's always the Lord's will for you, isn't it?" she interrupted. "You just can't think for yourself anymore!"

"Amanda!" said her mother.

"I won't take it back—it's true. It's true of both of you."

Charles was silent. What could words accomplish now? His daughter's ears were as plugged as her eyes were unseeing. Apparently other means than his own example would be required for the opening of them both.

"I'm embarrassed to be the daughter of someone who could help," she continued her tirade, "who could have an influence on world affairs but would rather walk around the fields and pray. What kind of religion is that, anyway?"

"Amanda!" said Jocelyn, who had finally had enough. "I want you to apologize to your father."

"Why? So I can be a nice quiet girl who does what she's told so she can go to heaven? I will not! When I'm older, I won't care about other people as little as you do! Mother, you could have helped Stirling Blakeley. Father, you could help the whole country. But neither of you do anything! I'm ashamed of you both!"

The words stung deep, burning like knife thrusts in the hearts of father and mother. Tears of anguish rose in Charles' eyes.

"When I grow up, my life is going to count for something!" Amanda shouted. "I *am* going to change the world, Father—even if you don't!"

She leapt up, spun around, and ran from the room, leaving her two parents crushed and her brother and sister utterly stunned.

As the door slammed behind her, the only sounds remaining inside were those of a mother's quiet weeping. The father, whose eyes were also wet but undimmed of resolve, was already on his knees.

George sat in shock. Catharine got up, went to her daddy, knelt down beside him, and laid her head against his shoulder and cried. Charles wrapped his arms around his youngest daughter and prayed softly, *"Lord, help us all."*

79

Thoughts of Far Away

*A*manda sprinted up one flight of stairs, thinking first of the refuge of her room. Face hot and breathing heavily, she paused briefly at the landing, then bounded upward again, taking the stairs two at a time to the top floor of the great Hall. Without a pause this time, she spun to her left and continued running through the long, dimly lit corridor.

At length she arrived at the end of the passageway, where a small single door sat framed by the stone wall at the end of the wing. She opened it and turned immediately right into a much narrower and even darker hallway, which led her moments later through another door opening into the tower staircase about three-quarters of the way up its height. Walking now, Amanda continued her ascent to the top. George had pestered her to join him up here in his recent explorations, but she hadn't been interested. She had not been here since the day she had visited it with Geoffrey.

The key still stood in the lock, though the door was unbolted. She pulled it toward her and walked inside. Here it was deathly quiet. Like a great bass drum Amanda's heart pounded out a cadence of discontent, while the snare of her emotions pattered in a high-pitched raging tumult. Their combined music was anything but pleasant.

Still trembling from the heated argument, Amanda walked slowly across the empty stone floor to one of the narrow windows and stood gazing out of it as far as her eyes could see. London lay somewhere in the distance to the east. She could not see the great city, but she could feel its pull.

As hard as she tried to act sophisticated and older than she was, Amanda was still a child in many ways, and the fancies of her childhood were still bright in her memory. Now, dreamily gazing out, she remembered the excitement of the day she had met the queen. She saw herself walking up the bright red carpet toward the royal dais, then ascending and curtsying before the ageless Victoria.

I'm going to be prime minister someday, came the remembered words from her lips.

The queen smiled, then turned to speak with her father. All around, the sounds and sensations of importance and royalty worked their magic in young Amanda Rutherford's consciousness, deepening the hunger to participate in it all herself. The connection between such participation and the respect and deference it would require never spoiled Amanda's daydreams. In the airy castles of her imagination, she could be a princess—or a prime minister—without anything being required of her.

The venerable queen's voice sounded again in her ears after a mere few seconds.

. . . turn the world on its ear when her time comes—won't you, my dear?
Yes, Your Majesty.

She had never forgotten the words. Her desire was to rule—to issue commands as she had done as a child and to have her entire world obey.

Amanda sighed as she recalled the memories and daydreams, longing to be part of a world she had only glimpsed. But now . . .

The present intruded once more upon her visions of the past.

Her father was taking the dream away! Not only had he stopped sharing the dream he himself had awakened in her, but now he was trying to take it out of her hands, to make its fulfillment impossible.

London! *There* was where great things happened!

Her father had been there only yesterday. He had been at the very center of power in the middle of the Palace of Westminster, with a chance to become the most important man in all England. His picture would be in the London *Times* every day. But he was going to turn it down!

What she wouldn't give for such an opportunity herself! She could see it, feel it, taste the thrill of having a hand on the pulse of the great city.

"Someday," Amanda whispered, *"you will be my home! It will not be so long from now. I will get away from this place where no one cares about me. I will get away . . . and then I will do what my father won't!"*

He used to be such a great man— But she had grown older. Perhaps now she was finally seeing things more clearly. How childish she must have been to idolize him when she was young.

Well, let her parents live their sedate country lives!

Let her father work in the stupid garden and walk about the hillsides and through the village like a bumpkin. Let her mother drink tea and entertain other ladies even more uninteresting than she. Let George stay here at Heathersleigh all his life. Let Catharine marry and have ten children.

She would make more of herself than any of them!

One day the name *Amanda Rutherford* would be on the lips of every man and woman in England. They would all wish they could be like her!

80

Overheard Prayers

That same evening, long after Amanda had retired to her room, a fit of restlessness seized her.

She should not have yelled at her father and mother. She knew that—knew it as an abstract fact. Little sense of remorse accompanied the realization. *I did wrong and should apologize for it*, were not thoughts that entered her consciousness.

Spontaneous apology had never burst forth from her lips in consequence of anything she had said or done. She had been forced upon occasion to utter the words *I'm sorry*. She always did so, however, through gritted teeth. Even the affair with Eunice had been carried out to ease her own guilt more than because she felt remorse for hurting the servant girl. Accompanying the words was always stubborn determination to yield to no softening of the heart following an extracted confession.

Yet it could not be denied that she was uncomfortable because of the scene.

She was, after all, a young lady of good breeding. She had been taught certain rules of decorum that were expected of a gentleman's daughter, and she knew she had violated them. Amanda's discomfort stemmed from having allowed herself to lose control and do what made *her* feel uncomfortable rather than from any behavior she would call *wrong*.

With that aspect of her personality capable of doing *wrong* she had not yet become acquainted. Besides, she was still irritated with her parents for putting her in the awkward position in the first place.

The whole thing was *their* fault, not hers. She told her father she hadn't wanted to come down for breakfast. If he had not insisted, the entire scene would never have happened. She had likewise later asked to be excused from dinner. With that request Charles had complied. At teatime she had left after eating one small cake and sipping a fourth of a cup of tea.

Amanda threw down the romance novel in which she had been half-heartedly trying to interest herself. She got up and paced about. A moment later she left her room with no particular destination in mind. She had no desire to see any of her family. It was too late to go outside. But she was not the least bit sleepy, and she couldn't bear to stay cooped up in her room a minute longer. It was a few minutes before ten. The rest of the house was probably asleep by now anyway.

Amanda made her way along the corridor with a vague idea of perhaps wandering to the library.

She heard voices coming from her parents' sitting room.

She paused and waited. The door was ajar, and though the voices were soft, she could hear plainly enough. Her father's voice was speaking.

"*. . . make a way for us to help the boy, we pray, Lord. Be the Father to him Rune does not know how to be.*"

It was her own father, praying for Stirling Blakeley. "*. . . give us opportunity, Lord God. However invisible may be our hand, give us some tangible way to bring both father and son your love.*"

Tiptoeing, Amanda crept closer, hugging the wall, listening intently. She could tell by the tone of voice that they had stopped praying and were now talking in low tones.

" . . . don't know what to do, Charles . . ." her mother was saying.

"He will take care of her . . ."

"She is so bent on her own way."

"That is true. Her self-will is strong. But the Lord will bring circumstances to force her to yield it by and by."

"I do not like to think what she may have to experience."

"Nor do I," replied Charles. "But of one thing we can be certain— we have given her to him since the day of our new birth. How it may have been different had we begun earlier, who can say? But we did not discover the truth until she was seven. If *we* are responsible for that lack, then the Lord will deal with us accordingly. But now she is fourteen, and he must deal with *her* accordingly as well. He will not cease knocking at the stiff door of her anger, nor cease bringing events and opportunities upon her to make her recognize it."

Her parents fell silent.

They're talking about me! thought Amanda as mingled anger and disgust began to rise in her once more.

Now they had started to pray again!

"Father, again, as we so often have," her father was saying, *"we commit our dear Amanda into your hands. We seem powerless to get through to her about yielding her will to a higher purpose than her own desires. Forgive us the inconsistency of our own example. Help her to forgive us for the changes she did not understand. Accomplish your purpose, whatever it may take. Bring circumstances into her life that will . . ."*

Praying! thought Amanda. That's all they ever did! But what good could that do Stirling Blakeley? What good would praying do if Father turned down being his party's leader?

She did *not* want them praying for her! And if they did, at least she didn't have to listen to it!

She turned and retreated silently along the corridor the way she had come.

The sooner she got out of here and away from Heathersleigh, the better!

PART VI

Crisis

1907

81

A New Century Accelerates Progress

••••

*A*s the new century advanced, changes for both men and women arrived and established themselves in the fabric of daily existence. Which of them could truthfully be called *progress* would be for history to determine, for progress in the ways of the world and in the realm of the spirit are two very distinctive things.

It was an age of technological advance far beyond even what nineteenth-century visionaries could have foreseen. Not only did motorcars rapidly replace horses as the preferred mode of personal transportation, now, as Sir Charles Rutherford had predicted, men also began to fly through the air. In every field from farming to communications, chemistry to astronomy, advances came at lightning speed. The human store of knowledge seemed to double every few years.

With motorcars and aeroplanes, telephones and electricity, faster trains, larger factories, telescopes that gazed deep into the universe, microscopes that probed the intricacies of the atom, machines that could do most anything . . . what a time it was to be alive!

Nor were men stretching their limits through invention alone.

Trends begun in the previous century accelerated. The way people *thought* continued to change.

Rationalists in all fields that probed the workings of the universe and human behavior left common sense behind altogether in their madcap pursuit of what they called truth. In fulfillment of Romans 1:22, they exalted their own small minds above him who had created reason and gifted it to them. Defying the very logic they deified, they thus cut off the source of their very power to think at all.

The influence of Charles Darwin became ever more pervasive as his theory of evolution now became commonly accepted by more and more of the scientific community. Increasingly, Darwin's zoological findings were illogically employed to bolster the notion that man's life on the earth was the result of chance rather than divine design.

At the same time, the influence of an Austrian physician named Sigmund Freud was spreading far beyond his native Vienna. Professor Freud's institution of an entirely new method of inquiry into the human makeup called psychoanalysis also had the effect of widening yet further the schism between will and action and absolving men and women from responsibility for present wrong because of past influences perpetrated by *others* upon their inner psyches.

The Viennese professor's influence, more spiritually subtle than Darwin's, was ultimately more dangerous as well ... for his inquiries into the sources of human motivation opened wide the door man had only peeped through till then. Now at last could sin be thoroughly justified. In the Freudian scheme, personal accountability was swallowed up by the id, the ego, and the superego ... and vanished from the human moral landscape. Increasingly, the thought patterns generated by Freudian thinking began to permeate the popular imagination.

The influence of Karl Marx likewise deepened the lethal errors which were being committed against truth. Marx's ideas, like those of Darwin and Freud, were destined to reshape the entire globe. The followers of the German founder of communism extended Darwin's views to their illogical conclusion and maintained that God did not exist at all. Upon this foundation of sand were Marx's disciples already envisioning a political system that represented the antithesis of the very equality they claimed to espouse.

Twentieth-century modernist thinking—led by Darwin, Freud, and Marx and their thousands of protégés—thus challenged all previous concepts of right, wrong, justice, equality, and truth, in the same way that invention and industry was challenging the technological limits of what machines could do.

In 1905, led by student unrest and striking workers, revolution against tsarist rule broke out in Russia. The unsuccessful attempt was repressed. But the foundations of Europe's political underpinnings had been shaken more violently than even its leaders recognized, and the house of its peace was about to crumble.

The handwriting of this collapse was written on the wall, of course. The European equivalent of MENE, MENE, TEKEL, PARSIN was a message to be discerned by the few Daniels extant in the land. It was not to the Medes and Persians that twentieth-century Europe would fall captive, however, but to the rising empires of the Germans and Russians.

For the women of the United Kingdom the changes ushered in by the twentieth century concerned a more foundational issue than technology or politics, psychoanalysis or revolution. On their minds was the fundamental question of what role *women* would play in the social fabric of this rapidly shifting new society. Did the new socialism of freedom and equality extend to all . . . or only to the male of the species?

Let men drive their machines, invent whatever they pleased, spin out their theories of personhood, origins, and revolution. Let men soar like birds . . . let them fly to the moon if they wanted! Most *women* cared less about such things than about taking their rightful place as human beings of worth and merit and equal voice. They wanted to be accorded the right to exert power and make decisions free from the dominance of male authority.

In order to exercise that power and ply those rights . . . women had to have the vote.

In the first decade of the new century, therefore, while invention, progress, and social upheaval occupied man's dreams, *suffrage* was the focus of woman's.

Besides what she read in the newspapers, Amanda Rutherford had not followed this cause of her kind with great passion. The topic arose occasionally in the most general of terms within family discussions. But she did not know the names of those at the forefront of the fight. She had heard of Richard Pankhurst, the radical Manchester barrister and political reformer who pioneered the woman's suffrage movement two decades earlier. She was also vaguely aware that Pankhurst's widow, Emmeline, had taken up leadership of the cause upon her husband's death, forming only two years earlier the Women's Social and Political Union as a women's arm of the Independent Labour party.

But Amanda was soon to learn more about this movement and its proponents. And her life would never be the same.

82
Fateful Encounter

It was February of 1907. Amanda Rutherford would turn seventeen the next month.

No plans had been made for an elaborate celebration on her birthday. Mention had been made of an extended visit to London in the spring so that Amanda could experience a portion of the social season. Neither father nor mother was eager for such a trip. But they were afraid that, without some concession in Amanda's direction, a greater revolt than they had yet seen would ultimately result. The proposed trip was a calculated risk, about which they were understandably apprehensive.

Anticipation of a London excursion had temporarily melted the ice between Jocelyn Rutherford and her eldest daughter, for at last Amanda saw some hope of expanding the horizons of a country life she viewed as dull, uneventful, and offering no future whatsoever to one such as herself. Ever since talk of London began, Amanda had grown considerably more cheerful and cooperative.

Buoyed by Amanda's improved attitude, Jocelyn found herself proposing a shopping trip to Bristol. An appointment required Charles' presence in that city. Jocelyn decided to accompany him and take the two girls along. The trip would give mother and daughters a chance to have fun together in the city and also begin the process of acquiring proper attire for the London season. If all went well, they would each come home with a couple of new dresses and hats, and perhaps a new pair of boots. Amanda brightened noticeably at the prospect.

Nineteen-year-old George, however, elected to remain at Heathersleigh with the servants while the others traveled to Bristol. Two years ago, George had left for university, but had neither enjoyed nor felt ready for the experience and had quickly returned home. Now he was making plans to reenter Cambridge the following year and continue with his engineering studies, honing his practical skills in the meantime by working on various projects with his father. Far preferring a few days of quiet tinkering to an excursion to the city, he waved good-bye to them at the door and, whistling, returned to his work while father, mother, and daughters made their way to the train station and northward to Bristol.

As soon as they arrived in the city, Charles left in a cab to attend to his business, while the women of the family sought the central shopping district. Three hours later mother and daughters were walking along Bristol's streets, packages from their shopping adventure in hand, chatting and laughing together as they rarely had in recent years, when they heard voices ahead.

Jocelyn immediately suspected their source. She attempted to lead the girls onto an adjoining street and away from the gathering crowd. But Amanda had already heard enough to cause her ears to perk up.

" ... is why we must make our voices heard," a young woman was crying out in a voice that *could* be heard.

"—men's *talk* of equality must become more than mere words," the voice continued. "Are women forever to be treated as second-class citizens, with no right or say in their own destiny?"

Entranced with what met her ears, Amanda took several steps in the direction of the voices.

"I say no!" the speaker went on. "The American colonies declared their independence from our own King George III over this very principle—that they had no voice of representation in Parliament. It has been more than one hundred years since then, and yet still the women of England and Great Britain—"

"Come, Amanda ... Catharine," said Jocelyn, "we must be on our way. We are to meet your father in thirty minutes."

"I want to hear more of this, Mother," insisted Amanda. Already she was halfway across the street, walking toward the thin crowd of listening ladies that had gathered in an open area. Reluctantly Jocelyn and Catharine followed.

"—still suffer from the same grievous lack of equality! The time has come for us likewise to insist that our voices be heeded, that we be granted the vote. If we are ignored indefinitely, we too shall declare ourselves in revolt against a system which grants so-called equality to some, but withholds it from—"

By the time Jocelyn and Catharine reached the scene, Amanda was already engaged in earnest conversation with a young woman not much older than herself. Nothing her mother said could tear Amanda away.

"Mother," said Amanda after a few minutes, "this is Sylvia Pankhurst." Her eyes were bright with sudden new enthusiasm. "She and her sister are in charge of this rally, which is about giving women the vote."

Jocelyn shook the hand of a lady who looked to be twenty-six or twenty-seven, then introduced Catharine.

"That is her sister Christabel speaking," added Amanda, pointing to the young woman whose strong voice still rang out from the center of the crowd.

"I am happy to meet you, Mrs. Rutherford," said the younger of Emmeline Pankhurst's two daughters. "Are you one with our cause?"

"I must confess," replied Jocelyn, "that I am not as interested in being able to vote as you apparently are."

"We must assert ourselves as women, Mrs. Rutherford. It is imperative that we demand our rights."

Jocelyn smiled but said nothing. She knew expostulation under such circumstances would be less than useless. She simply turned with the rest of them and listened to the remainder of Christabel Pankhurst's speech, watching with some trepidation the passionate glow that now lit her oldest daughter's face.

As soon as the speech was through, Christabel Pankhurst stepped down from the back of the carriage upon which she had been standing. Her sister introduced her to Amanda, Jocelyn, and Catharine, and the four of them conversed briefly—though Amanda and the Pankhurst sisters did most of the talking.

"We really must go, Amanda," said Jocelyn after a short time. "Your father will be waiting for us."

"Where are you staying, Mrs. Rutherford?" asked Sylvia. "We could bring Amanda to meet you later, that is—" she added, glancing toward Amanda, "if you would like to go with us. We have one other scheduled speaking engagement this afternoon."

"Oh yes!" cried Amanda. "We're staying at the Royal Coach. Mother, will you be able to manage my boxes?"

"Amanda, I would really rather you came with us."

"I want to go with Sylvia, Mother. We have nothing else planned today. You and Catharine can go have some tea or something."

Jocelyn sighed and took the packages from Amanda's hands. "Very well then, it looks like it's all been decided," she said reluctantly. "We'll see you back at the hotel this evening."

Amanda had already turned and was excitedly talking with Sylvia as Jocelyn and Catharine wandered off in the opposite direction. By the end of the afternoon, a fast friendship had begun between Amanda and the two Pankhurst girls. They exchanged addresses, and promised to remain in touch.

Throughout the train ride home, Amanda's eyes glowed—not from thoughts of the city or of turning seventeen in less than a month, but from the serendipitous exposure to people and ideas that were new and exciting . . . and that resonated so deeply within her own soul.

83

Birthday Reflections
────── ♦ ♦ ♦ ──────

*T*he hilly countryside north of Heathersleigh flew beneath the galloping hooves of a glistening grey by the name of Celtic Star II, a high-spirited filly named for her gentle grey mother.

Amanda Rutherford sat gracefully in the man's saddle, still the only kind she ever used. With eyes shining wide and her long light brown hair trailing wildly behind her, she urged the horse yet faster over the springy heath. She had become nearly as skilled on the back of a horse as her brother George, and twice as daring.

The family dinner on this, her seventeenth birthday, had been a happy one. No arguments had marred it, and everyone had been in good spirits. Her father had even stood to toast her health, her happiness, and her future.

Her future!

At last she was seventeen and could look forward to the chance— no longer years off but only a few weeks away!—to step into adulthood in her own right. She would go to London, meet new people, and face opportunities she couldn't even imagine.

Yet Amanda could not help being assailed by lingering doubts.

What *would* her future bring? She wasn't about to leap at the first man who presented himself and to marry at eighteen or nineteen as so many young women did in her position. She certainly wasn't interested in squandering the best years of her life as some man's submissive wife and housekeeper! Yet . . . what opportunities realistically lay available on the horizon to one such as her?

Never—save in her girlish daydreams of participating in Parliament—had Amanda thought of a career. Even now, she was astute enough to realize that, aside from marriage, the options for one like her were limited. She wanted to be independent from her family, but she really had no idea how to go about achieving it. The older she had grown, in fact, the more anxious she was about what would become of her.

It was the age of opportunity . . . but *what* opportunity would present itself to *her*?

She might well go to London for the season and then, when it was over six months from now, find herself back at Heathersleigh for another cold, boring winter with nothing to do. What if she *never* escaped this place? What if she was doomed forever to live under her parents' stuffy roof, hearing them drone on and on about the Bible?

It was a horrible thought.

In the midst of such morbid reflections, the faces of Christabel and Sylvia Pankhurst came to mind. She had already written to them once and received a lengthy reply. Here were two new friends who were not in any way part of her parents' world. Her parents would not even approve of what the Pankhursts were doing.

Perhaps the future was not so hopeless after all. On the threshold of entering into the very society her father had left behind, she had met two exciting young women who were *doing* something with their lives.

Maybe there *were* possibilities looming on the horizon of her future. Women *could* be involved in what was going on in the world!

How *she* might fit in with all that, Amanda could not see at present. But at least her prospects no longer appeared quite so drab and empty. More would come into focus during the London season in which she was at last old enough to participate. She would be a modern woman. Maybe she could be part of changing the world just like the Pankhursts!

Amanda urged Celtic Star on, though the way had gradually steepened and she now had to slow the mare's stride and exercise more caution. Gradually she worked her way in a northwesterly direction, toward a high ridge that overlooked the plain in which Milverscombe and the estate of Heathersleigh were located.

Everything would have been so different, she said to herself as she bounced along now at a more leisurely pace, had her parents not so thoroughly insulated their family from the rest of the world.

The thought brought a cloud over Amanda's countenance. She knew her parents frequently received invitations to parties and social functions. Yet they usually turned them down. Even if they didn't want to go to London, they could have found opportunities to let her mingle with the society of her peers right here in Devonshire. They could have introduced her to a dozen families or more of high standing. They *could* have taken her about during last year's season when she was sixteen. But they hadn't gone anywhere the whole spring!

There had been the Christmas party in Copperstone her parents had let her attend. That had been a wonderful night—the one bright spot all year. Why they had accepted the invitation she never quite understood. But it was the only such event she had attended in more than a year.

She had met Hubert Powell, the son of the Marquess of Holsworthy, for the first time that evening. He had casually mentioned a party his father was planning and said he would be sure an invitation was sent to Heathersleigh.

"I hope I might see you there," he said. "Tell me, will you be in London for the season?"

"I wouldn't miss it," replied Amanda. "I'll be seventeen in March."

"Ah, I see," he nodded, taking in her statement with interest. The information clearly meant more to him than that it offered Amanda her entrée into the season's festivities.

Hubert Powell was a dashing young man. A smile came to her lips as Amanda recalled the brief conversation. She had heard of him but had never met him before that night. No wonder every young woman in Devon knew of him—he was rich *and* handsome!

And true to his word, an invitation had arrived at Heathersleigh for the festive party to be held at the Holsworthy estate. However, it had been addressed to her father, not to her. That had been just last month. Amanda had seen the invitation and asked about it. "We'll see to it later," was her father's reply. But as in the case of nearly all the others, her parents had never even mentioned it again.

This year, however, would be different. It was so close she could taste it! Within two months the London social season would be in full swing, and she had to be part of it. She would not be left out again! Just let her parents try to stand in her way.

Even the attentions of someone like Lord Hubert, however, could not sway Amanda's head. She wanted influence, not romance. She hoped opportunities would come to her that would open all the right doors.

Amanda and Celtic Star entered a grassy clearing. She dug her heels into the mare's sides and galloped across it, then up the steep incline some hundred and fifty yards beyond. At last horse and rider crested the summit of the ridge she had been steadily climbing for thirty or forty minutes.

She reined in the horse, who was breathing heavily. They stopped. Slowly Amanda gazed about in every direction.

Northward, just beyond her sight, lay the sea.

Stretching around in the saddle, she looked behind her. Off in the distance, quiet and appearing so small from this vantage point, sat Heathersleigh Hall. Milverscombe lay just beyond it. Seventeen years she had lived in that place, seventeen years to the very day.

The reminder that today was her birthday filled Amanda with a curious melancholy. Her first seven years there had been so happy. Then everything had changed, and now . . .

She tried to force the unpleasant memories of the past ten years from her mind.

This is my birthday, Amanda told herself. *Freedom, that's what I want. Things are going to change from this day forward!*

She drew in a deep breath, and continued to slowly turn her head as she took in the view around her.

To the east beyond her sight lay London, city of her dreams. She often gazed in that direction. Now, at last, the future she envisioned there did not seem quite so distant, nor her dreams quite so unattainable.

84

Surprise Caller

*A*s Charles Rutherford had predicted ten years earlier, the new century brought advances in the development of electricity, and they came even more rapidly than he had himself imagined. Only ten years had passed since that ride when he and his son and daughter had discussed fuel and electricity and the future. Then, he had predicted there would be lights in every room at Heathersleigh when young George was lord of the manor.

But now George was a mere nineteen, and the future Charles predicted was about to come to Devonshire much sooner than expected. Charles and George were busily engaged from morning till night stringing wire up and down through the length and breadth of the Hall in preparation for the installation of an electrical lighting system. Heathersleigh would be the first estate house in all the southwest of England to employ the new technology throughout its walls. Charles had not been so excited about anything in years.

All winter and now into the spring, he had been scurrying about making preparations. He had gathered equipment and supplies, seen to every detail, refined his drawings and diagrams, and consulted with experts in Bristol and London. There was still no large-scale development of generation or transmission networks in England, although such was being hotly talked about in many circles. The Electric Lighting Act was under discussion in the House of Commons. Bringing electricity to Heathersleigh, powered by an on-site generator, was therefore as much experimental as it was practical. Many were watching to see how the Rutherford project, as it was dubbed, would fare.

The lord of the manor of Heathersleigh could easily have afforded for others to carry out the menial aspects of the labor. But neither he nor George was about to miss out on this project! Charles had designed the system himself. He and George and their servants had built with their own hands the small house in back that would house the generator. And they planned to install every inch of wire themselves.

As the project neared completion, and as word of it spread throughout the south of England, almost daily some visitor or another appeared at the Hall to observe progress and to question Charles about this or that aspect of his daring scheme. If it worked, and if lights indeed blazed throughout Heathersleigh Hall during the darkest of winter nights, the success would no doubt prompt far more than curiosity. Every wealthy householder who could afford such an installation would clamor for electricity, although few would be capable of understanding the scientific intricacies involved. Already Charles was finding requests coming his way to help with, design, or oversee other similar applications. His resignation from Parliament had not lessened his reputational profile. If anything, Sir Charles Rutherford was now in the public eye to an even greater extent than before.

He would consult, he said, but he was not interested in pulling wire up and down and throughout every castle and country manor in England! If George eventually required a lucrative occupation, here was one knocking on his very door.

The caller who arrived at Heathersleigh one afternoon about a month after Amanda's birthday, therefore, was not at all what Charles might have expected. Jocelyn found her husband in the corridor of the second floor of the north wing, boring a hole through the mortar of the stones in preparation for feeding wire through into his study.

"We have guests, Charles," she said as she approached.

"Who is it, Jocie?" said Charles from the floor. He continued to turn the auger.

"Mrs. Powell and her son."

A puzzled expression came over his face. He now glanced up from where he lay on his back. His hand stopped.

"Lady Holsworthy?" he said. "She hardly seems the type who would be interested in electricity."

"Electricity is not the purpose of their visit, Charles."

"What is it, then?"

"Our daughter," replied Jocelyn in a voice whose concern Charles could hardly fail to notice.

"Oh . . . I see. Well, is there any way you can handle it, Jocie? Tell them I'm filthy and smack in the middle of it. Give her my regards, and my apologies."

"It is Lady Holsworthy *and her son*," repeated Jocelyn with emphasis.

"Word of Amanda's seventeenth birthday has apparently spread more rapidly than we might have hoped."

"I see," said Charles. He sat up on the floor. At last the gravity of the situation began to dawn on him.

"Charles," persisted Jocelyn, "I want you to come down . . . I *need* you to be there with me."

His wife's imploring tone at last alerted Charles to the fact that there was more to the situation than met the eye. He set down the auger, rose from the floor, and slapped at his trowsers two or three times, mortar dust filling the air.

"You *are* filthy!" laughed Jocelyn.

"Let me just wash my face and hands and put on a clean shirt and trowsers. I'll join you in five minutes."

"Thank you, Charles," said Jocelyn sincerely. "This is not an interview I particularly want to handle alone."

Charles hurried back to his room to change, reflecting as he did upon the past few years and upon the daughter who had grown more and more distant as her teen years had progressed. He recalled his and Jocelyn's original talk with Diggorsfeld and the prayers they had offered in the heather garden since. Notwithstanding the almost cheerful disposition that had come over Amanda in the last couple of weeks, Charles felt a weight of renewed anxiety tugging at his heart. He thought of Timothy's exhortation not to be afraid to exercise the hand of parental leadership. What would this day bring? he wondered.

He approached the drawing room a few minutes later, his heart and mind full of the daughter in whom he had taken such pride only a few short years ago. Back then, Amanda had been so much like him. Now her outlook could not have been more different from his own. Even as he hurried down the corridor he heard his wife babbling on in a most uncharacteristic manner. He knew she was doing her best to keep the conversation lightly afloat until he arrived.

Jocelyn turned toward him as he entered with visible relief.

"Lady Holsworthy," said Charles, moving across the room and extending his hand, "how nice of you to pay us a visit. How is the marquess?"

Atworth Powell, the marquess of Holsworthy, presided over one of the grandest estates in all the south of England, lying some twenty miles northeast of Heathersleigh in the rolling hill country of Somerset. His hunts were legendary, both at his residence, Holsworthy Castle, upon his twenty-thousand-acre highland estate in Scotland, and, as Charles well knew, even in the countryside around Heathersleigh.

"My husband is well, thank you, Sir Charles," replied the woman, reaching up to take his hand. "He is in Canada at the moment.—You remember my son, Hubert," she added, gesturing with her hand, now free, to her right, where stood a young man of moderate height and muscular build.

"Of course—how are you, Lord Hubert," said Charles, "I haven't seen you for years."

"Very well, thank you, sir," said the visitor with the confidence and bearing of an adult of thirty, though he would just turn twenty in the summer of this year. The two shook hands, during which, already divining the purpose of the visit, Charles sought his eyes, that he might find what there was to discover within their depths. No mention was made, either now or throughout the visit, of their earlier difference of opinion in the matter of the fox, the sheep, and Mr. Mudgley's hens and the vegetables.

"Please be seated, Mr. Powell," said Charles.

The marquess of Holsworthy was reported to be one of the wealthiest men in England. His only son stood to inherit both fortune and title. Most fathers in the kingdom would have considered the lad a most excellent catch for any daughter. Besides his money, he was one of the best-looking young men in England, which fact he himself knew as well as did anyone who laid eyes on him. The lord of the manor of Heathersleigh, however, was no more in the habit of viewing such matters in the same way as did the world he had once so highly esteemed.

He and Jocelyn had known that such a day as this would come. Yet, as always seems the case, the moment had arrived sooner than they had anticipated. They had discussed the matter amongst themselves and resolved time and again to clarify their minds to Amanda. They wanted no misunderstanding over the future attentions of young men to arise.

They had not yet done so, however. Amanda did not make it easy for either of her parents to talk openly and honestly with her. In truth, they could not help being intimidated by her, afraid of what she might say or do. She had made it all too clear that their guidance in her life was anything but welcome.

Now the day had come.

Such visits were an inevitability when lovely young women reached a certain age. Most families and most young women looked forward to them. But Charles and Jocelyn Rutherford hoped for something other than the traditional avenue of romance for their son and daughters—a path perhaps trod less frequently, but whereon virtue and character were more highly esteemed than good looks, flirtatious personalities, and fat bank accounts.

This was the first such call to occur at Heathersleigh. It would doubtless not be the last.

On this particular day, Charles had just shaken hands with a young man whose previous actions had shown him to be of doubtful character. The reason for the visit was written all over the young man's face. Charles' own daughter sat with a silent smirk in her eyes, no doubt knowing what her parents were thinking, and enjoying their discomfort. As Charles took a seat, he thought to himself that he must do what was right, whether or not his daughter agreed with him or liked the result, and pray that God would somehow cause good to come of the consequences.

Lord Hubert now sat down. Charles turned and took a seat next to his wife.

"Is tea coming, Jocie?" he asked.

"Yes, dear—Sarah's on her way."

"Wonderful!—I've been working hard and could use a cup," he said in the direction of their guests with a smile. "What do you know about electricity, Lord Hubert?"

"Not a thing, I'm afraid, sir."

"Interested? I'd be happy to show you what we're doing here. My son George is up on the second floor right now, hard at work on it.— I believe you and he are about the same age."

"Uh ... yes, sir—I believe we are indeed," replied Hubert Powell. "But, actually, to tell you the truth ..." he added, glancing unconsciously in Amanda's direction, then quickly back toward Charles, "I'm really a bit of a dolt at such matters—usually leave all that to our servants. I really think I would prefer to stay here."

The crack of a private smile appeared around the edges of Amanda's lips, but she said nothing.

"I was just telling Lady Rutherford what a lovely young lady Amanda has become," said Lady Holsworthy. "Isn't she a pretty one, Hubert?" she added, turning toward her son.

Lord Hubert was the positive apple of his mother's eye. More important, however, he was his father's son and therefore a man of the world in the full sense of the word, even at nineteen. He did indeed find this young girl lovely, as everyone in the room recognized well enough. It was his attraction to her that had prompted this visit. His mother's presence was but a pretext. Rumors of certain oddities surrounding Sir Charles and his wife had reached Lord Hubert's ears, and he had been reasonably certain he would never secure an audience without his mother in accompaniment.

"She is like a flower ready to burst into bloom," he said in response to his mother's question. He turned briefly toward Amanda with a smile.

Amanda received the compliment as though she had heard the words for the dozenth time that day. Perhaps she was in the habit of saying just such sweet nothings to herself. She looked straight into the young man's eyes and nodded slightly with a coy expression in which was mingled a hint of haughtiness.

Jocelyn saw the nod, and it nearly took her breath away. Where had her daughter learned to behave so around men!

Tea and biscuits came. The usual small talk followed, including a discussion of the weather and recent trips to London. It was Lord Hubert who turned the shallow repartee to the subject of gardens. It hardly seemed a likely subject for the son of the marquess of Holsworthy. Yet neither of the elder Rutherfords was surprised when he skillfully led the conversation by circuitous paths to the grounds of Heathersleigh, then expressed his desire to see them.

"Perhaps Miss Rutherford might be good enough to show me around," he said, turning toward Amanda.

"A capital idea, Lord Hubert!" said Charles before Amanda could reply. "Why don't we all go outside and enjoy one of these last few days of winter together. I don't think it is too chilly for a stroll." He rose immediately and led the way from the drawing room and out of the house.

Knowing that to object would not help his cause, Lord Hubert swallowed his annoyance, rose from his chair, and followed Amanda's father outside with the rest.

Charles led the way as the party of five sauntered casually about the grounds. It was clear that young Lord Hubert had it in mind to break apart from the three parents with Amanda. But both Jocelyn and Charles lingered close by, and neither took their eyes off their guest.

Amanda was too at ease with the young man's attentions to make either of them comfortable.

By and by, as the day was a crisp one, by common consent they found themselves moving again in the direction of the front door.

85

Bold Proclamation

$\mathcal{A}$s they walked again toward the house, Hubert Powell moved close to Charles.

"I am hoping, sir," he said, "that you will do me the honor of allowing me to visit your daughter upon future occasions."

Charles nodded as the young man spoke, taking in his question thoughtfully.

"Let us go back into the Hall, shall we?" he said. "That will give me a few moments to collect my thoughts with regard to your question."

Charles had heard enough about the present marquess to make him more than just a little uncomfortable, if even half the reports were true. He would give any man the benefit of the doubt. If he were talking to the marquess he would be gracious enough. But that could not prevent the man's weaknesses of character from being well documented. He knew he would hesitate to engage in any business dealings with him or to allow his wife to be alone in the same room with him.

It was said the son was well on his way to following in the father's footsteps. The lad had already once been engaged to be married. The reasons for the broken engagement were obscure. But there had been talk, and the young lady had disappeared from public life thereafter for just something under a year. In any event, Charles felt confident that this was not the sort of young man with whom he wanted his daughter on friendly terms.

Lord, show me what to do, he prayed silently as they walked inside. *Give me the words you would have me speak. Turn my daughter's heart toward you. Accomplish good and bring about your purposes in Amanda's life. Open her eyes to who she is . . . and to the woman you would make her to be.*

Jocelyn rang for a new pot of tea. They reentered the drawing room and again seated themselves.

"To tell you the truth, Lord Hubert," said Charles once they were comfortable, "Amanda's mother and I are not quite ready to consent to her seeing young men on a regular basis. You see, we are a little old-fashioned in that regard."

"Old-fashioned!" exclaimed Lady Holsworthy. "Come, Sir Charles—everyone knows you for a progressive."

"I am afraid that was in my former life, your ladyship," smiled Charles.

"Your former life! Heavens, Sir Charles, are you a believer in reincarnation?"

"Not at all," laughed Charles. "Quite the contrary."

"Whatever do you mean, then?"

"I was referring to my life before I gave my heart to the Lord Jesus Christ."

An awkward silence filled the room. Amanda's face went several shades of crimson at her father's boldness. The future marquess took in the statement with analytical curiosity, wondering what such a revelation might mean to his plans with regard to the peculiar man's daughter. His mother shifted nervously in her chair and flustered about for some adequate response.

"I, er . . . that, is, Sir Charles," she said, "I see *now* what you meant, although . . . that is to say, it was not my impression—that is, I had no idea you were.—"

"Yes, Lady Holsworthy," said Charles jovially, "I am afraid I was altogether a heathen in matters of belief."

"Goodness, Sir Charles!" exclaimed the poor woman. "You do have a way of employing the strongest language."

"I am sorry. I hope I have not offended you."

"A *heathen*—gracious, Sir Charles, you cannot mean such a thing! How can you possibly be serious?"

"That is exactly what I mean, Lady Holsworthy. A heathen is no more nor less than precisely what I was. Like millions of others, I assumed myself a good and upstanding individual on the basis of the fact that I comported myself like a gentleman and had never robbed a bank nor murdered anyone like our ancestor Cain of old. But to my standing before the Creator who made me in his image, Lady Holsworthy, I had never given the slightest thought. Therefore, what could

I call myself *but* a heathen, an unbeliever? That was, as I say, my *former* life—a life of unbelief, a life lived for no purpose but to fulfill my own desires and do as I myself pleased."

Another brief silence ensued, interrupted by the timely appearance of Sarah Minsterly with a fresh tray of tea things.

"And you say your life is *different* now?" remarked Lord Hubert with feigned curiosity after everyone had been served. His question stemmed not so much from interest as from the desire to humor the fellow along and see what further outrageous thing he might say. He only wished his father could hear this. He would never believe it when he told him!

"As different as if suddenly a bright sun had exploded brilliantly over the landscape at midnight in the dead of winter. Ten years ago the light of that sun did rise in my life. It was nothing more nor less than the bright warming sun of God's love. I have been seeing things from an altogether different vantage point ever since."

"What might that vantage point be exactly?" asked Lord Hubert. He glanced over at Amanda. But now, mortified at the direction the conversation had taken, she did not allow him to find her eyes.

"It is the perspective," replied Charles, "of how God, my Creator, and his Son Jesus, who is now my Master, view things. I have taken *their* perspective for my own. I have relinquished my life into their hands. I now attempt to think, see, and respond as I believe it is their will for me to respond. That is not to say that I do so well or effectively, but such is my desire. In short, I became what is commonly called a believer in the Christian faith. As such, it is now my desire to order my ways— including my thoughts and decisions and attitudes and perspectives— accordingly. Again, this implies nothing of how well I do or do not do so, only that such is now the priority of my life."

"But does not everyone believe, more or less, in the Christian faith?" asked Lady Holsworthy, with just the slightest return to formality in her tone.

"Perhaps. One might say, I suppose, that many heathens *believe* in the way that you mean the word."

"How do *you* mean the word, then?"

"A man's faith is that by which he lives, Lady Holsworthy. One can hardly be said to 'believe' something if one does little practical about it in consequence. By *belief*, therefore, I mean that by which a man or woman attempts to order his or her every moment. For me, as I say, that is now a matter of finding the will of the Father and then doing my best to do it."

"How do you do that, if you do not mind my asking?" said Lord Hubert.

"I pray. I search the pages of the Bible for guidance as to how I should conduct my life. And I engage in a constant dialogue with the Lord, in which I ask him what he would have me do or think or say in a given instance and ask for his help in doing it."

"Did you ask him what you should say here—today . . . right now?"

"I did," nodded Charles.

Again the room fell silent. Amanda's embarrassment had by now turned to silent rage over her father's presumption at speaking so brashly to one who had come calling on *her*. Whatever thaw the past weeks had brought in the air between her and her father, a new cold front had immediately moved back in.

"And you, Lady Rutherford," said Lady Holsworthy after a moment, flustered again, "are you . . . that is, do you concur—what I am trying to ask is if you go along with your husband in . . . with these, I must say—well, they *would* seem to be rather unusual views, are they not?"

"I see nothing at all unusual in them, Lady Holsworthy," replied Jocelyn with a pleasant smile. "Indeed, I cannot imagine a more natural thing in all the world than that a creature should live in close and happy relationship with its Maker. How Charles and I could have been so blind to this central truth for so long we have wondered about and laughed about and wept about many times over the past ten years. In any event, to answer your question—I wholeheartedly go along with *everything* my husband has told you. I too attempt to order my life according to what the Father would have of me. I also am a *believer* in exactly the way Charles has described it."

"I see. Well . . . this—I must say, this is . . . it is most unexpected. I daresay, most people would find it as . . . as surprising as I confess it has been to me."

"No doubt you are right, Lady Holsworthy," said Jocelyn. "We do not make it our practice to be quite so forthright concerning our beliefs unless we are asked about them."

"I certainly apologize if my candor has made you uncomfortable," said Charles.

"No . . . not at all, Sir Charles . . . think nothing of it. I only say . . . yes, well, it caught me off my guard is all."

"Then perhaps we should move on to the practical matter at hand," said Charles. Lady Holsworthy again moved uncomfortably this way and that upon the plush settee, pretending to straighten her dress. "I want to answer your question, Lord Hubert," Charles continued, turning toward the young man, "as straightforwardly as I am able. Therefore, I must say this. I cannot at this time consent to the honor you request. Before giving you a decision one way or the other, as I have alluded to, my wife and I will have to discuss and pray about the matter. Such is our practice before all decisions. We will seek what is God's will on the matter as well as what we feel to be best for Amanda."

"I see," replied Hubert, shifting slightly and unconsciously straightening his lapels. He was not accustomed to being refused, and what he saw as Sir Charles' sanctimonious bearing was beginning seriously to annoy him. "And you take it upon yourself to speak for your daughter?"

"She is seventeen," replied Charles. "As I say, my wife and I are rather old-fashioned in these matters. In the matter of your request, as it was addressed to me, yes—I take it upon myself to speak for my daughter."

It was all Amanda could do to sit still for this. One thing she had begun to learn, however, was to keep her temper inside. She had not learned to rule over it, but she had at least grown capable of keeping silent when to do so suited her purposes. She knew it would not do to cause a scene here and now.

"Then clearly it is time for us to take our leave," said Lord Hubert, rising, "as it seems, Sir Charles, with all due respect, that you leave no room for any opinion on the matter but your own." The sarcasm in his tone left no doubt of his irritation, for he was one, not unlike Amanda, who usually got what he wanted.

Lady Holsworthy rose also and bade her respectful good-byes. The instant their visitors were out the front door, Amanda disappeared to her room.

In another two minutes the wheels of the departing carriage were crunching along the gravel drive, the mother relieved to get away from the place, the son silently fuming over the rebuff visited upon one who could have any eligible young woman in England at the snap of his fingers.

86
Mothers and Daughters
◆ ◆ ◆

*L*ater that same afternoon, when she had not seen Amanda for several hours, Jocelyn went in search of her daughter. She found her in her room.

She knocked, then opened the door. Amanda was sitting in a chair by the window. When her mother appeared, she glanced up, expressionless.

Jocelyn walked in. "I take it from your face that you are displeased," she said. "No doubt with your father and me."

"If the mortification of your speaking with such directness about your religious peculiarities wasn't bad enough," replied Amanda, "Father acted as though I wasn't even there."

"What would you have had him do?"

"Consult with me for one thing—it was *me* we were talking about."

"Are you honestly telling me, Amanda, that you want the young Powell to call on you?"

In truth, Amanda was not especially taken with Lord Hubert Powell. But the fact that her father disapproved of him automatically made her his defender.

"Perhaps that is a decision I would like to make for myself," she said.

"And perhaps it is one that we feel *we* are in a better position to make than you."

"What gives you and Father the right to speak for me?"

"We are your parents, Amanda. What greater right exists than that?"

"I am seventeen."

"Exactly."

"What is that supposed to mean?"

"That you *are* seventeen, and never more in need of your parents' oversight and guidance. You are a mere girl."

"I am old enough to decide for myself what I think is right."

"That is the folly of youth, dear Amanda. At seventeen you are capable of seeing almost *nothing* accurately—especially those things that have to do with yourself. If you had made a lifetime habit of wise choices, it might be different. But you have not done so, Amanda. You haven't even started yet. You *need* our eyes to help you see things as they really are."

"I *need* your eyes. Ha."

"That is the role we are supposed to occupy in your life—helping you learn to see accurately and truthfully."

"And I suppose you think that means deciding which young men I must associate with ... or if I am allowed to associate with young men at all?"

"In no more area of life are our eyes *so* important as that."

"Am I to have no say in the matter?"

"I said no such thing. But it is important that you trust us to know what is best for you."

"You only want to control my life!"

"We want what is best for you."

"What if I do not agree what that best is?"

"We are trying to help you mature so that you will blossom into God's flower, not become a weed that grows wild and never blooms."

"What if I *want* to see Lord Hubert?"

"Then you have to trust us above your own wishes."

"What gives you that right to say such a thing?" asked Amanda again.

"That we are your parents?" replied Jocelyn for the second time. "God has given parents authority in their children's lives."

"And how long is that authority supposed to last?" asked Amanda bitingly. "It seems I have endured it long enough!"

"Until a son or daughter is fully capable of making wise decisions and discerning the Lord's will on his or her own."

"And when do you think that might be? I'm already seventeen. Will I be capable at twenty? At forty? At seventy? How long do you intend to keep me under your thumb?"

"Amanda, please," implored Jocelyn. "Wise decisions involve learning how to listen to God's voice. That takes years and years. Everyone must continue learning it all their lives. There is no precise *moment* when a young person is suddenly wise and capable. It is a long process. We are only trying to help, trying to do our best for you because we love you so deeply."

"*We*—you keep saying *we*." Now Amanda switched tactics. "Surely you do not agree with Father about everything he said. You are only going along with him because you think you have to. How can you have become such a positive doormat?"

"What—where did you get such an idea?"

"I can hardly believe how you let him lord it over you!"

"Oh, Amanda—nothing could be further from the truth. I agree with your father completely."

"You were a girl once. Surely you understand how I feel more than he can."

"Perhaps I can. But I am still your mother. You cannot think your father loves you more than I do."

"What has that to do with it?"

"If he loves you enough to do what is best for you even against your own will, do you not think I would love you enough to do the same?"

Jocelyn's heart twisted as she gazed at her daughter's hostile face. This was not how it was supposed to be between a mother and daughter! She had hoped and dreamed of so much more!

———— ◆ ◆ ◆ ————

The young woman of fifteen lay on her bed, face down in her pillow, quietly crying herself to sleep. Poised between girlhood and womanhood, for the first time in her life, she had dared speak an objection to her mother.

"Why can't I go?" she had asked, trying to put on the confidence of the woman.

"We have an image to maintain, Jocelyn," replied Mrs. Wildecott. "Your father's position demands certain sacrifices from us all. There are those here in India who would simply not understand if they saw you with him in public."

She turned to go.

"How can you say such a thing, Mother?" said Jocelyn to her back, a hint of forceful annoyance in her voice. "Don't you care more about me than people we barely know?"

It was hardly a rebellious rejoinder. Yet hearing it from Jocelyn's usually timid mouth, her mother had spun around in shock. She stared at her daughter a moment in disbelief, then replied,

"Jocelyn, you may *not* accompany your father. It is only my love for you that forces me to such a decision. I am trying to keep you from being hurt. I do not want to hear another word about it."

Mrs. Wildecott turned and left the room. Jocelyn stared after her, desperately trying to pretend that her mother's words hadn't stung.

The little girl in her had now returned, pulling her back into her shell. Her mother had closed the door behind her, shutting Jocelyn into her refuge. This was the only place she felt safe from the stares, safe from the silent rebuke, safe from her mother's censorious glances.

"She doesn't care about me," Jocelyn whimpered to herself through her tears. "She doesn't care. She doesn't know how much it hurts. She only cares about what other people think of us. That's all she's ever cared about, what people will think of my face. She doesn't even love me."

The realization could not have been a more bitter one. She had never uttered the words aloud before this day. But suddenly out they had popped from her mouth. Had she been able to retrieve them, she would have continued to cry in silence. But they had been spoken. The sound of her own voice reverberated in her ears . . . she doesn't even love me . . . doesn't love me.

And now at last came the tears, if not quite in a flood, at least in full measure. For young Jocelyn Wildecott had long before this learned to swallow the hurt of her childhood with dry eyes and aching heart.

Mercifully, as they often do, the tears brought sleep. And if it did not altogether knit up the raveled sleeve of her care, for the next hour she was at least granted the peace of being oblivious to them.

When she awoke, it was not her mother's words that first came to her consciousness, nor even her own, which had deepened the heartache. Instead, though marriage had always seemed a remote possibility, she found herself thinking what it might be like to have children of her own.

"I will do everything I can to let them know how much I love them. I will tell them every day! I will be the nicest, most loving mother there ever was. Never will my daughter doubt my love. I will love her so much . . . love her . . . love her . . .

◆ ◆ ◆

Thirty-two years later, the memory only made her own daughter's words all the more unbearable.

"*Love!*" cried Amanda at her mother with derision. "Can you honestly believe everything Father said was from love?"

"Of course," replied Jocelyn. "What else could it possibly be?"

"Don't make me say it!" said Amanda.

"Your father loves you with all the depths of his father-heart, Amanda. Only a lesser love would give you your own way."

"Love me! All he wants is to keep me cooped up here, seeing no one, with no social life, maybe one or two parties a year, and turning away all the young men who come to call. He wants to keep me from the slightest freedom. He wants to rule my life and keep me here as if I were in prison! I can't wait to be in London this winter. When are you going to let me grow up and be an adult and stand on my own two feet?"

"When you are *ready* to grow up," rejoined Jocelyn. "When you *act* like an adult. When you begin thinking like a mature and respectful individual."

"I'm old enough for that now. Most parents let their children live their own lives by the time they are my age. Why, I am old enough to be *married.*"

"Your father and I are not most parents," Jocelyn replied. "We are *your* parents. And we do not happen to think that independence at seventeen is what the Bible teaches."

"I am sick to death of hearing about what the Bible teaches, as if that has anything to do with *my* life!"

"It has everything to do with it. Only someone who didn't love you at all would let you do whatever you pleased."

"You speak as if I were five years old . . . and an idiot besides!"

Jocelyn ignored Amanda's comment and continued. This might be her only chance to say some things, and she *would* say them. "Unfortunately," she went on, "when you were younger we often didn't love you as we should have. We let you do as you pleased. We are sorry now, for we see how harmful it was."

"Harmful—how? How did it hurt me!"

"Harmful to your character, Amanda. Look at you—you are completely full of yourself."

"I am not!" Amanda shot back.

"Oh yes," Jocelyn went on. "I'm afraid that Amanda Rutherford is the only person in the whole world you've come to care about."

For the briefest of seconds, a glimmer of uncertainty crossed Amanda's features. Then her face hardened. "Well, then, who else should I care about?" she spat.

"Now it is my turn, Amanda—don't make *me* say," replied Jocelyn sadly. "If you don't know, then that is something you will have to discover for yourself. If you truly don't know, then I pity you, and God forgive me for failing to teach you so basic a truth."

"Pity me?" repeated Amanda in mingled anger and incredulity. "You pity *me*! Look at your face—if you pity anyone . . . you ought to pity yourself!"

The words blasted against Jocelyn like hot air from a furnace. She turned and fled the room. Tears were already beginning to sting her eyes, both from her daughter's cruel words and from her own outburst which had prompted them. She could not even make it halfway to the stairs before the bitter weeping began.

Her mother's heart was pierced through with a knife, and she sobbed as she ran.

87

Parental Concern

The day following the visit from Lady Holsworthy and her son, Charles and Jocelyn walked out of the Hall into the chill of the evening. Their hearts were full of concern. By common consent they made their way hand in hand toward the heather garden.

"I'm anxious for her, Charles," said Jocelyn at length.

Charles nodded. His face wore a sober expression. He too was concerned.

Jocelyn now related to her husband the heated conversation with Amanda of the previous afternoon.

"Oh, Charles," she said as she finished, "I shouldn't have lost my composure with her. But she can be so headstrong and rude, I just couldn't help it!" She had not told Charles of Amanda's final words to her. She could not even bring herself to utter them again, even to him.

"We have taken her to the Lord time and again, Jocie," said Charles gently. "His plan for Amanda will not be thwarted because you are an emotional mother who feels pain for what she is doing to herself. Besides—what did you say exactly?"

"That she was full of herself, and that she was the only person in the world she cared about."

"There—you see. She may have taken offense, but you spoke the truth. As much as I love her, Amanda *is* full of herself."

"I just don't understand, Charles. Why has all this happened? I wanted so much to be a good mother!"

"You *have* been a good mother, Jocie. But we have to accept our share of the responsibility. We indulged our first two children. We followed the ways of society. George was somehow spared the self-centeredness such usually causes by finding much to satisfy his curiosity— or perhaps he has simply been granted the gift of a gentler temperament. But Amanda is different. She has always needed a firmer hand, and we did not use it with her."

Mother and father walked on some distance in silence. Gradually the conversation returned to yesterday's visit and questions of its purpose in the mind of the future marquess of Holsworthy.

"She was much too at ease with the attentions of that young man," remarked Jocelyn.

"You remember when we were walking outside," said Charles. "I could not help listening. I was surprised to see her so skilled at receiving his words, was even encouraging him."

"It was such an uncomfortable situation."

"I should not have agreed to let her attend that event in Copperstone last Christmas. She was different almost from the next day. I could see that the taste of the world got into her and made her yet more dissatisfied with us."

"What could you do? For years she has pushed and pushed for more freedom. You were only letting out the tether to see if it might make her less hostile."

"Perhaps," sighed Charles. "But sometimes parents have to put their feet down, even when their children are as old as Amanda is. The more I pray, the more I find myself thinking that now is exactly such a time."

"Are you referring to London and the upcoming season?" asked Jocelyn.

Charles nodded.

"I am having strong doubts," he went on, "that the round of London's parties and balls is in our daughter's best interests."

"I shudder at the thought of it," replied Jocelyn. "I do not think being at the center of society will be good for her in the least. It will only deepen her self-centeredness."

"I've been wondering if we should bring her out at all."

"That is the way it's done," sighed Jocelyn.

"Amanda's character is more important than the traditions of society, more important than what people think of us, more important than what *she* thinks of us."

"We need to pray further."

"Let's pray right now," suggested Charles.

He led the way to the nearest bench. They sat down and silenced their spirits for a few minutes. Jocelyn was the first to pray.

"Lord," she said, *"help us know what is in your heart for us to do with our dear Amanda."*

"We need your help, our God," added Charles. *"You are Father of us all, and you are Amanda's Father. You love her and want what is best for her even more than we do ourselves. Show us what that best is, Lord, and what you would have us do."*

"Develop her character, Lord. Turn her from independence."

"Break her pride, Lord, whatever it takes."

"Deepen virtue within her. Place in her heart a hunger for you, a hunger to be your daughter."

"Open her eyes to see our hearts, and our love for her."

"Tame her wild vines, Lord. Bring them under the tender pruning of your loving knife."

"Help Amanda to discover the mystery of the kingdom, the mystery of your life in her heart."

Their prayers drifted into the silent regions where both husband and wife dwelt alone with Father and Savior to them both. The prayer for guidance was one the Lord would not delay answering. It did not take long for both Jocelyn and Charles to recognize what his answer was.

"I think our course is clear enough," Charles said.

"It will not be easy," rejoined Jocelyn. "She has her heart set on going to London."

"You're in agreement with me, are you not," he asked, "that the time isn't right?"

"Absolutely."

"I want to make sure we're together on this. And on a related matter, what do you think I ought to do regarding the Powell boy?"

"He is certainly not the kind of young man I would want to consider as a potential son-in-law," replied Jocelyn. "Or that I would want to call on Amanda at all, for that matter."

"My sentiments exactly. I think that decides it for me. I will write him this afternoon, saying that I think it best to deny his request until further notice."

"We'll need to talk to Amanda about all this . . . and soon."

Charles sighed, then nodded. "I cannot say the prospect is one I look forward to. But you're right—we mustn't allow any uncertainty to drag on."

"I'll arrange a time tomorrow," said Jocelyn.

88

An Unwelcome Letter

━━━━━ ♦♦♦ ━━━━━

The future marquess of Holsworthy had just completed his luncheon and was dressing for a ride when the afternoon post arrived.

Noting the return address on one of the envelopes, and reminded of the mortifying conclusion to his interview at Heathersleigh Hall, he felt a temporary renewal of outrage for the insult which had been paid to him there. His first thought was to burn the envelope without opening it, which was certainly no more nor less than any correspondence from that quarter deserved.

He could not bring himself to destroy the letter, however, for he was certain it contained an apology. His injured pride demanded the satisfaction of reading it . . . and gloating that Charles Rutherford had come to his senses.

Already considering to what soirée he might escort the lovely Amanda Rutherford in the next week or two, the young man let a smile play upon his lips while his fingers tore at one edge of the envelope. If this was an invitation for a return visit to Heathersleigh, he would make sure to word his acceptance cleverly. He would show the pompous fool that he was not someone to be toyed with.

Dear Master Powell, the letter began,

Lady Rutherford and I wish to express our sincere appreciation to you and your mother for your kind visit last week to Heathersleigh Hall. I want especially to thank you for the honorable manner in which you paid us a gracious call to consult me, as Amanda's father, with regard to your desire to see more of her in the future. In these days of rapidly changing values and traditions within our society, I very much appreciate the respect demonstrated by your approach.

As I indicated to you on that day, my wife and I pray about all important decisions we face. We feel neither prepared nor qualified always to know what is best to do in every situation that arises. Thus, some years ago, as we attempted to explain to you and your mother, when we gave ourselves to our heavenly Father to become followers of Jesus his Son, we also placed into his hands the prerogative to make our decisions for us. I realize this is a difficult perspective to communicate to those who may not be likewise inclined. Notwithstanding this difficulty, this has been, and remains, the manner in which we order our ways.

In this light, and having consulted with our Father on the matter, and having both received from him the same sense of how he would have us proceed, Lady Rutherford and I must now respectfully decline your request to call upon our daughter in the future.

Please understand that this decision has far less to do with you than it does with Amanda. We simply do not feel she is prepared at this time in her life to receive the attentions of a young man such as yourself. Maturity of character must precede any such involvement. Toward such an objective, as Amanda's parents, we feel we must dedicate ourselves with steadfast vigor and prayer.

I am sincerely yours,
Charles Rutherford
Heathersleigh Hall,
Milverscombe, Devon

Before Lord Hubert had even completed the final paragraph,

Charles' letter lay crumpled on the floor, while the young man stomped outside to the stables in a rage.

He would get even with that arrogant religious fool one way or another!

The afternoon was anything but pleasant for the five-year-old piebald gelding that was dubiously honored to carry the young heir of Holsworthy on his ride. The poor beast returned to the stables exhausted, and with whip welts up and down its back.

89
Explosive Talk

*O*n the same afternoon that Lord Hubert Powell was tearing with reckless abandon over the Somerset countryside, Amanda Rutherford was making her way down a long hallway at Heathersleigh to her parents' private sitting room. Her mother had asked her there for "a talk." Immediately upon entering the room, Amanda knew the meeting would be anything but pleasant.

Recognizing in her father's expression a new determination to enforce the authority she so bitterly resented, Amanda instantly drew herself up. With sullen and haughty countenance she took a chair and sat erect. Her clear blue eyes stared coldly out from her face, seeming to focus on nothing in particular.

Her father stood across the room next to an oak sideboard. "Amanda," he began, "after the visit by Lady Holsworthy and young Hubert two days ago, we felt it imperative to have a serious discussion."

Amanda sat immovable, like a block of ice, revealing by no slightest twitch or expression that she heard a word.

"We need to talk to you," he went on, "about the future, about your life, about what will be expected of you . . . perhaps about what *we* expect of you. By your countenance and noncommunicativeness, it is clear you would rather not consider our points of view. I am certain you wish you were instead free to make your own plans independent in every way from us. However, we are still your parents, and we have an obligation to fulfill, and therefore we must do our best for you."

He paused briefly, then went on.

"Your mother and I have done much wrong as parents," he said. "To our great regret, we did not understand a great many things when you and George were younger. We did not see clearly the role that parents are to occupy in the lives of their sons and daughters. But as the Lord revealed our duty to train and discipline and guide your development, we did our best to carry it out. We have seen, however, that such efforts on our part have caused you some unhappiness and confusion. We regret this, and we sincerely apologize that the circumstances of the past ten years have been difficult for you.

"Be that as it may, the obligations of parental love still rest upon our shoulders. And there are two decisions we have made—your mother and I together—about which we need to inform you. The first is: Yesterday afternoon I wrote to Lord Hubert Powell, telling him that it would not fit in with our wishes for him to call upon you further."

At last Amanda made sufficient movement in her chair to show that she was alive, and that she heartily disapproved of her father's effrontery. She adjusted her position slightly, then spoke in a controlled and measured voice.

"You felt no need to talk the matter over with me?" she said stiffly.

"No, we did not," replied her father. "We felt in a matter such as this, in which you yourself were so directly involved, that your own judgment would be impaired. Your mother and I talked the matter over, prayed together, and we feel this decision is in your best interests."

"I see," said Amanda icily. "You think *you* are given to determine what is best for *me*?"

"In certain cases, yes. Young Powell is not a worthy suitor for you, nor for any young woman who values character."

"And as a Christian you feel it is right of you to judge and condemn him?" she said disdainfully.

"I neither judge nor condemn him. But your mother and I would be foolish not to exercise the discernment which our experience provides. We feel that you may be too blinded by motives of your own to see what is perfectly clear."

Amanda did not reply. She was furious. But the smoldering fire of resentment against her father's presumption was yet gathering heat, and was not quite ready to burst into flame.

Sir Charles resumed.

"Before continuing with the second matter," he said, "I want to say this, and I implore you, dear Amanda, to hear me. Please do not reject my words. If at all possible, put away your youthful pride for a moment and listen to this exhortation. It is simply this: There is no greater measure of maturity and character than the capacity to listen to the counsel of others about oneself."

Charles paused to give his words time to sink in. He could not tell from her posture or her countenance whether Amanda was still listening or not.

"You have always been a mature girl, Amanda," he went on, "—mature, that is, in the way of being able to appear older than you were. You are intelligent in many ways. But there is another and more important gauge of maturity which I now urge you to call upon, to enable you to listen to your mother and me. To hear unpleasant but necessary things about oneself requires the greatest of all kinds of maturity. Yet it is the most difficult thing in all the world for young people."

Charles glanced at his wife with an expression not unlike helplessness. His eyes conveyed that he would be grateful for any help she might give him.

"You can trust us, Amanda," said Jocelyn in the direction where her daughter sat. "We love you so deeply. We want only what is for your best. We want to *help* you work on aspects of your character that have been neglected. We want to help you mature. We realize our responsibility to teach you the qualities of virtue and maturity that young women need to possess as they grow into adulthood. We should have been teaching these things to you when you were younger. We overlooked much. You are nearly an adult, and we want to help you learn some of these things now."

Jocelyn paused, realizing, as it seemed, that she was talking to a brick wall.

"Please understand, Amanda," her father now went on, "we are not trying to hurt you by saying these things. We only say that everyone has aspects of their personality which require more work at some times than others. We want to help you, because we love you."

He paused and took a deep breath, then at last reached the point of what he and Jocelyn had been building up to.

"The long and the short of it," he went on, "is that both of us strongly believe that it is in your best interests that we do *not* take you to London next month for a formal coming out during this year's social season. Instead, we intend to spend this next year helping you learn what the Bible teaches in order to be a young lady of virtue and character."

These words fell like a great blast of icy wind upon Amanda's ears. For a few disbelieving seconds, she sat like a statue of stone.

"You are seventeen," her father was saying, "but you are not ready to be an adult. You are not mature in the things that matter most. We fear that participating in the social season, rather than contributing to your character, would in fact only deepen motives of self within you. Allowing this would be the worst thing we could do for you."

Her parents looked at one another, not knowing whether or not to go on. Nervously Charles continued.

"We feel you have grown self-absorbed, Amanda," he said, "and we are concerned for the person you are becoming."

The invisible fire was now smoking hot, and the statue coming to life.

"You are a lovely girl," added Jocelyn. "But your beauty and station in life have fed a pride and independent spirit within you that would only be made worse in Lond—"

"You keep saying you want to help!" cried Amanda suddenly. "You want to help me this, you want to help me that! Well, I want none of your kind of help!"

"We are your parents. We are *supposed* to help you grow."

"Says who?" spat Amanda.

"Says the Bible," replied her mother.

"Well, I don't care what the Bible says. And I don't want your help, I tell you. You've been controlling my life too long!"

"Amanda, please—"

"I won't listen to another word! You talk about responsibility—well I have no responsibility to live according to beliefs I do not hold. Yes, that's right! I *don't* believe as you do! Just don't expect me to go along with you anymore!"

"We are not trying—"

"The two of you are such hypocrites—trying to force everyone you meet to accept your ridiculous old-fashioned values. You're relics from some other century—no, you're worse, because you've *chosen* to live as relics! You condemn everyone who thinks differently than you. You don't even live in the real world. You're off in the clouds somewhere, and you think everyone can live that way. Most people can't, and I can't!"

"Oh, Amanda, we don't expect you to—"

"You expect me to go along with everything!" interrupted Amanda. "You always have, ever since you changed so much. You've always wanted me to become a nice little quiet church girl you could be proud of. I tried to tell you I wanted to live my own life. But no—you wouldn't listen. You never listened! All you wanted was for me to do what you said. I've had no say whatsoever around this house for years. I'm seventeen now, and it's time you let me grow up and be myself. I can't be like you!"

"We're not asking you to be exactly like us, only to be—"

"What else would you call it? Quit expecting it of me. Let me be myself!"

"Even if to give you what you want would hurt you?" said Charles softly.

"Maybe it is time for me to find that out for myself instead of having to take your word for it."

"Having to find out for yourself instead of trusting your parents is one of youth's most grievous follies. *Trust* is the doorway into maturity, Amanda . . . not finding things out for yourself."

"So *you* say! But perhaps I don't believe that anymore. I *don't* trust what you say. So what do you propose to do—*force* me to trust you?"

"No," sighed Charles softly, "we will not force you. No one can do that."

"You've tried hard enough!"

"We've only tried to turn your heart toward your heavenly Father. But the choice to become a man or woman of character is one no individual can make for another."

"Well, you can think whatever you want about me, that I have no character and that I'm completely selfish and terrible—"

"Amanda, dear—please . . . we don't think you are terrible," pleaded Jocelyn. But Amanda was no longer listening.

"Call it whatever you want," she said coldly. "As I see it, you *stopped* loving me when you went through your idiotic religious change."

"Oh, dear, but that's not true!"

"If I'm wrong, then you'll have to live with it. That is exactly how it looks to me!"

Amanda stood and slowly walked across the room. Before mother or father could utter another word, she was out the door without so much as a glance in the direction of either of them.

The room fell silent as a tomb. The two parents remained stunned, unable for several minutes to move or speak.

"What passage were you going to read?" asked Jocelyn softly at length, through the tears which were flowing freely down her cheeks.

Charles looked down at the Bible, still open to the page to which he had turned. *"Listen, my son,"* he read, *"and hear the instruction of thy father, and do not forsake the teaching of thy mother, for they shall be an ornament of grace upon thy head."*

"It is exactly what she so desperately needs to hear!"

"I'm afraid she will never hear it if it comes from me. She simply will not listen."

"Oh, Charles, what is to become of her?" said Jocelyn, crying now in earnest. "There must be *something* we can do."

"I am afraid all that is left us now, Jocie, is to continue to pray."

90

Another Letter and Its Result

The letter addressed to Amanda arrived exactly a week following the visit from Lord Hubert Powell and Lady Holsworthy.

For two days—ever since the explosive argument between Amanda and her parents—silence had reigned at Heathersleigh Hall. Two visits had been made by Amanda's parents to the cottage in the woods and a lengthy letter penned to Timothy Diggorsfeld in London.

Everyone at Heathersleigh knew of the incident, but none of the servants dared speak of it. Amanda had been seen by no one. When she ate, or if she ate, no one knew. Neither Charles nor Jocelyn was inclined to press her about *anything* just now. They feared enough for what they might have done already.

The evening after the letter arrived, however, Amanda presented herself to both parents in the drawing room at Heathersleigh. It was the first time in five days that Charles had laid eyes on his daughter.

He did his best to hide his shock at first sight of her. She appeared two years older than when he had last seen her.

"I received a letter from Sylvia Pankhurst today," Amanda announced with a formality that intimated to both Charles and Jocelyn the nature of what was coming. "I know you have not wanted me to correspond with them. But they consider your restrictions as unjust as I do. We have therefore continued to stay in touch despite your objections."

Amanda drew in a breath as her parents listened.

"The Pankhursts are moving to London and have invited me to come live with them and join in the movement," Amanda went on. Unable to look either mother or father in the eye, she therefore alternated her gaze between the floor at their feet and the wall behind them. "I have decided to accept their offer."

The words fell like an unexpected thunderclap into the room. A heavy silence followed.

"I . . . this is—you must realize this comes as quite a shock," Jocelyn at last managed to say. It was certainly no secret that Amanda had been on a different life's road for some time, and that she was angry and dissatisfied with her life at Heathersleigh. But never had either Jocelyn or Charles anticipated—not even after this week's events—that she would do something so drastic as to leave. "Surely . . . you must—" Jocelyn continued, "we need time to think it over."

"I told you years ago, when father resigned from Parliament," Amanda went on stiffly, "that I was determined to make *my* life count for something. I said I wanted to make a difference. I told you a few days ago that your beliefs were not mine. It therefore seems best that you be rid of having to worry about me further. This offers me an opportunity. The world is changing. The Pankhursts are in the middle of it. I want to be part of it too."

She sounded so much older than seventeen, so distant, so self-assured. This was a side of their daughter they had hoped would soften, yet this week it had come suddenly to stare them in the face. They had implored her to listen to their voices of counsel and instruction. During the days since their talk, she had apparently listened instead to the voices of pride and independence.

"Do you really think you are old enough to leave the protection of your parents' home?" asked Sir Charles quietly.

"I do," she answered, coolly confident.

Another brief silence.

"This is a mistake, Amanda," he said.

"In your eyes, perhaps. But can you not trust me enough to know that I would never do something I consider wrong? Why can't you trust *me* for a change? Why do you insist only that I trust you? Doesn't trust run in both directions?"

"You are young. And we are your parents. The sides of the fence are hardly identical. Young people are *supposed* to trust their parents. There is no injunction in the other direction."

"Do you have any idea how ridiculous and old-fashioned that sounds to me?"

Charles did not answer her question. Amanda's voice was so superior. She was talking to him as if he were a child.

"You are making a serious mistake, Amanda," he said, his voice yet softer than before.

"Not in my eyes."

"Your blindness won't make it less wrong, nor protect you from the consequences of it."

"You have both always treated me as a child since before I can remember," said Amanda with haughty disdain ... and no apparent awareness of the illogic of her own statement. "You cannot seem to give me any credit for being grown up, for being able to think on my own, for being able to take care of myself. When your beliefs changed, you assumed I agreed with them. When you decided politics was not for you, Father, you assumed I would share those feelings."

She paused and took a breath.

"Well, I did not," she resumed. "I *wanted* to be involved in the world then. And I *still* want to be involved in it. And I want to be involved in my own way. I am an adult now and perfectly capable of an independent life, though you continue to treat me as a juvenile who is going to be satisfied staying under your roof forever. That is precisely why I have no respect left for either of you. I know you do not respect me, so you might as well know that the feeling is entirely mutual. I'm not like George and Catharine. I'm sorry I've been a disappointment to you—"

"Oh, Amanda," interposed her mother in a heartbroken voice, "you've not been a disappointment to us. It's just that ..."

The sentence fell away uncompleted.

"What, Mother? Say it. I *have* been a disappointment. I haven't been what you wanted me to be ... and I'm never going to be. So I really think it is time I went my own way. You don't like me, and I can't say there is much feeling left in my heart for anyone around here either. I hate it here. I have hated it for years. The sooner we all realize that, the better for everyone. And yes, Father," she repeated, now turning to Charles again, "I think I *am* capable of taking care of myself."

Jocelyn looked down and tried to focus her eyes on her fingers, which were resting in her lap. She was doing her best not to cry, but the struggle was proving unsuccessful.

Charles was at a loss for anything to say. His own daughter had taken away his right to speak, into her ears at least, with hope of being heard. He might have uttered words of fatherly counsel and experienced wisdom. He had summoned everything within him for the attempt to do so a week ago, yet she had thrown his words back into his face. Deep and wrenching was the love it contained for his daughter. He knew this decision would reap dreadful heartache. Quite apart from the practical question of how Amanda could support herself, for her to leave home with such motives in her heart could *only* result in pain.

At this point, however, whatever he might say would be *mere* words, words that would make her despise him all the more, spiritual pearls cast before the swine of independence, and therefore less than useless. He remained silent.

"I am asking for nothing," Amanda continued. "I know George is the eldest and is your favorite—"

"Oh, Amanda—don't say such things," pleaded her mother, unable to contain her anguish. "You must know that we love you just as much as we do your brother."

Amanda drew in a deep breath of annoyance, but managed to conceal her frustration with her mother's miss-timed sentiment.

"I am not requesting anything from you, Father," she repeated. "I know Heathersleigh and all that goes with it will be George's someday. But if you do plan to give me any inheritance, I would like to ask you to give it to me now, so that I may use it to begin my new life in the city."

Again a lengthy silence followed.

"Whatever you wish, my child," said Charles at length. His voice was low. He could not keep from revealing the anguish prompted by his daughter's request. The man was wise enough, however, to realize the futility of attempting to keep her from the inevitable pain of her destiny. At least now, he thought to himself, she had a place to go in the great metropolis.

"Wherever you go and whatever you do," he added after a pause, "you will forever be our daughter. We will always love you with a depth and a fullness that, I fear, you may not appreciate as things presently stand. Be that as it may, know how inexhaustible is our love. When the eyes of your heart are opened, may you realize that we will always be here when you need us."

Amanda did not reply. She listened to the words but was incapable of apprehending her father's heart. She had long prevented the divine Voice access to her ears, and they had grown unhearing in consequence.

The strained interview did not last much longer.

Two months later Amanda Rutherford, with all her worldly possessions and a check from her father for three thousand pounds, was on her way from Devonshire to begin a new and exciting life in London.

PART VII

Heartbreak and Hope

1908

91

Dawn Through the Clouds

———— ♦♦♦ ————

*C*harles and Jocelyn Rutherford had now been walking with God eleven years. The past twelve months, however, had taught them more about trusting him as a good and loving Father than had all the previous ten years.

Amanda's abrupt, unexpected, and rancorous departure sent both Charles and Jocelyn reeling emotionally in a way that neither had ever experienced.

Weeks of doubt and self-recrimination followed for Charles, months of the same for Jocelyn. Both were forced back to the foundations of their faith. Under the strain of this great and personal crisis, suddenly their Christian beliefs seemed weak and newly fragile. Had they truly been Christians more than a decade, they asked themselves, or only a few days? With their strength so thin, the latter often seemed the case.

Charles especially found himself rethinking the most rudimentary tenets of and the intellectual basis for his whole belief system. This process, which he found necessary every year or two, was already an intrinsic part of his nature. Because his conversion to the Christian faith had contained a strong intellectual component, he found it continually necessary to reexamine the relationship between thought, belief, and actions in order to maintain his sense of spiritual and intellectual integrity. But now his daughter's wholesale rejection of God sent Charles' questioning roots deeper than had any personal circumstance since the encounter outside the Jermyn Street lecture hall. This was a more severe trial, he said, even than the death of his father.

For Jocelyn, the reevaluation did not so much concern the rudiments of being a Christian, but the nature of God's character. Suddenly her lifelong doubts about his goodness and his love gripped her heart again, filling it with resentment and pain. She had tried so hard to be a different mother than her own, but to no avail. How could a God of goodness allow such a bitter end to their attempts toward a happy and fulfilling home?

The day after Amanda's departure, the entire household was hushed, as if all Heathersleigh was in suspended motion while the rest of the world went on without them. The meals were quiet. George and Catharine were quiet. The staff was quiet. Even the horses and birds and sheep in the distance seemed quiet.

After tea that afternoon, Charles gathered the family in the library and asked Sarah Minsterly to bring the house and grounds staff to join the family there.

"We've all been through a bit of an ordeal in the last few weeks," began Charles once everyone was present. "I'm sure all of you feel awkward, as do I, not exactly knowing what to say or do. We must all admit that what has happened came as a shock, and it will probably take us some time to adjust to it."

The staff relaxed as he went on to explain a little more about what he and Jocelyn had been feeling.

"I suppose, in a sense, that for a long time this household has revolved around Amanda," he went on. "Amanda had a way of being at the center no matter what else might have been going on. Things will probably be different now. But the fact is—she has gone. She left angry. And her mother and I want to thank you all—"

He gestured about the room as he spoke.

"—including the two of you, George and Catharine, for your patience and long-suffering where Amanda was concerned. She made life a trial for all of us at times. Yet we love her deeply, and I know you all love her too and will miss her. Heathersleigh Hall will not be the same without our Amanda. And we will pray for her swift return."

He paused and cleared his throat.

"However, Amanda was but one individual. The rest of us are still here. I want you to know that you do not have to walk about as if we were in the middle of a funeral. Talk and laughter must return to Heathersleigh Hall. There has been something very much like death in this relationship. But we will move on with our lives, as Amanda will move on with hers. We will all go forward, praying for a hasty end to this period of separation."

Charles now motioned for Jocelyn to come stand beside him.

"We would like you all to join us," he continued, "in praying for our dear daughter. I include you all because I know you care for her."

Smiles and nods from around the room greeted his words.

"We would like you to pray with us now and to continue to pray for Amanda whenever the Lord brings her to your thoughts."

Husband and wife took hands and bowed their heads. The others did likewise.

"*Father in heaven,*" Charles prayed, "*we come to you now on behalf of our daughter and yours, our own dear Amanda. We can ask nothing more than that you accompany her wherever she goes, that you will be beside her and keep her in the care of your loving hands. Give us strength and courage to believe in your faithfulness . . . for Amanda and for ourselves. May she return quickly to us, and to you, with heart and mind open to our love and to yours.*"

As the weeks and months passed, in the attempt to trust God for Amanda, Charles' and Jocelyn's spirits were stretched into new regions of faith. Gradually, the opening verses of Romans five were impressed upon them: "We glory in tribulations also, knowing that tribulation worketh patience; and patience, experience; and experience, hope. And hope maketh not ashamed."

The focus of their prayers became, not the easing of their parental pain at this temporary loss of their daughter, but: *Lord, make these truths alive in us. Let us rejoice in this suffering, knowing that through it you will work the character of your nature into us. Give us the hope about which Paul wrote— hope for Amanda, hope for ourselves. Accomplish the full work of your will in all our lives.*

With such prayers on their lips, how could the sun of God's healing and restorative warmth and presence not eventually break through the clouds of their doubts?

Three months after her departure, the first word from Amanda arrived by post at Heathersleigh. What was the motivation or prompting behind such a letter, neither of her parents could guess. But their hearts were sore, as they read, to note the cold detachment in her words.

> *Dear Sir Charles and Lady Rutherford,* Amanda wrote,
>
> *Leaving Devon and getting out from under the stifling atmosphere of Heathersleigh and being with people of broader outlook has enabled me to see many things more clearly, both about you and about myself. I feel it is necessary for me to tell you that I have at last succeeded in breaking the bonds of control which you attempted to exercise over me. After the change in your lives eleven years ago, you tried to force me to follow you in every- thing you believed. I now see more clearly than ever how wrong this was*

of you. I did not then, nor can I now, endorse anything about the life you have chosen.

You will no doubt continue to live according to the narrow-minded and hypocritical ways and principles of the God you say you serve. As long as that is true, however, and until you recognize the hurt and damage you brought into my life, I see no basis for us to have a continuing relationship or friendship.

Knowing you as I do, I can conjecture at your response to my words. But I must ask you neither to pray for me nor to attempt to establish any connection with me. Such efforts, I assure you, will be less than useless. I am not interested in your God, in your prayers, or in either of you.

Amanda Rutherford

Jocelyn put down the paper, laid her head in her hands, and wept bitterly. Charles, after attempting to comfort her, sought the out-of-doors for the release of his tears.

For the remainder of the day they scarcely had words for one another, for what words could be found in light of such a communication?

Only anguished sighs came from the hearts of the two tender-hearted and hurting parents. The knife that was thrust into their hearts at Amanda's leaving had now been given an even more cruel twist.

92

Deeper and Stronger

◆◆◆

The morning following the arrival of Amanda's letter, Charles found his wife in the sun-room off the kitchen. She sat staring out into the morning's sunrise over her small terraced flower and herb garden south of the house. A cup of tea was in her hand.

"What are you thinking about?" he asked, taking a seat beside her.

"I'm remembering the happy times," she replied softly. "Remembering the hours of play out there on the lawn, the laughter, the games, Amanda's buoyant and bouncy nature."

She turned toward him with a smile, though it was a sad one.

"We *did* have happy times, Charles," Jocelyn went on with a sigh, as if trying to convince herself of a fact she had been wrestling with before he came. "We did . . . didn't we?"

"Of course we did," replied her husband. "Amanda had a happy childhood, though she is remembering it so differently now."

"That's what makes this all the more heartbreaking."

"What do you mean?"

"That Amanda really is hurting now too, just as we are. The pain she is feeling is real enough, even though it's based on an illusion of how terrible it was at home."

"But her memories right now aren't to be relied on," said Charles.

"I know. Yet in her own way, she's suffering as well. And knowing it just tears my heart in two."

"Our conversion threw Amanda's life out of balance. Perhaps she has to go through a period of doubt and question, even rejection of our values."

"But it's not as if we were bad parents, Charles, or as if this wasn't a home full of laughter, smiles, and fun."

"We did what we thought was best for them, Jocie. That happened to change midway through, but it was still their best we had in mind, mistakes we made and all. You have been a good mother, Jocelyn.— You *are* a good mother. All you have to do is look at Catharine or George and see the character traits we've built into them."

"We tried to do so much for them all. There is no sacrifice we would not have made for any of the three of them—Amanda included. Oh, Charles—how can she say those things about us? It hurts so even to think it!"

"You can't let yourself fall into the trap of thinking that Amanda's leaving is your fault."

"How can I not?"

"If anything," said Charles, "it's more *my* fault than yours. I am the focus of her resentment far more than you are."

"She resents my compliance with you," rejoined Jocelyn. "She especially hates the idea of my submission to your authority."

"Don't you suppose that it's actually not either one of *us* she's rebelling against? She simply hates authority in any form."

Jocelyn nodded and let out another sigh. "Here I thought we were doing well. I thought I was beginning to pull out of the despondency of her leaving. Now this letter's started it all over again."

Charles reached over and took her free hand. They sat some minutes in silence, staring at the lightening sky. Already the sunlight streaming through the windows was beginning to heat up the small room.

"Before you came in just now," Jocelyn went on, "I was thinking about what it would be like if Amanda decided to marry. It could happen, you know, Charles, now that she is in London. She is eighteen now."

He nodded.

"All these years I've imagined what it would be like to help one of my daughters plan a wedding. I always assumed it would be Amanda first. I thought how happy the day would be, so different..."

Her voice caught momentarily. Charles squeezed her hand. He knew what she was thinking. Jocelyn's mother had arranged to be out of the country and had not even attended her own daughter's wedding. It had been the final parental humiliation Mrs. Wildecott had inflicted upon her daughter. Jocelyn had carried it as a quiet, painful memory all the years since.

"I wanted so to be a part of it, Charles," said Jocelyn, dabbing at her eyes. "It's something a mother and her daughter are supposed to do with each other. But now I'm afraid ... I'm afraid Amanda's going to take that joy away from me too ... just as she's taking away the happy memories of her childhood by remembering them as awful."

"I'm sure Amanda will come to her senses long before then," said Charles.

"Perhaps ... yet I'm still afraid. I'm afraid of being shut out again—as I was shut out from her eighteenth birthday two weeks ago. I wanted to write, send her a gift, hold her in my arms and tell her how much I love her. But..."

Jocelyn glanced away. Only one who had suffered as had Jocelyn could feel such a disappointed grief in being shut out of a daughter's birthday celebration.

For some time they sat gazing out into the quiet morning. The house was so much quieter than when Amanda was young. But what would either not have given to hear her bossy, boisterous voice in the hallway at that moment?

"One thing we must do," said Charles, "as painful as this experience is—we absolutely must keep our hope and vision for George and Catharine alive. The fact that Amanda is gone doesn't make us any the less parents than we were before. The other two need us—especially Catharine, but George, too, even though he is practically a man and will soon be off to university. And Amanda may one day need us to be mother and father to her again as well. They all remain growing, feeling, sensitive, spiritual beings in need of a parent's love."

"I know," sighed Jocelyn.

"I suppose it is more difficult for you," Charles went on. "There is something about a mother's heart that probably suffers more when a daughter turns away, as perhaps there is for a father when his son turns against him. But we have been as good as parents as we knew how to be, at least. We tried to do our best for Amanda, and we will continue to try to do our best for George and Catharine."

Jocelyn nodded solemnly in response. He reached over and took the now-cooled teacup from her other hand, placed it on the floor and clasped both her hands in his.

"I love you, Jocelyn," he said fervently. "Nothing will ever change that. I love you more every year. I believe in you, and I care about you no matter what Amanda or your own mother has done."

Jocelyn smiled through the tears that had gathered in her eyes. "I am more thankful for you than I will ever be able to tell you," she said, sniffling a bit. "Actually, if anything, Amanda's leaving only makes me love you the more."

"God has been good to us, Jocelyn. We've had a good life—we must keep reminding ourselves of that. We must be thankful."

"I do try to keep telling myself that," she said with a wry smile.

"And it's far from over, Jocelyn. God will continue to be good to us . . . because he's a *good* Father. Remember all our talks with Timothy about just that?"

Jocelyn nodded. "How could I forget?"

"Now I believe we have been given the opportunity of learning to trust in that goodness, though this development in our lives does not *appear* good. We must hold on to our trust that he will turn it to good, because he turns *all* things to good."

Jocelyn was quiet for a minute. When she spoke, she did not respond directly to her husband's words. "Do you think Amanda will come back one day?"

"That is in God's hands. Only he knows what purposes his will yet contains for our daughter. But I know that we can trust him . . . and that good will result. We have to believe that."

"It's hard, Charles."

"I know. But look at it this way—we're being given the opportunity to feel a tiny portion of what God feels."

"How do you mean?"

"We're both prodigals, aren't we? We've both rebelled, gone our own way. We've said far worse things to God by our disobedience, even without knowing it, than what Amanda said to us. In a way, we can rejoice in this trial we are experiencing for no other reason than that—it enables us to know God's heart more deeply. Imagine *his* suffering over his wayward sons and daughters."

They were silent a long minute, gazing out together over the colorful gardens.

"You are right, of course, Charles," Jocelyn said at last with a sigh. "And I hope you will keep reminding me when I forget and fall into self-pity."

She smiled. "And you are also right that we have had a good life together. A few minutes ago I was remembering our wedding day. I suppose thinking about Amanda reminded me of it. Even though Mother wasn't there, it was still the happiest day of my life."

♦ ♦ ♦

For years, the eyes of many in England had rested on the handsome son of Ashby Rutherford, Lord of the Manor of Heathersleigh, and his wife, the Lady Anne. Not a few in London's social circles had dubbed him one of the finest potential catches available. And now young Charles Rutherford was about to marry the daughter of Colonel Wildecott, of distinguished service in India.

A few tongues wagged, it is true, over the fact—impossible to hide—that the young lady was . . . well, *different* of appearance than one would have expected to attract the notice of the heir to the Heathersleigh estate. To most, however, news of the announcement only confirmed what the young man's parents both knew well enough, as did Colonel Wildecott and his daughter— that Charles Rutherford was a man of integrity and worth, with a heart that valued character over appearance. If ever there was doubt that he was his own man and an independent thinker, his choice of bride put all notions to the contrary to rest. Charles Rutherford was surely a young man who would go far.

There was a bit of gossip, moreover, concerning the news that the bride's mother would not attend the wedding. She had chosen to remain in India, claiming that her health would not stand the long journey, and there were some who doubted her excuse. But the groom's mother had smoothly stepped in to take Mrs. Wildecott's role in preparing for the wedding, and Lady Anne Rutherford was widely respected. The murmurs regarding this slight change in protocol died down almost as quickly as they had begun.

Lady Rutherford had suggested one of the large London churches for the event. Her son, seeing little point in bowing to the customs of a traditional wedding, had argued in favor of the lawns and gardens of Heathersleigh. But Jocelyn Wildecott, swayed by a sentiment even she did not understand, had wanted to be married in a church. The perfect compromise had been reached by making plans to have the wedding ceremony itself at the parish church, with a gala party and reception to follow on the Heathersleigh grounds.

The scene at the small stone church at Milverscombe on the day of the wedding was such as had never been visited upon the humble edifice in the hundred years of its existence. Enough people were on hand easily to double the number that lived in the village and its environs—a lively mix of London society, for whom the event provided a welcome social break from summer's monotony, with local landowners, villagers, and even farmers, who rarely had the opportunity to witness such an event.

Dignitaries, noblemen and ladies, and other distinguished visitors sat in the church, whose tall double doors, as well as every window capable of the function after years of disuse, remained wide open so that the spectators gathered shoulder to shoulder outside might catch a glimpse of the ceremony in progress.

The crowd overflowed not only the church but the very churchyard as well. The day was so festive and jubilant, however, that no one seemed overly concerned with how close they could get. Being on hand for the celebration was enough, whether or not they heard the actual vows.

By the time Jocelyn Wildecott took her place on her father's arm, standing perhaps two hundred feet from the church door, they were surrounded by a press of beaming farmers and villagers and sheepherders and their wives, scrubbed as clean as soap and water could make their skin and clothes, and already proud of their soon-to-be new and future Lady Rutherford.

Never in her life had she felt so self-conscious. She glanced nervously around at what seemed to be ten thousand faces—all looking and smiling at her! And Charles at this moment, she thought, was safe inside the church and hidden from the view of these million eyes! If only he had let her wear the veil over her face. At least then she would have some protection from the thousands of eyes. But Charles would have nothing hidden, he insisted, especially the face of the woman he loved.

Little could Jocelyn imagine that it was the very scar on her face that made the villagers love her so. She might be a colonel's daughter, the locals thought. She might be accustomed to privilege and standing. They might always use the *Lady* when addressing her.

Yet her red birthmark, somehow, made her one of them.

At first sight, she became *real* in their eyes, approachable, vulnerable, down-to-earth. In her obvious humanness, she was a personal link between themselves and the well-off folk of Heathersleigh. From the day of this wedding onward, as long as she and Charles reigned at the Hall, she would be *their* Lady Jocelyn— no unapproachable aristocrat, but, like them, a fellow human creature, imperfect yet made in the image of God.

As she stood waiting, Jocelyn did not know what this wedding, and she herself, symbolized for the good folk of Milverscombe. Nor was she aware what she would one day mean to the happy older couple who had wriggled their way close and now stood but an arm's length away, and what they would mean to her. Maggie and Bobbie McFee were not merely beaming, but were also silently praying for the future of this young woman. Indeed she must be one in a million to have won the heart of their very own Master Charles himself!

Jocelyn stood erect, silent, jittery, happy, and waiting impatiently on the arm of her distinguished father. In grey tails and striped trousers, and sporting a huge mustache of the type generally associated with the wild regions east of Sudan, the imposing man would ordinarily have been his daughter's match for the attention of the eyes of the crowd. But today she was a bride, and every neck outside the church was craned to catch a glimpse of her.

Lovingly and painstakingly stitched by a gathering of local seamstresses, Jocelyn's dress reflected the Victorian spirit, and the ideals of its queen. Of the heaviest satin to be found, its collar rose high and encircled the neck. Tiny satin-covered buttons led from neck to waist in back, with a heavy satin bow tied at the small of the back. Each long slender sleeve ended with a delicate point of material, cut longer on one side to lie over the back of each hand. The skirt of the dress was plain, though the satin was luxurious in itself, without frills and lace. The filmy veil pinned to the back of Jocelyn's hair with a satin headpiece stretched the full length of the long train, now held carefully out of the dust by a pair of young attendants.

"The music's started!" shouted someone in the crowd.

From inside the church Jocelyn barely heard the faint strains now coming from the organ.

"Are you ready, my dear?" Colonel Wildecott whispered, turning and leaning toward his daughter.

"Yes, Daddy," replied Jocelyn. "I only wish Mother were here."

"You must forgive your mother, Jocelyn, dear," replied the colonel in an uncharacteristic moment of openness. "She has not had an easy life traipsing about the world with me. Down inside she is a good woman. One day she will come to her senses and will grow to love you as much as I do."

Jocelyn's eyes filled with tears at his unaccustomed tenderness. "Thank you, Daddy. I love you too. I am so glad that you are here with me."

"There is nowhere else I would be, my dear. All the tigers in India could not keep me from sharing this moment with you. Shall we be off on your new adventure?"

Jocelyn smiled up at him. The colonel stood erect once more and turned to face the church.

They now began the long, slow processional toward the open doors through the long narrow aisle of bodies. Never in Jocelyn's life had so short a distance seemed so interminably long! Every face they passed wore a triumphant and happy smile, as if she had grown up in the village and was personally a favorite with its every man, woman, and child. In truth, she knew not a soul among them. In time, however, she would be on personal terms with every one—and they would love her even more than they did on this day.

Inside at last, they walked keeping slow time to the processional. Flowers were everywhere, filling every corner with their delicious fragrance.

There sat Charles' cousin Gifford with his new wife of just eight months. A wave of new doubts swept through Jocelyn at the sight of the young woman's thin and graceful form. Already Martha Rutherford was part of London's high society and loving every minute of it. *What am I doing marrying into this family?* Jocelyn thought. *I'll never be Cousin Martha's match socially. I'll embarrass Charles. He'll be sorry he married me. . . .*

In the front row sat Lord Ashby and his wife, her future parents-in-law, old-fashioned yet progressive aristocrats. Already they had been so kind to her. Lady Anne caught her eye and gave her an encouraging smile. Jocelyn found herself just barely able to return it.

And then there was Charles . . . standing at the front of the church awaiting her, with his handsome, confident, and altogether disarming smile!

The music stopped.

She had arrived! This was the moment. She was about to be married!

The vicar of the local parish proceeded to perform the traditional Anglican marriage service. The words, the vows, the exchange of rings . . . it was all lost in a swirl of dreamy happiness.

Then came the words, "You may kiss the bride."

The tender moment of silence was followed by oohs inside. Outside, shouts and cheers erupted when news of the regal kiss was communicated via a local sheepherder named Mudgley, whose vantage point near one of the windows afforded him just the necessary view to corroborate the precise moment of contact.

Nor did the cheering and shouts and general hubbub diminish when bride and groom emerged from the open doors into the sunlight and hurried to a waiting carriage. The two horses had by now begun to stomp and snort impatiently. In the driver's box, young Hector Farnham had been sitting in stoic readiness, but now he lifted the reins and clucked to his charges that it was at last time to be on their way.

The moment they were off, the throng followed, mostly on foot. A steady stream of carriages bearing the more well-to-do of the guests steadily inched their way through the clogged road. But no one was in a hurry. This was a day to be savored.

The gala reception on the grounds of Heathersleigh Hall lasted all afternoon and into the evening. Lavish preparations had been made. Dancing, food, wine, and merrymaking were enjoyed by all. Following the example of the bride and bridegroom, who by day's end had personally greeted every guest, commoners and nobles mixed freely.

"I say, Rutherford," commented a friend of the father of the groom, "even the Tories you invited seem to be enjoying themselves!"

"Nothing like getting out and mixing with people of the earth, I always say," rejoined Charles' father.

At six o'clock, though none of the guests seemed yet inclined to leave, Charles and Jocelyn were whisked away by carriage to the train, which would bear them to Torquay.

There they would honeymoon for two weeks at the seacoast resort before returning to the stately home where they would spend their married life together.

———————— ♦ ♦ ♦ ————————

"I'll never forget that day either," smiled Charles. "And though there have been a few bumps and changes in the road since then, my love for you has only grown deeper and stronger."

93

Brother and Sister

*C*atharine, come here!" cried George, at home on holiday from the first term of his new tenure at Oxford. He called to his sister as he ran down the first-floor corridor of Heathersleigh's east wing.

Fourteen-year-old Catharine jumped up from her chair and hurried from her room. She saw her twenty-year-old brother coming toward her.

"I think I found what's causing the spooky noises!" he exclaimed.

He immediately turned. Catharine answered his cries and they hurried back the way he had come.

"Is it really ghosts, George?" said Catharine, following closely on her brother's heels.

The slight tremor in her voice betrayed nervousness. She would have trusted George with her very life. But if he was going to show her some creepy old bones with cobwebs all over them—or something even worse ... something that maybe wasn't altogether dead yet!—she wasn't sure she liked the idea.

George glanced back with a smile and wink but said nothing further. Already they were climbing to the second floor. Within another minute they entered the library.

George moved quickly across the floor to the movable bookcase he had discovered years before. In one motion he swung it aside. He lit a candle and then led the way into the darkened labyrinth of passageways behind the library wall.

"George ..."

"I promise, Catharine," he said, "there's nothing to be afraid of."

He took her hand, and she followed.

George now led, more slowly, back eastward in the direction of the hidden tower staircase. He knew every inch of this passageway by now and could have negotiated the whole thing with his eyes closed. One level above them, the passage had been walled off from the rest of the garret. This fact had led to George's original discovery of his great-grandfather's shrewdly contrived maze. It was to this region of the house that Catharine expected George to take her. Instead, when they reached the tower, George turned in the opposite direction and began descending the hidden staircase which paralleled the one that held communication with the rest of the house.

Down he led . . . down . . . down . . . until Catharine was certain they must be below the level of the ground outside. Not a word was spoken. At last they reached their destination, a small basement chamber which George had also discovered some years earlier.

A brief explanation followed.

"I don't see what this has to do with the ghosts," said Catharine after George had revealed the basement portion of today's discovery.

"You will after I show you what I found in the garret. Come on."

He turned and led her back up the way they had come. In three or four minutes they had arrived in the upper portions of the Hall. Then George proceeded to explain his findings, patiently pausing for her many questions and explanations.

"You see, the wind coming up from the cold basement all the way to the top of the house into the garret—that's what causes the noises."

"It's too bad Amanda isn't here to see this," said Catharine at length, sitting down in the semidarkness of the confined space.

"She wouldn't be interested, anyway," replied George, joining her on the floor. He set the candle down beside him. The flame danced and flickered about, casting eerie shadows that made Catharine glance around uneasily. George might explain everything to the perfect satisfaction of his rational mind. But it was still spooky here.

"You're probably right," she said. "But I still don't understand why Amanda became so stuffy. Even before she left, she'd hardly smiled at me in years, and she never wanted to have fun with us."

"I don't understand it either. We used to have such fun playing together."

"She was always telling me what to do, since before I could remember."

"She ordered me about too."

"But you're a boy—and you're older than her, too!"

"What difference did that make? That never stopped Amanda. She even told Mother and Father what to do."

"You never treated me like that, even when I was little. Why did she?"

"That's just the way Amanda was."

Brother and sister sat for a while in the candlelit darkness. Thoughts of Amanda caused both to grow pensive. Their sister's leaving had affected them too, though each in different ways.

"Why is Amanda the way she is, George?" asked Catharine at length.

"She wanted to grow up too fast," her brother replied. "That's how it seemed to me at least. I enjoyed being young. I still do. I don't feel at all as if I'm twenty."

"You always seemed like a grown-up to me."

George laughed. "That's only because I am older. But I feel just as much like a boy as ever. It seems to me that you and I are practically the same age."

"So why did Amanda want to grow up too fast?"

"I thought all girls were in a hurry to grow up. Aren't you?"

"I don't care about being seventeen and wearing fancy dresses and going to balls in London."

"I can't see you doing it either!" laughed George again. "Can you imagine you and me going to some society thing—you in a gown, me in tails and a top hat!"

Now they both laughed.

"We'd probably stand out like two country bumpkins," added George. "I don't know about you, but I love the country—I miss it the whole time I'm at university. I wouldn't trade Heathersleigh for anything. I don't see why Amanda was so stuck on London."

"I never want to leave Heathersleigh," said Catharine. "I like being fourteen too. It's a little like being halfway between a girl and a woman. I don't want my life to change any faster than it should. I want to enjoy every age as much as I can."

"Amanda sure didn't feel that way. I can't imagine why she hated it here so much."

"I sure wouldn't want to be without Mum or Papa."

"Me neither. I never understood why Amanda became so annoyed with them."

"She once said to me that they were trying to control everything she did."

"She said that to me too. But I didn't know what she was talking about. Mother and Father give us plenty of freedom, don't you think?"

She nodded thoughtfully. "Except of course, I've never been that interested in all the things Amanda wanted to do . . . like go to London or march with the suffragettes."

"I must say," he added, "I'm worried about Amanda."

"I really love her."

"So do I," George replied, then looked up with a sad smile. "After she got to be older," he went on, "she always thought everyone was against her. But really we all love her. But when she was seeing things so mixed up, how could she realize it?"

"Let's pray for her, George."

"Good idea."

A deep silence fell. A presence was indeed with these two young people who were in the process of making their parents' faith their own and thus passing it afresh down into new generations of the ancient family. It was not, however, a ghost of some ancestor who was with them at this moment, but the Spirit of their Father.

"God, we pray for Amanda," said George at length. "Make her want to be part of our family again. Show her down deep that we all love her. Help her not to be too foolish while she's in London. I'm sorry if I wasn't always as good a brother to her as I should have been. And help Amanda someday to look inside herself, to see that she's got some problems she must face if she's ever to have a happy life."

"Help Amanda not to be so angry at Mum and Papa because of what they believe," now prayed Catharine. "And help her not to be angry at us either, if she is. Help her know that we love her. We do still love her, especially now that she's gone. Take care of Amanda, Lord. Be with her even if she doesn't know it. Don't let anything bad happen to her in London. Amen."

"Amen," added George.

As they fell silent, they heard footsteps approaching from the stairway below. A second or two later, light from a second candle began to flicker toward them.

"I thought I heard voices," came a familiar voice. The next instant Jocelyn's face appeared.

"Hallo, Mum!" said Catharine. "How'd you find us?"

"I came into the library for a book, and there was the bookcase pulled back. I poked my head in to investigate, heard the two of you, and decided to have a little adventure of my own by following you. What are you doing?"

"Well, first we were talking about ghosts, and then we were praying for Amanda."

"That's wonderful. I know that pleases the Lord. It pleases me too."

She sat down between them, placed her candle holder next to George's on the floor, and took each of their hands. "You know," she said, "the two of you really mean a lot to your father and me—you know that, don't you?"

"Of course we do, Mother," replied George.

"When something like this happens—with Amanda, I mean—of course it hurts us as parents. But our grief over Amanda doesn't mean we aren't more thankful for you than you can realize."

She squeezed their hands and smiled sincerely at them both.

"Whatever Amanda might say, we believe in you and Papa," said Catharine. "You're the two most wonderful people in the world to us. Aren't they, George?"

"I couldn't have said it better," replied her brother.

"Catharine . . . thank you!" said Jocelyn. She leaned over and embraced her daughter affectionately. When she drew away, tears were falling from her eyes. "That's one of the nicest things anyone's ever said to me.—Thank you, too, George," she added, turning and giving her son a hug. "You both have really helped your father and me to endure this time of sadness."

It was silent for a few minutes, and they all sat quietly together, watching the candle shadows flicker. Now, with her mother present, the little room seemed warm and cozy to Catharine, not spooky at all.

"I know that in one way Amanda hasn't done anything so very dreadful," said Jocelyn. "You may wonder why her leaving has caused your father and me such grief. It isn't as though she has committed a crime or has done something that society would count so terribly wicked. Have you wondered about that?"

"I don't know, Mother—not really," replied George. "I think what Amanda did is pretty awful. The things she said to you are unforgivable, especially after all you've done for her."

Jocelyn nodded.

"We do forgive her, of course," she said. "Or we are trying. But what she has done *is* very serious, even though she may still appear perfectly respectable on the outside. And the worst of it, of course, is not what she has done to us, but what she has done to God. Rebellion of the heart, even though it sometimes remains invisible, is the worst sin a human being can commit against God. Seeing our own daughter do so is more painful than it is possible to say."

Again the comfortable silence fell for a time before Jocelyn went on. "You know, it could be one of you, or both of you, who will be the ones to help Amanda come to her senses."

"How could *we* do that for her?" asked Catharine.

"I don't know. But if you pray for her and ask God for an opportunity to show that you love her and believe in her—not in what she may have done, but in the person she could be—and to tell her that you believe in *us* and trust us, and God too, then you never know what God might be able to do."

"Do you really think Amanda might come to one of us first?" asked George.

"Right now her heart is closed to your father and me. But I know she loves the two of you. Her heart may open back to one of you before it does to us."

"That doesn't seem very likely," said Catharine.

"Don't lose patience with her," said Jocelyn. "Try to keep a forgiving heart. I know she's hurt you in the past, and she has said and done cruel things. I know you share our hurt over her leaving. But you must keep praying for her. Then wait for whatever opportunity the Lord gives. You never know how those heart-doors will open. Your father opened doors for me that I didn't even know I'd shut."

"What kind of doors, Mum?" said Catharine.

"Doors down inside myself, doors of doubt, of guilt—and places, too, where I was holding back, refusing to grow in areas he knew I *needed* to grow. If it hadn't been for your father, I wouldn't be as close to God as I am."

"How did Papa do that?"

"He believed in me. And he prayed for me. It helped me to see things I'd never seen about myself. And he still does that when I'm struggling. I do it for him, too."

"I guess . . . I never really thought of you and Papa having to struggle with God."

Jocelyn's face held a tinge of sadness. "Oh, my dear, of course we struggle. It's not always easy to be God's people."

Mother and son and daughter sat in the stillness of the garret talking for another hour. Never had the three of them felt so close. Catharine and George seemed somehow old enough, perhaps for the first time, to know and understand their mother not merely as their mother, but as a fellow human being engaged in the universal struggle to know herself. Seeing that side of her made them love and admire her all the more.

"Oops! There goes my candle," exclaimed George, as the fading wick finally gave up the ghost and became a thin trail of dying white smoke.

"Then mine isn't far behind!" said Jocelyn.

They rose then, and returned to the library.

94

Unknown Connections

*C*harles Rutherford sat down to peruse the morning edition of the *Times*. Some five or ten minutes later an announcement on page four caught his attention.

"I say, Jocelyn," he said, "it seems old Lord Halifax died yesterday."

"I don't think I know the name," she replied.

"Burton Wyckham Halifax—been a stalwart in the House of Lords as long as I can remember. Though I understand he's been slowing down for years. He and my father were somewhat close, actually. Politically and professionally, I mean. Can't say I ever recall seeing Lord Halifax here at Heathersleigh for a visit."

"When are services?"

Charles scanned further down the page.

"In three days," he said.

"Will you go?" asked Jocelyn.

"I don't know," mused Charles. "I must admit I haven't thought of the old fellow in years. But perhaps I should."

"Do you know his widow?"

"No. Lady Halifax—his first wife—died years ago. I heard he'd remarried years back, when I was still in the Commons—a year or two after the Diamond Jubilee, as I recall. A widow from the Continent, I believe. I never knew her.—Curious," he added thoughtfully, "the paper makes no mention of her."

—————————— ◆◆◆ ——————————

Meanwhile in London, the widow of whom Charles spoke was at that moment engaged in conversation with her son, now twenty-four years of age, concerning a future that would in time draw the two families together in ways the Rutherfords of Devon could never have foreseen. Their tones were thoughtful and subdued, though they would hardly be considered those of mourning.

"Now that your stepfather is gone," the lady was saying, "it may be time to reassess your plans."

"I am content with my position at the *Mail*."

"*The Daily Mail* is hardly worthy of you, nor is it why I sent you to Cambridge," rejoined Lady Halifax.

"Journalism offers its opportunities, Mother. I am able to travel widely. That is something I am not eager to relinquish."

The woman nodded. She knew far more about the nature of her son's travels than he realized, but was content that such knowledge remain private for the present. The time would come for disclosure. Perhaps one day she and her son would even work side by side for the cause. But the boy was still young. He had to be handled carefully as events on the Continent developed. In the meantime, it would be useful to explore more actively what infiltrations on this side of the Channel might be open to such a wealthy and eligible young man.

Both had more to consider than they were willing to let on. For this mother and son were involved in a game where secrecy and information were the commodities to be bought and sold and where one's allegiances were best kept fluid ... and to oneself.

Nor were they the only sleepers in England who yet remained in their hidden slumber. The time for the revealing of this clandestine network would come. Before that, it would draw many unsuspecting English men and women into the webs of their schemes of deceit. But the full story of how such as these would change Europe's future, and in the process that of the Rutherfords of Devon, lay yet ahead to be told.

All would come to light ... but not until its appointed time.

95

Privilege of the Prodigal's Parent

❦he tears at Heathersleigh gradually lessened. Over the months, Charles and Jocelyn took hope on behalf of their daughter and began the long process of covering her with prayer.

One weekend far into the fall, Timothy Diggorsfeld came from London for a visit. Since Amanda's departure he had tried to get down to Devon as often as was practically possible to reassure his dear friends. He knew both had searched long and hard within themselves to find whatever responsibility lay upon their own shoulders—willing even in their grief to spare their daughter.

Though he had never had a child of his own, the pastor understood a father's heart—because he knew God—and he could therefore empathize with Charles and Jocelyn. But because he was not personally involved, he could also see much that his friends could not. He was keenly aware that they had been privileged to share in the ageless retelling of Jesus' story of the prodigal . . . and to live out the loving and prayerful parental role in it. He hoped, by his presence, his encouragement, his friendship, and his prayers, to help the mother and father come to see the blessing contained in such a sharing of the divine grief.

The three friends talked late into the Friday evening of Timothy's arrival about matters of high import in their hearts.

"Sometimes, Timothy," Charles said, "I find myself wondering if we are making too much of all this. I pick up the paper, and I read of an axe murder or a bank robbery or some other atrocity. Then I think of the parents of the individuals who commit such crimes, and I realize how much greater must be their suffering than ours."

Timothy nodded as he listened.

"You make a valid point, I suppose," he replied. "It is no doubt good to remind yourselves that there are those who have it far worse. Such a realization is always an aid to gratefulness when we begin to feel sorry for ourselves."

He paused momentarily.

"On the other hand," he resumed, "all parental grief is unique, in whatever form it comes, and whatever the circumstances giving rise to it. No one's pain can be rightly compared with any other's. Your Amanda has rejected you, your faith, your life as a family. She has rejected your influence as a father and mother. She has said cruel things to you. Of course, in your hearts you have already forgiven her. You await with open arms any change she might make. Yet who can say that the pain you feel is not deep and genuine—fully the equal of what the parent of a criminal, for example, might feel? The parent of a robber and the parent of the silent rebel are both parents together. It grieves the parental heart when a son or daughter walls himself or herself off from parental love—*whatever* form that wall may take. Our heavenly Father has sons and daughters in many kinds of rebellion against him. Who is to say his grief is not just as great for those who turn from him quietly and invisibly as it is for those whose rebellion is more visible?"

Charles and Jocelyn listened intently, seeking whatever fresh understanding might help them grow and trust God more completely.

"Your experience," Timothy went on, "has caused me to read the story in the fifteenth chapter of Luke with, I pray, new insight. I see in it a family situation far more similar to yours than, say, that of the axe murderer you have mentioned."

"Why do you say that?"

"Look at the parable more closely, Charles. It is, quite simply, a story about a respectable family, a family of means, whose son leaves home."

"I never considered it in that light before."

"The story follows the prodigal to what is called the far country," Diggorsfeld continued, "where we see him foolishly spending his every penny. How much time passes, we do not know. Was it months, years . . . ten years? And all that time, the Lord gives no hint as to what the lad's dear parents were suffering. What was the father thinking as he waited on the road, scanning the horizon for the return of his son? And the mother! Not a word about her—but oh, how deep must have been the parental grief! How she must have wept for his immaturity!—"

He broke off with an embarrassed look on his face. "But I did not come out here to give you a sermon," he said. "I suppose it is a hazard of the trade, to wax eloquent. But I came to give you help and support, not to review my Sunday sermon notes with you."

"No, no!" protested Charles. "You must go on. I find this extraordinarily helpful."

Timothy glanced at Jocelyn. She nodded solemnly. So he took a deep breath and continued.

"Well, then, you must understand that the boy became no criminal. He was not thrown in prison. We have no indication that he was an excessively wicked young man. Well, it says he lived riotously—I suppose that doesn't sound very good. But his chief immaturity was simply that he wanted his inheritance prematurely. He suffered from that malady that is at the root of all sin—the pride of independence. And for that alone he is known for all time as the prodigal. He *left* his father's home. He squandered his inheritance. He lived out in one life that great story of the human race. He did that which we all have done toward our Father in heaven."

Here Timothy paused. The silence was lengthy. They were all thinking of Amanda.

"And yet," he went on at length, "a moment came when, as the Lord says, the young man *came to himself.* He came to his senses. He woke up. The fog of self-delusion lifted. He matured. He began at last to *see* things clearly. And the first truth he saw was his *father.*

"Suddenly he saw the truth to which he had been blind—such an obvious truth, no doubt obvious to all who knew this family. The son's rebellious independence had caused him to turn from it. But now he saw what a fool he had been. The eyes of his heart were opened at last to see that he had been hasty and unwise.

"Actually," continued Timothy, "I believe he perceived two huge truths. He saw that his father was a good man. And he saw that things had not really been so bad at home. And with those realizations, already he was on his feet. His rebellion was behind him. The image of his father was before him. '*I will arise,*' he said, '*and go to my father.*'

"To my mind, these are eight of the most beautiful words in all Scripture, encapsulating the one and only solution to the entire human dilemma.

"'*Father,*' the prodigal says, '*I have sinned against heaven and against you. I am no longer worthy to be called your son.*' It is the salvation prayer. And here is salvation indeed! Such is the prayer we must *all* pray—we are not worthy to be God's sons and daughters, for we have sinned against him. Yet he accepts us, his arms thrown wide to embrace us!

How great indeed must be God's love!

"Does not your heart swell to envision the scene? The dusty road ... the father waiting ... the figure approaching in the distance. The father's heart leaps! Can it ... but ... yes! Already he is beginning to run, shouting behind him—'*Wife ... wife!*' he cries. '*Come ... come quickly!*'

"Now the figure in the distance throws bag and staff to the ground ... he is running forward ... there is no mistaking him now!

"The woman emerges from the house. There before her eyes she beholds the scene about which she has dreamed night and day, only half believing the day would ever come. She runs after them now ... tears flowing down her face ... her son's name on her lips. Ahead of her, father and son embrace in the middle of the road. She weeps with such joy that she can scarcely continue. . . ."

A sob broke at last from Jocelyn's lips.

"Oh, Timothy—if only I could believe such a moment will come to us!" she said.

"But you can believe it ... you *must* believe it."

"But how can I?"

"You can believe it, Jocelyn," replied Timothy, "because God is good. *He* is the father, and it is *he* whose house Amanda has left and whose inheritance she is squandering, not yours."

"*His* house?"

"Of course. Amanda is *his* daughter first of all. She has only been given to you for a few brief years, but she is his for all eternity. The two of you have been granted the wonderful privilege of joining in the divine fatherhood, of sharing in the pain and joy depicted in Luke fifteen. I truly believe it is a privilege, an opportunity to partake of the heart of God, to pray a prodigal back into the family of God. It is not a privilege the Lord gives to the faint of heart, for it is a high calling."

They considered his words for a minute in silence.

"What exactly do you think God wants us to do?" asked Jocelyn at length.

"He calls upon you and Charles merely to wait, patiently and prayerfully and expectantly—gazing down the road in hope, feet ready to run, smiles prepared to break from your lips, forgiveness alive in your hearts, arms aching to embrace in welcome, fatted calf waiting in readiness.

"Ah, but *he*—the Father whose bosom Amanda has left even more than she has left yours . . . he is already pursuing her to the far country. There he will woo her among the swine husks. You must *wait*, but he will *woo*. Silently and invisibly will he speak truths into her heart about her Father's home and the inheritance that awaits her there. He will woo her, and *win* her . . . as he woos and wins all prodigals in the end."

Quietly Jocelyn wept. Timothy said no more. The three rose. Their hearts were full of many things to contemplate before the Lord.

96

Father and Son

*T*he next day, Saturday, Charles, Timothy, and George went for a long ride into the hills. Ordinarily Jocelyn and Catharine would have accompanied them. But on this day, knowing from their boisterous spirits that the three men were ready for a romp and would lose no opportunity to tear off over the Devonshire downs at breakneck speeds, mother and daughter remained behind. They planned to take a small carriage over to the McFees', where everyone would meet later for tea. By the time the men left for the stables, Jocelyn was already packing a basket with sandwiches and some of Sarah's pastries and jam. Both Maggie and Bobby were beginning to show signs of their age, and Jocelyn was determined not to put Maggie to any extra work.

As mother and daughter made their preparations, the three riders rode hard. Some five miles north of Milverscombe, they neared a crest from which they would just be able to make out the blue of the sea in the distance.

"Race you to the top!" cried George. The next instant his mount, a chestnut gelding named Admiral, was tearing over the grass with such speed that huge clumps of turf flew up into the faces of the two who followed.

Charles, on Celtic Star II, dug his heels into the grey mare's sides. He called out in exhortation, and bolted after George. Timothy followed, though at some distance. He was a fair horseman. But when father and son set themselves head to head in a challenge, no one for miles could keep up.

Charles turned the mare to the left to escape the pelting clods, then cried and whipped and kicked and urged her up the hill after his son. George glanced back. He knew his father would cover his sudden sprint, for his father had faster legs under him than his own. George could only hope to hold him off long enough to gain the summit.

"George!" cried Charles after him. "That was a daring ploy, but dangerous!"

George laughed, but threw his energy into the race rather than a reply. He bent low over Admiral's neck. The only sound now was the thunderous beat of hooves over the ground.

Slowly Charles gained. By the time Celtic Star's nose came within whisking distance of Admiral's tail, however, the race was over. George reined in, and Charles drew even. They cantered up onto the crest. Both were laughing in sheer delight.

"Why was that dangerous?" said George, turning in his saddle.

"Jumping out to a quick sprint like that," replied his father, "—you know I'll always make up the ground."

"Getting a quick lead is the only chance I have!" rejoined George. "I may be half your age, but I'm still no match for you in a dead sprint—at least, not when you're on Celtic Star. Besides—it worked, didn't it? I beat you to the top!"

"That you did, George, my boy!" laughed Charles. "You will be gone soon," he added, growing more serious. "I am going to miss our rides and long talks when you go back to university."

"So shall I, Father," replied George as Timothy rode up.

"The two of you are a couple of madcaps in the saddle!" he cried as he approached.

"Just say *race*, and all bets are off—it's one of us tearing after the other," replied Charles. "I'm afraid, however, that George has age on his side of the fence now."

They sat a few minutes in silence, all three horses breathing heavily.

"It's beautiful up here!" exclaimed Timothy quietly. He gazed all about, gradually taking in the complete 360 degrees of the panorama. "The gentle hills and fields of the Devonshire downs spread out behind us, the faint blue of the ocean in the distance, mingling with the sky so that you can't quite tell where one leaves off and the other begins . . ."

"This *is* one of my favorite spots," said Charles. "Jocelyn and I used to ride up here often when we were younger."

After some minutes, they turned to head back down. The pace remained leisurely and the dialogue increased, George adding to the discussion not only his spiritual insights, but also his own developing youthful wit.

By the time they arrived at the cottage in the late afternoon, their mood had grown more thoughtful—this owing perhaps to the fact that they had worked hard along with their three exhausted mounts. Bobby ambled out to meet them. He took the three sets of reins as they dismounted. The horses would make vigorous use of the respite of water and grain and would enjoy the cool shade of Bobby's barn. Later in the evening, George would accompany Catharine in the carriage back to the Hall, while the three friends would ride the horses home.

When the men entered the cottage, a sumptuous tea was already spread out upon Maggie's kitchen table. Jocelyn poured, and conversation flowed freely and jovially as they enjoyed the pastries and sandwiches.

Timothy Diggorsfeld was gratified to see everyone's spirits high, though Jocelyn still seemed a trifle wan. The previous evening's conversation, though portentous, had put much into perspective for Charles, and Timothy felt sure that Jocelyn's peace was not far behind.

An hour later, as the sun moved toward its appointed daily burial behind the trees west of the cottage, the seven friends, truly brothers and sisters now, though their ages ranged from fourteen to almost seventy, sat in the McFee sitting room. And gradually the talk, as it usually did these days, turned to Amanda.

97

Prayers for a Prodigal Daughter

ou know," said Jocelyn as the discussion progressed, "I was praying for Amanda this morning, and a thought came to me that I haven't been able to get out of my mind since. I'm wondering if it may be a truth from God."

All the rest waited expectantly.

"I was awake early—you remember, Charles . . . you asked me how long I'd been up when you came down for tea."

"I found her in the sun-room," Charles added, toward the others. "I could tell something was up. I knew she'd tell me when she was ready."

"The moment I woke, I felt a strong tug in my heart for Amanda," Jocelyn continued. "Before I even left the bedroom, I sat down on the edge of the bed and began to pray. *'Father,'* I said, *'look after our daughter. She is so blind right now to who we are and to the depths of our love for her. Yet she's your daughter even more, Father. Fill up the holes caused by our parental mistakes and shortcomings. Make up for the gaps in our training and our love. Fill the places in her that we weren't able to fill. Draw her to you.'"*

Jocelyn paused and drew in a breath.

"Of course, we've all been praying for Amanda," she went on. "I pray for her every day, sometimes almost every minute. She is constantly on my mind. I know all of you are praying too. Charles and Catharine and George and I pray for her together at every meal, and sometimes more often. But there was something different about this morning. I felt the Lord might perhaps be revealing a new way for me to pray.

"I left the bedroom and went downstairs. As soon as I got to the sun-room and it was barely light, I found myself praying again, this time for clarity and focus. *'Lord,'* I said, *'perhaps it is too much to ask that Amanda's whole life be turned around miraculously in huge repentance and vision. I know you can do so. But perhaps you want her eyes to open slowly, so as to grow used to the light by degrees. Perhaps a brilliant flash of illumination all at once would blind the eyes so long accustomed to shadows. So I am going to ask you simply for a tiny miracle—not for you to change her life all at once, although I hope that will come in time . . . but for one moment of clarity. Give her just a glimpse, Lord, of the reality of what she is doing, even if just for a second. Send in just the amount of light she is capable of seeing today. As Amanda's mother, even though she is not here with us, I take authority and bind any deaf or blind spirit that is preventing Amanda's seeing and hearing the truth, so that God's light might penetrate, however briefly, the darkness surrounding her. Allow clarity to penetrate. Give her illumination of truth, one small bit at a time.'"*

The cottage fell silent.

All seven felt the prophetic impact of Jocelyn's words.

"I knew almost immediately," she added, "and somehow in a new way, that God was indeed watching over our daughter. I felt a deeper sense of peace than I have felt since she left. God *loves* Amanda. Everything you said last night, Timothy, is true. *He* is her Father. He *will* care for her."

"Amen!" said Timothy. "We can be certain of that. He has promised—"

He paused and glanced about.

"Is there a Bible handy?" he asked.

Maggie rose and took her mother's Bible from the ornate secretary. She handed it to Diggorsfeld. He opened the ancient book carefully and flipped through the pages.

"Yes, here it is—Psalm 121," he said. " 'He that keepeth Israel shall neither slumber nor sleep,' " he read. " 'The Lord is thy keeper.' "

He glanced up, closed the Bible, then added, "He has promised that he never sleeps in his care for us. I believe this is especially true for his lost sheep."

Again silence fell. It was Bobby McFee who broke it, speaking in his unrepentant Irish brogue.

"I'm thinking," he said, "that 'tis a true revelation ye've had, Jocelyn. Fer from a thousand instants o' clarity like the one ye're describing, one added t' the other, will come the insight t' make bigger repentance possible. They all pile up. From one moment o' true seeing, the next such moment can add a little more light. 'Tis a way o' bringing yer prayers down t' something ye know God can do right now, this very day. What do ye think, Master Charles?"

"I was reflecting along those very same lines, Bobby," said Charles.

"I think the Lord may have given Jocelyn a word of revelation to help us all to pray for Amanda with greater faith. In fact, the more I consider the thing, it may have more power for *us* than for Amanda."

"Why, Papa?" asked Catharine. "Why us?"

"Let me ask you a question, Catharine," replied Charles. "When you pray for Amanda to wake up and see God and herself in a true light and to come back home, do you truly believe she will do so tomorrow or, say, next week?"

"I don't suppose so," replied Amanda's sister. "I pray, but it *is* hard to think of Amanda changing all at once."

"Exactly. But can you envision her having just one tiny *instant* of seeing—maybe remembering a happy occasion from childhood?"

Catharine nodded. "That's not so difficult to imagine."

"That's it—of course!" now exclaimed Timothy. "Praying for such tiny slices, as it were, helps *us* increase our faith to believe our own prayers. You've hit upon it, Charles! We can pray, *genuinely believing*, that God *is* going to send that momentary flash of light, and that it *will* penetrate."

"My whole attitude has been different today," said Jocelyn. "For the first time, I really do *believe* as I pray for her. I can sense God's answer on the way immediately—the loosing of an arrow of clarity from his bow."

"A good analogy, Jocelyn!" said Timothy. "You ought to be a preacher!"

"But it's true," said Jocelyn. "I've never felt anything quite like it when praying ever in my life. There is a strong and deep assurance that it *will* happen. I truly think that Amanda *has* had such a moment today. You're right, Timothy—it's *my* faith to believe my own prayers that has suddenly grown."

"Which is why I believe the Lord gave you this revelation," rejoined Diggorsfeld, "that we might all join in praying arrows-of-clarity prayers."

The others nodded in affirmation.

"This is exciting," Timothy went on. "I think the Lord has truly spoken to us. I'm convinced this is his way of telling us that Amanda's eyes *are* going to open."

"And it doesn't matter," now said Maggie, "if the fog gathers back over her heart the next moment. For the arrow of clarity has done its work. She will have seen something, remembered something, experi-

enced some brief *seeing*. In time another such moment will come ...
and another ... and like my Bobby says, they will all add together."

"I'm going to start praying for Amanda like that tomorrow," said
George enthusiastically.

"Why wait until tomorrow, my boy?" said Charles. "Let us pray for
her now—all of us. With seven people praying for one moment of clarity, who knows what God might show her!"

As of one accord, the seven began joining hands, gathering and
shifting themselves closer together, until the circle of prayer was complete.

"*We thank you, our God,*" prayed Timothy Diggorsfeld, "*for this dy-
namic and down-to-earth word of insight you have given our sister. May each
of us wield this weapon of prayer warfare as David wielded the tiny stone with
which he slew a giant. May we be bold to pray with new faith for tiny stones—
or arrows—of clarity to penetrate the surrounding fogs with which the enemy
has encircled our dear Amanda. Send our prayers to their mark, heavenly Father, that your perfect will may be done in Amanda's life.*"

"*Give the lass a glimpse o' truth this very day,*" prayed Bobby.

"*And another tomorrow,*" added Maggie.

"*I add my prayer to Bobby's, Lord,*" said Jocelyn. "*Part the fog in her
heart and let in the rays of sunshine.*"

"*Help Amanda to see the truth, God,*" said George. "*Open her eyes.*"

"*Open her inner eyes,*" added Charles, "*the eyes of her heart.*"

"*And her ears too,*" prayed Catharine.

"*Bring memories to her mind,*" said Jocelyn, "*good and happy memories
of our family, and of Charles and me. Help her to see and feel our love, even
now.*"

"*And may she be given arrows of clarity about you most of all, Father,*"
said Charles. "*I know what it is like to be spiritually blind. But you sent a
moment of clear thinking to me, and it eventually changed my life. Do the same
for our daughter.*"

And thus, in the very cottage which held the secret that would open
the door to her own personal future, did these seven loving family
members and friends offer up prayer for the daughter of Charles and
Jocelyn Rutherford.

It was a secret that was intertwined with Amanda's own destiny. Its
disclosure could not come until after the day of her awakening ... for
she only could bring it to light.

Until then, the secret would remain silently hidden between the pages of truth.

98

Thank You!

*T*he next morning Charles and Jocelyn, with Catharine, George, and Timothy, drove slowly up to the small church in Milverscombe.

After last evening's time of prayer at the cottage, an expectant hush had remained with them all. Breakfast had been subdued, and no one said much on the drive into the village. For the first time since Amanda's leaving, a renewed sense had come over the four Rutherfords that they *were* a family, and that Amanda was still one of them. They were praying now with confidence that their prayers were indeed finding the mark. And this fact at once brought Amanda nearer their hearts than she had been in months. She was newly *present* with them, because they were praying for her with new faith.

As they got down out of the carriage, Jocelyn smiled to one of the village women. She nodded shyly in return and continued inside. Behind the woman now came Bobby and Maggie, full of smiles and greetings as the Rutherford carriage emptied. How glad Jocelyn was that they could all be here on this morning and that Timothy had been able to remain with them through the weekend for a change. It was the first occasion upon which he had been able to attend church with them. Usually, his responsibilities to his own flock took him back to London on Saturday evenings. Today, however, he had managed to obtain a substitute.

Jocelyn glanced upward. A deep blue sky was dotted with lazy clouds which thickened as they extended toward the sea. A warm sense of God smiling down filled her heart.

A new season in their lives had begun.

Yesterday had brought a breakthrough. For Amanda, for their family, in their prayers . . . and especially for her, thought Jocelyn. What might God be about to do, not only in her daughter's life, *but in her own!*

Everything was different. Change had come to Heathersleigh. But maybe, in the long run, the change would turn out to be good after all. At first it was painful. Amanda's final words and letter had broken her mother's heart. But Jocelyn could feel a new peace coming in the wake of the pain.

They walked inside the church where they had been married, where they now attended services every Sunday, knelt in prayer as they readied themselves for worship, then sat down.

The service began. The familiar and lovely opening sentences descended comfortingly on Jocelyn's ears. In recent years they had taken on the gleam of deepened meaning and relevance. And then, as the service progressed, the congregation rose to sing from the psalms.

"O give thanks unto the Lord,
    call upon his name . . .
O give thanks unto the Lord, for he is good;
    for his mercy endureth forever . . ."

"O give thanks unto the Lord;
    for he is good . . .
O give thanks unto the Lord;
    for he is good . . ."

Jocelyn recalled the day of the wedding when she walked down this aisle on the arm of her father, flowers filling every nook and cranny with heavenly fragrance. So much had happened since that day. There had been disappointments. But today she was thinking how much she had grown. As she now sang, Jocelyn's heart soared. She was no longer the self-conscious Jocelyn Wildecott as she had been that day, but Jocelyn Rutherford, child of God.

"O give thanks unto the God of gods . . .
O give thanks to the Lord of lords . . ."

"O give thanks unto the God of heaven;
    for his mercy endureth forever!"

"A lesson from the fifth chapter of Paul's first letter to the Thessalonians," the vicar now announced as the congregation took their seats. He began to read. "Rejoice evermore. Pray without ceasing. In everything give thanks: for this is the will of God in Christ Jesus concerning you."

The next words were lost on her as Jocelyn's mind repeated the words she had been singing and had just heard—*in everything give thanks . . . give thanks unto the Lord . . . give thanks unto the Lord, for he is good . . . in everything give thanks . . . in* everything *give thanks . . .*

The service progressed.

Jocelyn's mind filled with memories as she sat and absorbed the morning's service . . . her years with Charles . . . the memorable discussions with Timothy. And throughout, the Scriptures about thanks continued to echo in her ears.

She realized that her entire life had been a struggle over this one simple yet momentous truth—giving thanks. In it was bound up her past, her identity, her struggle to come to terms with who she was. Now that struggle had taken on new dimensions. She must carry it beyond herself and try to summon thankfulness even for Amanda's present plight. That was just as difficult as being thankful for her birthmark. More difficult, perhaps.

Yet if she could not move past this roadblock, which for so long had prevented *her* from intimacy with God, how could she expect *Amanda* to be thankful for circumstances that were not to her liking?

Fragmentary words from the vicar's homily intruded into the edges of Jocelyn's consciousness.

" . . . the same profound truth with which Paul opens his epistle to the Romans," the priest was saying, "instructing his hearers that the first step on the road toward spiritual darkness is failing to give God thanks as Creator. In not giving thanks, the apostle says, did their foolish minds become darkened . . ."

Jocelyn had told George and Catharine that they might perhaps be doors for Amanda. Now it dawned on her with brilliant clarity—that the principle could be applied to her as well. Perhaps in her own way *she* was being given opportunity to gain victory over the very thing with which Amanda was struggling. Perhaps, in the mystery of the spirit realm, it was necessary for her first to learn the truth of gratitude and apply it in her own life, *before* the way would open for Amanda to pass through the same spiritual doorway—out of rebellion and into gratefulness.

" . . . the injunction toward a grateful heart is found on every page of the New Testament ... in Colossians, in Hebrews ... in nearly all the psalms ..."

What makes the thought of gratefulness such an internal battle? thought Jocelyn. *Why is it so difficult to give thanks?*

Then it occurred to her that the whole issue could be reduced again to the two questions that were at the root of every question in life: *Who is God? What is he like?*

Was he truly a *good* God whom anyone might trust in any circumstance, no matter how sad or bleak or hurtful ... no matter what one's daughter said or did ... no matter what one's face looked like ... no matter what blemishes of body or personality or temperament one was born with?

If so, if God truly was *good* ... then truly could one give him thanks in all things!

Deeper caverns in Jocelyn's heart continued to open to the sunshine.

Again into her mind came the words of the Scripture from earlier— *In everything give thanks, for this is the will of God in Christ Jesus ... in everything ... in everything!*

Quietly she began to weep. She couldn't stop. Tears began streaming down her face. But she was now unconscious of the red scar on her cheek. She only knew in a deeper place of her being than ever before that God loved her ... loved her!

"... *how do we enter the Lord's gates?*" now came the vicar's words in conclusion. "*With thanksgiving.* It is the resounding message of God's Word—give thanks, give thanks, give thanks! Give thanks unto the Lord, for he is good!"

The homily drew to a close. The service continued. Jocelyn stood and knelt and sang and followed along with the familiar service almost without being aware of where she was, those final words of the homily continuing to ring in her ears.

After the benediction and the recessional, the congregation knelt in prayer, then filed out of the church.

Jocelyn was uncharacteristically quiet as the Rutherford family walked back toward the carriage. Timothy and Charles exchanged glances but said nothing. Both could sense that Jocelyn had been moved by the service, and neither wanted to intrude upon the holy ground where she was now walking.

"Charles," said Jocelyn, "I think ... I think I need some time alone."

"What can I—"

"I think I will walk home, if you don't mind."

She turned and now walked away from the church toward a lonely side street. She made her way through the village, then through the woods and fields back in the direction of Heathersleigh Hall.

A lifetime of doubts and confusions and uncertainties now rose to a climax within the heart of Jocelyn Rutherford. She had been walking with God for years, learning gradually to give him her pain and her fears. Now at last came the final relinquishment. As her daughter had been wrenched away, now too final lingering doubts about the God to whom she had given her life were about to be cast from her. She had finally opened the bottommost doors of her being and allowed him to burn away her final hesitations.

At last, more than a decade after coming to the Lord, she was ready to give him her all.

Halfway home, in a small clearing of meadow grass, unseen by another soul, suddenly Jocelyn was overcome with God's presence.

The next instant she was on her knees, face bowed to the ground, weeping freely.

"*Oh, God ... my Father—I know I've been slow to learn what you've wanted me to see about you,*" she prayed. "*Forgive me! I'm sorry for being so stubborn to hang on to my doubts about your goodness. At last I am certain that you are good! Timothy and Charles have said it over and over, but there was part of me that just couldn't believe. But now I do. I believe you are good. I'm so sorry for taking too long to see it. I love you, Lord ... I want to be your daughter—not just with part of my heart, but with my whole heart, my whole being. At last I am ready to say it ... and to mean it from the depths of my heart ... thank you!*"

As the words came from her lips, a great cry erupted from her depths. The release sent heaving sobs through her frame. She remained on her knees, sobbing with the anguished joy of liberation.

For several minutes she wept.

Gradually her spirit calmed. The catharsis was nearly complete, the butterfly of her personhood was at last ready to take wing.

"*Thank you ... thank you, Lord!*" she said, more quietly now, though the tears continued to flow. "*At last it feels good to say the words. Thank you that you have put gratefulness in my heart. I feel so new, so different, even more than when I gave my heart to you for the first time. I truly feel thank-*

fulness inside! I am thankful for that! It feels so good and clean to have a grateful heart."

Now, it seemed, the "thank-yous" were bubbling up from a deep place inside of her. *"Thank you for how you made me, thank you for my face . . . thank you, God, for placing the fingerprint of your love on me for all to see. What a privilege you have bestowed on me! I carry your fingerprint for the whole world to see! At last I truly mean it—I am thankful, dear Father, for I see it has been for my good, and has drawn my heart closer to you, and it has brought me to this moment."*

She paused and sighed deeply.

"And, I thank you for Amanda," she added. *"I am not quite ready to say that I am thankful for the hurt she has caused or for what she is presently doing. But I am willing and eager for you to make me truly thankful. Until then, I will thank you, and I will keep thanking you . . . for I know now, beyond any doubt, that you are* good. *Thank you . . ."*

For several more minutes Jocelyn remained where she was, then slowly she rose. She breathed in deeply several times, then slowly continued on her way. She knew the change that had just come was one from which she would never look back.

———————— ◆ ◆ ◆ ————————

Back at Heathersleigh Hall, Charles stood in the northeast tower gazing down upon the grounds and surrounding countryside. He was waiting expectantly.

The moment he saw his wife's approach across the field from the direction of the village, he turned and hastened down the staircase and outside. He ran all the way to meet her.

She continued to walk slowly toward him, smiling contentedly as he ran up and took her in his arms.

"I finally know it," she said. "All the way to the deepest part of myself, I know what you have been telling me."

"What is that?" he asked, taking her hand.

"That God is good," Jocelyn replied with a smile. "I finally was able to tell him . . . and say *thank you* . . . and *mean* it without holding even the tiniest corner of myself back."

They walked some distance before either spoke again.

"You've thanked God before," said Charles at length.

"Yes," replied Jocelyn. "But always for specifics, for some certain thing that has happened. This time was different. This time thankfulness welled up inside of me ... for *everything*—for all God is, for his goodness, for how he made me, for our life, for my life, for salvation, for my birthmark ... even for Amanda. It was the first time I've ever been able to be *completely* thankful to him."

"I can see the difference in your eyes, all over your face," said Charles. By now he was beaming.

"Why does it take some painful circumstance to show us that God truly is good in all things?" sighed Jocelyn as they walked across the grass toward the Hall. "But if Amanda's leaving was what it took for God to finally get that truth into me, then I truly can be thankful for it. And that makes me know all the more that Amanda truly is in his hands."

"How so?"

"If God has been with me all this time," smiled Jocelyn, "and if he loved *me* enough not to stop trying to get his goodness through to me, surely he will do the same for our Amanda."

Still holding her husband's hand, she turned to gaze up at the powerful grey walls of Heathersleigh Hall, then sank into his offered embrace.

"I just know it, Charles," she murmured. "The Lord is good. And he will never rest until Amanda's eyes are opened to his goodness ... just as mine have finally been."

Epilogue

———— ◆◆◆ ————

$\mathcal{V}$ictory does not always lie in the happy conclusion to every chapter of life. Eternal endings are more significant than temporal ones. And the whole story of the family Rutherford has not yet been told in this volume. Indeed, many threads of that story have only begun.

Happiness comes from a heart of gratitude and thankfulness. Victory lies in the recognition that God is good. And with that deep and joyful knowledge this chapter of the tale of Heathersleigh draws to a close.

Meanwhile, the legacy of the prodigal lived on.

In forsaking her birthright, the daughter of Charles and Jocelyn Rutherford now sought that illusive thing called freedom, which she imagined the great center of civilization would bring her.

Faithful continued to be the prayers on this daughter's behalf. Seeming happiness would be hers for a season, yet her smiles and laughter would have little joy to sustain them . . . and the chastening that followed would be severe.

For alas, Amanda Rutherford was a plant that had sprouted a multitude of wild shoots, a plant in need of stringent discipline if she was to grow and bear fruit. Winter's harsh blasts must accomplish their cleansing and invigorating work, freezing roots and branches to prepare them for a new springtime of growth. The divine pruning hook must then probe to the depths, removing these untamed vines so that the beauty envisioned in the eye of the Gardener might blossom forth in its glory.

Throughout this sojourn of independence, however, Amanda was not alone, for around her proud shoulders was wrapped a cloak of prayerful familial love. Unseen by her unseeing eyes and undetected by her unfeeling heart, this covering kept her safe and protected until the appointed time should come at last for a more vigorous rustling of the Spirit's stormy and wakeful winds.

Meanwhile, the events that would engulf the European family of nations in its greatest conflict sped toward their climax. Sleepers remained in their places of slumber while drawing silent invisible nets around those they would eventually use to advance their cause of revolution.

And still the secret of Heathersleigh Hall lay hidden in the cottage that had once been part of the Rutherford estate, sealed away in the book that holds all the questions and mysteries, answers and revelations, of the world. And there it would remain for yet a season.

But nothing is hidden that shall not be revealed.

The Rutherford Family Lineage

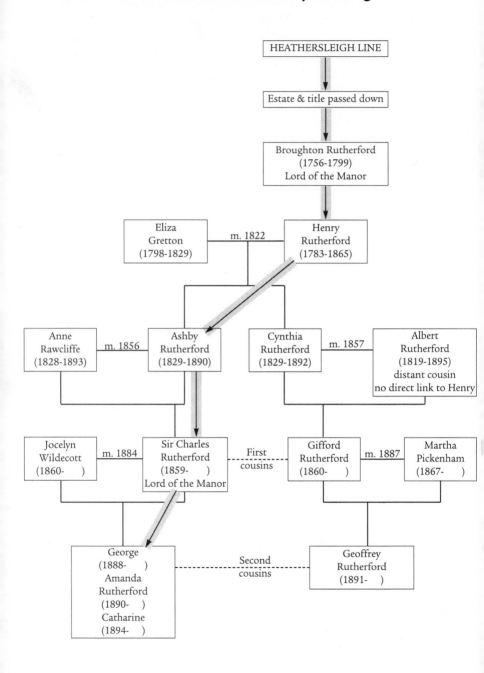